HAR

Also by Edwin Tipple

eBook: My Thai Eye

Edwin Tipple

HARROWING

is also available in eBook

Dedication

This novel is dedicated to those who died on October 8th 1952, in England's worst train crash at Harrow and Wealdstone.

*

For Elizabeth, my lovely wife, who has survived being an author-widow with great fortitude.

***

I would like to thank my Alpha readers Julie Hewitt, Shelagh Brinsdon and Terry Read who picked up my mistakes in my early drafts and made real suggestions.

My thanks, too, to my Beta readers, Roger Ward and in particular Carol Ward, who has read this work almost as much as I, hunting for improvements and corrections. Her sterling work, quite rightly, earned her a place in the story appearing as herself.

It would be remiss of me not to include reference to some of my friends and staff at the Writer's Workshop. Emma Darwin, Debi Alper and Lesley McDowell each deserve my special thanks.

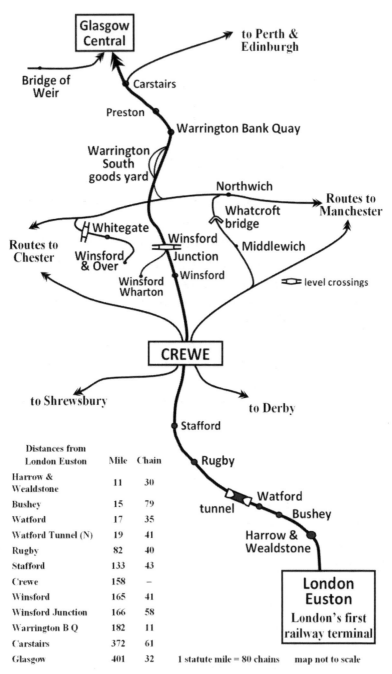

Glasgow Central

to Perth & Edinburgh

Bridge of Weir

Carstairs

Preston

Warrington Bank Quay

Warrington South goods yard

Northwich

Whatcroft bridge

Routes to Manchester

Whitegate

Winsford Junction

Middlewich

Routes to Chester

Winsford & Over

Winsford

level crossings

Winsford Wharton

CREWE

to Shrewsbury

to Derby

Stafford

Rugby

Watford

tunnel

Bushey

Harrow & Wealdstone

London Euston

London's first railway terminal

Distances from London Euston	Mile	Chain
Harrow & Wealdstone	11	30
Bushey	15	79
Watford	17	35
Watford Tunnel (N)	19	41
Rugby	82	40
Stafford	133	43
Crewe	158	–
Winsford	165	41
Winsford Junction	166	58
Warrington B Q	182	11
Carstairs	372	61
Glasgow	401	32

1 statute mile = 80 chains   map not to scale

1952 British Railways' West Coast Route from London to Scotland

1

BRIDGE of WEIR, SCOTLAND, 1939

HER THIN REFLECTION IN THE WINDOW OFFERED NO COMFORT. Outside, the mist still looked ominous — was it deliberately hiding something? Lorna shivered and turned to switch on the wireless and, as if learning Hitler had stomped mob-handed into Poland wasn't enough bad news that first day of September, her headstrong sister marched into the kitchen to announce she was going to wed Vincent Sylt, a nefarious twin from the East End of London.

'Why, Mary? For goodness sake? You're not preg—'

'No, Lorna! I'm not. Anyway,' said Mary, preferring to address the window, 'Vince says we should. He wants us to marry, in case he gets called up.'

'You mean, he's not volunteering for the chance to be bloody and brutal for the sake of his country? Wants to keep those skills for their *business* I suppose.' Lorna turned away to check the mist again, disturbed to see it still skulking. 'You needn't worry, Mary. Those cowards won't be going to war. They'll no doubt rough-up a doctor to give them bad medical reports.'

Which, as it turned out, was exactly what happened — once the doctor had recovered — allowing the Sylt brothers to exploit the black market of the war years to the full.

Lorna's closest relatives refused to accept Mary's foolhardy act would trigger the destruction of their family. But thirteen years after her wedding, the process began.

Vincent died in 1952, just a month before the Harrow and Wealdstone train crash. So, Daddy argued, he couldn't be blamed for the family's loss.

Lorna doggedly refused to agree, asserting that if Vincent had lived, their nearest and dearest wouldn't have been killed at Harrow: they'd be alive today and living right here, in Scotland.

But die he did — such is the way of fate — leaving his brother Lance to gore his way through the rest of his repulsive life. A life that, by rights, should have withered in prison. Or better still, Lorna wished, would soon perish just like his brother's.

***

Lorna had forced her loathing of the Sylts aside, braced herself and went to Vincent's funeral for Mary's sake.

As his coffin was lowered to consign one Sylt a little closer to the devil, Mary, dry-eyed, turned to her sister, 'A loving father they all say. A complete stranger actually said so in his, so-called, eulogy! I couldn't believe it. But I've lived the truth, Lorna. Vincent was vicious, verbally and physically. Had been for years. But not, of course where it would show.'

Lorna put her arm around her sister and gave her a hug. Mary winced — a cracked rib; Vincent's final souvenir.

'If only I'd had the nerve, I'd have walked straight up to that bloody pulpit and faced the ignorant scum-bags. While he was speaking in glowing tones about Vincent, I'd have removed my bra and revealed my bruised breasts. Admittedly,' said Mary, 'they ain't quite as colourful as the church windows, but they sport several shades of blue, black and yellow.'

Lorna often recalled that moment; Mary sounding a little tipsy, though she hardly touched a drop. Lorna understood, too, Mary's release, so long overdue.

It was the last time they laughed together.

'I'd shout at the top of my voice, tell the ignorant congregation what a brutal coward he'd been. But what would be the point?' Mary searched her handbag for some lipstick. 'Like father, like son. That was Vince all right. His sodding brother still is!'

The sodding brother took a step towards Mary and grabbed her, as if ready to hurl her into her husband's grave, but thought better of it.

Unusual, Lorna thought, for Lance to recognise unseemly behaviour. Anyway, contact with the Sylt mob, she felt sure, would cease as soon as they left the churchyard.

Lorna had enjoyed the last few days she'd spent with her family. But soon, half of them would number among over one hundred who would die in England's worst train crash.

||*

Lorna was dreading that in two days, it would be the seventh anniversary of the devastating tragedy. For years, her nightmares of the crash were becoming much worse; each dream more vivid, more bizarre, more frightening than the last.

And they were not just restricted to her sleeping hours. Merely looking at a photograph of Mary, or seeing that damn mist threading its way through the garden, might bring them on.

Unless she could find the real reason behind the train crash, she knew she would never be free of their terrors. But this morning, while tidying away the newspaper cuttings her father had saved about the tragedy — the reading of which triggered last night's ordeal — she found something new, something to give her hope.

Carefully separating two articles stuck together, by what appeared to be damson jam — Daddy's favourite — she discovered a cutting which repeated many of the facts already imprinted on her brain. But, in addition to the Ministry of Transport investigation in London, it revealed enquiries into the crash also took place at Crewe.

How had she missed that?

The Railway Detective in charge at the time was one Inspector Oliver Crosier. And his office, it occurred to her, was over half-way back to London.

Assuming he still worked there, a break in her long journey home, at Crewe, might just prove to be informative.

2

CREWE, OCTOBER 1959

LAST WEEK, PROMOTED TO THE DIZZYING HEIGHT OF DETECTIVE Inspector, I left my family in York and returned to Crewe's British Transport Police. Famed in part by the music-hall song '*Oh Mr Porter*', Crewe was the railway's busiest junction on the westerly route from London to Scotland. The town seemed to me less important than the railway serving it, which probably explained why the lay-by, provided to drop off and pick up travellers, was so small for such a large station.

The first few days in my new job had been easy enough. Monday I spent getting to know everyone. Gardiner, the scruffy and excitable desk sergeant, still worked here. I remembered him, from my short stretch seven years ago, sporting, as now, a piece of pork pie in the corner of his moustache. Perhaps it was the pie that kept him on permanent nights and away from most of the travelling public. How he'd retained it all those years I'll never know. I suspected dried mustard, but didn't ask.

And there were two guinea pigs in a series of staffing experiments: Carol Ward, recruited six months ago, to do the day shift on the front desk had minimal contact with Gardiner, much to her relief I suspected. Mrs Ward was not a police officer but a civilian who fell well short of regulation minimum height. Just how she'd perform in unarmed combat with villains was irrelevant, but something about her told me she'd prove tough in other respects.

On Tuesday a theft of pottery — by a helpfully incompetent thief — from a railway warehouse in Stafford had made my job both entertaining and a little profitable. Today, the J H Weatherby Pottery Company of Hanley – grateful its shipment had been so quickly recovered – presented me with a dozen of its Falcon Coronation mugs for the staff. Considering the Coronation was six years ago, I was surprised they still had stock. They'd told me, that if we kept them with their boxes, they'd be worth a lot of money one day!

I had just returned with them and passed on Weatherby's advice to Ward, delegating her to dole them out. Nobody in the office had the patience to find out if they would bring them a fortune and put their mug to immediate use. I'd keep mine back at my digs.

I was arranging my new overcoat on its hanger on the back of my office door when the other guinea pig suddenly kicked it wide open and marched to the middle of my office. Sergeant Cardin, finding me bending to recover and shake out the crumpled garment, tried not to smirk. Remarkably, the coffee the sergeant held in each hand wasn't spilt across the floor.

'Do you always dash into a room with hot coffee, or were you hoping to trip and throw it all over me and my desk?' I tried once more to hang my coat properly. 'What's all the rush anyway?'

'I forgot to tell you, there's an appointment at four, sir, with a Miss Todd-Dunscombe.'

I checked my wristwatch. 'That's in less than half an hour.' I glanced at the pile of paperwork on my desk, and wondered if Dunscombe's arrival would scupper my plan to clear it. 'And anyway,' I said, brushing the last specks of dirt off my coat, 'who is this Dunscombe woman, when she's at home? What's this all about, Cardin?'

'Insisted she'd be here at 4 o'clock; said she must see you.'

'She did eh? Why?'

'Something to do with your investigation here, years back. Said she was at Harrow and Wealdstone and saw the crash?'

I slapped the back of my neck a couple of times. It always helped. Cardin, still not used to my habit, tried again not to smirk. A second or two later, the memories of Harrow began to crystallise as I went behind my desk. 'That was before you started,' I said, making a space for the coffees. The imperious gaze of the young Queen Elizabeth II — guarded by her British Lion and Unicorn — eyed me through the newly crazed glaze of Cardin's hot mug as I sat. 'I was sent here from York on the 8th of October, 1952 ... seven years ago—'

'To the day. Uncanny, eh, sir?'

'Augurous more like.' The only thing uncanny was this Dunscombe woman, even in her absence, now had my full attention. I could recall just one Dunscombe, a Tory politician the Socialist press had in their sights; a sex scandal or something. I wondered if there was a connection between them and if I'd have to meet him if there was.

'But why send you, sir?'

'Sorry?' I picked up a file and turned its pages without absorbing a single word.

'Why send you here?'

'Anonymity, in case someone had something they didn't want to tell the local boys.'

'Welcomed you with open arms, I suppose?'

'Most were all right after a day or two. I was just a fresh-faced inspector in those days,' I said, studying Cardin's face.

Without asking, Cardin took one of the two seats

opposite and sat eagerly waiting for me to elaborate. The sergeant had the looks of a boy I once knew. Both in our early teens, we'd become very fond of each other, *too* fond in fact. He'd probably have a black moustache or beard by now, features which certainly would not grace the swarthy-beauty of the sergeant sitting opposite. It would be interesting to get to know her parentage one day; I just hoped she wouldn't be subjected to racial abuse; something not uncommon in British police forces.

Her smile told me she was considering something else. 'A bit of a long shot, I'd have thought, sending a green inspector? What did you find out?'

'Their hopes and mine that Crewe might hold the secret, the cause of the tragedy, were dashed after a month. Having found nothing significant, my investigation was shut down. The main one, however, continued at the crash scene eleven miles north of London, and I returned to York.'

'But how was Crewe involved?'

'Crewe was the logical place to start asking unpleasant questions; after all the relief train crew, who took the Perth overnight sleeper forward to London, had lived here.'

'What went wrong?'

'They passed danger signals ... several danger signals.'

'Any theories?'

'Many were bandied about. None conclusive. The driver and fireman were experienced. Worked the London route dozens of times, making the crash even more difficult to comprehend. Less than four hours after they steamed out of here they lay dead. And we'll never know *why*.'

I closed the file, went over to the window and looked down into the station. The electrification work — promising us new and clean high-speed trains — was well underway. Shafts of afternoon sunlight, paled by the grimy glass roof, lingered on a group of passengers as if to invite my closer inspection. Had they noticed the "bright new future" under construction, or were they more interested in the blood-coloured paint the decorators were applying to the café's window frames?

'How bad was it?'

I'd forgotten Cardin was still in the room. 'Bad ... very bad, Claire.' I cast an uninterested eye over the waiting passengers, as I gave her the bare facts. 'Three trains; more than three hundred injured. The final death toll well over a hundred.' I turned to face her. 'I don't suppose you got anything else out of Dunscombe?'

Her cheeky smile gone, she picked up her coffee and stood ready to leave. 'No, other than she'd read about you in some old newspaper cuttings her father saved.'

I looked through the window again. Newspapers! Newspaper men, each one desperate for a story, hounded me every time I set foot out of the office. Insensitive bastards even camped out on the dead train-crew's doorsteps.

'She's on her way back from Scotland,' Cardin said. 'Lives in London. I'll bring her through when she arrives.'

I didn't reply and, a moment later, heard the door gently close.

The loose pane of glass in the metal window frame began buzzing; a train was arriving, hopefully Dunscombe's. As it screeched to a standstill, clouds of smoke drifted across the station and I wondered if the imminent demise of steam could ever heal the deep wound Crewe had endured since that fateful October morning, when far more than a lick of paint was needed to hide the scar.

And any minute now, this Dunscombe woman was about to walk in and open old wounds.

Could she have new information? I doubted she'd have anything to add to the little we'd gleaned. So why had she chosen the anniversary of the crash to come and see me?

Five minutes later Claire threw the door wide open and marched her in.

I turned to meet her. We made our introductions as we shook hands and Cardin left to fetch us tea.

Dunscombe selected the sturdier of the two spare chairs and slung her coat over its back, an action which denied me the chance to help her out of it and hang it properly.

With more than a little disdain, she sat and examined my spartan office. True, its colour had leached away over the last decade but at least she hadn't run her finger across the top of the door, as my mother-in-law did on the rare occasions she visited us, to check for dust. Miss Dunscombe — I assumed, by her ring-less fingers — had invited herself here and could make of it whatever she wished.

Her ash-grey plaid suit, appearing pre-war to me, certainly made my attire look like I'd chosen it — as indeed I had — to be in vogue. I didn't want these Cheshire johnnies thinking I was some sort of Yorkshire tyke. An unpleasant odour, mixed with something or other — perfume, sweat? — had travelled with her.

Cardin arrived with refreshments, and sat by her. As the tea ceremony progressed, I studied my visitor's thirty-something face; long and weary, topped with a grey hat retained by a pin through her white hair. Her blue eyes suggested she might have once been blond. I guess shock had stolen that from her.

Dunscombe's scrutinising eyes set in dark sockets were one moment analysing me, the next studying the poster above the dented green filing cabinets. She was either making up her mind about me, or being tempted to visit Skegness, where it proclaimed the air to be *So Bracing*.

Given a choice, I'd take the sea air right now. A seaside holiday might be what she'd need, if she decided to recount her experience, yet I doubted it: this woman exuded authority, and would be made of stern stuff — no wonder Cardin didn't get much out of her.

'So, why have you come, Miss Todd-Dunscombe?'

Her eyes returned to mine. 'You can call me Lorna, Mr Crosier,' she said, ignoring my station.

Her voice carried a pleasant Scottish-lilt heavily diluted, sadly, by plummy English. I slid my card across the desk. She eyed it, then me. It made no odds.

After a moment of rummaging inside her handbag, she took from a small tin a miniature cigar, found an ornate lighter and flicked it into action. As smoke drifted from her mouth towards me, she said, 'I'm searching for closure, if that's at all possible. I rather hoped you'd have something from your investigation to help.'

'I'm not sure I do.'

I bent to retrieve the ashtray I'd hidden below the waste basket under my desk. 'The case is closed. You do realise that?'

'Nonsense. I'm doing all I can to find out exactly what must have happened. I have to, why aren't you?'

'Why do *you* have to?'

She took a mouthful of smoke, held it for a second. 'It's my nightmares,' she said, exhaling the smoke towards me. 'They are getting much worse. Merely looking at a photograph of my late sister can bring them on, even during the day. And mentally shutting out the noise of freight trains, to prevent those triggering them, can make rail travel fraught at times.

'But there's something about them ... something buried, hidden ... deep down,' she said, wistfully.

'Maybe the reason it happened? I suggested. 'Have you taken medical advice?'

'Yes, but they just want to drug me, fill me full of all

sorts of poisons. I'm not going down that particular track.'

'Hypnosis perhaps?'

'You are not the first to suggest it. I'm not convinced it helps. 'Look, can we get back to the matter in hand?'

'What little we found, was forwarded to the accident investigation board. All relevant data was included in the *Ministry of Transport Report*. I assume you've read it?'

'Of course I read it. Every survivor must have read it as soon as it was published! The waiting for it was not easy. Our hopes the investigators would find the real cause, the reason why the driver passed those danger signals, turned to despair when they didn't. Yes, I analysed it all right. It didn't help me, no matter how many times I read it and newspaper reports.'

She paused and took a long draw from her cigar.

'You get used to trawling for information when studying for my line of work, Inspector. The crash put paid to it, for a year at any rate. And anyway, I had to make sure daddy was all right.'

'And what line of work is that?' I said, to nudge her along.

'I'd just started my finals in '52, at Girton.'

She saw my eyebrows rise.

'Girton?' said Claire, trying not to titter at the sound of it.

'Girton College Cambridge, to you my dear. I was reading law.'

My eyebrows rose further.

'Unusual for a woman you're thinking, Inspector? How right you are. Even now there's still only a few of us in general practice, me probably being the only female solicitor in Britain familiar with railway operations. A study, I might add, I would have preferred not to have made.'

She allowed herself a brief congratulatory smile. 'Tell me what you do know, if you feel up to it.'

Her piercing eyes warned me I'd underestimated her and, most likely, insulted her with my caveat.

'Will it help?'

I shrugged.

She studied the poster of Skegness while she considered my suggestion.

After a moment or two, I think she decided I was a suitable recipient for her memories, so to ease her into her story, I asked Lorna how she'd been caught up in the crash.

'A funeral, Inspector,' she said, treating us to a few seconds of that smile again.

Now Cardin's eyebrows were raised, too.

Another intake of smoke, then: 'We buried a useless relative a few days earlier. He'd been shot.'

'Shot?' Cardin said.

'You heard correctly, Sergeant,' Dunscombe said, as if responding to a gormless crook in the dock.

Then, after waiting for what seemed an eternity, while she stirred her tea and dropped more cigar ash on the lap of her skirt, she leaned forward to rest her free arm on my desk and look directly at me. 'My brother-in-law Vincent Sylt,' she said, clattering the teaspoon back into its saucer, 'wasn't just shot.'

'He was murdered, thank God.'

3

'IS HIS DEATH RELEVANT. LORNA?'

'Seeing as he died the best part of a month before the crash, I find that a little difficult to believe, don't you? Either way, I still hold him responsible for the deaths in my family.'

'But why, if he didn't cause the crash?'

'Simple logic: if he hadn't died, we wouldn't have been in Harrow.' Her thin lips tightened across her jaw, her piercing eyes held mine again.

I nodded, accepting her stark argument, and wondered how Sylt could possibly have caused the crash.

A heavy goods train lumbered through the station, setting the loose pane of glass rattling once more. I'd quickly become accustomed to its single note every time a train passed, but as Lorna lifted her tea to her lips, her right hand trembled a little. Some colour drained from her complexion. Unnerved, she quickly supported the cup with her left hand before it was slammed into its saucer, more sugar added, and vigorously stirred. Her eyes stared at the spinning tea as she took another mouthful of smoke.

Cardin almost offered support, by putting a hand on her shoulder, but changed her mind as now cigar smoke headed her way.

'I ... I was with my niece Emily,' Lorna tried again, 'and my brother Robert. My sister Mary brought that damned awkward daughter of hers, Phyliss, to wave us off. We were sitting on the northbound platform waiting for Daddy to catch us up. He'd stopped to buy something to read on the journey. He walked slowly in those days ... even more so now,' she said, almost smiling, 'but we had a good fifteen minutes before the local to Watford was due to arrive.'

Beneath us a crescendo of clanking and squealing trucks, as the freight train jerked to a stop, immediately froze her; she just sat there, eyes unfocussed, trance like.

'Lorna, are you all right? What's wrong, Lorna? Where are you?' I said, but she made no response. I tried once more, 'Lorna?' but she was gone, mumbling to the fairies . . .

'My thin reflection in the window offers me no protection. I see through it and the early-morning mist. I can just make out my family now. They're beckoning for me to join them, to wait for the train at Harrow ... the train that will never come. I must save them . . .'

A look of panic spread across Cardin's face. She was about to touch Lorna, but I quickly raised my hands to signal she shouldn't. Lorna didn't react to my gesturing. I feared she had already slipped away to some place where neither Cardin, nor I, had any experience with which to help her. To shock her now might prove dangerous. It seemed to me the sound of the crashing trucks had hypnotised her, but if it had, I'd no idea how we could get her back.

'The evil mist is here. His intent is deadly. One moment he lurks by the signal box, the next he'll be slithering back into the wings to hide and wait. His return always unsettles me: I know he wants to repeat the havoc. But this time I'll beat him, he'll not win. I wish I could blow him away. Try as I might he stays put, laughing at me, his knowing sneer plastered across his misty face. He's waiting for the freight train, hungry to consume it.

'The lovely enamelled Underground map behind us is quaking at its approach, vibrating noisily in her wooden frame. She's remembering she'll be smashed to pieces very soon. I lay a soothing hand on her old, varnished timber, to no avail. Still she trembles and thrusts a splinter deep into my flesh, ungrateful thing she is.

'Smoke pours from the engine of the goods train to cloak the noisy rake of trucks, as if it's embarrassed by their presence. They thunder past us eager to feed their misty friend. The platform shakes violently — is a wagon about to come off the track and crash into us?

'At last, they are spirited away by the churning mist. It smiles, pleased with its trick, then slinks back into the wings. I hope Daddy will be here soon. He'll know what to do.

'The station is silent, bereft of trains. Nobody moves, each person a frosty statue. I feel alone. Cold grips me. I tighten my red scarf around my neck.

'Everyone across the tracks is staring at me. Damn them. They must know by now I can't make it right.

'I jump at the stage manager's metallic voice scratching in my ear. "Time for a platform alteration!"

'I think the mist has put him up to this. "No" I say, "you mustn't. What about the express? You'll be killing—"

'"Oh, it's much more exciting this way."

'I put my fingers in my ears but now I've trapped him inside my head!

'"If they're lucky, the passengers may get to London."

'"They weren't lucky last time" I shout. "Why should I believe you now?"

'"They'll just have to take their chances."

'"Murderer."

'"My mind is made up. I'm in charge here, not you. I'll line them all up on the fast-line platform."

'"No!"

'"You just watch me."

'I reach out, trying to grab the evil voice, but there's nothing but a wisp of mist which dissolves through my fingers; I was right after all. It's too late anyway. He's already rushing around the station telling the London-bound passengers to move to the fast line. But he shouldn't be laughing at them. This isn't vaudeville.

'Everyone across the tracks spring to life — an army of office workers, soldiers and shop assistants — to muster along the platform's edge, ready for their daily scramble. Just as they'd rehearsed, they stand well away from the stone-faced, bowler-hatted bankers and managers, each armed with an umbrella. They'll not let the riff-raff board first-class! Quite right.'

Someone knocked on my office door. Cardin sprung to her feet to slow whoever was about to enter. Fortunately, Ward had far more consideration than Cardin when she came into a my office. She entered quietly, bearing papers she'd typed up ready for me to check before they were copied.

Ward seemed shocked by our guest's state of mind but made no move to leave, preferring instead to guard the door as Cardin returned to sit with Lorna.

Lorna carried on as if nothing had happened ...

'Smoke, from the locomotive of the Euston train, wafts over everyone, causing Emily to cough, as it slowly clanks its way across the points.

'Even before stopping, boarding has begun.

'Faces of anonymous performers appear, framed in tall, narrow carriage windows.

'Some immediately hide behind newspapers — as if steeping themselves in the news of Queen Elizabeth's Coronation plans will afford them royal protection!

'But most are staring at me, seeking my confirmation that the next scene can begin. I see they are ready, and wonder if they know . . .

There was a long silence, before Lorna returned to her story. Cardin moved to pull her back to the present.

Again I stopped her.

Ward put a hand on her shoulder and said, 'She has to come out of it on her own, Claire.'

'Emily asks Robert if Granddad will arrive in time.

'Robert points to him, standing on the footbridge.

'As one, the heads in the carriage windows swivel to follow the direction of his finger.

'Emily waves. Her face breaks into a smile. Evil Phyliss turns away in a huff and picks at the peeling paint on our seat-back.

'I hope Daddy has spotted us. I can't tell; something is obscuring his face. I hope he remembers to stay put.

'Carriage doors bang themselves shut while red-faced guards compete to see who can blow their whistles loudest. The happy engine toots her friendly response. I think it will be okay, the train will leave the station in time. But what's taking it so long? What is her driver—

'The bells in the signal box sound very angry, rapidly dinging their warning, announcing for some their final call.

Ward perched on my desk so she can study Lorna's face.

'On cue, the poisonous-mist materialises, like a magician from the wings, and prepares to do his terrible trick right in front of us. But what? I've seen the show before but now my brain is blocking out my memory. So, why am I shaking?'

Before I had a chance to stop her, Ward grabbed Lorna's shaking hands.

'Robert grasps my hand, squeezes it tight. Thank

goodness young Emily has remembered the scene; she's stamping her feet up and down on the platform. She's trying to shout the warning. But ... it won't come!

'The stupid faces, framed in the carriage windows, are pointing and laughing at her. Those selected to die won't laugh for much longer. Some have already begun their transformation. Their movements are slowed as blood-red discs bloom on pure-white cheeks. Tears of blood leach from the station nameplate.

'Some actors look as dead as my china dolls.

'Emily moans, her words remain stuck in her throat. Furious, she waves her arm towards the mist.

'The inanimate faces in carriage windows still manage to swivel to follow Emily's direction!

'Everyone on the platform turns to see the mist rapidly changing shape. I fear he has beaten me again; clouds of smoke and steam are growing inside him, thrusting high above his evil shape. Deep inside him, an ominous form is looming, moving fast, very fast, towards us.'

Lorna became more agitated, her unblinking eyes darting around my office. Yet she didn't seem to notice Ward was holding her hands.

'I must stop the express in his thirst for death.

'I'm running backwards along the track, all the time pushing against the express's engine. It's no use. I can't stop his angry tons of steel. I have to warn and save everyone.

'I'm standing on the running board of a carriage, banging on the window, looking in at the performers. Most are fixed to their seats, but one spotty youth, still supple, leans over to his mate to laugh at the mannequins beside them. He hasn't attended the rehearsals and will have to pay the price. His cheeks have already begun to turn white. Soon, their red discs will come. He stands, and tries to leave, but is stilled by those dreadful sounds; first the detonators — placed on the track by the signalman to warn drivers of danger — explode with ear-piercing cracks; then the continuous whistle of the sleeping car express from Perth, screams loud her belated warning for everyone to get clear. Some about to board the Euston train stop and look towards the sound. Selfish ones push past, eager to get a seat in which to die. Others know they must escape, and turn to make a frantic dash for safety.

'Some just stand watching the express, shooting from the mist at fifty miles-an-hour, and coming straight for them.

'A man in the next carriage has remembered his part and lowers a window to lean out and look back along the track. Hasn't he seen his cue to leave the carriage — Catherine wheels of red sparks flying from every squealing brake of the express? He is supposed to warn others, get them out. But he just stays leaning from the compartment, his face slowly losing all colour. He'll be smashed to pieces if he doesn't wake up and move, *now*.

'Two men in dark boiler suits jump from the footplate of the express, arms outstretched. They float alongside the engine as their faces begin to register death.

'"Jesus, it's not going to stop", Robert shouts. "We have to get clear. *Now*." He shepherds everyone from the tracks. Except Emily!

'I yell at her to run. The express engine is screaming a series of blasts on his whistle. He's much louder than me. Why can't he shut up long enough for me to tell Emily to dash for her life?

'I run to her as the express slams into the back of the standing train. The thunderous sound of the crash rams into the pit of my stomach. My ears ring so loud they hurt.

'The wooden coaches splinter into matchsticks.

'Performers inside the local train lose all protection. They and lethal shards of glass, fly wide.

'A pale-faced man, still clutching his briefcase, falls from an open door of the express. He somersaults alongside the halting train. His performance is excellent, but as his case bursts open, the deadly red signs appear on his cheeks.

'He misjudges his roll, swerves under the carriage's wheels, and is snapped in two. His pin-striped legs, still wearing their polished shoes, are trying to walk. The toes of his shoes kick and kick at the trackbed, until they shatter. His papers dart about searching for his missing body.

'The express engine hauls several sleeping-car coaches over what remains of the local train to collapse onto the actors trapped inside.

'Exhausted, the locomotive completes his murderous task by thundering onto one side to straddle the north-bound fast-line ... the track our train will be on!'

Cardin, Ward and me are silent, stunned by the graphic way Lorna has told her harrowing story. I can picture everything as it must have happened: the fog; the detonators going off; the engine crew falling from the footplate; the wooden carriages being shredded by the screaming engine. I now understood why her dreams were so bad, but not why she refuses help — help I wished I could give.

'For a moment, everything is silent. Everyone just stands, gawping, speechless ... until the china bodies, strewn everywhere, begin to revert to their human form.

'The unjustly injured, crushed or suffering the loss of a limb savagely snapped off, begin screaming loudly.

'Emily sits shaking, her hands clamped over her ears to shut out the hideous sounds. I run to her as she starts coughing, breathing in the dust hanging in the air. All colour has drained from her face, but she's alive.

'"Stay here", Robert says. "I'm going to Dad ... see he's all right." He dashes towards the steps leading up to the footbridge, sees Daddy through the dirty windows and stops short of the staircase to frantically wave, trying to show him we are all right. But Daddy doesn't notice Robert. His face is still obscured by something.

'Mary runs to Robert's side to wave. I'm relieved they've survived the terrible first act, but I see their faces are turning white. Robert leaves Mary on the platform while he charges up the steps to Daddy.

'No. Stop, you won't reach him in time.

'Why don't they take notice of me? Their cheeks will turn red at any moment if they don't move to safety. Have they forgotten about the danger that's coming?

'I can hear splashes, like rain falling onto the platform. But it isn't raining. They're splashes of blood; blood falling from the station nameplate. The station's name is crying blood! Gradually the drops are coming towards Emily. Before I can drag her away, the overture to an even more monstrous act has begun. Oh God no. Oh, God, please no!'

'The duet of rising mechanical screams petrifies everyone. The northbound express, hauled by two locomotives, is rushing ... suicidal haste ... towards—'

The goods train below my window moves off, each truck pulled forward by its tightening couplings. A series of loud clanking sounds seems to be pulling Lorna from her trance. Cardin risked placing a hand on Lorna's shoulder, who having returned, seemed puzzled by the presence of another woman, holding her hands.

Ward released her grip. Lorna slumped forward over my desk, knocking two glasses of water across it and spilling the contents of her ashtray over my trousers.

Ward and Claire grabbed Lorna and eased her to the floor

before she hit it. Ward placed Lorna into the recovery position.

'Where did you learn that?' Cardin said.

'The Girl Guides; I even have a Women's Health badge to prove it.'

Ward splashed Lorna's face with cold water.

I opened the window to let in some fresher air and prevent the window from buzzing again.

Cardin and Ward helped her back to her seat, where she sat looking completely unaware of what she'd said or done over the last ten minutes.

'Now, where was I?' she said, ready to continue.

After a moment of questioning myself of the wisdom of her carrying on, I said, 'You told us about the first crash, then you fainted.' I thought that would have been enough for her but without any delay she set off again. Fortunately, this time, she was wide awake; no sign of a trance.

'We'd sat at the north end of the platform — anywhere else and I'd have been killed. All of my family on the platform died in the second crash. All except Phyliss. Trust her to be so lucky.

'I didn't much like the girl before the smash, and I've hated her ever since. But not because she lived, mind. Plainly the girl had had enough of us, and no doubt wished we'd already gone. She didn't know then most of us would be soon enough.'

Cardin was taken aback by Lorna's grim humour but I'd become hardened to her forthright style and intrigued by the name she mentioned earlier — Vincent Sylt.

I'd been sifting through my memory while Lorna had been recovering. It wasn't to be jogged. Be patient, I told myself; you'll remember him when you're in the bath.

'An eerie silence pervaded the station for a few seconds after the second crash,' Lorna said. 'A bizarre peace, except for the racing pulse banging in my ears. I stood, sweating and panting, in the cold air. I turned round and saw Emily trapped under a demolished cast iron lamppost. I walked to her, knowing there was no longer any need to dash. I slumped down beside her and held her hand ... so limp in mine.'

Lorna's eyes moistened. I doubted she would break down and sob but still proffered my laundered handkerchief.

She declined and rooted in her handbag to find her own.

'Staring at the tangled mass of steel and wood, I struggled ... struggled to understand why we deserved this. Which one of us had done something so dreadful that so many should die?'

It was a powerful concept: that someone wrought this carnage as payment for some, as yet unknown, horrendous deed.

'There's not a day goes by when I don't search my mind for an answer, when I don't relive the crash again.'

I, for one, was relieved she'd chosen not to give us the gory details of the second crash.

She stubbed out her cigar and picked up a pencil from my desk. Studying it, she rolled it between her fingers and spoke softly. 'The vast engine which caused Emily's death lay at a crazy angle across the tube line, hissing gently as if relaxing after its murderous work was complete. The fireman tumbled from the footplate and sat, stiff-legged, leaning against the cab roof. He seemed to be looking around for his driver. Dazed, he put his head in his hands and wept. His chest was heaving with grief, as if he already knew his mate had perished, like so many who'd survived the first crash.

'Moans from the newly injured joined in the chorus for help. People gingerly emerged from buildings, then scrambled over tracks and climbed, like enormous ants, over the mechanical carcasses in search of the living. Bewildered, they didn't know who to rescue first. Orders were shouted. Ladders appeared, were extended and propped against the mangled mechanical corpses towering thirty feet above us.

'I remember well the frantic ringing, as distant bells-of-rescue approached. No matter how loudly they rang, poor Emily was beyond their help.'

Cardin plucked up the courage to squeeze Lorna's shoulder.

I felt lucky to have her with me. I cleared my throat and said pathetically, 'I believe everyone within two miles of the station heard the crashes. Some even raised their eyes to check the sky was clear of enemy aircraft.'

'But this was not war,' she said, slamming the pencil onto my desk. 'This was England's worst railway tragedy!' Then, with a distant look in her eyes, she said, 'I looked up at the clock on the tower ... its dead fingers pointing, reminding us: eight-nineteen — lest anyone should forget.'

In the absence of hot tea, Lorna took a long drink from a fresh tumbler of water. 'Phyliss came to kneel on the platform beside poor Emily who hadn't deserved to die; she was only twelve. Any notion Phyliss may require comfort soon evaporated. "Mum won't be coming for me" she said, dry-eyed. "Nor will your brother for you. They'll both be dead. Maybe Granddad survived but I don't care about him. He's a bossy old fool. And anyway, I still have Uncle Lance. I suppose you know he's rich? So if nothing else, he'll be fun. Yes, I'll be just fine with Lance."

'I stared at her, my mouth gaping, astonished at how heartless she was. She'd just witnessed her mother killed! Most around us lost friends or relatives, but all she cared about was her uncle's money, and having a good time.

'She began stroking Emily's hair, saying how good it felt and how the mard-thing would be no trouble to her any more. She began to paint patterns with her finger on Emily's blooded cheeks. I knocked her hand away. She said she'd never touched a dead person before, never been so close to one. Then: "I wonder how many dead people are here? Didn't you find it thrilling, Lorna?"

'And that was it. I couldn't stand being near her any longer. I slapped her face hard. So much so, I hurt my hand.

'She got to her feet, and turned to sneer at me. "I'm going to Lance's place" she said. Not even Uncle Lance now! She gave me her stupid little wave, wiggling her fingers covered with

Emily's blood. I stood, ready to hit her again. She just walked away, and never looked back. It was the last time I saw her, though I wasn't surprised when I heard she'd been in remand ... somewhere in Cheshire, I think.

'I stayed with Emily. I don't remember for how long, until rescuers decided it was our turn to be dealt with. I remember a black woman, a nurse in military uniform. I watched her attend to the fireman slumped against his engine. She gave him an injection, probably to calm him, then, with her lipstick, she marked a red cross on his forehead, before coming to us.

'After searching for Emily's pulse she shook her head. She told me her name, in an American drawl, was Lieutenant Sweetwine. She asked me if I would be okay to stay with Emily until someone arrived to take her to the mortuary.

'She stood and looked back towards the signal box at two men — separated by some thirty feet — who lay between the tracks. They were dressed in dark navy boiler suits, not the pale grey jacket worn by the fireman she had just attended. She watched them, then must have decided they, too, were beyond help. She selected a closer survivor instead and left us, with the lamppost still pinning Emily to the platform.

'I hoped Phyliss might come back having regretted her behaviour. Two hours later, she hadn't returned. I suppose she'd been in shock, but I'd always known the girl was evil. Perhaps that's unfair of me, considering her upbringing. Lance, not having any children of his own, spoiled her rotten. How right the accuracy of that expression!

'I cannot forgive her, though. In my opinion, she was old enough to behave better. I hoped then, that one day, she'd rot in hell with Lance. And I still do.'

Lorna noticed my frown. 'Lance Sylt is a bastard, Mr Crosier. Sorry, Detective Inspector. He remains an East End villain. A thug who brings his violent work home, who can't control himself enough to stop beating up people. His inability to distinguish between villains and his wife forced her to leave him.'

'Did he ever strike or molest Phyliss? Uncles have been known to. He'd obviously made a favourable impression on her.'

'We don't usually talk about such things do we, but the child has always been impressionable.'

'Did his wife ever consider divorce?'

'Mr Crosier, I know we live in a different world since the war. Everything is changing, rapidly I'll grant you, but one thing still drags its feet: the ordinary person's view of divorce. Few of my colleagues represent such clients.'

Her short lecture had restored some colour to her cheeks and after the briefest of pauses she returned to the Sylts.

'Like two peas in a pod, him and his brother. We were all so happy when we learnt that Vincent had been murdered.'

Cardin looked directly at me not daring to even glance at Lorna, whose hatred for her vicious in-laws was indeed palpable.

Lorna knew we were shocked by her anger and seemed pleased with its result. I reckoned this woman was much harder now than her original character had been destined to become.

'One bad Sylt down, one to go. We only went to Vincent's funeral for Mary's sake. Why go for the dead? But the bastard couldn't even turn up on time.'

'I beg your pardon?'

'Vincent Sylt wasn't just dead, Inspector. He was dead late for his own funeral!'

I had no need to wait for bath time: like the proverbial ton-of-bricks, it struck me who he was.

4

I DON'T THINK LORNA HAD NOTICED MY SURPRISE. I'D SEEN HER seven years before, when she was indeed blond.

More tea arrived. Cardin instantly took to being mother again, perhaps more for light relief than hospitality.

I had nothing to rush home for, so I decided to take Cardin for a drink after work, and tell her the juicier bits about the funeral.

After small-talk over tea, I made a note of where I could reach Lorna if, in the unlikely event, I had news for her. She hadn't found what she came for and looked forlorn. To divert her thoughts I said, 'You seem very familiar with the technical side of the railway, Lorna.'

'I had to be, Inspector. Not knowing how the crash happened wasn't an option, so I studied the official report. I never realised there was so much to running a railway.'

'And lot to policing it, too,' Cardin chipped-in.

Lorna tilted her head towards her and smiled at me as if a cheeky child had spoken out of place. Her frown returned. 'The trouble is, for all the information telling us how, the report doesn't tell us, *why?*'

'None of us know that,' I reminded her.

'It blamed the Perth train's relief-crew,' she went on. 'I suppose it was the only conclusion to be drawn. But it couldn't explain why they passed those danger signals. We'll never really know, will we?'

'Both the driver and fireman died, so no ... I'm afraid not.'

A long silence followed. Like me, I guessed, we were each churning over what might have gone wrong on the footplate.

It was time for her to leave. 'I'm truly sorry for your loss, Miss Todd-Dunscombe,' I said, helping her into her coat and wishing there was some way I could help her.

'You have my sympathy, too,' said Cardin, who this time received a more favourable smile. 'Look, there's ten minutes before your train. Why don't I accompany you onto the platform?'

'That's kind of you, sergeant. And send me the cleaning bill for your trousers, Inspector.'

I assured her there was no need, thanked her for coming, and said goodbye as we shook hands. Cardin escorted her to meet her train.

I closed my office window and a moment later I watched the two women, roughly the same age, as they descended the steps to one of the south-bound platforms. Lorna, it appeared, was chatting with Cardin as if they'd known each other for years — they'd obviously relaxed outside my company.

Signalling the arrival of the London train, the window pane began its buzzing. I looked at it, questioning whether it performed its monotonous tune when nobody was in the room, then returned to my desk to mull over Lorna's story.

She'd hoped I had an answer for her, but I didn't. Perhaps coming here was part of her therapy to deal with her loss. Through appalling tragedy, apart from her elderly father and horrid niece, she had lost all her family and needed the closure I was unable to provide.

'I offered to put her in first-class,' said Cardin, somewhat miffed when she stomped into my office. '"I always travel first, Claire". Well bully-for-her. One moment you can rub along just fine, chatting about anything and everything, and the next—'

'You get the big put-down. Comes of being a lawyer: the easy ability to run rings around a witness in the dock.

'How does the Crewe Arms hotel sound, Cardin?' I said, noting it was a proposal with which she had no trouble.

Relaxing in a couple of wing-backed armchairs, Claire sipping a G-and-T, me a pint of Wilsons, I prepared my tale.

'Come on, I can see you're itching to tell.' She waggled a finger in a circle. 'I saw the wheels going round in your head when I poured out the tea.'

'Do you have a couple of hours?'

'For you, sir? Always.'

I must have grinned like a Cheshire cat. Claire was so comfortable to be with. She must have sensed I liked her and I hoped my feeling was mutual. 'Have you met many people, Claire, who have died within a week of your last being with them?'

'None I can recall. And you?'

'Yes — but I only knew it an hour ago. And it ... feels strange.'

'How do you mean?'

'Lorna didn't seem to notice we'd seen each other before,' I said, 'outside the church of St Mary-the-Virgin, in Stanwell — at Vincent-bloody-Sylt's funeral. I didn't speak with Lorna but I did have a few words with Mary, her sister.'

'But why didn't you say?'

'No point. She has enough on her plate.'

'So what happened?'

'Okay, Lorna was right. Sylt arrived over half-an-hour late for his funeral, and I was pissed-off. It was my last day of a three month stint with The Yard. Before that, a six-week course at Tadworth, training to be a railway detective. They thought, as I showed promise, they'd send me to London for—'

'Promise?'

'I got top marks, if you must know.'

'Well done, sir,' she said, raising her glass.

'Oliver please, Claire, when we're out of the office.'

'I was an experiment. Afterwards, they didn't think it warranted the cost. To my knowledge, nobody from the RP has been seconded to the Home force since. A week before

Tadworth, Alice and I had just finished our honeymoon in Eastbourne. So I hadn't seen her for over four months.'

'Bit desperate eh?'

'You could say that. I was under Detective Inspector Hunt, who'd been trying to nail the Sylts for well over a year. He decided it would be good experience for me to go to a mob-funeral.'

'And was it?

'At the time I didn't think so, too eager to get on a train back to York and, I hoped, my equally desperate wife. Long-distance telephone conversations, however steamy they might become are not the best way to start married life. Or maybe, they were. When I eventually got home, we started all over again; a second chance for us to, well ... exhaust our lust and gradually replace it with something enduring. That was the plan, for me, anyway.

'Then, five days after I returned home, they sent me here for a month. Being away again wasn't easy for either of us. Our marriage had to survive me being a copper, too. Time, was all I needed. Some time with Alice, just to be certain.'

'Sounds to me like you knew, even then, it wouldn't be easy.'

I looked into my beer for a moment, and took a long drink. Comfortable to be with or not, I shouldn't have told her. Now she'd be coming onto me even stronger. Perhaps I should let her, an extremely capable and attractive woman in the same game who understands all that goes with the job. Was this the start of a seven year old itch which needed scratching? I heard her cough politely. 'Sorry, Claire.'

'The funeral?'

'Ah, right. Hunt and I were sheltering from the teeming rain, with six uniformed officers, under the lychgate roof; all getting cold and weary with the wait and stamping our feet to keep the blood circulating. To anyone passing by, they might think we looked like a lost Irish dance troupe too tired to practise our steps. If only we'd had a ceilidh band, dry clothes, and an awful lot more co-ordination. But Hunt was more concerned about the delay. He didn't trust the mob one little bit. "Now you know, Hawksnose why I wanted you to come. I guarantee it will be worth your wait. You'd be surprised what turns up at mob-funerals, and who".'

'Hawksnose?'

'Play on words, Claire; crow's-ear? One of Hunt's inventions.'

She burst out laughing.

'Sylt eventually graced us with his decaying presence,' I said, once Claire had quietened down. 'The lychgate was a good spot to observe who came to pay their misplaced respects to Vincent And Hunt had hidden a police photographer inside the church to take pictures of all the mob's ugly mugs.'

The more I told Claire about the Sylt funeral, the more my mind went back. It was surreal, like watching a film . . .

'So who do you think will manage the firm now?' I asked, checking my wristwatch again.

"I doubt Lance can", Hunt said. "Poor sod wasn't blessed with his brother's brains ... unequal in that respect. A dearth of thinking-glands meant they had to fit a large piece of snot instead. He has all of Vincent's other skills, mind".

'My heart bleeds for him,' I said, empathising with a spider busily wrapping up a meal for later.

"He'll lay low for some time, might even switch to another mob. Lance will get involved in something, I'm certain of it. Keep your eyes open, lads", Hunt said, to the uniforms, "see who the bastard talks to. There's bound to be someone feeling sorry for him, for a price".

'I wonder what life must have been like for Mary and their daughter.

"Unpleasant, would be putting it mildly", chuckled Hunt. "It's obvious from her last interview she's glad this bit of lowlife is out of their way. He beat her up regularly. I wouldn't worry too much about her, though. The house will be paid for, a secret pile of cash no doubt somewhere, so unlike you or me, she won't have to work for a long time to come".

'He's here,' I said, nudging Hunt with my elbow, so I could keep my hands deep inside the pockets of my overcoat. We all stopped stamping and turned to watch the hearse crawling along Lord Knyvett Close.

"I'm surprised they didn't lay on a gun-carriage pulled by six white horses,' observed Hunt. 'The arrogant bastards usually behave like they're fallen-heroes or, worse still, royalty".

'The Ford hearse came to a stop outside the porch. Pallbearers, self-conscious in their formal attire — but no doubt at ease wearing the grim faces they used when battering people — climbed out of a second matching Ford and prepared to hoist Vincent onto their shoulders.

'Hunt and I stood apart, so the expensive-looking coffin could pass between us, its bearers sneering as they went by. Hunt, always ready to taunt villains, raised his trilby in acknowledgement then nimbly, he stepped into the path of a couple, who had dashed out of a detached house opposite and were trailing behind the coffin.

'The short, thickset man's grey-eyes, sitting well back in his skull, gave him a shifty appearance. They seemed too close to his large nose, and — like his character, I was soon to learn — would give him an unbalanced view of the world if he lost an eye. He had dressed immaculately for the business in hand. His jet-black Brylcreemed hair, glistening with drops of rain, was cut well above his collar: military fashion. I assumed he was the undertaker escorting a female mourner, but the pasty-looking man turned out to be Vincent Sylt's twin.

"My sincere condolences, Lance, Joan", said Hunt, chirpily. "Vincent will be deeply missed". Hunt had deliberately blocked their passage so they had to stand outside the shelter of the porch. He eased to one side so the woman, much taller than her brother, could step out of the rain. Lance, rapidly becoming soaked, peered venomously up at Hunt.

"I'm sorry, Lance. You seem to be getting a little wet. I don't believe it, boys", he said, turning briefly to the uniforms while waving a hand towards Sylt, "all his money and yet Lance here isn't considerate enough to buy an umbrella to keep his sister dry!"

The uniformed officers were having a job keeping their faces straight.

"Tut, tut, where are my manners today? Please come inside, Mister Sylt".

Sylt ignored Hunt's invitation, and studied each smirking face; probably remembering them so he might be able to exact pain at a future meeting. Then he hissed: "Found my brother's killer yet, Cun—"

"Now I like droll, Lance, I really do ... but please, no shop-talk; this is a funeral after all".

Hunt's words made Lance even more annoyed, and he smashed the fist of one gloved hand into the palm of the other. But Hunt was for the moment, at any rate, on safe ground. A punch-up here would be most unseemly and besides, Sylt's men had their hands full. With a sweep of an arm, Sylt eased Hunt to one side, grabbed his sister's hand, and marched her along the short path after their dead brother who now was well inside the church.

I'd been studying Joan Sylt. Unlike her poison-dwarf brother, she didn't look a bit shifty, her features were plain but not unpleasant. Did she have the same views about the twins as Mary? If she did, I doubt she was fortunate enough to voice them with Lance around.

"Come on", said Hunt. "Act two is about to begin, and remember, lads, look out for who the short-arse talks to".

A waiter was clinking glasses as he put Claire's fresh order on our table; my reverie must have taken longer than I thought.

'Oliver? Are you doing a Lorna on me?'

'Sorry, Claire. I was remembering the funeral. Weird how events stay with you. Nothing happened inside the church. It got a bit delicate at the graveside afterwards, though. Vincent's wife was giggling with Lorna. Even began powdering her nose!

'And Phyliss didn't like the way her mum bid her dad farewell by throwing soil hard onto the lid of his coffin. The kid was in a right old-strop as they left.

'The rain had stopped while everyone was in the church and Mary looked much better as she left her husband for the last time. She paused for a moment with us inside the lychgate, her face briefly stern. Then she smiled, removed her black hat, screwed it into a ball and stuffed it into a rubbish bin.

'What will you do now? I asked. She said "We're going to spend a few days together, and try to forget Vincent. On Wednesday, we'll see the family off home". Sadly, we know what happened.

'She shook out her hair, a clear sign the Vincent-phase of her life was now history. She smiled as we bid them farewell.'

'Well, whoever shot Vincent Sylt obviously did her a big favour,' said Claire.

'Dead right. I watched them from the lychgate, as their car moved off then disappeared on its way to Harrow, wondering what life might have in store for them.'

'As you said, now we know.'

'We certainly do. But that's not quite the end.'

Claire wriggled her bottom into the cushions, getting herself comfortable for my next instalment.

'I watched Hunt's eyes surveying the churchyard. It had emptied within minutes. The funeral cars had left, thankfully without any trouble from Sylt's men.

'Hunt posted two uniformed officers at the lychgate and sent the others around the grounds to be certain they were clear of onlookers. The photographer emerged from the church and confirmed it was empty; the vicar and organist had hastily left through a door at the back of the vestry. The other officers returned to report all-clear.

'I was curious; what was Hunt's game?

'I didn't have to wait long before he announced, coolly "Time to get the bugger up, boys, before the gravediggers get back from their lunch". He could see I was stunned. "The mob were late, Oliver. I don't trust them. I must be certain of who is in that coffin", he said, pointing towards the mound of wet earth in the distance, "and what might be inside it with him"

'He needed to nail Lance, and like he'd said earlier, you never know who or what turns up at funerals. "When we confirm it's Vincent", he said, "and he's taken nothing with him he shouldn't have, I'll drop you at Kings Cross and you can catch a train home".'

'But what about the gravediggers?' said Claire.

'My point exactly.

'Hunt checked his wristwatch, and turned to look along the close, checking for men in overalls who might be approaching the churchyard. He said "They'll be starting their last pint, courtesy of The Yard, I should think. I must remember to put their beers on my expenses". Reluctantly, I had to agree with him, however risky lifting the lid on the dead without an exhumation order might be.

'Vincent Sylt, if Lance was anything to go by, had probably looked bad enough alive and I had no desire to gaze upon the dead version of whomever might be in the coffin. The church walls instead attracted my attention — an interesting mix of stone, brick and flint unscathed by the Luftwaffe's attempts to bomb the developing RAF transport base at Heathrow — and were, unwittingly, to be privy to a most unusual exhumation.

'But trying to guess how old any church might be, for me, Claire, is pointless. I can still remember the look on my mother's face, one evening, as she read my school report; her questioning eyes settling on the history section rather longer than its brevity required. The master had simply written, *who is he?* Another, a year later in the same hand, bluntly exclaimed, *he cannot even remember any of the vital of dates!* Twenty-odd years on, I still can't. How relevant is history anyway, when you were going to become a copper?

'The graveyard was peaceful; all but one below ground at rest. Blackbirds made the most of the damp soil, and urgently heaved up worms, lest they too, should go on ration.

Cold winds gusted from the north, twirling leaves into miniature tornadoes, which rustled away, like rowdy children, to find others.

'I looked towards Sylt's grave, impatient for progress. Hunt was giving instructions to the officers, a hand jutting out from time to time to emphasise a point. He saw me watching, and beckoned me over. I went across thinking, I could do without this; it's not even my sodding case.

'The wind greeted me with a strong smell of rotting flesh as I approached the opened coffin. I hoped my stomach would hold-out. Fortunately it was pretty empty; I'd be okay. Sergeant Jones wasn't so lucky. He chucked-up under the coffin — most considerate of him.

'Two sawn-off shotguns recovered from the coffin were being stowed in the boot of a Wolseley squad-car. They looked pretty clean in Hunt's opinion. Said he'd have them checked for dabs anyway, then went on: "It's been known for mobs to bury victims with the weapon that killed them. Not in this case, though; just a single entry mark above his left eye. Ballistics at Woolwich might be able to tell us who Vincent used them on to maim or kill. Apart from the guns, there wasn't anything else. His pockets and mouth empty, nothing underneath him".

'And it was definitely Vincent inside the coffin?' said Claire.

'Oh yes, it was him all right. A face of grey skin sagging over cheekbones greeted me, its flesh beneath putrefying. Surprisingly, he still resembled Lance. If anything, he looked even more shifty. The stench of his decaying corpse was wedged in our noses as we left the grave.

'Hunt took a deep breath, turned to me and grinning said, "But unlike Lance, Vincent is beginning to rot away nicely".

'On cue, my stomach rumbled. Hunt rolled his eyes, sensing my need, but to be certain he understood, I asked if he knew any good fish-and-chip shops on the way to Kings Cross. At least they hadn't been rationed throughout the war.

'Half an hour later, the squad-car stank of fish-and-chips. The smoke from the driver's Woodbine didn't help, and it made me feel a little sick, so I wound the rear window down for some fresh air. "He has connections up north in Manchester", muttered Hunt through his last mouthful of chips, "so you might well come across him one day, if the competition down here closes ranks on him. I want to know if you do". Who does? I said, my mind focused on Alice. "Lance-bloody-Sylt, that's who". I screwed up yesterday's newspaper that had held our meals, pondering why I would ever again have anything to do with the Sylt dynasty.'

'So,' said Claire. 'Here we are, seven years on, and—'

'His name resurfaces.'

For no reason, I felt a little uneasy about that fact; the timing of the murder, the funeral, the crash and now Lorna's visit.

Claire saw the wheels going round again.

'Come on, Oliver, tell.'

'It's just my imagination. Picture a grubby bed-sit in East London. Vincent's killer is sitting at a rickety table having eaten his fish-and-chips. With greasy hands, he's counting out hundreds of soiled five-pound bank notes, uncertain of how to dispose of his stash of hit-money. He'd have no idea that if he'd waited a week or two before he shot Vincent, Lorna's family wouldn't have been involved in the crash.'

'From what I've seen of Lorna today, I think she was only one step away from killing Vincent herself.'

'Or paying for someone to do it for her. Come on, I'd better walk you home, Miss Cardin before you get any more fanciful ideas.'

It was the quickest of glances, but I could see my proposal was another with which Claire had no trouble. She knocked back her second G-and-T as I finished my beer.

'Are you feeling hungry, Oliver? I could just do with some fish and chips. I know a good chippy and, as it happens, it's just a few doors from where I live.'

5

WHILE CARDIN AND CROSIER WERE GETTING TO KNOW EACH OTHER a little better, courtesy of a local café, Lorna is well on her way to London.

Her train sings its clackerty-clack, clackerty-clack song as she drinks wine with her evening meal in the cosy restaurant car. Weary, but replete, she sways, with the motion of the carriages, her way back to her compartment where she sits alone.

She can just make out some dimly-lit station name plates as they streak by in the darkness. The train however, doesn't consider Rugby a town worthy of its stopping. It whistles its determination to be passed as quickly as it can. After jolting across the points south of the station, it sets off in earnest to reach the capital as soon as possible. 'Suits me,' says Lorna, to herself, 'another hour and I'll be in London.'

She thinks back over her meeting with Crosier. 'Why didn't he have something, anything, which might help me?'

Clackerty-clack.

Sleep calls and, aided by the wine, Lorna is away in seconds. But the hallucination of the afternoon isn't quite finished ...

My thin reflection in the window offers me no protection. The Liverpool and Manchester train, pulled by two screaming engines, hits the Perth locomotive laying in its path. The first engine has jumped the wreckage and is flying towards the footbridge: the bridge my Daddy is standing on!

It punches a gaping hole through it, cutting it in two. I can't see if Robert reached Daddy in time.

But Mary must have, for she stands screaming.

But she must run, not stand looking for Robert.

She realises, too late, she has to outrun the locomotives descending towards her.

They land with an almighty crash onto the platform. Their hundreds of tons of steel instantly transform into colossal bulldozers and slide to easily demolish everything in their path.

Petrified travellers are flattened.

Jets of high-pressure steam shoot from broken safety valves, to scald anyone who hasn't moved away.

The roar of twisting, crushing metal, is deafening.

Emily remains frozen to the bench. She has forgotten her part. Oh, God. I can't leave her here to die. I scream in her ear again and tug at her coat.

At last she sees the danger but just sits immobile.

I drag her off the seat and along the platform until eventually she gets to her feet and runs with me.

Phyliss — looking after herself as usual — has almost reached the platform's ramp. Her cheeks look normal. She can witness this act play out from a safe distance. But for now, Emily and I must bolt for our lives.

I look over my shoulder, amazed to see Mary is still running towards the 'tube' lines, to take cover by jumping over the platform's edge — onto the electrified tracks!

But Mary slows. Her legs have stiffened. Perhaps next time, her cheeks would keep their natural colour.

The first engine is still aiming for me and Emily. Desperately we run, trying to reach the end of the platform.

Emily slows now — will she never learn? Her hand suddenly feels as cold as steel in mine. I lose my grip on its smooth surface.

I look back at her once lovely face. A face now marred by pure-white cheeks. Oh no. No!

She's still able to run, but not fast enough. The monstrous locomotive is nearly on her.

The seat on which we'd been sitting, less than a minute before, has disappeared. The frame holding the Underground map is being flattened.

Luggage piled high tumbles, from a porter's truck, into Emily's path.

She tries to jump, catches her foot on a suitcase, and falls into the parcels and trunks.

I scream at her to get up and run, but the engine flips a cast iron lamppost out of the platform, and hurls it, like a huge truncheon, across Emily's back as she tries to stand. Her transformation to china wasn't complete.

At least she stayed in one piece to die.

My legs are numb, are jelly. I can run no further. I'll just stand and wait for the life to be crushed from me.

A shower of sparks whiz passed my head. I turn to meet my death but the engine has veered onto the electrified lines and . . .

Lorna is woken by the engine, screaming its piercing-warning, as it enters the station ... the station she will never forget: Harrow and Wealdstone. She throws herself to the floor; the safest place to be if the train is about to crash.

The ticket inspector slides the door of her compartment open. Astonished to find her on the floor, he says, 'Come on, Madam, up you get. Sit back down here. That's better. We'll be in Euston within twenty minutes at this lick.'

Lorna tries to smile back at him.

He stares into her face, gives her a knowing look. 'I was here, too,' he says. 'We survived.'

He must have remembered punching her ticket. 'May I suggest next time you go to Scotland, you take the train from Kings Cross? It's a longer way round to Glasgow, but you won't have to come through here. I'll get some tea for you. Make you feel better.' He tips his cap and quietly slides the door shut, leaving Lorna alone, with her memories, and her resolve to be able to travel this way again without fear.

6

EDINBURGH, ON A FINE, BREEZY AUGUST MORNING. HE EASILY smashed the quarter light of the Ford Consul. Then, once inside, he forced the ignition lock with a special tool he'd made. She looked out for the pigs.

'Easy see, just like I told you,' he said, fiddling under the dashboard with a piece of wire. The starter-motor turned, the engine fired. Revving it hard, he engaged the column-shift, slipped the clutch and shot out, without warning, into the busy traffic. A fast-approaching bus behind was honking long blasts.

She swung around, alarmed to see the bus had almost hit them. The steel mesh of its radiator grill, just inches behind the car, filled her view through the back window. 'Jesus, take it easy,' she shouted, breathing heavily now and beginning to regret this scheme of his, 'you'll get us both bloody killed!'

'Shut it. I can't hang around waiting to be nicked, can I?'

***

Moira, Elspeth and Sidney had visited the castle, and were now desperate to find somewhere to lunch. They'd spent far longer in the castle than intended.

It was important that Moira must eat soon. Her husband and daughter had spotted the telltale signs; increasing bad temper, irritable and argumentative with them over trivial things. They were resigned to her cycle of ups and downs brought about by lack of food. Sidney pointed across the street to a small café.

'No, Sidney,' said Moira, 'I want somewhere nicer to eat. We are on holiday after all.' Stubbornly she ploughed on, gradually leaving them behind, until she spotted a Lyons Corner House. She'd read about them in a magazine at their hotel and was determined to find one while they were here. And now she had. She turned, stepped into the road and sharply beckoned for them to follow.

***

They were going fast, far too fast, down the cobbled hill. Tyres thrumming, they approached the lights. 'Hang on.'

She turned forward and saw the amber light turn red. He put his foot to the floor and blew the horn. People, who had started to cross, jumped back onto the pavement, some shouting and waving their fists at him as they shot past. He swung the steering wheel one way, then the other, swerving around the cars already crossing their path. He turned to her, laughing madly.

She wished he'd keep his eyes on the road. She saw a woman step into it.

He didn't, until the last second.

***

Sidney saw the car jumping the red lights, weaving through fleeing pedestrians. It was heading straight for Moira. The driver wasn't even looking where he was going! 'Moira, look out,' he shouted, rushing to drag her back to the curb, 'no, no, *NO!*'

She turned, saw the approaching car and froze.

Sidney reached out for her hand and pulled her back. He lost his grasp as the car skidded across the cobbles and hit Moira broadside. She fell heavily after banging her head against a lamppost.

The car continued to swerve, spun around, mounted the opposite curb and crashed backwards through the front door of the Corner House restaurant. Broken plate glass windows fell like guillotines. The car stopped. Trapped beneath it, a child. The stunned occupants were unable to move. Their short game was up and, this time, they'd be sent down.

Sidney rushed to Moira's side. A man dashed into a chemist shop, shouting he was calling for an ambulance. Moira lay unconscious in the gutter, her breathing slow.

Blood seeped from the gash on her head.

***

The ambulance had arrived quickly, although it seemed to have taken an age. Another was dealing with the boy trapped under the car.

Sidney and Elspeth travelled to the hospital with Moira. Sidney was talking to the first-aid officer as they shot along, swaying from side to side.

'She's diabetic. She will need food and insulin very soon. I'm worried her blood-sugars are too low, especially after the shock of the accident. Surely there's something you can give her now?'

The first-aider made a note on his form and placed his hand on Sidney's shoulder. 'She'll be all right, sir, don't you worry. The hospital will test her before she's operated on.'

'What do you mean, operated?'

'Her right arm appears to be fractured as well, I'm afraid. She'll need to have it in plaster for a while. Like I said, sir, she'll be all right.'

Sidney turned away from Elspeth and spoke quietly, 'But if the doctors want to operate on her arm straight away, she might not make it.'

'She'll probably be given glucose to stabilise her condition before they take her to theatre, sir,' he continued, trying to reassure Sidney.

Sidney nodded and smiled weakly.

Elspeth held her mother's hand and told her she'd be okay.

Moira gave her a feeble smile, closed her eyes then drifted off, unconscious again.

7

SHE SAW THROUGH UNFOCUSED EYES THE PALE GREEN CEILING
rolling by. New-fangled fluorescent strip-lights punctuated the
drab view with their long fingers of blurred brilliance. A sudden
pungent smell of disinfectant accompanied the clatter of a
bucket and a cheerful exchange between the porter and cleaner
was over as quickly as it began. A few more bumps. A crash
through rubber flaps of swing-doors.

A round inverted-pan of spotlights slid slowly into view and
stopped above her to mark the end of the ride to the operating
theatre.

Heads each side of Moira bobbed about, mumbling to others
with masked voices. Garments rustled. An x-ray flapped into
view, was briefly held up, against the overhead lights. An order
was given. Instruments clattered into metal trays. A hissing mask
of gas, as if produced by a magician, was held firmly over her
mouth and nose until the spinning began. Spinning, and
spiralling, down into a giddy darkness.

***

'Mum'll be all right, Elspeth. Very lucky really,' said Sidney.
'She'll wake up with a plaster cast on her arm. You'll be able to
draw pictures on it tomorrow.'

Elspeth nodded, unsure.

'An older, experienced nurse, has been specially appointed
to take care of her after her operation. So she'll be fine, you'll
see.'

Elspeth insisted they come back to meet the nurse and check
to make sure the doctor had told them the truth.

***

At last, the spinning was slowing but the sickly smell of the rubber mask lingered. One arm felt heavy, her whole body limp. Hushed words floated around. They were growing louder, coming closer. Curtains swished open, their brass rings scraping along the metal rail. The noise hurt her ears. The darkness vanished.

'Ah, there you are, lassie. How are you feeling now?' Moira blinked a few times. A look of panic came across her face. Where was she? And who's this woman in uniform?

'Where ... w ... where am I?'

'Now, don't you worry your wee-head about that. I'll be looking after you while you are here. I'll make sure you have everything you need.' She smiled at her patient as she fiddled with the arm-cuffs over her rolled-up-sleeves. 'Why on earth we have to wear sleeves rolled up in the height of summer and hidden with this frilly elastic-cover is beyond me. I ask you. What's wrong with ordinary short sleeves? Now your husband will be able to come and see you for ten minutes tonight.'

'My husband ... am I, err, married?'

'According to this you are.' The nurse waved Moira's charts then hung them back on the white, metal bed frame. 'You have a daughter too. I saw them earlier. Can you remember your name, my dear?'

'Yes, I think so.'

'Are you going to keep it secret from me?'

'Moira. I'm Moira Scott,' she said, her voice trailing off, uncertain.

The nurse nodded and double-checked the patient record.

Moira Scott was not the name at the top of the page.

8

THE RECORD SAID THE PATIENT WAS MOIRA CURZON. SHE'D HEARD, or seen, the name before. Was she famous? She didn't look it; but who would after what she'd been through today?

Back at the nurse's station, in the middle of the ward, she checked again the names on the day's admission sheet: Moira Curzon, born 1920, married to Sidney Curzon, husband and next-of-kin; has one female child. Medical conditions: a fractured right wrist; concussion; and as she's diabetic, takes insulin. No family history of diabetes or amnesia, as far as her husband could remember. All other conditions fine, apart from her dangerously low blood pressure.

The last visitors were leaving. A shift change soon and she could be off home. When Sidney and his daughter came earlier to see Moira, the nurse told them she was sleeping and they left after a few minutes. Before they did, she'd asked if they had enjoyed their time in Edinburgh. Sidney had smiled at her saying they had, until the accident, adding they'd come from mid-Cheshire. He named a town she'd never heard of. The child had piped up that they got free train travel, because her granddad had worked on the railway. My, oh my, weren't some people lucky? Precocious little brat!

The bus ride back to her bedsit lasted only twenty minutes. It was long enough, long enough for her to remember. Staring out of the window, it suddenly came to her: where she'd seen, not heard, the name before. She'd have to read the article again in *The Scotsman*, to be sure. To be dead certain.

If she was right, tomorrow she would take a few extra things in for Moira. Yes, some very special things. Things from the hospital, collected over the years, and hidden away in *her secret cupboard*. She longed for the chance to put them to good use.

And now Moira had popped into her life, and presented her with the ideal opportunity. If it went well maybe others would come along for some special treatment, too. She smiled. Isn't coincidence amazing?

The nurse slept well, pleased her memory hadn't failed her. A short article in the *Scotsman* from the thirteenth-of-June 1953 had confirmed her suspicion and, amazingly, it had named Sidney. So it was only fair that Moira should die.

***

She arrived at the hospital early and made for the laundry, wondering how long it would be before accountants decided nurses should wash and iron their own uniforms at home. She changed, and placed into her apron pocket the special items hidden inside a tea-cloth.

As she strutted briskly along the pale green corridors leading to the women's orthopaedic ward, the tails of her unstarched white cap fluttered behind her as if finding it hard to hold on. She was happier today, a new experience lay ahead. Indeed, a new duty to carry out.

Occasionally, she checked her pocket making sure the glass phials were safe. At last she was on the ward. The night-nurse's report informed her that Mrs Curzon had slept well, but continued to use her maiden name, so it was assumed she was still delirious from the blow to her head.

'How are you today, Moira?'

'A bit better, thanks, nurse. My arm hurts and this pot is driving me mad.'

The nurse smiled at her and returned a few moments later with a long knitting needle. 'Here, try this.'

'Ah, that's wonderful, nurse. Thank you,' said Moira, pushing the needle inside the pot to where her arm itched 'Can I have some breakfast, please? I'm starving.'

'I'll see to that. And I'll get your injection prepared, too. Back in a wee-while.' She collected a large syringe from the instrument cupboard, hid it in her apron pocket, left the ward and headed for the ladies toilet.

Inside a cubicle, she sat and hitched her skirt over her knees. Carefully, she broke open a glass phial of insulin, held it between her knees and began to draw its contents into the syringe. She selected another and broke it open.

The ladies door swung open and crashed against a cubicle partition.

The nurse froze, almost dropping the phial. She heard high-heeled shoes enter.

The wearer clip-clopped over to the washbasins. Water flowed. Whoever she was started to hum a tune, in no hurry to leave.

The water stopped running.

The nurse held her breath.

The humming eventually faded away as the visitor departed.

The door closed.

But there were still five more phials to transfer into the syringe and breakfasts would be arriving soon. She'd have to work quickly.

At last, the syringe was full. She checked there were no other women about, flushed the toilet, and left without washing her hands, walked straight past Moira's ward and went outside.

She found the rubbish bins, and dumped the six phials, wrapped in the tea-cloth, into the one marked *No Medical Waste*. She stood looking back at the hospital. Felt the adrenalin coursing through her veins.

It was time.

***

She quietly drew the curtains around the bed and looked down at Moira, deep asleep again, her breathing shallow. Ideal, it would be a quick death. She held Moira's wrist, counting her pulse, against her watch. Very slow. She smiled, savouring the moment. Told herself to keep calm, and prepare herself.

'Not long now, Moira Curzon,' she whispered, 'just a few more seconds.'

The curtains were suddenly pulled open. Sister thrust her head through the gap. The nurse, startled, gasped and dropped Moira's arm and turned towards the head. Surely she hadn't been caught out already? Her hand went to the apron pocket, checking the syringe was still inside, not lying on the bed.

Sister eyed the nurse up and down as if looking for evidence. There was none, no crime had been committed, yet.

'Nurse, when you've finished here, Mrs McCain needs help. Wants a bedpan again.' The nurse nodded. Sister's head withdrew.

She waited a moment to check that Sister had returned to her rounds, heard her talking to another patient further along the ward. She removed the syringe from her pocket. Holding it needle-up, she tapped the glass cylinder to collect any air, then squeezed the plunger until insulin spurted out.

She examined Moira's right wrist. Couldn't find a vein. But with insulin, that wasn't a problem, plenty of flesh to go at inside the plaster. Enough to absorb the insulin. The syringe punctured her skin. Steadily, she pressed the plunger. All the way.

Now the syringe was safely back in her pocket. She held a small piece of cotton-wool over the puncture until the bleeding stopped. The pin prick wouldn't be spotted under the plaster.

It was done.

Moira hadn't made a sound. What a good patient.

The nurse pulled back the curtains, and holding Moira's records, checked to see if anyone was watching.

Only Sister glanced back at her from the top of the ward and briefly inclined her head in the direction of Mrs McCain.

Sometimes nursing was a shitty job, but dealing with Mrs McCain would help take her mind off the dying woman opposite. It was the first time she'd killed anyone and, although she thought she was in control, she saw to her surprise, as she removed the bedpan of urine and excrement from under Mrs McCain, that her hands were shaking. The smell, of Mrs McCain's ample deposit, made her want to vomit. She placed the bed pan on the floor then sat for a moment on the visitor's chair.

Mrs McCain was on her side, staring into the nurse's eyes and said, 'Aren't you going to clean me up?'

The nurse's hand slipped inside the pocket of her apron. The syringe was still there, her hand steady on it now. Had it been full, Mrs McCain might have had a dose of Moira's treatment. She took a deep breath, found some toilet paper and smiled sweetly at Mrs McCain.

Moira's breakfast arrived. The orderly was about to serve it, but seeing Moira was asleep, told the nurse she'd keep the porridge hot and return it in an hour.

The nurse nodded to her, thinking how inedible reheated hospital-porridge would be by then. She would have to act shocked if Moira was found dead now.

She looked across at Moira. Her breathing should be much shallower. She hadn't woken and she never would. Hypoglycemia, a brief diabetic-coma, then death would be the order of her going. A post-mortem would be unable to trace the insulin overdose.

The nurse went into Sister's office to report that everything was normal with Mrs Curzon.

An hour later a young orderly, new to the job, returned to give Moira her reheated porridge. Everyone in the ward heard the dish smash to the floor.

The orderly screamed. She'd never seen a dead body before.

It was time for the nurse to start acting.

9

MID-CHESHIRE

LISS HAD MADE HER SELECTION THREE YEARS BEFORE: THE ONE that stood out from all the other boys. Tall, ginger, vicious — and obviously destined for failure — Boyton, she knew, had promise.

Already he possessed many of the qualities she was searching for in a growing man; a plodder, single-minded, meticulous, and yet dim, who if commanded, she felt sure, would watch paint dry.

Mentally he was ready for what she had in mind. He'd be physically fit for her task one day; she was in no rush, could wait. His spaggy-eyes might become a problem. On the other hand, they certainly unnerved everyone — never sure of which eye was doing his looking.

Like her, he'd gone back a year. They were the oldest in the school: each given a pointless second chance to gain a GCE, maybe two. She'd observed him closely during every spare moment in class and out; learned as much as she could about him. It wasn't a long process. He didn't notice how every boy avoided him, that none wanted to become his friend. He seemed unaffected, too, by how each girl he approached had heartlessly turned him away — no doubt revolted by the prospect the copper-knob would soon attempt to grapple with her for sex. But he had noticed her. They'd become alike. She'd made certain of it.

Since school, she'd stayed near, hung around him to gradually reel him in, manipulate him until he was ready, and to ensure any desire to lay other females remained undeveloped. Now she owned him. His only hope of demonstrating how manly he might be, would be at her bidding not his.

It was on their last day of school, certain that he'd accept her challenge, she'd told him in her matter-of-fact way she would be his reward when he completed the task.

He'd stood looking puzzled for a moment, said nothing, then smiled. He wore the smile for the rest of the day; almost wore it out. It proclaimed she was his, from the moment he'd heard the name — the name of the man she wanted dead.

***

Darkness outside, rain drizzling against the living room window. Inside he was double-checking her demands.

'You sure, Liss?' he said, getting up to turn on the stolen television set. Then, as if he'd given the matter considerable thought, he said: 'Wouldn't do to top the wrong bloke.' He returned to the tattered brown leather sofa, slumped down and rested one foot on the opposite knee, to wait for his favourite programme to start: *Dragnet*.

'How many times do I have to tell you? That's who I want dead first,' she said, watching him. His right eye was studying her face; the left, unable to lock focus on her for more than a few seconds, seemed to be checking the television.

'Because they've got money?'

'That's part of it. Good enough reason, for me anyway.'

'And the other part?'

Would she really say why old man Gilmore was her first choice? He'd tried to squeeze it out of her several times. He sensed there was something more to it, something unfathomable, but just what, she never revealed. As far as he was aware she didn't really know the Gilmores — or the others she'd named — she just went to school with their bloody kids.

'Besides, I could never stand his lanky son either,' she'd said, folding her arms and pouting. 'He kept making passes at me.'

'So that's it, eh? Lanky bloody Gilmore. Who'd have thought

it. They have money and a lanky son who kept asking you out. Randy little bastard; good job he never touched you. Maybe I should do Lanky instead,' he said, warming to the idea. 'At least if I did him instead he'd be out of the way.'

He kept his good-eyed-stare on her, but decided against forcing her to tell. He wanted her and wasn't going to throw away the chance to have her after all this time.

She'd told him at school she was a virgin. He wanted to believe her. True, she'd never had any boyfriends since she'd joined the school, but it was common knowledge in class five-D that she'd arrived after spending a year in remand, and anything might have happened there. The fact that she never talked about it reinforced his doubt.

There was something about her, though. He couldn't tell what exactly but it had put all the other blokes off her. Without the aptitude to read her true character, he would never know what it was. None had propositioned her, except Lanky. She isn't a bad looker. Was that it? Not attractive enough for 'em? Has a nice figure, though. He'd keep his cool and hopefully tonight she'd reveal all of it — so long as Lanky's dad did what they wanted.

'Lanky's all right,' he said, 'just smells a bit. He needs a bloody good wash occasionally but other than—'

'How would you like some stinking bird keep coming up to you, wanting you to take her out, and then grope you, eh?' A finger was waggled at him, teasing him. Hips swaying, she moved towards him. 'I don't think you're as smart as you think you are.'

She pulled the zip of her black PVC bomber jacket down and leaned forward to give him a peek of the future, pushed the foot off his knee and sat squirming astride his leg. He felt her hot breath convey the whispered words to his ear, 'I think you're getting scared, don't want to do it for me.' She clamped his leg between her thighs.

He saw her looking into him through his good eye; saw that

she understood he wasn't scared, saw that she knew how vicious he could be when provoked — even by someone just glancing at him the wrong way, which they did often.

He felt the weight of her arms around his neck, smelt her jacket filling his nostrils, heard the crumpling noise its sleeves made as their folds reformed.

Her cleavage blocked his view of the television which had warmed up. *Dragnet* had started.

'Leave it out, Liss, I want to see this. I might pick up some ideas.'

'But we've planned it for over a month. Too late now for *ideas,*' she said, venting her frustration that Gilmore never took the shortcut.

'Liss, our chance will come. He'll take it one night. Now shut-up and watch this.' His temper rose just enough.

Heavier rain beat against the window. She sat close, rested her head against his shoulder and toyed with the zip of her bomber jacket.

He sensed the last thing she needed tonight was an argument that might postpone the kill.

10

I HAD BEEN IN CREWE FOR TEN DAYS, THE FIRST FEW TAKEN UP with sorting out our new home — at least, I hoped it would become our new home — before reporting for duty. Ever since I'd applied for the DI post at Crewe, Alice had made it abundantly clear that she was not keen to move. She cited all sorts of reasons why we'd be better off staying in York; schooling, being close to her family — not that they ever visited — and losing her part-time job headed an increasingly long list of objections. The fact I had a big pay increase, which more than covered what she earned, didn't seem to be relevant. But then it wouldn't be, would it? After seven years of marriage, I still hadn't figured out how my wife thought things through. Ever since Alec was born, Alice's reasoning defied logic, and seemed even more mysterious once Ruth arrived. She even said I could make use of my free rail travel by coming back to York for the weekends!

Nevertheless, I was beginning to miss them all and hoped to be able to tell Alice my late night call-outs would be fewer in Crewe than they'd been in York. Her cooking was far better than mine, which would become a serious problem for me if she stayed absent for long.

After draining the last of the Grouse, I turned off the light and snuggled down under the covers, wondering how long it might take for Alice to be convinced I'd made the right move for us. I'd give her until Christmas.

I was glad I'd opted for an early night. Tomorrow I planned to be up bright and early to do some more decorating and find a longer bed. My landlady was short and probably assumed everyone else was too. I lay diagonally across it, blissfully unaware a series of events were falling into place to scupper my early night and plans for the weekend.

11

TEN MILES NORTH OF DI CROSIER'S WARM BED, THE CREW OF THE last train from Winsford & Over station to Northwich, on this miserable Friday night, were ready to leave on time; but not to kill.

Bentham the guard, checking for last-minute passengers, stepped out of the dilapidated clap-board hut which served as the station master's office. Judging by the way the boards were sagging, they didn't look like they'd serve their purpose for much longer. He blew his whistle and waved his green flag for the off to Robinson, the new driver. He dashed into his compartment in the rear carriage as the train pulled slowly from the terminus. Fireman Warburton grabbed the token from the signalman who stood outside the signalbox. The token prevented other trains running towards them on the same track, having locked their signals to danger.

'Got it,' shouted Warburton.

With the regulator less than half open, the Stanier tank engine ambled along the uneven track, past unseen rock-salt barges moored at the Imperial Chemical Industries' wharfs. The track turned due west leaving the River Weaver at Falk's junction, a point where — so it was rumoured — just a quarter-of-a-mile away, the Crown Jewels were hidden during the last war: deep below ground in the Meadow Bank rock-salt mine.

The train comprised a rake of two elderly third-class non-corridor carriages which had seen better days. Their upholstery was torn, the bench seats were either too springy or not springy enough and any pictures, originally in the broken glass frames above the seats, had long since perished.

Two male passengers sat together, steaming gently, in the only compartment of the rear carriage possessing a working light and some heating. They were soaked to their skins having not anticipated the cloudburst on their way from the Red Lion pub.

It wasn't long before condensation obliterated any view, then trickled down the inside of the windows to form dirty pools of water in the bottom of the frames. The windows hadn't been cleaned inside or out for months or longer and probably never would be again.

There was plenty of talk about closing this and many other branch lines. At one-shilling for the return journey to Cuddington, everyone who worked the line knew that this level of custom was not enough to support it much longer.

12

BILL GILMORE WAS VERY PROUD OF HIS NEW FORD ANGLIA 105E. He liked its two-tone colour and the cut-back rear window, but most of all he liked its white-walled tyres. They really made it look sporty. Keeping those clean would become quite a task.

Now he didn't have to cycle to work, which pleased him immensely; winter was on its way. Even if he took the shortcut, the eight miles to the salt works was becoming too tiring. At sixty-four he was glad to have a bit of luxury. Getting in and out of the car was a tight squeeze; he really had to lose weight.

He was punctual leaving work at the end of his ten o'clock shift and wobbled his broad frame across the car park as quickly as the laws of physics permitted. It was heavy rain tonight and he was soaked before he reached his car.

He'd seen the motorcyclist and his girlfriend every night this week, but he wasn't surprised they weren't around tonight.

***

Oh but they were, just. They'd pushed their luck getting here in time. He'd wanted to see the end of Dragnet and this episode of criminal life in Los Angeles had a new twist; the killer kept the victim's hands.

'OK, Liss, he's just coming through the gates,' he said, pointing into the distance with his gloved hand, 'dead on time.'

The Anglia edged out onto the road leading to the dual-carriageway, its white tyres easy to spot in the near-darkness.

Liss took the pillion seat, he kicked the motorbike into life.

She sat hugging his waist, wishing he didn't make her wear her crash-helmet. At least it would keep some of her hair dry. Once he'd let her ride his machine on the open-road alone. She loved the excitement: at eighty the vibrations became orgasmic. Maybe she'd have her own bike one day and wouldn't need to rely on him for any of her thrills — well sex, maybe, if they pulled this off.

She'd watched Gilmore every night this week. Every night he waved a meaty hand as he turned out of the factory gates. How he managed to squeeze into his small car always surprised her.

She could feel it in her bones; tonight was going to be special. He wouldn't have to squeeze into the car ever again. Tonight they were going to kill him.

***

There was one stop before the junction with the main line at Cuddington. If anyone wanted the train at Whitegate they had to request the driver to stop. Warburton worked this line almost every day. Always surprised to see passengers waiting here, he was often amused by the techniques some deployed to catch the engine driver's attention. 'I can still see that woman last year ... looked like she was waving her mother's red bloomers for us to stop,' he shouted, to Robinson. They both laughed at the recollection.

The timetable allowed for passengers to board or alight at Whitegate, but on this wet and gusty night it was unlikely Robinson would have to bring the train to a stop. As they approached the halt, he cut the regulator, a little, allowing the engine to slow. He reckoned if anyone waved them down at the last minute he could still stop the train within the platform.

Nobody wanted their services tonight. By not stopping they'd be one, maybe two minutes early.

***

He was keeping a good distance behind the Anglia, not wanting to alert Gilmore. The road was surprisingly busy. Sane persons, he thought — as if he knew what they were — would be sitting at home in front of a roaring fire listening to the wireless; *Friday Night is Music Night* for the fuddy-duddies or, if you were "with-it", Radio Hilversum — if you could hear it! The faint signal faded and swelled, in sympathy with the prevailing atmospheric conditions, to make for a very frustrating listen. When would the BBC start to broadcast popular music?

***

Sheets of rain tested Gilmore's nerves, and his new-found driving skills, beyond their limits. The dazzling headlights of oncoming cars blinded him. To avoid them, he turned into the shortcut.

***

Was he getting close to the Anglia, or was it slowing down? Yes, it was slowing to turn left into the lane, Gilmore failing to indicate.

'Yes,' he shouted punching the air, 'we're on, Liss.' He felt her slap his back in celebration then turned into the lane and accelerated hard. The unmetalled road was full of potholes. Liss clung to his waist. He overtook the car easily as it splashed through the deep puddles.

Slowing at the top of the cobbled ramp, that led up to the level crossing, they made the tricky left turn and stopped just past the track. They laid the bike sideways to look as if they'd skidded and fallen. So far they were on plan, but it suddenly occurred to him the scene looked staged; they were too clean — there was no blood.

'Take your crash helmet off, Liss.'

She frowned at him but still removed it. 'Why?'

'You need to look like you're hurt.'

'How?'

'Dead easy, Liss. Like this.' He clenched his fist and punched her, right in her face! She recoiled violently and blood gushed from her nose as she tumbled backwards onto the muddy road.

'You bastard.' She moaned and raised a gritty hand to her face. Her lip was bleeding as well.

He saw her flicking her tongue over her teeth and hoped she still had them all. Was her nose broken? 'Give over woman — it was only a tap. Just lie there. At least its stopped raining.'

Gilmore's car headlights were feeling their way towards the crossing.

'He's coming, be still.'

'I'll get you for this.'

He got down on one knee and grabbed her throat and whispered in her ear. 'Shut you're gob, Syph,' he said, not caring that he used the nickname she loathed so much, 'or do you want another one?' He showed her his clenched right fist.

***

Gilmore was nearly at the tricky left-twist in the road as it rose to cross the railway. He crawled the car up the hill, just making out the warning sign at the top. *STOP, LOOK, LISTEN BEFORE CROSSING* it commanded, flickering into view through the smeared windscreen. No way was he going to heed it tonight — he'd just dash across. He revved the engine hard and turned sharp left onto the crossing. The car levelled out and the headlights dropped to reveal a motorbike across his path! He stamped the brakes hard, but forgot to depress the clutch. The car stalled across the line. Automatically, he applied the handbrake and tried to restart the engine; nothing. He could see a man was kneeling beside a body. He opened the door, released the handbrake and put his leg out to heave the car back off the crossing.

***

'Great,' he said, still kneeling by her, stifling a laugh. 'The idiot's stalled his bloody car right across the track! Nearly hit my bike, the dozy-git.' He studied her face for a moment and ran a finger through the blood still streaming from her nose and drew red lines round her cheek. 'Now you look a real clown,' he laughed, pleased with his artwork.

But she didn't seem to find it funny and quickly turned her head away.

Perhaps he had hit her too hard. Why did she always have to question everything?

He stood holding his back, acting as if it was injured. He

turned awkwardly towards the car expecting to see it straddling the crossing. It wasn't. Somehow Gilmore had moved it off the crossing.

'Jesus, Liss he's pushed the car back, and now he's coming over!'

'Is anyone hurt?' asked Gilmore, breathless.

'She'll be all right, she's just coming round I think.' He realised Gilmore might recognise him and quickly pulled his goggles back over his eyes.

Liss started to moan and tried to sit up. She was acting her part very well.

But what was the point now? He'd have to think of something fast. 'Give me a hand to get her to one side.'

Supported between them, she staggered to the grass verge, slowly turned and sat.

Liss watched Gilmore studying the face behind the goggles. Had he recognised him? 'Ow,' she gasped to distract him.

Gilmore shook his head then sat on his haunches to look at her injured face. 'It's a nasty gash you have there, Luv.'

She'd never heard him speak until now.

'You'll need to get it stitched I think. A few bruises tomorrow I shouldn't wonder.'

His voice was kind, but she mustn't have second thoughts about him. Not now, after all this time. He still had to die.

She tried to smile. Her cut lower-lip stung like hell. This wasn't supposed to happen. He didn't have to hit her. 'I'll get you, you bastard,' she moaned softly.

He just shrugged his shoulders and went to his bike. His boots sounded uneven on the cobbles, exaggerating his pretend limp.

Her head ached and she closed her eyes as Gilmore examined her face. His left hand held it steady while his right stroked the blood-art from her cheek with his handkerchief; so tender a touch from such a meaty hand. He smelt salty; clean and fresh. She began to feel a little better.

She heard the boots marching back from the bike, but now they didn't sound as if he was limping. They stopped, silent for a second. She opened her eyes in time to see the thin rope pass across Gilmore's face. It was quickly looped around his neck and pulled tight.

Instantly Gilmore was spluttering. His spit showered her face as his rapidly turned purple. He dropped the handkerchief as he tried to free the rope. His mouth opened wide as if to speak, but no sound came out.

She could see the gaps of his missing teeth. His extended tongue flapped about like a swollen piece of purple chamois-leather.

She watched as Gilmore was hauled backwards off his feet to sit on the cobbles, legs straight. He was staring back at her with confused eyes pleading for her help. His boots desperately struggled for purchase on the wet cobbles.

She looked at the hangman and shouted, 'Let him go. This isn't in the plan.'

'He knows me,' he said, wrestling with the weight at his feet struggling with the noose. 'Could tell the way he looked at me,' he gasped. 'And he touched you. Only me touches you. Nobody, but nobody, touches you ... except me. Understand?'

She nodded and looked back into the dying face. They'd planned to fake his suicide, to die instantly when the train hit him, not for her to witness — within spitting-distance — his prolonged struggle for life.

Yet to be so close to his death was enthralling, exhilarating and she felt once again the feeling she'd experienced all those years ago. She smiled at Gilmore as she watched his hands trying desperately to free the noose.

Gilmore made a final struggle to free himself. His hobnail boots tried again for purchase, but this time they had to struggle against her weight, too — she had sat on his knees.

He opened his eyes: saw her give him a little wave, just wiggling her fingers. Slowly, Gilmore's hands lost their power and fell one at a time to the road. His head lolled sideways.

Breathing, she thought, had stopped.

The noose was released.

Gilmore slumped onto his side.

She watched the killing hands calmly roll the rope into a neat circle. 'Here, Liss. Trophy for you,' he said, as if nothing had happened and slung the rope in her lap. She fondled it then stuffed it into a pocket, to keep for later.

He began searching through Gilmore's pockets, found his car keys and slung them, too, in her lap. 'Stop staring at him, Syph and get his car over here. Now for god's sake!'

She looked up at the killer. After all her years of manipulating, he'd done what she'd wanted: he'd murdered. He'd taken Gilmore's life, in a way that satisfied her more than anything she'd experienced. She'd show him in bed tonight how much she'd forgiven him for hitting her; so long as he stopped calling her by that sick nickname he used when he was angry with her.

'Do it, I need to move the bike out of the way,' he shouted. 'The train will be here any minute!'

She picked up the keys with shaking hands and stood.

'For god's sake, Syph,' he shouted, clenching his fist again.

It was enough. She walked unsteadily across the track to the Anglia, still annoyed that he kept calling her Syph. A minute later she parked the car alongside Gilmore.

'If we can get the car back on the crossing, with him behind the wheel, everything will be fine.'

She just nodded, remembering the body dying just inches from her face; her face which still carried Gilmore's spit mingled with her blood.

They struggled, forever it seemed, to move Gilmore's dead-weight into the car, stopping twice and laying him flat while they caught their breath. They left him with his head lolling to one side as they pushed the car back across the track.

She wiped her bleeding lip again with the palm of her left

hand and, while he stood behind the car to stop it rolling back, she reached inside to pull on the handbrake.

They heard the engine whistle; it was almost at the crossing. 'Well done, Liss. Let's get out of here.'

She felt his strong grasp around her arm, as he led her to the bike.

He paused to double-check the Anglia was still in place, felt relieved to see it parked on the crossing. He was too far away for him to notice that Gilmore had opened his eyes.

***

The view from the footplate hazy with smoke, beaten down by the wind, cleared briefly as they completed the right-hand curve, to show fireman Warburton a car with white tyres straddling the line. A mere two-hundred feet away!

He looked at Robinson, frozen in panic. 'Jesus, man, do something.'

Warburton knocked Robinson's hand off the regulator and looped it over the whistle chord. The engine immediately started screaming a warning. Warburton shut off steam and applied the vacuum brake. They were thrown forward as the engine rapidly lost speed.

But he knew it was too late, knew they were going hit the car.

'Brace ... we'll not stop in time.' He was thankful they didn't have a tender full of loose coal behind them. If they had, it could crush them on impact.

***

Gilmore was trying to fathom what had happened to him. Everything in view swam, making him feel sick. His neck was so tender. His head throbbed like hell.

He recognised a sound ... a train whistle? Strange. His neck hurt as he turned to look along ... along a railway track! How had he got here? He vaguely remembered a motorbike. Yes ... there was definitely a motorbike.

An engine was revving. It roared once more and he saw a

red light disappear into the darkness.

He heard something screaming. Was he dreaming? The ignition keys were beginning to jangle. He put a hand on them to quieten them — it was no dream.

He turned back to see a train coming around the curve towards him, its engine rapidly consuming the short distance between them. At last, he realised he had to get out of the car. He only had a few seconds — just five short seconds.

The ominous shape, lit orange by the level crossing's arc-light, was rapidly expanding to fill his view through the window. The continuous whistle was making his headache worse. Everything was so fuzzy, going in slow-motion.

Four seconds: he fumbled with the door handle: he must get out and run, or his new car would be crushed with him inside. The door clicked open. Relief.

Three seconds: he swung his rubber legs out as fast as he could and pulled himself upright using the top of the door for support.

Two seconds: in shear panic he stared at the locomotive's growing red buffer beam, its towing-hook aiming straight for his chest.

One second: he decided he'd be safer back inside the car and began to sit. He prayed for the train to stop, but it refused. His time had come.

Gilmore's agonising yell set a barn owl screeching in harmony, but their eerie resonances reached no human ears.

Zero seconds. There was no alternative: his instant death had arrived. One-hundred tons of steel slammed into the car at thirty-miles-an-hour. Every window shattered on impact. His left leg was roughly severed below the knee, the door closing around it like blunt shears, as the top neatly sliced his head from his body.

Sounds of scrunching, twisting metal continued as the train propelled what was left of Gilmore and his beloved car, sideways along the track.

Robinson was flung around the cab and released the whistle.

Minus four seconds: the train squealed to a standstill.

The car hung from the engine's buffers.

The engine hissed quietly.

The owl screeched in disgust.

Bentham arrived at the car, panting, to find the driver and fireman standing, appalled, by the scene. He switched on his torch and flashed it over the wreckage.

They took a step closer. Blood ran from bits of flesh and bone jutting out from the top of the car's cream door.

The two passengers arrived to stand dumbstruck.

Robinson, getting the feeling he was being watched, turned slowly, then pointed towards the engine. His open mouth failed to speak.

Bentham swung his torch round to illuminate Gilmore's head, standing upright, trapped behind the white oil lamp on the engine's buffer beam. Its accusing eyes stared straight through Robinson. Its jaw, wide open, looked ready to shout abuse at the engine driver.

Robinson, seeing streams of blood begin to trickle from Gilmore's eyes, turned and threw up. He tried to stand upright, but his knees buckled, and he fainted, tumbling backwards into the wet brambles bordering the line.

Bentham, disgusted by Robinson's collapse, was the first to speak. 'I'm going to call Cuddington box — tell 'em what's happened. They'll need to get the railway police and a meat-wagon here as soon as possible. You'd better keep an eye on 'im,' he said, pointing to Robinson's legs protruding from the brambles. He turned and trotted back to the telephone mounted on a post by the crossing. The waving beam of light from Bentham's torch disappeared towards the crossing, accompanied by curses as he tripped over lumps of coal flung from the engine.

Robinson came round and was helped to his feet by the two

passengers. They escorted him back to the cab, trying not to look at Gilmore's questioning gaze, where they found Warburton had already started brewing strong sweet tea for everyone.

Two-minutes later, Bentham had told the signalman in Cuddington box what had happened. As he turned to go back to the train, the light from his torch caught something on the level crossing. It was a black left boot; its bright metal studs glinted in the torch light. He was about to pick it up, but changed his mind when he saw it was spattered with blood and contained the stump of a leg!

He stood for a moment studying the boot, then remembered it was his duty to fix warning detonators to the track some two hundred yards behind the stationary train.

On his way back some ten-minutes later, he stopped again at the crossing. Puzzled, he scratched his beard. The boot wasn't where he'd last seen it. Had he imagined it? He stood shining his torch over the crossing. Relieved, he saw the boot nearby. But now it was on the road, not between the rails. He hadn't imagined it after all. He went across to check it.

The boot's laces were undone and the boot no longer contained the stump of Gilmore's leg.

13

BLEARY-EYED I CAME TO AND TURNED ON THE BEDSIDE TABLE LIGHT, checked the alarm clock and went downstairs to silence the annoying ringing. I knew Alice wouldn't be calling, especially at 11 o'clock at night.

'Suspicious circumstances,' said Gardiner, plainly excited about the possibility of some juicy tale.

I pictured Fred's lips competing with the morsel of pork pie clinging to his moustache to deliver the message.

'They've not told me any details. A car's on its way. You'll be in Whitegate within the hour. Sorry to call you, but I'm told that prat at Manchester 'as already got wind of it.'

Great. I knew about the new boss at Manchester. Newall, the pompous idiot, would be wanting a nice, neat report on his desk come Monday morning regardless of the scale of the incident. But I also knew — which soothed my irritation a little — he'd have to wait until I was ready. 'Thanks for the tip-off, Fred,' I sighed. 'You just made my night. I'm on my way, that is, once I'm fully-clothed.'

By the time I'd dressed, found my torch and put on some wellingtons, the arranged car had arrived. We drove without speaking, allowing me some time to speculate about the incident.

The driver broke our silence to give me something else to think about. 'You're new here aren't you, sir?'

'Yes, landed here this week.'

'You get to recognise most of the officers.'

'This is my first late-night call-out, at the end of an easy week; well it was, until you turned up.'

'Um, looks like it's not done yet, sir. Do you mind being called out late at night?'

'Probably a lot more than you do I suspect?' The driver smiled, no doubt calculating the overtime he would be getting paid.

'Why the railway branch of the Transport Police, sir?'

Uncertain whether to continue this conversation or not, I knew full well the answer. 'Simple really. I like trains. Got the bug off my brother.'

The driver nodded, but didn't ask any more questions. He probably loved cars.

I stared through the window into the darkness. Unseen countryside slipped by and my mind went back twenty-five years. Yes, David's fault, if fault was the right word. Of course we both wanted to be engine drivers. But when dad had taken David on one side and lectured him hard about the folly of such a job, we both began to have second thoughts about a railway career. "It's extremely hard work, son" dad had said, "dangerous and very, very dirty. Look at the engine drivers and the firemen. See how grimy their faces and hands are. And you'll have to do years of backbreaking service as a fireman to be able to even start learning to be a driver! If you qualify, you'll have to walk the track to learn the routes. You'll be away from home most of your life and run the risk of being killed or injured by someone else's mistake. Think again, son".

David took dad's advice and much to everyone's surprise he opted for a career in the Civil Service. The last I heard, he'd been posted by the Foreign Office to America. He didn't say why; something hush-hush I suspected. I envied his opportunity to travel around the States by train and hoped, that one day, I'd get a chance to visit him.

Dad was right about being killed on the railway. The appalling images of the Harrow and Wealdstone crash came flooding back. I'd taken Alice to the pictures. *Monkey Business*, the film's title I remembered, not because it was a cracking film, but because of the horrendous footage of the *Pathe Newsreel* which preceded it. The tragic grey scenes, projected through thick clouds of cigarette smoke onto a nicotine stained screen, had silenced the entire audience. The stern monotone voice of the newsreader described the scene and the British resolve to rescue as many lives as possible.

"And soldiers from a nearby US army base helped our own boys, the police, the Red Cross and the ordinary man-in-the-street to find and pull out survivors. Even the boys, from the famous public school of Harrow, pitched in and helped by distributing refreshments, prepared by the Women's Guild, to the rescuers. The tragic scenes resembled those not witnessed since World War Two."

Yes, dad had been right ... very right indeed. A collection box, to raise money for the victim's families, was at the door when we left the cinema. As I was in the service of the railway, we felt obliged to contribute and decided to forego our usual fish-and-chip supper on the walk home. Alice had held my arm tight throughout the film report. I sensed on our way home she was still uncertain about my chosen career.

It was then she told me she was three-months pregnant.

I was jerked from my reverie by the car bumping its way along the pot-holed lane which led to the scene of the incident.

'Sorry, sir,' said the driver, 'we've arrived.'

So, what was I likely to find here? Suspicious circumstances Fred had said, which usually meant foul play. The Railway Police had to attend accidents, indeed all incidents on the railway, be it theft or a tree blown across tracks during a storm. The safety of the trains and their passengers was paramount.

I set off to meet the local Bobby who was first on the scene. He looked like he was ready for retirement, and eager to talk to a new face.

'It's a bit lighter now the clouds have uncovered the moon. You come about the crash?'

I nodded, and produced my warrant card, which he ignored. 'Do you know what happened?'

'That's easy enough ain't it. A train's run into a car.' His bicycle was propped up against the post carrying one of the cast iron warning signs. 'A fat lot of good they turned out to be,' he said, pointing to the sign. 'Car driver's dead.' Smiling, he ran a finger across his throat to emphasise the point but he didn't bother to warn me the driver had been decapitated.

I was about to walk to the train, when the Bobby coughed. I looked at him waiting for the snippet he'd kept secret until now.

'There's one more thing, 'fore yer goes. He pointed to his cape which lay on the roadside.

'What?'

'It's under my cape.'

'What is?'

'Evidence, sir. I turned me cape inside-out to keep it dry for you.' The Bobby's expression reminded me of the type found on the faces of obsequious waiters expecting a big tip.

'Show me.' I wondered what was in store and bent to lift the cape. Underneath lay a blood-stained handkerchief. One corner carried the embroidered initials WG. I thanked the bobby, who coughed quietly into his fist to complete the waiter-image.

I carefully placed the handkerchief into one of my brown paper bags I always carried, making a mental note to pass it on to the Coroner's doctor. I couldn't leave the handkerchief in case the weather turned to rain again. I pulled a red peg from my pocket and pushed it into the soft earth to mark the spot. Gleaning nothing more from the bobby, I set off along the line to examine the wreckage and meet the train crew.

I stopped first at the twisted car, turned on my torch and examined the inside of the car through the broken window of the passenger door, which was jammed shut. The driver seemed to be standing, with his back towards me, as if ready to sit. But he wasn't standing. He was hanging; trapped by the driver's door which had closed around his neck. I leaned into the car and sniffed, and detected a faint smell of urine, and something else: salt? Clouds covered the moon again making a thorough assessment of the scene impossible.

I walked around the car and shone my torch onto the driver's door. It was then I discovered that the driver was headless.

I found the missing head quickly enough; the shock made me take a step back before I moved closer to inspect it. Blood from its neck and eyes had congealed to form a sticky mess, gluing the head to the engine's buffer-beam.

It was time to talk to the train crew.

***

'BTP coming up,' I shouted and climbed the steps to the footplate. Five heads turned, as one, to watch their new guest slowly revealed. I was always amused how the new people I met reacted to my six-foot-three stature. They remained silent as I looked down on them and produced my warrant card.

None of them looked at it. Instead, they carried on smoking and supping tea as if waiting for their break to officially finish. After a short pause their eyes searched mine, waiting for me to start asking probing questions; after all, it's what I'm paid to do.

The guard startled everyone by suddenly springing into action, snatched the mugs from the two passengers, then flung their tea out onto the track. Looking much like a school boy, caught out by entertaining guests not permitted on the footplate, Bentham introduced everyone and offered me a mug of hot sweet tea. I gratefully accepted. It was a tight-squeeze inside the cab with six men inside, so the tea-less passengers returned to their carriage while I prepared to question the crew.

Robinson, the driver, was still finding it difficult to explain exactly what he'd seen. Even in the red glow cast from the open firebox door he looked visibly white and was still shaking. His tea splashed onto his boots as he raised the enamelled mug to his lips with nicotine-stained fingers. I doubted he'd be much use to my enquiries until his shock left him.

Bentham was much more helpful and precise about what he'd witnessed. 'We left Winsford & Over station bang on time, sir,' he said, standing as if to attention but swinging pompously back and forth on his toes, 'and made good running. Nobody flagged us down at the Whitegate halt so we didn't have to—.'

'So, if you had stopped, you would have arrived here a bit later?'

'That's true,' said the driver, standing his ground, 'but only by a minute or so at the most.'

'So whoever he is might have managed to move the car, or get out of it at any rate?'

'Assuming he wanted to?' You can't blame me because he didn't succeed. It wasn't my fault, inspector. I was only doing thirty at the whistle sign.'

Warburton looked at him then quickly turned away. The driver had probably knocked ten off his actual speed.

Robinson became more distraught, so I raised a hand to calm him, but he went on. 'Surely the chap in the car would have heard the whistle,' he said, before giving us all something to think about. 'It's a bloody good job we stayed on the rails!'

We looked at each other in turn, pondering on what might have happened if the engine had derailed.

'God man, that's right,' chimed Warburton. 'From what I saw, whoever it is didn't look like he'd tried to escape until the last moment.'

'Did either of you see anyone else about?'

'No,' said Robinson.

Warburton shook his head.

'Are you sure? Someone on the crossing as you approached; a passenger in the car; another vehicle perhaps?'

'Not that I could see. By then we were almost on top of the car and the body of the engine obscures the view anyway. Take a look and you'll see what I mean.'

I shuffled around them to take up a position where the driver would have been standing and peered forward through the small window of the cab. Robinson was right. Although the scene was lit by the moon, the smashed car was completely obscured from view.

Bentham explained how he'd found a boot and that its leg had mysteriously gone missing.

We left the cab and went back to where the boot lay near the crossing.

The bobby stood as if waiting to direct traffic, an unlikely event at two in the morning. Bored, he came over to listen.

'And where, originally, did you find the boot with its leg?'

'Here, sir.' Bentham pointed to the middle of the crossing with his torch.

I could just make out a thin trail of blood leading back to the train. 'And you are quite certain it did have part of a leg inside?'

The guard looked at me, affronted. 'Certain of it, sir. The dead bloke,' he said, pointing back along the track, 'only has one complete leg.' Bentham had proved to be more observant than me on that point.

I slipped a pencil through the loop on the back of WG's boot and took it back to the car. The evidence was stacking up; evidence pointing to a probable murder.

Not a lot more could be done here. I'd go and speak to the two passengers and take their addresses before allowing them to leave. I'd have to return at daybreak, with Dobbs, when it should be light enough to see the true picture and piece together what had happened.

Someone from a Coroner's office would have to come and identify what had caused the death of W G, whoever he was. The train crew would have to ring in from the phone at the crossing to organise a fresh staff for the morning. A railway crane would have to be brought in, and reversed back down the line from Northwich, to clear the track. Fortunately, this incident had taken place on a branch line and not a busy main line. If it had, I'd have to deal with the additional problem of several delayed trains.

I set off back to the train. I was about to go and interview the two passengers when the tank engine suddenly let off a shrill blast of steam, startling me. I heard a scrabbling noise in the bushes on the embankment above the train and put it down to a startled rabbit dashing for cover. At least that was what it sounded like.

14

IT WAS A DRY, DARK, MORNING WHEN WE SET OFF FOR WHITEGATE. I had telephoned PC's Dobbs and Smith at six o'clock to advise them their weekend, too, or at least Saturday was cancelled.

On our way to the incident an hour later, a promising dawn had broken. By the time we arrived at eight o'clock, the rising sun in a clear sky cast long shadows over the scene.

Considering this incident had taken place some distance from habitation, there were a surprising number of rubber-neckers mingling with a few pressmen. Some reporters I recognised, in particular Herbert Jabberson, the crime reporter from the *Manchester Evening News*.

'Morning, *Detective* Inspector Crosier,' called Jabberson, as he moved away from his photographer taking pictures of the crowd. He was as eager for news as I was for information.

'Morning, Jabberson,' I said, while gesturing to Dobbs and Smith to go and examine the wreckage. 'How did you know I'm a DI now?'

Jabberson leaned forward slightly and tapped the side of his nose a couple of times with a forefinger. 'Well, Oliver, how about you tell me what's happened here, and I'll tell you who told me,' he said, stabbing the finger into my chest.

'Nothing at present, so don't even ask. I think it's going to turn messy. I'll keep you posted.' I'd known Jabberson for many years and he'd often been a source of useful information for the BTP when I'd been based in Manchester, ten years earlier.

A car door slammed.

'Detective Inspector Crosier?' said a young man, who had just arrived in a black Wolseley police car. 'Inspector Davidson,

CID Chester. Congratulations, I hear you're Crewe's latest railway DI, and we have some interesting facts to discuss.'

'Indeed there are.' I took an instant liking to this young and well-spoken inspector, but I wondered how he too, knew I was new to Crewe. It had to be Gardiner. I went over what I had learned from my nocturnal interviews as we walked towards the wreckage.

'So, what's the cause? Any theories?'

'I think he was targeted. Another worrying aspect is the missing foot.'

'Sorry?'

'Didn't they tell you? That's why I dragged you in here.' I rapidly stroked the front of my neck up and down. Davidson looked at me, curious: Alice told me once about my unconscious habit of displaying frustration deployed when others didn't do as I'd asked. 'The victim lost his left foot during the collision. And it disappeared within ten minutes. There's a slim chance a fox might have taken it, but with all the commotion I doubt any would dared come anywhere near.'

'I doubt if foxes can undo laces without shredding them and the boot to bits,' Davidson said, a broad grin on his face. 'A trophy killing then?'

'Certain of it, though just what sort of prize was worth killing an old man for, I've yet to discover.'

'I can't recall any, but I'll check our records. See if we have any similar unsolved cases in the district.'

'The only means to identify the driver, assuming it's his car is by its registration; nothing else on him as far as I could tell.'

'They'll have a name and address for us any time now.'

'Be interesting to see if the owner's initials are WG. A handkerchief with those initials was found near the crossing.'

'Could be the killer's,' said Davidson.

We reached the car, and I stopped to block Davidson's view of the gargoyle stuck on the engine's buffers.

'I should warn you, as well as losing his lower leg, the driver also lost his head. Luckily we found it.' I stepped to one side, watching Davidson, and waited for his reaction to this unusual introduction to the deceased. Its bloodless face glared at him.

'And his leg stumped off in disgust, I suppose,' he said, recovering well.

We both grinned.

'The brief search I made last night revealed nothing. We might find something on him once we allow his body to be removed. There's a faint smell of piss, and salt which I considered a bit odd.'

'Probably something to do with the brine workings. They're all over this part of Cheshire. I'll get onto the local boys. Get them to call the works. Someone may recognise the car's description.'

'The pathologist should be here by now,' I said, 'but let's take a butcher's-hook inside the car before he arrives.'

Davidson grimaced at my use of the slang I'd picked up from my time with Hunt in London.

'We'll have to wait for the railway crane to arrive before we can remove the corpse. Shouldn't be too long now.'

Apart from the remains of the victim, and discounting the broken glass which lay everywhere, the inside of car looked surprisingly clean, almost new. There were no documents inside the car, and very little blood. A few drops had soaked into the victim's clothing about his neck, none on the victim's hands, yet some, I noticed, had dried on the handbrake lever. I made a mental note to remind the pathologist, when he arrived, to take samples of both. If they were different, we might have a sample of the killer's blood.

Leaving Davidson at the car, I climbed up to the cab only to be informed that the engine driver was asleep in the first carriage. Warburton had kept the locomotive company all night, keeping enough heat in the boiler to heat the carriage where Robinson, Bentham and the bobby had taken it in turns to rest. Now, some ten hours after the incident, the level in the water tanks was getting dangerously low.

A whistle sounded in the distance, heralding the arrival of the crane followed by a few flat-bed wagons, pushed along by a locomotive. I sent Bentham to wave his red flag, and stop the train before it could damage any evidence.

It would be at least half-an-hour before there'd be enough pressure for the steam-driven crane to lift the car, so I suggested to Dobbs and Smith we take this opportunity to have breakfast of salmon-paste sandwiches I'd made-up this morning, and mugs of sweet tea from my thermos.

***

The crane's jib had finally been raised and swung into position. The crowd and reporters scrambled into the field, the other side of the fence, eager to get the best view.

Ropes were fed around the car as cameras clicked.

The steam crane hissed and puffed, as it clattered into action to gradually hoist the wrecked car off the engine's buffers.

Someone in the crowd cheered; some clapped.

The car swung twenty-feet above the rails.

Making space for the car to be lowered, Robinson reversed the engine a few feet towards the crossing then began to damp-down the fire.

I waited.

The crane operator, misunderstanding what I required of him, engaged the slewing mechanism. The crane jerked and began to swing the car round in front of the crowd. The sideways motion dislodged the corpse, which slumped to expose its headless torso through the smashed window of the driver's door.

A woman in the crowd screamed and keeled-over.

I ran to the operator, shouting at him to stop.

He did suddenly, causing the car to swing wildly, unbalancing Gilmores corpse even more.

The car slipped in its ropes.

The driver's door swung open.

The crowd gasped.

Cameras clicked enthusiastically, as Gilmore's corpse eased itself from the car to somersault twice before hitting the verge, neck-first. Some evidence would almost certainly be destroyed.

'Fucking great,' I said, to Dobbs.

The pathologist arrived too late to witness the drama. After his cursory examination of the corpse, the cause of death, he announced, "was bloody obvious, even to a blind man dashing by on 'orse". He'd examine it later in the mortuary for any other signs of booze or foul play. I requested he take a sample of blood from the car's handbrake and gave him the blood soaked handkerchief the Bobby had found. I demanded the pathologist's report by Monday lunch time.

He left, as did most of his type, in a huff.

Ten minutes later the corpse was stretchered away to the ambulance waiting in the lane. Before its journey to the mortuary, Davidson and I went through its pockets. We found a half-crown, two three-penny-bits and an empty Wrigley's chewing-gum packet. No name tags on any of his clothes, nor was WG carrying his driver's licence or insurance papers. Result: nothing with which to identify him.

Davidson and I watched as the crane placed the wrecked car onto a flat-bed wagon. The recovery train moved a few yards forward, so my constables could begin searching the track.

Keen to replay the crash through my mind's eye, I went back to the crossing then looked back towards the two trains. Thick black smoke wafted towards me from the tank engine as its fire gradually died down. If WG had simply broken down on the crossing he would have surely got out of the car in time. If this had been a prank gone wrong, would the perpetrators have stayed to witness the smash and then remove vital evidence? At that time of night, a wet one to boot, they'd no doubt get as far away as possible. The sound of the smash alone would scare seven sorts of the proverbial out of them. Nor would they be likely to keep WG's foot as a memento.

On the other hand if this was premeditated murder, to me the most likely option, would the killer or killers want to make sure the job was done? And if they were really sick bastards, they might well have taken a piece of WG away as a souvenir. I didn't like the direction in which the evidence continued to point.

I moved around the crossing. Where might be the best vantage point be for the suspects to see what had happened? If they wanted to be sure WG was dead, then they'd need to be on the side of the crossing facing the direction of the engine's travel. To one side, the embankment fell away steeply. The other climbed gently in the direction of the main road, about half a mile away. But it was wooded, and might afford the watchers, if there ever were any, a place to hide. I sent Dobbs and Smith over to do a thorough search of the hillside between the crossing and the point at which the train and car had come to a stop. With luck, they might turn up something.

After a few minutes, I heard Dobbs shouting.

I signalled to Davidson to join us then walked along the track, clambered up the bank and climbed over the crumbling wooden fence — which left two large splinters in the palm of my right hand.

There weren't many trees, but by one Dobbs had found cigarette butts. The grass was trampled down, too, whereas it wasn't behind the other trees. Fortunately the crowd had been moved away before they had a chance to trample on this potential evidence. I collected the butts which felt soft, so recently dropped, and bagged them.

This spot would afford the killer a good view to check the victim was dead. Grass was broken down in a line which led back towards bushes near the main road. It certainly looked like one or two persons had been here very recently.

We followed the track, taking care to walk either side of it. Below some bushes were imprints of a motorbike's tyres in the soft mud. Its tracks led back to the main road. And there were definitely two sets of footprints where the bike had been hidden.

Davidson dashed off to take a call on the police car's radio-phone.

I sent Dobbs and Smith to continue examining the track then stood to examine the two large splinters in my hand, and think about young Davidson, who strictly speaking didn't need to be here. The railway police was the oldest force in the land and today the BTP was well able to carry out its own investigations into all criminal acts taking place on the railway, though it was good policy to involve the local CID forces in serious cases. Davidson didn't seem to mind assisting me; something I doubted, his older colleagues would be likely to do. I hoped if any more of these suspicious incidents turned up, I'd have the pleasure of working with him again.

From my viewpoint by the bushes, I could still see the top half of the two trains. Smoke had almost stopped from the tank-engine that hit the car, now secured to the flatbed wagon with chains. The heads of Dobbs and Smith bobbed up and down as they searched for evidence. At night the view would not be so clear, the car would almost certainly be obscured by the drop of the hillside and if you wanted to be certain WG was dead, then you needed to be a lot closer, and the bushes up here were an ideal hiding place for the bike.

I decided we couldn't do any more here and that the two trains should be coupled together and leave for Northwich. By the time I walked back to the crossing Davidson had WG's name: William Gilmore. He had live at an address in Winsford.

The local force had already called round to break the news to his widow and pick up any other descriptions to confirm William Gilmore was the dead man.

Dobbs and Smith had taken statements from everyone concerned and with any luck we'd all be home by mid-afternoon. I would have to write up my notes in readiness for the case meeting on Monday. I'd report to 'know-all-Newall', once I'd read the pathologist's report. Newall would just have to wait until I was ready.

I still had Sunday clear, so I might be able to redecorate the children's bedroom before the family arrived, but the prospect of finding a longer bed before the shops closed at five-thirty looked impossible. It looked like I'd be sleeping diagonally for at least another week.

***

It was early afternoon when Davidson's photographer returned. 'Here's your set of photographs our man took this morning.'

'Thanks,' I said, taking the envelope. 'Better get him up the bank to take some shots of the bike tracks. Smith will dig up a section afterwards so we can make a cast.'

The photographs were good; several wide shots of the scene; a few of the crowd; details of the wreckage and Gilmore's empty boot — which I'd brought along this morning.

Pictures of the corpse, suspended inside the wreckage, an amazing shot of it falling from the car and the close-ups of his head resting on the buffer-beam, were not photos to show his widow.

15

RELIEF: THE VERDICT IN THE CASE OF GILMORE WAS NOT DEATH BY misadventure. I didn't like unsolved cases, especially murder. And this was my first.

I went with Dobbs and Smith, to the funeral service in Winsford Methodist Church, partly to pay my respects and partly to see if anyone of interest might show-up. Cardin, Dobbs and Smith, dressed in uniform sat at the back next to me in my plain dark suit and black tie.

Apart from Michael Gilmore, all the mourners were of his parent's generation; none of his school friends were present.

'Quite a turnout,' Smith observed. 'I've counted fifty-three so far, apart from us.'

When it came to singing *Onward Christian Soldiers*, the mourners gave a hearty rendition. Perhaps they thought it could speed up the process of dispatching the dead and get them to the tea and sandwiches sooner.

It didn't seem likely we'd glean anything here which might help our investigations. The same, too, at the burial at Wharton Church, half-an-hour later, where only a handful of close relatives went inside for the brief service.

I stood with Dobbs inside the lychgate while the burial took place. Despite Dobbs' expectant looks, I declined Mrs Gilmore's invitation to participate in a bun-fight back at the Armstrong Hall. I hoped she would be all right and reassured her the investigation would not stop because her husband's funeral had taken place.

Some standing within earshot looked at me curiously; I couldn't tell if they thought I was lying or if they were simply upset. Whether they believed me or not wasn't relevant. One certainty however, was that in a week, Mrs Gilmore would be spending Christmas without her husband.

I watched her, walking with her son to the funeral car waiting to whisk them off to the Armstrong Hall. Within a few minutes everyone had gone, the churchyard quiet once more.

As the gravediggers began their task it struck me: I'd been in this scene before, when I attended Sylt's funeral, seven years ago. True there wasn't an exhumation this time, but the similarity was eerie; the conversation with chief mourner under a lychgate roof, then watching her depart. And, as far as I could recollect, the uncanny resemblance Mrs Gilmore had to Mary Sylt, thirty years her junior.

16

MONDAY, JANUARY 4TH 1960, WAS A SAD DAY FOR THE TOWN OF Middlewich. There had been a lot of talk about cutting back services on little-used lines, and the route from Sandbach to Northwich became one of the earliest victims in Cheshire.

Today, passenger services would cease and the line kept open exclusively for goods traffic. Despite the local uproar, the British Railways Board had concluded that this service must go and Middlewich station be closed.

I decided to go with Dobbs to the gathering organised to bid farewell to the last train to Northwich. It got us out of the office, though officially, we went to ensure the event passed off peacefully and protect the travelling public right up until the last moment. A sad affair; what was the British Railways Board thinking?

We arrived, about half-an-hour before the last train arrived from Sandbach, amazed by how many people had turned up.

At least eighty, according to Dobbs. 'I think we'll need reinforcements?' he said, grinning.

'I doubt it. I don't see any BRB members here, otherwise I might agree with you.' I looked at those around us, a mixed bunch of local business people; mothers with children in prams; kids from the local primary school; the two station staff and some train-enthusiasts.

Of course the Mayor — who, highly organised and punctual — hadn't arrived ten-minutes after the train came in. The press were there, reporters from Winsford — now the nearest service, only a 'mere twenty-minute' bus ride away! — Northwich and Crewe. Even Jabberson from the *Manchester Evening News* was here accompanied by his usual photographer. All were hoping for an interview with the Mayor — not that he would have anything of relevance to say!

The Mayor arrived and the crowd gathered by the engine decked out with flowers, bunting and, to add insult to injury, a British Railways flag. The thick-skinned Mayor climbed onto a makeshift podium, tapped the microphone a few times, coughed, then delivered a dreadful speech. Apparently, he deplored this closure, and others made since the war, whilst everyone knew he had never travelled anywhere by train, even before he had access to the mayoral car.

Lots of photographs were taken. I wished I'd brought my camera. I'd have to buy all the papers when they came out on Thursday and make do with them for my scrapbook.

The train left twenty-minutes late, which on this occasion wouldn't bother anybody. Those on board, leaned through windows to cheer and wave to those who weren't.

I didn't cheer or wave. I couldn't understand why everyone else did.

The crowd eventually dispersed in an orderly fashion much to our relief.

And that, we assumed, was all this sad scene at Middlewich had to offer.

17

APRIL 1962

YOU SIT ON CREWE STATION, RUMMAGING THROUGH YOUR HAND-bag, looking for a handkerchief to dry your moistening eyes. You tell yourself you have done all you can for your mother. And just when you hoped to be on your way, you have to wait another half-an-hour for your train.

You have nothing to really rush back to London for. Work tomorrow will still be there, whatever time you turn the key in your front door tonight. You may as well be calm, and observe the travelling-world as it passes you by.

You relax to watch those not so lucky, those that have to be on their way *now*, not when British Railways sees fit to take them. Their frustration will turn to anger soon, while you smugly decide whether to have your hair done after work tomorrow, or the next day. Even your — a-year-to-live, if she's lucky — mother found the strength to tell you as you said goodbye: "Curls suit you much better, my dear". So you'd better get it done before your next visit.

A train pulls in from London, nosily stealing the rays of sunlight in which you'd been warming. Several passengers are deposited onto the platform. Most know where they're going but your eye catches a small man as he leaves a second-class carriage. His foxy-looking eyes seem to peer into your mind. Does he recognise you? You don't know him.

He scans the platform, checks his wristwatch against the station-clock then walks to the timetable standing in the middle of the platform. It's so big its shadow will cover you within the hour if you are still here.

Your eyes stay with him, but why? Was it the way his drilled beyond yours? He studies the timetable. You can almost read it from where you sit. He looks up, checking the platform's number.

Whistles are blown, distracting you from your noseying, as doors bang shut. Green flags are waved and as the train departs the station master — or his assistant? — cranks a handle to raise all the timetable's letters as one. Reference to the London train is erased and your sunshine returns.

Foxy's at it again, checking everything: he's clearly worried and you ponder upon what it might be; a business meeting missed, though he carries no briefcase, not even a bag; an assignation, with a now-frustrated lover; perhaps he expected to meet his wife. Or is he a crook come for the payoff? You may find out: he's walking towards you. Surely he's not going back to London?

Reluctantly you make space, so he can sit, by moving your small overnight-case to one side. His eyes are definitely wrong. You casually move your handbag to the opposite side. He can't have come all this way to steal from you? Thinking better of him, you rest it once more on your left.

His clothes have seen better days. His suit, expensively tailored many years ago, looks very tired despite its fine red lines. Its cuffs and turn-ups are frayed and the top button of the jacket is missing. His greying-hair is held firmly to his hatless head by Brylcreem. You'd recognise that smell anywhere and wish you'd never bought a pot for your husband.

Foxy, you hope, will be travelling second-class, so there's no need to worry, but you take your ticket from your purse to check it still says *First-class*.

An announcement hurries around the station roof.

You're good at the local dialect and learn your train will be here in two-minutes.

Foxy seems to have understood, too. He sighs. You can't be

sure if he's relieved or resigned. He hasn't spoken — not even a good-afternoon.

At times like this, you wish you'd not left your *Penguin* in the Crewe Arms hotel. Still, *Murder on the Orient Express* didn't exactly thrill you, even though Hercule in his fastidious — no, tedious — way gathers all his suspects together to reveal the killers. You, being good at solving crime novels, had already worked-out more than one person was involved. Anyway, it's too late to go back for it now: your train is arriving.

Foxy recognises someone in the train — a pensioner? — briefly waving a limp hand from a first-class compartment, his tartan suit doing nothing to reduce his years. Strange he didn't smile.

You stand, overnight-case in hand hoping the train has a dining car. Ah yes, it does. Foxy reaches its door-handle first. You say thank you, as he opens it, and you look into his wild eyes, hoping he hasn't noticed your shock when, to your horror, you realise he's hungry, too.

Choosing where to sit isn't difficult; the carriage is empty. Seated, you look through the window to see a man in overalls tap each wheel, of an adjacent train, with a long-handled hammer. What on earth is the point? Wiping condensation from the glass to get a better view, you tut-tut at the black stain on the serviette. When was this window last cleaned?

Almost imperceptibly the ground begins to slide, briefly unbalancing you and stealing the wheel-tapper from view; your journey south has begun. Rails, like the strands of a steel-rope, gradually wind together as the train clatters across points and gathers speed. You turn, astonished to see Foxy has chosen the table opposite yours.

The old man in the tartan suit arrives, unsmiling, and slams a ragged old newspaper onto the table, knocking an empty wine glass over in the process. Oblivious, he swings his backside into a seat to face Foxy. Tartan, by way of introduction says, 'Makes interesting reading, I hope you'll agree. Blowback, what a load of old-bollocks,' he says, stabbing at the headline with an arthritic forefinger.

Like most old people, he doesn't seem to care who overhears him, which is good because you're curious about what they are up to. But what, on earth, is a blowback?

'You have just over five clear months,' he continues, 'to button this up. Enough time even for you.'

Foxy raises an eyebrow at the insult.

'I've given the matter considerable thought, and I've come to the conclusion it's time you balanced the books. I'm not up to it any more,' Tartan says, holding up his ancient hands as evidence. 'It's your job now.' An arthritic finger is pointed directly at Foxy. 'Make a plan and *see it through, man.*'

Foxy is frowning.

You're intrigued.

'Don't worry; whatever your solution, it won't cost you a penny.' Tartan withdraws a fat envelope from inside his jacket and slips it into the paper. 'I'll come back to approve your scheme before I get off, two hours hence. And I want this newspaper back.' He turns the paper face down and slowly stands. As an afterthought, he fumbles in his trouser pocket and says, 'Oh, and here's a tenner for your lunch. I'd heard you're on hard times.'

You were right about that.

'I recommend the roast beef. It's Angus, best in the world. You'll find a half-bottle of the fifty-eight claret suits just fine.'

Tartan turns and walks back to his first-class seat.

The attendant arrives, stands the wine glass upright, and takes Foxy's order for lunch before asking what you would like — whatever happened to ladies-first? Though you fancy some fish you decide on the beef instead — well, it does come highly recommended.

Foxy leans across the table to pick up the paper. He reads the headline, seems deep in thought. But not for long.

The waiter brings his wine and your water.

Claret is poured to half-fill a glass which is quickly emptied before Foxy searches for the envelope, knocking the glass back over in the process.

Then you realise, apart from giving his order, Foxy hasn't uttered a single word and, you note, he hasn't come to meet his wife or girlfriend after all.

18

MAY

THE PARTY WAS IN FULL SWING. JOAN WAS KEEPING FAIRLY SOBER, not easy when every guest brought a bottle and expected it to be opened there-and-then. Taking the wrapper off yet another bottle thrust into her hand by Jane and John Jones, whose paper shop was at the end of the street, she wondered if any of her guests actually knew her taste in drinks.

She smiled, said thanks, took John's coat and threw it over the banister then led them along the hallway into the back room, where the drinks table was groaning.

'Now, what would you like to drink, Jane?' she said, placing their gift alongside four other bottles of rum. Ugh!

Jane and John arrived late after closing the shop and counting its takings. But they weren't the last to arrive, as proven by another knock at the front door.

She went along the hall to open it for a most unexpected guest. 'Well blow me down. Fancy seeing you here.'

'You know me, Sis. I never forget a birthday,' said Lance.

'So how come I don't get any cards or presents every year?'

'Sorry love, pressure of work. I couldn't forget your fortieth.'

'Don't give me all that flannel. Get your backside in here and give me a kiss.'

'With pleasure, come 'ere.'

The lingering kiss complete, he said, 'I expect you've got enough booze, so I got you this.' He rummaged through several pockets before he found the small gift-wrapped cube.

'Oh, this looks nice, wrapped it yourself did you?'

'You know me. Very practical with my hands,' he said, hitting a clenched fist into the palm of his other hand, 'but not for tiny work like this.'

She was shocked by the sudden violent action. Unpleasant memories returned. A sudden roar of laughter from the back-parlour returned her to the present. She hoped that ripping the paper from the unexpected gift would mask her worried expression.

'Don't worry love, not much of the old stuff going on these days, I'm too old anyway. I leave it to the younger hot-heads now.'

She smiled, not meeting his eyes, and dropped the final wrapper. Inside the box, the diamond ring sparkled. She gasped. 'I hope this is legit,' she said, regaining her composure. 'It's lovely.'

'Of course it is, love — I saved up all year. Go on, put it on.'

She did as he asked. It was a bit too big. She'd have to have it adjusted, if she could find a trustworthy jeweller.

'Lovely,' he said, raising her hand so he could kiss it.

She smiled, studying his face. She guessed what he wanted to ask.

'So, Sis. Is she here?'

'Yes, she's here.' She flicked her eyes towards the back room.

'Behaving I hope?'

'She's not a bad kid, Lance. Remand seems to have worked. She's not in any trouble now, as far as I know. She had a bad start, that's all. What's wrong with this family, Lance?'

'Cheer up, Sis, it's your birthday. How about a drink?'

'Give us your overcoat first.' She took it from him and threw the heavy coat over John Jones', not noticing their similarity, but shocked by the heavy thud of a revolver in an inside pocket as it hit the newel-post. She swung round to face him. 'Please, Lance, tell me you're not carrying?'

'No,' he said, checking the coat. 'It's a half bottle of rum.

Then I remembered you don't like it, so I'll make use of it later.' He made sure the gun was safe, buttoned up in the inside pocket. He knew Joan had seen through him, she always did.

She led him by the hand to join the party. Maybe she'd hide the gun later. 'Wait there,' she said, releasing his hand, and went to find her niece. 'Look who the cat's dragged in.'

'Lance, what the ... ?' The likeness froze her, just for a second or two before she pushed through the guests to meet him. 'You're looking all right. Going a bit grey, though. Where did you pick this up?' she said, stroking his tailored suit. 'Or should I say, from whom did you take it?'

'That's nice. This what you call a Mancunian greeting? I'd heard people are friendly up here.'

'We're very friendly up here, Uncle ... very friendly.' She bent her head a little to kiss him full on his mouth. 'See. And this is Salford, by the way. Much better than Manchester.'

He stood holding her, examining her. She was taller now, confident, every part of her stunning. He could feel himself becoming aroused by the deep green eyes looking straight into his. 'I think I'll have a stiff-one after that greeting.'

She giggled, took his hand and led him to the drinks table. 'What will it be? There's plenty of rum.'

The party had continued until three on Sunday morning. Eventually people drifted off. He didn't know any of them, but they'd shared a joke or banged on about United or City. Being a rugby man, they'd bored him to death. Round-ballers! He'd been sympathetic about The Busby Babes, though. After four years, the air crash was still fresh in everyone's minds, especially when football became the topic of conversation and you were in a maudlin-mood having had a few too many drinks. He'd smiled when necessary, had clinked his glass against theirs on cue, told a few jokes and waved everyone off as they left.

'Bloody good party that, Sis, bloody good.'

'Thank shoe, Larnce,' she slurred, raising a glass of rum-and-black to him, swaying gently. 'So, it's time for me bed, I think. Yes, that's it ... me bed.'

'Too right, old girl,' he said. 'Leave this lot for us to clear. You shouldn't have to do this on your fortieth after all.' She swayed a little more as his offer sank in, turned slowly then left the room, glass in hand. They heard her climb the stairs, one heavy footstep, then another.

They looked at each other, just the two of them now, in the silent room. He smiled, 'Come on, let's make a start, and then you can make up a bed for me on the sofa.'

'Okay,' she said, 'but when we've cleared away, I have a much better idea'.

***

He woke about ten, leaned sideways, reached for the last cigarette in the packet and lit it. He lay back smiling, nicely tired from their exertions.

Disturbed, she stirred then curled up beside him and tucked her head under his arm. Her free hand found the black hairs on his chest. Warm sunlight streamed onto them — she'd love to stay in bed with him all day, but didn't want to offend his sister. 'Lance,' she asked. 'Tell me why my dad was killed.'

He wasn't sure at first whether to tell her or not. She's old enough now to know, he thought, looking into those eyes again. He took a deep breath. 'Well, it's complicated really.'

'That doesn't surprise me. But you know everything about him. Nobody else seems to know anything, or want to tell me.'

'Okay,' he said, playing for time, 'maybe if you ask me about the things you don't know, I might be able to answer them.'

'So, what did he do, where did all the money come from?'

'Your dad made his money from many things, mainly protection rackets. You know, collecting so much a week from owners of small shops so they wouldn't wake up the next day and find their stock trashed or nicked.'

'Is that a reason for someone to kill him?'

'Competition from other agencies is fierce, in every sense of the word. They're always trying to take over each other's patch. Sometimes it could get out of hand. People were beaten up, but rarely killed. I always tried to stop him getting in too deep. He never took any notice of me. Said, as I was the youngest, I should do as he wanted.'

'So he was older than you?'

'Yes. By five minutes. I couldn't believe him. He was always dreaming up new ways to make, what he called, easy money. God knows where he got his ideas from. Always taking risks, some very stupid, big risks.

'His last, a gent's outfitter, quite a large shop actually — Jacobs of Tottenham — was privately owned and a long-standing client of a rival. The owner got well behind with payments. Your dad got to find out about it, went in and made the owner a sweeter offer. Word got out. Vincent had upset the opposition a few times before, but never this bad. They decided enough was enough.'

'So they had him shot?'

'Yes. They will have paid someone. Cowards. Simple, that's how it works. Keep away and you're okay. Interfere, and ... ' He could see her mulling it over and hoped she would be satisfied. 'So, tell me about life up here. What have you been up to these last few years?'

'Oh this and that. Not much of either really.'

'No job?'

'Tried a few, shop work mainly, but they didn't like me. Said I didn't fit in and I was too blunt with the customers. I suspect they thought I'd been up to my old tricks again: taking stuff home.' She laughed. 'It's their loss.'

'What about remand?' He could see she was disappointed he'd asked.

'How do you know about that?'

'Joan. Well, she is my sister and probably needed someone close to talk to. Go on, tell me. What was it like?'

She sat up. 'Short. I don't want to talk about it.'

'No boyfriend?'

'Sort of. I don't see him much.'

'What do you mean, sort of. Either you do, or you don't.'

'Well, I suppose I do. We don't meet-up so much these days. He's all right, bit like you really.'

'Oh aye, what's that supposed to mean?'

'He's vicious at times, gets very moody and can't hold a job down. Thinks the world owes him a living.'

'A bit like you too, then.' He held his arm out for her to snuggle back under.

'Yes, we are similar,' she said, settling down under his wing once more. 'But I wouldn't actually kill anyone.'

Lance sat up fast and started coughing. When he'd stopped, he said, 'Kill someone, you mean, he has done, or is going to?'

'When you frown at me, you look just like my dad,' she said.

'Fortunately, I'm not your dad otherwise what we've been doing all night would be incest.'

'That's where you are wrong,' she said, slapping his chest. 'What we did was—.'

'Don't change the subject.'

'Oh, he murdered right enough. I told him to.'

'What?' he said, uncertain if she was teasing or being honest. But since when had being honest mattered to him, or any other Sylt? He looked at her, trying to weigh-up this ... this new side of her so unexpectedly presented. 'You have proof he did?'

She was staring through the window while she decided whether or not to tell him any more. 'Yes,' she nodded slowly.

'What proof, girl?'

She placed her right hand back on his hairy chest, but instead of playing with those hairs slid it down over his stomach. When she reached the hairs of his groin she looked into his eyes and said, casually, 'I helped him.'

An hour later he went downstairs to look for breakfast. He'd promised her breakfast in bed after her sterling performance half-an-hour ago, but first he needed another cigarette. The last hour had been very revealing and he needed a smoke to help him think.

Should he find her boyfriend and ask him nicely to leave her alone. Perhaps he wouldn't be nice to him and just get rid of him altogether. Yes, that way he'd be certain she wouldn't become involved. She needed to be on the straight and narrow and not be sucked down by the likes of those who'd spoiled his life.

In a couple of years she'd inherit her parent's house in Harrow. Vincent had made him executor of his will. So with the help of a solicitor he decided to put it in trust for her for when she was thirty. He surprised himself that he'd begun to think like a parent. Perhaps she was the daughter he never had. A daughter who took you to bed.

He stood looking through the kitchen window onto a typical terraced-house back-yard; small, grey and not much sky to look at. The Victorians had definitely liked things dark. It might be glorious outside but you'd never know. The stale air of last night needed freshening. He leaned across the sink to raise the sash window, but after seeing someone had painted it in, he settled for opening the back door instead.

Cigarettes, the gnawing in his stomach told him. He walked along the hall to get a fresh packet from his overcoat. He picked it up and instantly realised how lightweight it felt. Quickly he searched in the pocket for the gun, hoping Joan must have taken it last night and locked it away somewhere. She knew exactly what was in the pocket. But there wasn't a pocket where the gun should be. It looked like his coat but it wasn't: the lining light, not dark. Someone had taken it last night, by mistake probably, with the gun still in it.

He dashed back upstairs to get dressed. 'Who was the last to arrive before me last night?'

She propped herself up and saw him dressing. 'I think it was the couple from the newsagents. At the end of the street. Why?'

'I think he took my overcoat by mistake.'

'What's the rush? John will probably bring it back himself later when he's got a minute. Come back to bed.'

'I need some more smokes. And there's something important in one of the pockets. I'll need it soon. Where did you say your boyfriend lived?'

19

SUNDAY'S SPRING EVENING AIR TASTED SWEET. INSIDE, I WAS mellow, satisfied by a large dinner and copious glasses of red wine. As I waited for the nine forty-five to Manchester, sitting on a bench-seat at New Mills Central station, it struck me how quiet it was here. Some rustling in the bushes behind me — a hedgehog perhaps, or mice — and the occasional hooting from a pair of owls, one very close.

I could hear the station master's radio and listened to its distant sound as an orchestra played the end of Delius' *Summer Night on the River*. I love Delius' orchestral music. This piece — masterfully interpreted by none other than Sir Thomas Beecham — the silent warm night, the wine, soon had me nodding-off.

My head must have dropped onto my chest. With a jerk and some snorting I sat bolt upright, briefly wondering where I was. Then from the radio came the chimes of Big Ben — I counted ten — followed by: "*This is the BBC. Here is the News, and this is Alvar Lidell reading it.*"

Ten o'clock! And no train!

Had it come and gone whilst I was sleeping? No way ... but where was it? If it came now there was still time for a connection at Manchester. I listened intently, straining my ears for the sound of a steam engine or even, God forbid, a diesel. More rustling in the undergrowth, the sound of a car crawling up the steep hill the other side of town: little else. Five-past-ten: nothing. Time for action.

I hammered on the ticket office window. I didn't care if the Station Master's heart missed a beat. The owl hooted in disgust. From inside the sound of shuffling was followed by the scraping back of the wooden door behind the booking office window. The BBC was telling the country how the radio telescope at Jodrell Bank had made contact with a satellite over four-hundred-thousand miles away.

'What are *you* doing here?' said, the station master, flabbergasted that someone was actually waiting.

'I've come for the nine forty-five.'

'Nobody ever comes for that train.'

'But I'm booked on the sleeper to London!'

※※※

I just made it to the sleeper as the guard blew his whistle. I was shown to my compartment by a short bald-headed conductor, dressed in a dark uniform, who was stewing pots of strong tea at a stove in the carriage vestibule. Cups rattled as the train moved off. Station lights cast moving shadows into the dimly lit compartment. The lower berth was already occupied by a fat man who seemed sound asleep.

Now wide awake after the excitement of making my connection, I turned off the light. The shadows swung by faster as the train gained speed then disappeared altogether when it left the station. I took off my jacket and, in near darkness, hauled myself as quietly as possible onto the top bunk — not easy as we rattled at speed across points.

I decided I should have taken off some clothes — it was so hot up here — and removed my trousers, banging my head on the ceiling twice in the process. My trousers ended up at the foot of the bunk, along with my tie.

The fat man set about snoring, heavily as the train jerked away from Stockport. Stewed tea, on a trolley full of rattling cups and saucers, moved past my compartment on its way to poison the newcomers.

I tried to settle down again but began thinking about Alice. I had hoped she at least, would have travelled over from York for the weekend, perhaps leaving the kids with her mother. But she didn't. Said her father had influenza and she didn't want the kids to get it and be off school. I'd asked her to bring them over to avoid the bugs; they could join in the fun this weekend at Malcolm and Susan's place in the country. They had two children of similar ages; they'd get along fine.

But Alice refused, saying she'd better stay in case her dad got worse. I felt she wasn't being entirely straight with me; perhaps that was why I'd had a little too much to drink at dinner.

My hosts, becoming concerned about my relationship with Alice, kept dropping hints or asking questions about her continued absence. I said it was because of the children's education, but could see they weren't convinced.

Kids ... when they came along, everything changed. They were the centre of attention for Alice now, not me. It was understandable, maybe even the way nature intended. Alice, once outgoing, entertaining with her wicked sense of humour, happy and loving, was now introverted, short-tempered and focused solely upon bringing up the children. I could work and provide the money, but beyond that, I didn't seem to count for much in her life. And now, being so far away had made the prospect of a happy marriage dwindle. She seemed happy with this arrangement. I wasn't and wondered if the kids were. She must move to Crewe soon.

****

I woke with a start. 'Euston, Euston station, Euston; all change,' the conductor's voice boomed as it moved passed my compartment. Then, in the distance again, 'Euston, Euston station, all change.' Euston at last, at six in the morning!

I heard noises below and squinted over the edge of the bunk to see the fat man was up and fully dressed in his pinstripe-suit, which didn't look a bit creased.

He was checking his briefcase before leaving. Sensing he was being watched, he glanced up at me, smiled, tipped his hat, placed it back on his head and left without saying a word.

The conductor was back. 'I brought you some tea, sir. You'll just have time to shave and dress before the train gets moved into the sidings at six thirty.'

***

Platform-one Euston, at six thirty. I'm half-asleep, on a chilly Monday morning, watching the sleeper moving off to the sidings; the sleeper with my warm bed and my tie. Oh well, never again.

The gnawing in my stomach was shouting breakfast, so I wandered along the platform in search of some. I wondered if this would be the last time I'd see London's first railway terminal in one piece. The pioneering spirit of the London & Birmingham Railway — symbolised by the Doric Arch and The Great Hall built over a hundred and twenty years earlier — was to be swept away, along with the rest of the station buildings. The worst of the sixties-construction was about to be foisted onto the travelling public, along with years of upheaval.

***

By nine, smartly uniformed Regional Detective Superintendents from all the BTP English divisions had gathered with their plain-clothes DIs in the relatively new and ugly offices hired for the quarterly meeting. The depression this modern pile caused me was matched only by the subject matter in hand.

This was the first that I and the idiot Superintendent Newall were both attending. By all accounts, his had been a promotion upstairs to get him out of Bristol's hair. I scanned the large meeting room as I entered, wondering which of the several Supers was him. I noticed one in particular was eyeing me up and down disapprovingly. Maybe he didn't want to be associated with this dishevelled detective from Crewe who, God-forbid, had arrived without a tie! Our eyes met. He turned his back on me and began talking again to three men who each eyed me in turn.

Chief Superintendent (London Division) Herbert Mullard called the meeting to order and then dawdled through its agenda. Suicides, theft, damage to railway property, trespass and staffing were reported by the delegates from Manchester, Birmingham and Bristol.

The most interesting report was from the Derby Superintendent about the success they were having with dogs — another policing first for the force — on football excursions, to keep the bladder-kicking rabble in order.

I wondered if anyone would be interested in Crewe's staffing experiment which was working out really well, but decided against it; the meeting was dragging on far too long as it was.

I was the only DI present in charge of a murder investigation and, during the short break, I'd made some strong coffee. The overnight journey was telling on me and beginning to make me irritable, not good when I was due to tell the assembled officers the progress my team had made on the Gilmore case. It wouldn't take long: we hadn't made any.

I coughed to get everyone's attention, my left hand slowly drifting up to my neck where my tie should have been. 'I have to tell you that progress in solving the Gilmore murder has regrettably come to a full stop, even with the help of the boys from Home.' This at least raised some laughter around the room, as everyone knew it was the BTP's role to solve its own cases.

Newall, obviously a humourless git and realising at last that I must be his senior DI from Crewe, looked disapprovingly at me and made a note in the notebook he'd just pulled out of his breast-pocket.

'It may have started out looking like a case of suicide, but for the fact that the Gilmore's lower leg had disappeared within ten minutes of his death. I'm convinced this is a trophy murder. CID, Chester has no record of any such cases in Cheshire. As yet there are no leads as to whom the culprit is, though I suspect two people are involved. Gilmore had no history of stress. According to Mrs Gilmore, he was happy and looking forward to his retirement. Apart from being overweight, he was in good physical health. There were no signs of a heart-attack.

'I further regret that this case has gone cold since Gilmore's death three years ago.'

A hush went around the room.

Newall made another note in his book.

I gave some more details and wound up my brief presentation as soon as possible, having not been able to add much to what was already known. Some had asked me questions. Others made suggestions.

I sat down and glanced at Newall who was deliberately ignoring me — he doesn't want to know me, I thought. Not in public anyway.

I yawned through some more presentations, none grabbing my attention. I wondered what Newall had written in his notebook and didn't think we were going to get off to a good start. Mullard rambled through a pep-talk then, at long-last, brought the meeting to a close. A meeting that should have finished by twelve gasped its last at half-past-one!

The press were snapping at both police forces' heels over all sorts of issues. But articles deploring the lack of progress in solving the Gilmore murder appeared regularly over the years, particularly in the Sunday gutter-press.

Yesterday's edition of the *News of the World* had focused on the BTP and its so called *specialist railway knowledge* — or lack of it, as the article propounded — and caused Mullard to collar me at the end of the meeting. 'Before you go, Crosier, we need a word.' He turned to the door which led to his office.

I followed Newall inside and was not invited to sit.

Mullard sat behind his large mahogany desk, Newall sat to one side. This was as close to him as I'd been. He looked much older than from a distance, in his early wrinkly-sixties at least. His bulging eyes were his most curious feature. Lurking under dark eyebrows, the top eyelids looked as if they were permanently descending, while the lower ones tried their best not to make contact.

I'd heard the tone in Mullard's voice many times at these quarterly meetings. He always dragged someone in at the end of the meeting and now it was my turn. Before speaking, he stiffened his tunic by tugging it downward a few times, just above his trousers. Maybe his wife hadn't used enough starch in her wash tub. I'd heard from other unfortunates that this performance was the usual precursor to a bollocking. I stood waiting for the first salvo.

'We're being made to look like fools, Crosier. I know everyone is doing their best up there with other crimes, but what have you come up with so far on this one, other than a missing foot?'

'True, sir, but—'

'This is your first murder case. If you want to keep your position, then I suggest you get some answers PDQ. Understand?'

'Yes, sir.'

Newall's head was nodding, as if someone had turned on an electric motor buried inside his neck.

'It looks bad when we have to listen to the same old report at each meeting,' Mullard went on. 'What do you think the new recruits will think? This is the oldest police force in Britain, but they must think they've joined a bunch of idiots.'

I looked at Newall, still nodding, and was inclined to agree.

Mullard had changed gear since the meeting broke up. He was now getting stuck into me with some force. The trouble was, I had never liked him in all the years I'd had dealings with the man. Mullard, in my view, was there to take the applause and he didn't like it when things prevented the clapping.

It was after two when, somewhat scathed, I emerged from Mullard's office. At least this wasn't a full-blown public bollocking — as was his usual style — in front of entire meetings, grandstanding for the benefit of his arse-lickers, who watched the unfortunate officer's humiliation with glee, at the same time hoping they were not to be next.

Newall had sat sour-faced and tight lipped throughout Mullard's blathering. He'd made a show of writing several notes.

The most important to him, no doubt, being the absence of my tie.

At last he'd spoken, saying he would visit Crewe next week to "try and chivvy things along a bit".

***

Glad to be out of the building I was now heading so see my old friend at New Scotland Yard. Mullard & Newall would have to wait a bit longer for a successful collar, something that secretly pleased me. Although I had to admit, Mullard had already been waiting three years.

My meeting at The Yard had been a rather brief affair in the reception, where I'd waited for almost an hour.

Hunt arrived, but spent only five minutes with me before being summoned upstairs. 'Looking unusually dapper today, Oliver. Must have been a big audience for you back at Euston.'

Hunt always commented on my appearance — he probably wondered how someone from the north had the slightest idea about dress-sense. I never took the bait. Instead I ran my latest theory by him who, after listening for two minutes, simply burst out laughing.

'Let me get this straight, Oliver. You've come all this way to tell me you think the motive is jealousy. Who'd be jealous of an overweight salt worker about to retire, eh? Nice suit Hawksnose. I hear the crumpled look is all the go.'

***

I cheered myself up on the train back thinking about the prospect of Alice and the kids coming over for the Whitsun holidays They would be off school for almost three weeks. Perhaps she'd start to change her mind about Crewe and move in permanently during the summer holidays.

I hated the continual travel back and forth to York most weekends and my marriage, as far as I was concerned, wasn't working!

On each visit to York, or when they rarely came to see me, she'd ask about the job. I reassured her it was much quieter here. The only serious crime I'd had to deal with was that of the unfortunate Mr Gilmore's death — I hadn't been involved in anything remotely dangerous at all.

But I couldn't stand our situation for much longer. Alice had to move to Crewe, and soon.

20

24th MAY

HE WENT ROUND TO NUMBER EIGHTEEN, TO CHECK FOR ANY MAIL and feed the cat, letting himself in through the back door. Mog was supposedly being fed next door, yet the silver-grey cat still slept here even when nobody was at home. She bounded down the stairs and pestered him to be fed. It didn't matter at what hour he came by, Mog always wanted feeding. With a tin of cat food dutifully opened, and its contents placed in a dish on the kitchen floor, he went to the front door to check for mail and found a solitary letter addressed to him.

Puzzled, he went back into the kitchen to make some coffee. While the kettle boiled on the gas hob, he opened the letter and began to read the note.

> We know what you did
> We know who you are.
> Kings Arms Saturday 1p.m.
> Be there. Come alone or you are
> DEAD

And that was it. Five typed threatening lines. He read the missive again. No name other than his on the envelope. The envelope! He picked it up to examine the post-mark. Partially smudged, he could still make out the date, the twenty-second.

The kettle began to whistle. He turned off the gas and tried to spoon two large teaspoons of instant-coffee into a mug. His hands were shaking and most of the contents of the second spoon fell onto the draining board.

The cat, seeing a feline face the other side of the transparent cat-flap, shot through it, the sudden commotion causing him to drop the spoon. He raised his hand to his forehead, now damp with sweat. Somehow he managed to pour hot water into the mug and added two more spoons of coffee. He reached for a cigarette. He had to think.

Reading the note again was virtually impossible: his hand shook so much, he had to lay the paper on the table before the words would stop dancing around the page. A threat for sure, but who would send him such a letter? And who knew this address anyway? He couldn't remember telling anyone about it. He didn't live here. Perhaps it's a mistake and should have been delivered to next door — postmen were only human after all and did make mistakes — but the envelope still carried his name. As much as he wished it to disappear, when he looked again, the envelope had stubbornly refused to remove it, or the number eighteen; the number on the front door.

There was a smudged London postmark; he'd have to look at a map of London to see which district ----- -ross might be. But what would be the point? He didn't know anybody from London, except his sister. And why would she do anything like this? Okay, he hadn't seen her for years, didn't want to either, but she wouldn't do this. And she didn't have this address anyway. The letter could have come from anywhere, even here in Warrington, posted to someone in London in another envelope, its contents to be forwarded.

He had no option but to go to the Kings Arms on Saturday and meet whoever had sent him this threat. Saturday, another three days to wait. He started to shake again and took a lungful of smoke to calm down. Without thinking, he washed up the cat's plate and his coffee mug and all the stuff piled up from his previous visits. Therapy?

He stepped outside and locked the back door. Walking along the side of the house, he stopped dead. The note said, *We know who you are.* Was he being watched? Only one way to find out! He reached the front gate and fiddled with the catch as if it was stiff. It gave him a second or two to scan the street. Apart from a couple of parked cars, it was empty. In half-an-hour the street would be teeming with kids on their way home from school.

He'd walked a few paces and heard the front door of the house directly opposite number eighteen close. The handle below its letterbox tapped out a few metallic notes as it was released.

He turned, as casually as he could, to see who might be following.

It was that busybody woman. She seemed to be making a show of pulling on her leather gloves, an unnecessary act this mild day. He'd seen her several times before, hiding behind her net curtains which always twitched when he shut the garden gate. He could believe she might be spying on him. Probably every nosey bugger in the street was, too. But surely, she'd not be clever enough to make up this letter and send it? What reason could she possibly have?

He decided to go around the block and back to the house again to make sure he wasn't followed.

He passed the two parked cars, both empty; no one slumped down hiding behind their steering wheels.

He turned right at the crossroads.

The woman went inside the 'phone box standing on the corner and squinted at him through a dirty rectangle of glass as she dialled a number.

21

26th MAY

THE NOTE HAD SAID HE SHOULD BE THERE AT 1 P.M. HE'D BEEN watching the Kings Arms pub, since nine-thirty, from the coffee bar opposite, but hadn't seen anyone he recognised or who looked suspicious. The Wilson's dray had delivered six wooden barrels of beer and the postman handed some mail to the landlord who stood, arms folded, watching the draymen.

But one can only drink so much coffee, so he'd crossed over the main road and ordered a pint as soon as the pub opened at eleven. That was an hour and-a-half ago.

He'd ordered some ham sandwiches to soak up the beer; three pints already. He couldn't negotiate with a fuddled brain.

The bar girl brought his sandwiches and a newspaper over to him. 'Thought you might like this as you're on your own,' she said, handing him the paper. 'Are you waiting for someone?'

'Yes, I think I am. Thanks.' He regretted his reply instantly. It was a dumb thing to say. She looked at him puzzled, then retreated to safety behind the bar.

A woman came through the door at the rear of the bar and said something to her, waving an envelope as she spoke. Both women looked towards him.

He lowered his eyes pretending to read the paper.

'I think this is for you.' The landlady, now standing at his table, slapped an envelope down. 'It came in another envelope yesterday. Said some bloke fitting your description would be here at one-o'clock for it. It's you, right?'

'Could be, I'm not sure. I was expecting someone to come

here, but I might have misunderstood.'

'Well if it is you, you can tell whoever sent it, I'm not in the habit of delivering mail. Understand?' She, too, returned to the bar and stood behind it, glowering.

His hand trembled on the envelope. No name or postmark.

He fumbled to light a cigarette then took a long drag before he dare open the letter. He counted to ten, then decisively opened the envelope. Another typed note said,

CHECK THE CAT

And, the warning not to tell anyone was repeated.

The door to the snug opened and he was stunned to see the busybody woman enter and start talking to a woman already at the bar. She removed her gloves, glanced over to where he was sitting. Their eyes made contact.

He smiled.

She turned her back to him.

The woman she was with looked over her shoulder at him, her eyes resting on him for a few seconds, before returning to her conversation with the busybody.

The girl came back to the table to take his plate away, noticed he was shaking and asked if he was okay.

He said he'd had bad news, and ordered a large whiskey.

She went back behind the bar and brought his drink.

He threw it down in one desperate gulp. It wasn't satisfying. He considered ordering another, but the bar girl had returned to her post.

He'd wait until one-fifteen.

Nobody else had approached him so he prepared to leave as instructed.

Mrs Busybody and her friend turned to watch him go, then went the window to make sure that he had.

He was almost at the house. All the way back, he was trying

to figure out what was going on. Somebody was playing with him, but why? He'd teach them a lesson for sure if he found out who the hell it was.

Was he being followed?

He'd taken the long way back, stopping occasionally and suddenly looking behind, but never saw anyone who looked like they were following him.

But then he wouldn't: nobody was.

He parked his motorbike a few streets away and walked up to the house. The garden gate squeaked as he opened it. He closed it, while glancing at the house opposite. Its net curtains remained undisturbed.

The back door was still locked and the windows looked secure. Hands shaking, he managed to unlock the door and tried to push it wide open. Something was stopping it from opening fully. The cat? Was it dead behind it? Had someone been to kill it?

He knelt down and opened the cat flap. There was a loud meow and the animal shot out at startling speed.

'Jesus Christ. You stupid bloody animal.' He stood, took a deep breath, forced open the door and stepped inside.

There was a something wrapped up in newspaper on the floor. It had obviously been pushed through the cat flap. He picked it up and, feeling the weight of it, took it over and placed it on the kitchen table. This whole thing was getting stranger by the hour.

He needed some more liquid strength before he opened the package, so went to raid the drinks cabinet in the front room. He poured a large glass of Bells into a cut glass tumbler and turned to look through the front window.

The busybody woman and her friend had just clambered out of a taxi and were about to go into her house. They looked up and down the street then across at him standing in the window, clearly visible. He raised his glass to her. They turned away, entered and closed the front door.

It was time to open the package.

He ripped off the newspaper to reveal an oily cloth which, when unrolled presented him with a handgun, a silencer and six bullets. His pulse quickened.

There was an envelope, too. Inside, another page carried three type-written lines. His lips moved as he scanned the words.

A warning. A date. And a name.

A bigger smile now — he knew the person named. He was already on their hit list.

He finished the glass of whiskey and washed the glass.

The cat flap banged shut; the cat had returned and was shouting to be fed.

He picked up the gun, pushed the silencer over the long barrel and placed a bullet in the chamber.

He took aim at the cat, the barrel targeted on the animal's nose.

The cat sat patiently, its head cocked sideways questioning his every move.

His finger tightened on the trigger.

If he fired here, the bullet would pass straight through the animal and bury itself in the cupboard door.

Bad idea. He settled for making a noise as if he'd fired.

The cat shot out of the kitchen.

He wouldn't take the gun away today. Instead he took it and the spare bullets upstairs to hide.

A few minutes later he'd left some fresh food for the cat, locked up the house and had reached the garden gate. It squeaked when opened.

The net curtains opposite twitched.

He could see the shadows of two people and as he walked back to his motorbike he heard the familiar sound of Mrs Busybody's front door closing.

22

8th OCTOBER 1962, 8 pm

EDWARD BRIGHT, SON OF ALEX AND JUDITH BRIGHT, SEEMED TO have everything he could ever want in life. He was the only child of doting parents who both worked and could afford a nice semi-detached house, a nice new Ford Zephyr and take their son away with them on nice holidays twice each year.

His record at school had been his saving grace in that he was not bright at all, regardless of what his mother and father thought of him. He'd always be showing off, or back-chatting teachers, bullying younger kids and worst of all flaunting yet another flash watch the very next day after he smashed one fighting in the school yard.

She'd fancied him a lot when she first came to his school but so did many other girls, most from a better background than her. He'd turned her down immediately she asked him out. She remembered the way he looked down his nose at her. Something would have to be done, one way or another, sooner or later.

***

Boy told her of his decision in the snug of his local late one night. They were sitting opposite each other at a round table.

'Liss,' he said to her, trying to be very casual, 'you always fancied Edward Bright at school, didn't you?'

'What if I did? Wot's it got to do with you?' she said, crossing her legs. Her short skirt had ridden right up her thighs. She turned away from him to scan the bar for eligible men.

He had a job to keep his eyes off them. 'Well,' he said,

nonchalantly trying to see what colour knickers she had on, 'you know it's been three years since we did Gilmore.'

She didn't face him and tried hard not to look excited.

'I wondered if you were interested in doing another.'

She couldn't ignore him now. Her head swung round. Her eyes locked on his. 'Go on.'

'This isn't the place to discuss it, but I've worked out how we could do his dad.'

They drank up and went back to his place for a more private conversation, and for some more intimate excitement.

***

Alex Bright — who like his father had worked in the railway engine sheds in Northwich — was a short wiry athletic type who cycled to work to keep him trim. His white Ford Zephyr would remain on show, parked on the driveway of his home.

They'd watched him for several weeks before putting their plan into action. He seemed to have a couple of routes home from work.

They preferred the one which took him along the quiet lanes that ran through Whatcroft to Davenham. The narrow road crossed the Trent and Mersey canal, then dropped down past the flashes, before rising steeply to the bridge crossing the single line railway.

He'd usually be at the bridge by seven thirty. The problem would be hiding the body, and its bike, until nine o'clock when the empty goods train came up from Middlewich. They'd just have to work it out *if* he chose that way tonight. It was time to go to the crossroads and see.

***

Bright left his office at the engine sheds where he was in charge of the staff roster. He'd worked there for a few years, first dropping the engine's ash pans as they came out of service, then cleaning the engines, a slightly less dirty job.

His boss liked him, thought him efficient, mixed well with his workmates. When the supervisor, old-George died, he was his natural successor.

Not done too badly for myself, he thought; been here less than six years and now almost running the place. Time to go, and he smirked at those getting ready for the late night rush of engines based at shed 8E. A clear moon-lit night too, bit of a frost though; he shouldn't be too late getting home.

··*

Passing the crossroads he noticed again the two bikers in their leathers. They've been here at this time every night lately. A bit odd — there's nowt to do around here.

They returned his wave before mounting their bikes ready to decide what to do next. Tonight they were in luck. Bright took their chosen route.

Five minutes later, they started their machines and set off, she following him from a safe distance, while he went along the dual carriageway towards Davenham. He then turned left and circled round so the two bikes would meet on the Whatcroft bridge, just as Bright would be puffing to the top.

··*

Bright was making good time on his new six-speed bike, crossing the canal and working the bike hard down the short hill ready for the long climb to the top of the railway bridge. He was sweating now and weaving across the road as he stood on the pedals for extra weight.

Then just as he reached the top, horror: a motorbike, with its headlight on full beam, was approaching on the wrong side of the road!

Bright swerved too late.

The motorbike rider pushed him hard aside as he went by.

Bright struck his head against the wall of the bridge and collapsed, out-cold.

She arrived just as Bright went down. Between them they heaved Bright across the seat of the heavier bike and wheeled him back down the hill. To the right were plenty of bushes and trees to provide cover. She collected her own bike and guided

Bright's bicycle alongside. Pity the front wheel was buckled. She'd have liked to take it as a souvenir.

They hid the body and bike under some bushes and sat in the shadows.

'Is he dead?' said Liss.

'I don't think so, I'll see.' He crouched down and put his ear to Bright's mouth. 'He's still alive.'

She pulled out a large oily rag from one of her bike's pannier-bags and gagged him while he bound Bright's hands behind his back, then tied his feet together. It was to be a long cold wait for Bright on the frost-hardened ground.

They sat waiting, getting colder in the damp night-air until at last he heard the distant sound of an engine. 'It's coming! Help me get him over my shoulder, then I'll go and dump him over.'

'I've been thinking,' she said, holding onto his sleeve, 'don't you think it would be better if we killed him now and left him here?'

'No, Liss, that isn't the plan. We agreed to work the plan didn't we?'

She nodded, still uncertain.

'The train has to kill him and get him away from here. The train is our friend. The trains always help us. The train will be disappointed if we don't give it his body while it's still alive.'

She could see the sense of what he was saying but said, 'I'm worried we'll be spotted on the bridge.'

'Jesus, Liss, nobody will be here at nine o'clock at night. Every night we've checked this place out, nobody ever came. We'll be fine. Now help me up with him before it's too late.'

Reluctantly, she helped haul Bright out from under the bushes. Boy staggered towards the road with Bright across his shoulders. Bright was fairly lightweight but it was still a struggle carrying him.

Soon be a dead weight. The drop head first would do for him.

He moved as quickly as he could up the hill to the bridge.

The train, coming closer with every step, grumbled along — a mechanical creature, its heavy breath matching his.

A final dash for the top of the bridge complete, he stopped over the track panting for breath. Everything, so far, was going to plan.

The engine chuffed under the bridge. Thick black smoke engulfed them. Bright disappeared from view.

Below, the wagons grumbled along.

Bright started coughing; he was coming round.

The smoke slowly cleared to show Bright staring like a drunk, at his captor, trying to focus. A glimmer of recognition formed on Bright's face. His tongue, trapped by the gag, struggled to form a name. 'Lon?' He tried again, 'Lonnie?' but was forced round and lifted onto his stomach to lean over the thick wall of the bridge. He saw the empty open trucks as they slowly moved along and realised what Ronnie was about to do, but couldn't think why?

Boyton worked feverishly to release Bright's legs, his hands then the gag.

'Ronnie,' shouted Bright and, no longer like a rag doll, he kicked out. He grasped the wall with both hands. Could he jump into a wagon?

He swung his legs over the wall and dangled over the moving train, ready to fall. To escape.

A hand grabbed his right wrist.

Had his captor changed his mind?

He looked up, into the barrel of a revolver.

Behind it, Boyton's spaggy eyes danced across Bright's face.

Bright stopped struggling.

The revolver disappeared.

Bright was being hauled up and now his right arm was almost on the top of the wall. It was then that Bright saw the moonlight glint on the blade of the raised axe.

He tried with his left hand to free his right, bending back the fingers which held him like a vice.

He heard to late the sickening sound of his flesh and bone being hacked above the wrist of his right hand.

Blood gushed from the wound and poured over his face.

He felt the searing pain as the axe worked again to remove his right hand. Heard the bones in his arm crack then snap. Felt the pain as the tendons stretched then finally, as he grabbed the top of the wall with his left hand, the axe hit the wall.

His right arm swung uselessly over the train, blood spraying its wagons as they passed below.

He saw the glint of the axe for the last time.

His left wrist was severed in one clean chop. It no longer held Bright.

He fell.

His scream was short, and ended with a dull thud.

His face smashed into the cold-steel front of a wagon, which removed his nose and part of his scalp. He'd landed on his back and, slid head first, down the slope of the outlet chute.

Neck broken, he would never know when or where he'd be seen again.

Ronnie heard Bright's dull-thud. He secured the axe to the leather strap around his waist. He looked at the loose hands and smiled; their fingers still gripped the side of the wall. He collected his trophies and wrapped them in the oily cloth she'd used for the gag.

Pleased with the way the killing had gone, he smiled again, until he heard the crash of metal on metal, as Bright's bike fell into a wagon.

'What the ... ?' He turned astonished to see her there, a wide grin on her face. 'What the fuck have you done, Syph?'

'I didn't want them to find his bike, silly. And besides, the front wheel was buckled. No use to us.'

'But this was supposed to look like a suicide,' he said, knowing she hadn't seen his last-minute butchery. 'It's why I untied him! Did you ever hear of a dead man throwing his bike into a train? After him!' He turned away from her and felt for the gun in his pocket.

She was seriously worried he'd hurt her.

His grip tightened on the gun. He looked at her very hard, trying to decide what to do with her.

They stood, the only sound the *clank-clank, clank-clank* of the trucks fading into the distance. It was too late to shoot her and throw her in, too. Besides, he needed her help for the next killing. And she was good in bed.

***

Inside the guard's van, Thompson was happily drinking tea and eating cheese-and-pickle sandwiches, not wanting to share them with anyone when the train arrived at Northwich. Unaware his train was no longer empty, as far as he was concerned, everything tonight was just fine.

***

She turned away and started walking down the hill.

He took the gun from his pocket, made sure the silencer was fitted tight and followed her. The moonlight would give him enough light to do what he had in mind.

She kept a safe distance from him in case he swung out at her. Her hand touched her nose — he'd hit her last time they'd killed. At least he hadn't thrown her into a wagon. She had to admit what she did was dumb. Now he might think of her as a liability. That really frightened her. To placate him, she tried to think of someone else they could kill.

They reached their motorbikes. It was darker here, but enough light for her to keep an eye on him.

He raised the gun and pointed it at her face.

She was shocked to see he had a gun, uncertain if he dared use it. Trembling, arm outstretched towards him, she pleaded with him not to shoot her. Perhaps if she stripped off her clothes it might persuade him to think again? But he could still shoot her afterwards.

He flung the oily parcel at her feet. 'Pick it up,' he shouted, no longer concerned if he was heard.

'Why, what's happening? What are you going to do to me, Boy?' Tears rolled down her cheeks.

'Pick it up.' He waggled the gun at her. 'Now.'

She bent.

'Take the cloth off.'

She did. Was stunned by what she saw.

'Pick up a hand.'

She touched one, cool and rubbery.

'Hold it by the wrist, palm towards me, next to your ear.'

She did, shaking.

He moved a few steps back.

She saw the gun, still aimed at her head.

Then with a move she couldn't see, he moved the gun off her face and shot the severed hand through its palm.

She felt the bullet pass inches from her face, felt the slight movement as it passed through the hand. Heard it disappear into the bushes behind. She stared at the hand shaking in hers, saw the bullet hole in its palm; the bullet hole that could easily have been in her face.

She saw, in the full-moon's light, the pale, evil smile on his face.

He knew he didn't have to say anything.

She knew, at last, he's completely mad.

23

TUESDAY 30th OCTOBER 1962

MY INVESTIGATION, INTO THE MISSING ALEX BRIGHT, HAD YIELDED only three clues: one, some green garden string, two; recent footprints and three; motor bike tracks. The last two, confirmed by laboratory tests, matched those found at the Whitegate crash — or should it now be called the Whitegate murder?

It had all started some two weeks earlier when Northwich Police had contacted me saying they had a new missing-person case on their hands, but were not progressing very far with their investigations. As the vanished Alex Bright worked at the local railway engine sheds they thought there might be a connection with my unsolved Whitegate case.

Was every missing persons case suddenly to be on my shoulders? 'Yes it *appears* the Whitegate crash might be murder. But that doesn't link it to every missing person, does it?'

'No it doesn't, DI Crosier,' said the Northwich inspector, 'but it may be worth your while looking at the route he usually took home, where it crosses any railway.'

Reluctantly, I went along with the idea after reading the report Northwich police had sent over. It outlined two possible routes the missing Bright might have taken home on the night he went missing, assuming he intended to go home that night. Both meant crossing the Middlewich to Northwich single track which was only used for goods traffic since passenger trains had stopped over two years ago. One crossed at Whatcroft, an isolated spot and the other a half a mile north where the line ran under the busy Northwich bypass road. Logic suggested the isolated Whatcroft bridge was the most likely place to carry out — carry out what exactly? Was the case a kidnap, or a murder without a body? 'Come on then, Dobbs,' I said, and took him to Whatcroft in a spare pool-car.

***

Arriving at the point where the road climbs over the railway by a steep narrow bridge, we started to search for any clues that might show how a crime may have been committed here.

'There are some recent scratch marks on this wall, sir,' said Dobbs, 'but if they mean something, well, I'm not sure what. Anything could have made them.'

I checked the top of the wall and found a few deep scratches stained by what could have been blood. 'Interesting? Let's check out the ground either side. Wouldn't want the Northwich lot saying we missed something they found later and turned out to be important. God, we'd never hear the last of it. It might be worth getting a dive team into that lake,' I said, pointing to where a solitary fisherman sat smoking a cigarette.

'It's called a flash, sir,' said Dobbs. 'They might come up with a corpse or a bike.'

'Remind me to talk to Hatton at Northwich about it will you, Dobbs?'

'Yes, sir.'

We walked down the hill towards the canal and I went to speak with a man fishing while Dobbs went rummaging through the undergrowth beside the line.

'Good afternoon, sir. I wondered if I might ask you a few questions?' I said, producing my warrant card.

'Go ahead,' the fisherman said, ignoring my identification. 'I'm doing nothing — like the damn fish.'

'Sorry to hear that, what do you normally catch?'

'Oh, carp mainly. I get a few eels, too; very tasty in a stew.'

'I'll bet. Do you come fishing here a lot?'

'Most days when it's fine, can't stand it when it's wet. It's a toss-up between getting drenched sat here or staying at home and listening to her-indoors prattling on about somat-or-other.'

'We suspect someone went missing here Tuesday night three weeks ago so I'm making enquiries to see if anyone saw or heard something. Would you have been here that Tuesday evening in particular?'

'Sorry mate, no. I'm all'as gone be five. But Bill was.'

'And who might Bill be?' I said, expecting a worthless answer.

'Billy Jenkins.' The fisherman stood and pointed to the cottage on the right. 'Lives there, 'as done all his life. If yer wants to know owt about what 'appens 'round here, which 'ain't a right lot mind when all's said and done, he'll know; nosey bugger.'

I thanked the surly fisherman and, buoyed by the hope that Billy might live up to his reputation, set off to ask him a few questions. I had to hammer on the door three times before Jenkins deigned to answer. An even more surly man stood blocking the open doorway eyeing me through bottle-bottom glasses. My expectation evaporated instantly. It was doubtful this "nosey bugger" had seen anything at all in recent times through those glasses. He was here now so I may as well ask.

'Good afternoon.' I tried.

'Irit now? Whot yer wantin'?'

It was pointless showing this man my warrant card so I said, 'I'm from the Crewe Transport Police. I was wondering if you saw or heard anything suspicious here or on the line Tuesday night three weeks ago?'

'Three weeks! Can't say as I did, 'cos I didn'a.'

And with that, the door was slammed shut in my face. I turned away and went to find Dobbs, hoping he'd fared better than me.

Dobbs was smiling when I found him.

'Come this way, sir. See what you make of this.'

24

INTERVIEWING GRIEVING FEMALE RELATIVES, WAS NOT NEW TO either Cardin or myself. Cardin had done it many times, usually in cases of children killed by playing on the railway — an easy thing for them to do with so many miles of broken wooden fences lining the permanent way.

I'd telephoned Judith Bright, to tell her to be in when we arrived, an impossible task for Mrs Gilmore's appointment who we'd be visiting next: the Gilmore household hadn't come to telephones as yet and now with the man-of-the-house dead, probably never would. We'd just have to take a chance.

Of all the houses on Hewitt Avenue in Winsford, the Bright's house at the end of the cul-de-sac, bordering open fields, certainly lived up to its name; the place had recently been repainted to match an immaculate new Ford Zephyr standing on the driveway between beds of similar coloured roses.

Before my hand reached the door bell, the door was quickly flung wide-open by Mrs Bright who bundled us into the house without saying a word. She looked along the avenue to make sure none of her neighbours were watching. Although several Friesian cows were interested, it wouldn't do to have police officers seen entering her house; what would the neighbours think? Of course the neighbours would know exactly why we were there but it seemed Mrs Bright, in the few weeks since her husband had been missing, had almost forgotten.

'The kettle's on, make yourselves comfortable. I've made some Dundee cake for you. I like Marks and Spencer's almost as much as my own, even though they're shop-bought.' Bright was busying herself in the kitchen, before we could reply. 'Do you like butter on it? Yes, I thought you would,' she answered, before we had a chance to respond. Bright was stalling for time, acting as though entertaining her WI friends, not the railway police. Tea and cake duly arrived.

Claire commenced proceedings. 'We're very sorry to have to come and see you, but we need to explore your husband's disappearance further.'

'That's fine,' said Bright, who knew it wasn't and suddenly shrunk back into herself, knowing it was all going to have to be pawed over again. 'Please, carry on,' she said, timidly.

'Can you think of anyone, anyone at all, who might have had a grudge with your husband?'

'Not really, no. I know the neighbours think we're a cut above them, which we are of course, but no. I can't see why anyone would want him out of the way. Can you?'

'Well, each case we deal with is different. In a case of murder, the killer usually knows the victim.'

'Are you suggesting Alex has been killed?'

'It is possible,' I said, 'although, the killer might have had a grudge against you or your son, not necessarily against your husband.'

'I'm not sure I can help you there, officer. I didn't really know any of Edward's friends, or Alex's come to that. They were all a bit — you know, how shall I say, err ... well poor really.'

'Could jealousy be a motive?' said Claire.

Bright shook her head, slowly.

'You know Mrs Gilmore lost her husband?'

'Yes, I had heard. Poor woman, I know how she must feel, though I don't really know her. She lives the other end of Crook Lane, if you know what I mean. Would you like some more tea?'

She'd picked up considerably once she reasserted her social status over those less well-off. We were dealing with someone suffering from delusions of grandeur here and declined her offer of more tea, wanting to get away as soon as possible.

'Her boy went to the same school as Edward, but of course, he was always in a lower form than Edward's.' This information was imparted as if it was perfectly obvious to all, the correct order of things, each in its rightful place in the Bright world.

'You say a lower form, but in the same year?' asked Claire.

'Oh yes, the same year. Not the same set, not the top set. I heard Mrs Gilmore lost her husband in their new car,' she said, fishing for more gossip on the Gilmores, 'a Ford Anglia of all things, two-tone, too! Ernie would never have had one of those would he?'

'And why would that be?' I said.

'It's obvious, isn't it? You can't get golf clubs and large suitcases in such a small car.'

'I think we can leave it there for now, Mrs Bright. Thank you for the tea and the lovely cake,' said Claire, rising to her feet. 'We'll be in touch if we learn anything or need to ask you any further questions.'

'Do you know when? I have a hair appointment next week before I go up to the lakes for a fortnight with Ernie. He's been very kind to me since Alex has been gone. I like to look smart for him when we get away.'

'Ernie?' said Claire.

'Yes that's right, do you know him?'

'No, I don't. I thought at first it was your husband's middle name, but that's Ernest, isn't it?'

'Did I, I don't remember. Oh, yes how silly of me. Ernie is Mr. Bingham's christian name.'

'Does Mr Bingham have a telephone number where we could contact him?' I said.

'Yes, it's Winsford two-five-six-one. That's his office number for Bingham's shoe shop on the High Street. They're coming up for their autumn sale and he always wants to get away and leave that sort of thing to *his girls*.'

Bright suddenly shut the front door on us without saying another word. Claire looked at me and raised her eyes. 'It seems the promise of Bingham's special shoe-shine technique has made her life very bright very quickly,' said Claire. 'What a creature. If she weren't looking through her front window I'd trample her bloody flowers down. What a creature!'

***

I turned right off Station Road onto Crook Lane. 'So you think there's a jealousy thing going on here, Claire?

'It's a possibility.'

'You know, if I was Alex Bright, I might just disappear to get away from the dingbat.'

'They can't have had much of a relationship. I wonder if he knew about Ernie Bingham. It's something we should have asked her.'

'It's pretty obvious that if Bright and son were out of the same mould as her, everyone around them would want to do them in,' said Claire.

***

Five minutes later we arrived at Mrs Gilmore's house, hoping our recent experience of interviewing females was not going to be repeated. We had a tenuous link; both boys went to the same school and they were in the same year, something we could explore now, so long as Mrs G was at home. It turned out she was, and very helpful, too.

'I expect you've come to ask me more about Bill's death,' she said, after seating us in her front room.

It had been at least two years since we were last here. They'd certainly taken their toll on this poor woman; her life must have been miserable since William's death. She would probably have had support for a month or so from friends after he'd died, but so often in these cases support faded remarkably quickly — as if the bereaved carried a contagious disease.

'Yes,' said Claire, as gently as she could.

'Right ... that's all right.'

'We've been to interview Mrs Bright.'

I noticed Mrs Gilmore stiffen at hearing the woman's name.

'She said your boy went to the same school as hers.'

'Michael, was at the secondary modern with Edward, but they didn't really mix well.'

'That's a shame. Why was that?'

'Well, the Bright's are better-off than us. They're too posh, so even the boys didn't want to know each other as—'

'I see. Did they have other friends in common?'

'There were a few who knew each other but not in the same gang as far as I know. It's a while ago now. They've all grown up and left home, well most of them have, I think.'

'Can you remember any of their names? Especially those who stayed locally, Mrs Gilmore. It might help us if we can talk to them.'

'I can remember a few. There's the Saunders boy, he works in a bank in Nantwich, I think. There's Sidney Jones who did all right and got a job in Stockport; Tony Adamson — I don't know what he does; Frederick Curzon went off to join the army, or he might have gone to London. He has a sister Elsie, or something like that. Nice girl from a very well-to-do family, that I do remember. She lives in Northwich.'

'Yes, how about girls, Mrs Gilmore,' said Claire. 'Were there any they mixed with?'

'Only a few girls, Joan Dobson, Carol West and Elsie Curzon of course. They have all moved away. Well, there's not a lot here for young ones. There's talk of expanding the town, to take in folk from Manchester and Liverpool and bring in industry. I don't understand it. Why can't they stay where they are instead of coming here? It's not big enough here is it?'

It looked as though this interview was not going to reveal much more information of use, until Claire said: 'One more question, Mrs Gilmore, if you don't mind. Were any of these kids unruly, ruffians or spiteful?'

'Oh yes, there were a couple of bad-apples. Let me see now.'

We waited while the cogs in Mrs Gilmore's head engaged. I

studied the hideous rose-patterned wall paper to see if I could spot where the pattern repeated. I found it.

'Ronnie Boyton, I think, and somebody Sylt. Yes they often hung around together. Up to no good most of the time, but they've both gone away. I never heard of them since Michael left school. Those who couldn't find jobs here just seemed to vanish.'

'Thank you, Mrs Gilmore, you've been very helpful,' said Claire.

*****

I leaned back in my chair and slapped the back of my head. 'Okay then, let's question the people named in your book Claire, particularly Elsie Curzon.'

'But Mrs Gilmore said she lives in Northwich, sir, not Winsford.'

'I know that, but she's apparently "well-to-do" so she might even be on the killer's jealousy list.'

'Okay, okay ... I'll speak to her first,' she said. 'Once I find her address.'

'I'm going to set up an interview with Davidson at Bingham's shop first thing tomorrow morning. Then we'll decide if we need to bring them in.'

*****

Later that afternoon I received a call from a booking office clerk saying a parcel had arrived by hand for me. 'There's an unpleasant smell about it. Something messy if you ask me, sir.'

Why had someone sent me a foul smelling package. Did I upset people that much?

In the enclosed space of the small brew room, I caught the first whiff of something horrible. I cut away the damp brown paper carrying my handwritten name and put it to one side before it became too wet. Peeling back the remaining wrapping paper and cellophane sheets exposed a block of ice. One end was melting much faster than the rest. The smell, definitely dead meat — old sausages perhaps? — became much stronger. I ran the cold tap over the ice to melt it.

Gradually, as the water drained away, one end of the sausages gradually grew finger nails. Then a complete hand appeared, with what looked like a bullet hole through the middle of its palm.

25

THURSDAY 1ˢᵗ NOVEMBER

BINGHAM WASN'T DUE TO OPEN HIS SHOP UNTIL 9A.M. ANOTHER five minutes. Squinting through a gap in the back of the display, he was surprised to see me studying the array of men's footwear on display. A well dressed customer waiting for the shop to open, I assumed, was very unusual and his hopes of making an early sale must have risen.

He stood on his tip-toes to check on my current shoe style, but my feet were obscured by the low window frame. I could see the wheels going round in his head: he'd certainly need a large size, maybe twelve or thirteen considering at my height. I doubted if he'd have much stock my size, a thought which seemed to be confirmed by his frown.

Davidson joined me, we shook hands and entered the small triangular shop which stood on a corner opposite the Co-operative furniture store. The bell over the door was broken and made a dull *clunk* noise rather than a clear *ding*. The smell of new leather hit us as we stepped inside.

No announcement of our presence was necessary. Bingham, a short bald-headed man in his early fifties, had figured out who we were and greeted us after breaking off a discussion with one of his assistants.

Bingham wore a pin-striped three-piece suit without its jacket. Vivid-red braces matched his dickey-bow. The reflection of the overhead light in his black shoes matched the one on his bald head. A very snappy dresser — I suppose one had to be in his line of work. 'Good morning gentlemen. I assume you are the officers who telephoned yesterday?'

'We are, sir,' I said, as we simultaneously presented him with our warrant cards.

Bingham's assistants stopped what they were doing and turned to look at us and then each other.

'Is there somewhere private we could talk?' I said, glancing at the two girls.

'Yes indeed, officers.' Bingham turned on his heel to disappear behind a curtain the colour of his braces. He gestured for us to follow him up the stairs previously hidden from view. Davidson shot me a look as if to say, what can the Bright woman see in this bloke? I shrugged my shoulders and we followed the shopkeeper upstairs.

Bingham's office was the area of the entire shop downstairs, with a large mahogany desk at one end and two old rickety wooden chairs reserved for visitors, most likely shoe-salesmen, or his female assistants. Photographs and advertisements of various shoes hung on the two walls. The effect would have been quite grand had it not been for the stacks of shoes in boxes, which stood in columns from floor to ceiling, covering the rest of the floor space. We had to manoeuvre quite carefully to prevent them from being pushed over like dominoes, as we moved towards his desk. Bingham had obviously shelved his plans rather than his shoes. He squeezed around his desk to take up his plush leather revolving chair. Plainly Bingham kept the nice things in life — like Mrs Bright — for himself. We gingerly sat opposite, at each end of his desk.

'Mr Bingham, as you know we're investigating the disappearance of Alex Bright,' I began. Bingham nodded. 'How long have you known his wife?' Bingham's face rapidly turned bright red. 'Did you know her before Mr Bright disappeared?'

'Er, well, yes I did, as a matter of fact,' he said, swinging his revolving seat so he could look directly at me, 'I've known her for about two years.' He stroked the side of his nose with a finger tip. 'She buys a lot of her shoes here. I met her husband at a Clarkes' dinner dance in Altrincham. She'd spent a lot in the shop and I offered her two free tickets as a thank-you. We seemed to get along very well, so we'd occasionally meet and go out for meals or to the theatre in Chester or Crewe.'

'We, Mr Bingham?' said Davidson.

Bingham swivelled again. 'Yes, the four of us,' said Bingham, fumbling with his dickey-bow, 'my wife and I, together with Mr and Mrs Bright.'

'Mrs Bright tells us that you like to go golfing as well. Did you play golf with Mr Bright or was it just with his wife?' I doubted Bingham's podgy face could get any redder, but it did.

'After my wife died last year, Inspector, the Bright's were very kind and helpful and we decided to continue our outings though now there were, obviously, only three of us.'

Davidson said, 'And did Mr Bright play golf too?'

'No, he didn't like the game at all. Mrs Bright had never played. She'd often said she'd like to learn, so I helped teach her.'

I had an image of the short balding Bingham standing behind the taller Mrs Bright, his arms wrapped around her waist, with his hands over hers on the club, rocking together as she practised her swing.

'She joined my club near Chester,' continued Bingham, 'and took some lessons there. Occasionally we played together.' My image flashed up again, causing me to cringe at the very thought of it.

'A foursome or just the two of you?'

'The two of us mostly, occasionally we made up a four.'

'But not with Mr Bright?' I said.

'No, as I said, he didn't go for the game at all. We'd play most Wednesdays: it's half-day. The girls usually look after the shop while we, er—'

'How did Mr Bright feel about you taking his wife out?'

'Ah well, in the beginning he, err ... well he didn't know.' Bingham smirked, then realising he was still being interviewed by two police officers presented us with a serious expression.

'When did he find out?' said Davidson.

'About six months ago.'

'And what was his reaction when he found out, Mr Bingham?'

'He wasn't best pleased. Actually, not pleased at all.'

'In what way?' I said.

'He became aggressive towards his wife. And me. I think he hit her once, but of course, she denied it.'

'And you continued to take her out golfing?'

'Sometimes we would. Others we'd go walking in Delamere forest. She liked it there; we'd take a picnic or go for lunch in Chester.'

'Mr Bingham,' I said. 'Thank you for being so open about your close relationship with Mrs Bright, but you do realise you could be accused of foul play towards Mr Bright? You could be implicated in his disappearance.'

Standing quickly to his full five foot-four, he slapped his hand down hard on his desk, a move that probably startled both girls downstairs. 'How dare you insinuate,' his spittle flew in my direction, 'that I have murdered Alex Bright? I have done no such thing. True I have grown closer to Mrs Bright since my wife died—'

'No one has said anything about murder, Mr Bingham.'

He stared hard at me for a moment then slowly sat down.

'You know he's been murdered, do you?'

'I ... I don't know anything. I just assumed that he must have been, having disappeared for so long.'

It was now over three weeks with no sign of him. 'How has Mrs Bright been since he disappeared, Mr Bingham? Is she depressed, worried, concerned, happy even?'

'Well I shouldn't say this, but she doesn't seem to miss him at all. It might be because he's not around to hit her any more.'

This agreed with Claire's opinion: she didn't seem a bit bothered her husband wasn't around.

'Is she a wealthy person, Mr Bingham?'

'She's what they call comfortable, Inspector Crosier. I don't know any real detail as to her finances other than she inherited some money which is why she stopped working.'

I nodded. 'Thank you, Mr Bingham. We may need to speak with you again at the station. Do you have a home number at which we can reach you?'

Bingham, obviously shocked at the possibility this might go further, managed to stutter out his home telephone number. We both noted it in our books, stood and the three of us went downstairs.

Davidson and me went to the door without saying goodbye and turned in time to see Bingham dash back upstairs.

The two shop girls looked at each other, then us. They had a job to stop tittering when we heard boxes of shoes crashing to the floor above. Their services would be called for later, no doubt, to sort out the mess; once Bingham had called Mrs Bright.

'I think it's time to bring Mrs Bright into Crewe for further questioning,' I said. 'I'll have a car pick her up now.'

***

An hour later, I, Davidson and Judith Bright — whose get-up was more suited to attend a race meeting at Ascot, rather than a police station — were in the main interview room at Crewe.

The police station offices were not obvious to most travellers who were naturally more intent on getting down onto the platforms to catch their trains. It occupied the floor above the buffet on platform five. The LMS Company, which added it, saw no sense in continuing the elaborate and ornate cream and orange brickwork design of the buffet up to the first floor. Instead, it was made from plain drab purple-grey coloured bricks capped off with a grey slate roof. However, its proximity to the buffet below often provided me with ample opportunity to escape from the office when I felt hungry — which I did often during serious cases.

Everyone was seated on uncomfortable wooden chairs around a large wooden table, its surface stained with cup-rings, its edges split away almost everywhere. Narrow grimy windows high up near the ceiling let in a dull light which had to be aided by two bare one hundred-watt light bulbs. WPC Cardin came in to take notes, and be the female officer present for the interview.

'Judith Bright,' I began, 'you are not under arrest, as yet, but I should warn you that your demeanour since your husband's disappearance does make us think you might be involved, maybe with the help of Mr Bingham?'

Bright looked coldly at each of us in turn. On further questioning, it turned out Bingham had telephoned Bright as soon Davidson and I left his shop. He told her we suspected they'd both planned Bright's disappearance and that they might be his murderers. She'd reassured him there was nothing for them to worry about at all.

'What do you mean by, "my demeanour", Inspector?'

'You don't seem bothered much about your husband's disappearance. When we visited you yesterday, we left with the distinct impression you cared more about getting your hair styled and going off to the lakes with Mr Bingham. This doesn't fit the usual pattern of a loving wife, wouldn't you agree?'

Bright, who had been glaring at WPC Cardin as I spoke, turned back to face me.

Below, an express from Liverpool roared into platform-five causing the whole room to tremble slightly.

Mrs Bright raised her voice, without any difficulty, over the noise. 'It's true, officer, I didn't much like my husband. Yes we had a good lifestyle, but that isn't everything is it? He didn't like me seeing Mr Bingham after his wife had died. He became angry and we argued a lot. When he didn't come home that night, I wasn't too bothered. Truth be known, Inspector, as you have so rightly observed, it hasn't worried us at all that he never came back. I was a little uncertain at first of course about what might he be up to. Then as the days drifted by without him, I felt as if I had my freedom again. I have become used to it. And I like it.'

'Was he violent towards you? Has he ever struck you?'

'Not at first. We argued more and more and, as I refused to stop seeing Ernie, he became much more aggressive; violent too. He hit me twice, not where you'd notice, though.' She put her hand across her stomach. 'That did it for me, Inspector; once possibly, but not twice. I didn't want to be around him at all. Then he disappeared. If Alex has walked out, or if someone has killed him, so be it, Inspector. But neither I nor Mr Bingham played any part in his disappearance.'

Everyone was silent for some seconds after she'd tried to acquit herself. Could anyone believe her? She seemed very confident. If she had been beaten by her shorter husband, and they would never have proof unless her son had witnessed it, then maybe she was truly glad he'd gone. Whether she and or Bingham were instrumental in his going, had to be investigated further.

'So you won't want this, I assume?' I said, opening an envelope containing the gold wedding ring which had fallen off Bright's hand yesterday. 'I'm afraid you can't touch it. It's needed for forensic evidence. It's engraved—'

'J & A,' said Mrs Bright, calmly. 'Yes, you are right on two counts, Inspector. It did belong to my husband and it is starting to look like murder, isn't it?'

I nodded slowly, watching her for any reaction.

She sat looking directly into my eyes, the colour drained from her face.

I broke eye contact and placed the ring back in its evidence bag. 'Mrs Bright,' I said firmly, making her start. 'We're going to have to look into your personal finances. I need you to produce bank statements and any insurance policies covering Mr Bright.'

'Fine, Inspector, do what you must. There is a joint-life policy taken out about ten years ago. I think now, it would be worth about two thousand pounds.'

'And what about your house, does it have a mortgage?'

The sound of carriage doors slamming shut could be heard below. An engine whistled twice.

'No, Inspector it does not. I wanted it paid as quickly as possible and when my father died three years ago, we used my inheritance to pay it off. I couldn't bear to be, like all the others around us, in debt.'

Claire looked like she was ready to punch her. Once again this woman was more concerned about being a-cut-above her neighbours than what had happened to her husband.

A distant whistle blew. The interview terminated and Mrs Bright was to be driven home by Dobbs and Claire. Once there, she'd have to hand over her bank statements to them.

Guards were blowing their whistles again.

'I have one more question, before you leave the interview room.'

Bright turned to look at me. The relief she'd briefly felt, on hearing she was free to leave, deserted her.

'Would the house come to you in the event of Alex's death, Mrs Bright?'

The room was trembling again as the Liverpool train set off for London.

'Yes, Inspector, it would. I made certain of it.'

26

3rd NOVEMBER

IT WAS THE WEEKEND AND I'D PROMISED TO TAKE THE FAMILY OUT for a day-trip, if the weather looked promising. It turned out to be just the opposite and nobody wanted to set foot outside.

In the absence of that distraction, the possibility Elsie Curzon might be on a hit list was playing loud in my mind. I was going through the case files yet again hoping the more I reread them, the more likely I would find that elusive something to lead me to the killer. The files contained all sorts of information, consisting mainly of reports from those who attended the scenes of the crimes, railway personnel and witnesses, coroner's reports, official photographs of the scenes and press cuttings.

I was working in the upstairs box room, not that it was any form of office, but it at least allowed the kids to play downstairs without disturbing me.

Alice brought up coffee and biscuits and asked how I was getting along.

I explained how frustrating the whole investigation was, with so little to go on. I turned to reach for my coffee, and in so doing, the files perched on my lap fell across the floor.

'Let me help,' said Alice. They were completely mixed up, I having failed to neatly file them in order.

'I must get Carol to sort them out properly,' I said, frustrated by my own disorder.

Alice arranged them as best she could and finished up with all the loose press cuttings in a stack. 'That's strange,' she said, glancing through them. 'All these pictures of crowds. Were they taken at different places?'

'Yes, they were.'

'So where is this one?'

'Let me see. Oh, it's a cutting from the *Chronicle*. It's the send-off for last train from Middlewich. I went, but forgot my camera. It shouldn't be in this lot. I keep meaning to take it out and put it in my scrapbook.'

'Perhaps you shouldn't. Don't you think it odd that on this one and the Whitegate pictures, the same two people appear?'

'Where, let me see,' I said. 'Blimey, you're right.' They looked to be in their early twenties but weren't standing together. 'Thank goodness for women; they see all the things us chaps miss.' That was a thing about me, well one of them, according to Alice. My photographic memory was pretty good, but as for faces; that bit of my brain needed development. Was Alice's discovery relevant? Were they some ghoulish type fascinated by trains and crashes, or could they actually be connected to the cases? If they knew each other they'd probably be standing closer together, unless they were being devious, of course. Could they be my suspects? To eliminate them from my investigations, I needed to find out who they were, and soon, before another murder case landed on my desk.

I looked closely at them again. The head of the female was just visible as she stood at the back of the crowds in both pictures, her garments hidden. The male however, although standing behind others at Whitegate, seemed to be wearing motorbike leathers at Middlewich and Whitegate.

I'd almost raised the cup of coffee to my lips when it occurred to me, that Dobbs and I might have stood by the very man who killed Gilmore and Bright.

27

HE DECIDED TO PICK UP ANY MAIL AT NIGHT SO THAT THE NOSEY woman across the street might not see him. It had unnerved him: her turning up in the pub. Was she connected? Should he confront her with his suspicion?

He left his old motorbike parked around the corner so she wouldn't hear him arrive; it had been backfiring a lot recently. He kept an eye on the house opposite as he approached his destination. A quick dart along the side of the house, then in through the back door. With luck he wouldn't be noticed.

'Hello, Mog,' he said, as the cat bounded downstairs for another supper. He closed the hall door, switched the kitchen light on and fed her before turning the light off again and checking for any mail. At the front door, there was a large fat padded envelope and one like the first. He could see by the glow from the street light they both bore his name, but the addresses were written by different people. Both post marks looked just same as the first letter, though; even smudged in the same way. Was the padded one in a woman's hand writing? He went into the front room and peered at the house opposite.

The cat left the kitchen at speed, its cat flap closing with a single loud bang. He cursed the animal and opened the padded envelope. He couldn't believe his eyes. There was no message. A broad grin spread across his face. He could get used to this.

In the normal envelope, he found a small strip of paper with the typed name *Elspeth Curzon*.

He needed no direction. He knew who she was and where she lived. The posh cow had been at school with him.

28

5th NOVEMBER

IT WAS VERY EMBARRASSING, TO PUT IT MILDLY, BUT IT WAS NOT MY fault: I wasn't in charge of train movements. A diesel goods train lumbered along below my office. I closed the window to prevent the sickly fumes coming inside and to shut out the noise of the offensive locomotive. Back at my desk, feet up on one corner of it and slapping the back of my neck again, I was thinking about the two cases, trying to tease out anything we might have overlooked or any reason as to how they might be linked.

I was looking at the framed pictures on the office walls — all railway posters — scenes of destinations the railway companies commissioned artists to paint, in the hope of attracting people to travel to them by train. One advantage of my job was I was able to get the posters for nothing — they'd only have been thrown away — when they were replaced with new advertisements. A word in the right ear was all that was needed to rescue them and add them to my growing collection. Some day they might be worth something. I still had three at home that required framing and soon I'd have to start hanging them there, too, if Alice allowed me.

Alex Bright had been missing for four weeks. His wife, though initially suspected, never seemed concerned. His son, whom Claire and Dobbs had interviewed, showed little sign of shock that his father was missing. The short-arsed Bright probably knocked him about as well.

So why wasn't there a body? I couldn't be certain there

should be one, though, until it appeared. Maybe Bright had decided to clear off, an affair or something. Having met his wife, I wouldn't blame him.

A thorough search of the area — including a team of frogmen sent into the flash — didn't turn up either a corpse, or Bright's bike. It was a safe bet the old codger living in the vicinity hadn't heard or seen anything since the last war. But Dobbs had found motor-bike tracks and green string in the area covered by bushes at the foot of the hill leading to the bridge. None of the potential witnesses, traced on the list that Claire compiled, had anything to offer. Some were still in Winsford and didn't seem to be particularly well off. Claire had visited the Curzon household in Northwich in search of Elsie, whose real name turned out to be Elspeth. She was told their daughter had moved to Warrington over a year ago, so whether she was at risk seemed less likely than if she'd stayed locally. I'd get Claire to see her or telephone a warning anyway.

I was staring at a view of Edinburgh — the sun shining on the railway's Caledonian Hotel at the western end of Princess Street, with Edinburgh Castle high upon its rock in the background — pondering my next move when the telephone rang. I must take the family up there one day.

'DI Crosier.'

'It's Bill here from Control.'

'Thanks for calling me back. What have you got for me?'

'Well, there's not a lot of traffic that time of night. The only train after seven o'clock was an empty-goods of thirty five wagons, from Crewe via Sandbach to Northwich.'

'What time would it have passed under the Whatcroft Bridge?'

'Be around nine. It usually clears the main line through Northwich station before the nine-fifteen Chester to Manchester service comes through. It was held in the sidings at Northwich overnight. Then next day, it moved to Warrington south sidings where it is now, waiting for its next schedule.'

'You mean it will still be there? Even after four weeks?'

'Should be, Oliver, I've no record of it leaving and I would have if—'

'So I could get over there with a team now and search the wagons? This might turn out to be a murder investigation, Bill, so get onto Warrington to hold them. What about the train crew, the driver, fireman, guard? Where will they be now?'

'Yes you can go there. I'll get yardman Phips to show you the wagons. The engine crew, as it turns out, are off duty today but they'll be back on in the morning, about six at Northwich sheds. You'd have to ask Northwich about the guard's whereabouts.'

'Okay, Bill, I'll see them then. Have them standby for when I arrive. I love these early-starts. And get Yardman Phips waiting for us at Warrington. If we get cracking now we should be there by two o'clock. Thanks, Bill. Oh one more thing, get Phips to get a few ladders for us.'

I set off with Dobbs, Smith and Long Len — always a good man to have on ladder work — on the next train out of Crewe which stopped at Warrington Bank Quay station. It would take some time to go through a rake of thirty five trucks, but for once I was feeling good: I had something at last to investigate.

*****

After a tramp of about half a mile, down a narrow lane following the line from Bank Quay station, we entered a small wooden shack made of railway sleepers and set into the side of an embankment, which hid our view of the sidings beyond. Its corrugated-tin roof, we saw once inside, had leaked in places. There was a coal burning stove at one end keeping warm a large pot of stewing tea. But of Phips there was no sign.

The door swung open, startling everyone, and narrowly missed Dobbs' elbow. My optimism evaporated when a small scruffy man entered, wearing a flat cap and a boiler suit, that much like its occupant, needed a wash. A whiff of strong body odour followed yardman Phips, causing Dobbs to turn fast in search of some fresher air. Phips placed his shunter's pole in one corner of the cabin, then barged passed us and poured tea into a chipped enamel tin mug.

Seated at last, by the cabin window, he opened a pack of sandwiches and stuffed one into his mouth and stared chewing. 'Tha've come to take a gander at rake o' wagins, aye?' he said, spitting bits of egg towards me.

'Mr Phips? I'm DI Crosier, Transport Police.'

Phips taking on this news looked like he was about to give birth. His face gradually reddened, he stopped chewing and his jaw slowly dropped to reveal egg and tomato mixed with soapy white bread and saliva. Two rotten front-teeth were on display as well.

'Which line are they on? Did you get the ladders ready?' I followed Phips' gaze to the shunting yard through the cabin's rear window. My optimism hit rock bottom. Across the main line the sidings contained less than ten wagons.

'So where the hell are those wagons, Phips?'

'Well, er, I dun know like. Yer sees, the rake were split up some time back and stuck ont' others like, so I ain't that shurwer really like.'

'Okay, Mr Phips, who does know where the hell they are? You can't just lose them, can you?' I knew he probably could, though: British Railways were scrapping more than three hundred-thousand trucks of one sort or another. Twenty five was a very, very small percentage in the scheme of things; small enough to lose.

'Well, it's like this thou knows. Some would have gone back t' salt works at Winsfo'd, maybe some to brine at Winnington, ant rest, well could be anywhere really, maybe Sandbach. Bit of a bugger ain't it like?' Phips smiled uneasily.

'Bugger is not how I'd describe this, Mr Phips. So, pray tell me, who does know?'

'Not me, that's for shurwer.'

'Mr Phips, you might have a degree from the school of the

bleeding-obvious, but I don't. This is a murder investigation and I need to know *now* who can tell me where those wagons are likely to be heading? What records have you here?'

'These,' said Phips, somewhat chastened as he went to forage about in a drawer in a tall wooden desk fixed alongside a wall. He passed me the record book thick with grime.

'Thank you indeed.' Steam, with enough pressure to pull the missing wagons, was almost coming out of my ears. Scanning through the record book, it was obvious it was not religiously completed each day with details of trains which arrived and departed. 'Why aren't these records up to date, Mr Phips?

'Well, I don't rightly know like. Depends on who was on duty I suppose. Sometimes they clock off thinking they'll write it up next day like.'

'No I don't like, Mr Phips. Who was on duty on the 9th of October?'

'Let me think now, the 9th. Wer' it a Tuesday?'

I nodded.

'Oh, that'd most likely be me then, I suppose. I do Monday's t' Thursday's. Aye, me,' Phips nodded as if pondering on some new scientific discovery. 'Aye, me,' he muttered again.

Turning to the page marked the 9th of October, I could see some numbers relating to the wagons which had arrived that day. Whether they came from Northwich or Timbuktu was anyone's guess. There were at least two hundred. And none were listed as having left!

I sent Dobbs off to Winnington and Smith to Winsford Meadow Bank rock salt mine, each with a full set of the numbers. Long Len could do the climbing work with me.

I phoned both yard managers asking them to check all wagons were empty before any load was placed inside them. If anything was found, they were to stop loading at once, and call the investigating team. Deep down I knew I was far too late.

A southbound express thundered by; the vibration of it causing ripples to appear on Phips' rapidly cooling tea.

***

After fruitlessly climbing up the single ladder Phips had provided to inspect the eight remaining very empty wagons, we left Phips to his cold tea and egg butties and walked slowly along the lane back to Warrington Bank Quay station. It was a mild day and I could hear birds in the grassy banks. *The Lark Ascending* played in my head while blackbirds sang their rainy song. The weather was going to turn.

Len and I had ambled along deep in thought and angry at Phips. We missed the next train by five minutes. Still, plenty of time for a cuppa and cake before the four-ten, something which consoled us both.

***

Back at the office, I took the opportunity to call Davidson and bring him up to date with the missing trucks scenario and my suspicion that Bright was dumped into a passing goods train as it went under Whatcroft Bridge, hence no body.

'A case of naughty trucks eh, Oliver?'

'Yes indeed, very naughty trucks. I'm flagging with you the possibility that when or wherever they turn up, we might have our missing corpse and his bike, too.'

'Okay, Oliver, I'll monitor anything that comes in with a body or a bike in a railway wagon. Talk again.'

After a moment of brooding, I picked up the telephone and called Bill-in-Control. It was time he realised that he wasn't and that his system, to put it mildly, was crap.

29

AT LONG LAST, I HAD THE LABORATORY REPORT ON THE SEVERED right hand. It was difficult for the lab to say exactly how long ago the hand had been hacked from its owner but it looked as though it was frozen soon after its removal. The lab' were able to confirm it was male and estimated it had belonged to someone about five-feet-two inches tall.

The bullet wound had traces of powder marks suggesting it was shot at close range, probably by a point-two-two round. The reports on the green string, the footprints and motor bike tracks discovered at the Whatcroft Bridge, matched those found at the Whitegate incident.

The chances Mrs Bright and her admirer, shoe-shine-Bingham, were responsible for Bright's disappearance were reducing rapidly. I knew also, I definitely had two murders to solve — so long as Bright's corpse turned up.

I was certain they were both caused by the same person, or persons. It would take some effort to heave a body, especially if it were fighting back over the bridge wall. And whoever did it, would have to have timed the drop of the body to land inside the wagons, then pick up the bike and time its drop, too. If either fell between the wagons they'd end up on the track close to the bridge or be spotted by someone as the train passed through a station. The stretch of track from the bridge to Northwich had been searched on foot by Dobbs and Smith. They found nothing. No reports of unusual items hanging on trains had come in either. The crew of the train had been interviewed when they reported for duty. They estimated it would take just over a minute for the train to pass under the bridge. The driver of the 'crab' engine had seen nothing as he approached and passed below the bridge. The fireman was busy stoking the fire and the guard had no reason to be looking out from either of the van's side observation bay-windows. Even the sound of a lightweight bicycle falling into a wagon would be drowned by the noise of the empty wagons clanking along the single track to Northwich.

The rumble of a train below, as it sneaked its way towards platform-six, made rings in my cold tea. Dobbs and Smith came in and went through their visits to Winsford and Winnington works. Some wagon numbers they'd seen, matched those on the scrappy list of Phips' numbers. Once inspected they were allowed to be loaded. Collating their numbers suggested we were twenty-two wagons short and nobody interviewed could say for certain where they might be. I slapped the back of my neck. Where the hell were those missing wagons?

'So now what else links these two cases?' I said, desperate to find a new angle on them.

'They're in the same district, sir,' said Smith.

'That in itself doesn't take us far, does it?'

'The MO's similar,' continued Smith, 'both late at night and at deserted single-track locations.'

'It had occurred to me, Smith.'

'Do we know anything about the bikes, sir?'

'Not yet. We are talking to dealers. I suggest you chase that line of enquiry along, Smith.'

Claire entered. 'I've spoken to Elspeth on the telephone.'

'And?'

'She couldn't think of anyone who would want to harm her or her parents. I advised her to be vigilant of anyone who might be watching her and to call us if—'

'Okay, Cardin, we get the picture.'

30

10th NOVEMBER

THE TRACK RECONSTRUCTION SOUTH OF RUGBY WAS WELL UNDER way. Jason Coles, lean and fit, was the civil Engineer In Charge of the stretch between Rugby and Wolverton. The weather today was with him and his team were making good time laying the new track. Trains were diverted via Northampton to give the track laying teams an uninterrupted weekend. They'd reached the point where the new track was laid and additional ballast stones were needed between the sleepers.

A ballast train of thirty wagons was called forward. It moved slowly along the track. As the wagons reached the point where the ballast was required, the trap-doors were opened to dump the stones over the sleepers. Teams of men would manually fill the gaps between the sleepers with ballast once the train was moved away.

Wagon M3429 was brought into position, its chute opened and it dumped five tons of stones, along with the crushed body of a dead male, onto the track bed.

Jason ordered the ganger to stop the train while they scrambled under the wagon to take a closer look at this unusual deposit. The corpse looked a real mess and flat, as if run over by a steamroller. Showing all the signs of being crushed by forty tons of stones, it would never again match any photographs taken previously. Its eyes had been forced from their sockets, and its limbs took up a contorted position, as the body came to rest on the track-bed. All its bones seemed to be broken. Dried blood covered what remained of his face and was crusted into its clothing, but at least it wasn't festering with flies, yet. The left arm was jutting from the stones, its hand missing.

'I think this is what the RP have been looking for all week,' said Jason, to his ganger. 'Better hold work on this stretch until they arrive. I'll go and make the call.' He marched off to the nearest signal that carried a telephone and called the BTP at Rugby, knowing his schedule was now shot to pieces. It would very likely be a few hours before the police arrived and released the body to the nearest mortuary.

::*

Herbert Bishop, at the Rugby RP, took Jason Coles' call. Aware Crewe division were looking for a corpse dumped in a goods wagon, he got the home number of the DI leading the case from the Duty Sergeant at Crewe and then put a call through to Crosier.

::*

I was digging up an apple tree which was in perfect condition. Why I was doing this was not questioned by Alice. She'd seen me do it several times with the other six trees too. I guess she put it down to stress relief. This physical activity certainly made me a happier man by the end of the exercise. I looked at her as sweat ran down my face.

She had her here-we-go-again look about her and I knew instantly what to expect. 'On Saturday morning now; at least it isn't Sunday!'

I left my muddy boots by the back door and entered in my woollen socks to take the call.

'Bishop, BTP Rugby. Sorry to trouble you, Inspector.'

'What can I do for you, Mt Bishop?'

'I think I have information about your missing body.

'Really. And what might that be?'

'It's turned up south of Rugby.'

'Rugby?'

'They're laying new tracks. The corpse fell out of a wagon when they dropped ballast. Looks a right-mess by all accounts'

'Who's in charge, Mr Bishop?

'Jason Coles is the EIC. He just called me.'

'Get hold of him and ask him if there are any of these wagon numbers in that ballast train.' After searching in my briefcase for the file, I read out a series of twenty-two wagon numbers. 'And ask him not to drop any more from those trucks until I get there. It'll take me about two or three hours, so I should be there just after mid-day. Have a car waiting to take me as near as possible to where they're working.'

I walked into the kitchen where Alice, having overhead one side of the conversation, was already making up a pack of ham sandwiches and a flask of tea.

'Don't make a habit of this, Oliver. You'd better put a change of clothes in your case, too.'

***

I arrived on site just after one. Jason Coles was understandably miffed at having his schedule stopped until the corpse was removed. But there was nothing anyone could do about it. Dead bodies — not that they had any say in the matter — demanded procedures be followed. I would have to brief Rugby CID, as a matter of courtesy, about the background to this case.

Coles took me up to the train which had brought the suspected missing body of Alex Bright on its last rail journey. Coles confirmed that all the wagon numbers Bishop had relayed to him were indeed part of this train.

'Well, Mr Coles, the fun isn't over yet. I suspect you will find a bicycle in one of these wagons. A red Raleigh sports model.'

'That's just what my boy wants for Christmas.'

'I'd let you have it for him, but if its suffered half as much as its owner, he'd have a bit of a job riding it. Once the Rugby blokes are happy to remove the corpse you should be able to resume your work.'

We arrived at M3429, below which the mangled remains of a man lay partially obscured by the pile of ballast stones. His face was in view, but damage to it rendered identification impossible.

Other than his hair colour, it didn't look a bit like the photograph I had in the file, but then it wouldn't after the stones had been dropped on it from a great height. His clothing although in tatters did match the description of what Mr Bright was wearing on his way home that fateful night, and his ID was confirmed by the absence of his left hand.

The CID inspectors were already at the site, and had removed as many stones from around Bright as possible, revealing that his right hand also was missing. Photographs were taken of him and the immediate location. There was nothing else to be done so the body was removed and stretchered off to a waiting ambulance. There was no doubt this was the missing Mr Bright and no doubt now I did have two trophy murder cases to deal with.

I gave the all-clear for work to proceed. Knowing it was only a matter of time before the bicycle was found, I perched on a pile of old sleepers and set about Alice's sandwiches. The weather was getting cooler now, and I was grateful for the hot tea she'd made.

I hoped the next discovery would be revealed before it got dark in a few hours. My wait was not long; just long enough in fact for me to polish off my refreshments.

'DI Crosier,' called Jason. 'I think you can have your bicycle back now.'

I wandered up the track to where M4712 was trying to discharge its load.

'I don't think you'll get very far on it, though.' Coles smiled.

Indeed I wouldn't. Bent and buckled it was jamming the trap-door opening and restricting the fall of the ballast. Jason signalled the driver to proceed forward slowly.

'Once it's empty I'll get a man to climb inside and pull it out for you to try, Inspector.'

Coles' humour had returned despite his four hour delay to his work schedule. They could still get the job done this weekend if they worked right through.

I bid them goodbye and set off back to Rugby. I'd see if I could inveigle my way into the Station Master's office and change out of my dirty work clothes — can't sit in a dining car in scruffy clothes can one?

31

SHAW JUST CAUGHT THE BUS TO THE RAILWAY STATION. HE WAS A man-in-a-hurry and a full-blown panic. Panic came easy to Archie Shaw and he told himself to calm down, it will be all right soon. But would it be? It had happened. It wasn't his fault: he couldn't help it.

He hoped he wouldn't draw attention to himself on the bus, but it wasn't easy. It was full of shoppers going home for the evening and somebody was bound to notice the man carrying a suitcase and sweating profusely in this cold weather. He sat with his small case on the seat beside him, praying nobody would want to sit next to him and start up a conversation. How could people start talking to complete strangers?

The bus drew in to pick up more passengers standing outside a post office. Most clambered noisily up the metal steps after glancing briefly along the lower deck for a vacant seat; some, more than likely, disappointed that during their journey they'd be shrouded in smoke.

The bus started up again as the conductor came along. 'Tickets please, if you don't mind, tickets please. Do you have a ticket, sir, if you don't mind?' He stared into Archie Shaw's face waiting for a response.

Shaw felt the man's breath on his face and pulled away. 'Er, no I don't have one. I'm going to the railway station. How much will that be?' he said, fumbling for some money in his trouser pocket.

'It's nine pence, sir, if you don't mind? That's the little silver one and that knobbly bronze one, if you don't mind, sir. Not too much to ask for a two mile ride to the station is it, sir?'

Shaw handed his money over and the clippie wound the handle on his machine strapped around his neck and passed over a pale blue ticket. 'Be there in ten minutes, sir. Going far, sir? I see you have your case with you.'

'Er, no, not really, well I don't think so anyway. Why do you want to know?'

'I'm making conversation, sir, if you don't mind, sir. If that seat is needed, I'll stow your suitcase under the stairs for you if you don't mind. Safe journey, sir, wherever you are off to.'

There it was again, a complete stranger wanting to talk to him. He knew he should have 'phoned for a taxi; but then taxi drivers always wanted to talk, didn't they?

Shaw, uncertain of what to do if someone wanted the seat, felt panic rising from deep within. If the conductor took his case he'd be bound to remember him if questions were asked. He didn't like the way the conductor had studied him.

'Station, railway station, anyone for the station, if you don't mind?' announced the conductor.

In his panic Shaw hadn't realised how far they travelled and the bus was slowing for the railway station. I just have to buy a ticket for Glasgow, he thought, and then things would be fine.

He didn't like the way things had gone today and was depressed by the speed at which news of the latest murder had reached the *Evening Crier* so quickly. Lucky then, that earlier when he'd been sitting in a rather grubby coffee house on the High Street, he saw the newspaper-van pull up outside. Bundles of newspapers were tossed onto the street and after some banter with the news vendor the driver climbed back into his van and shot off to his next drop.

Shaw watched the man as he unfurled the latest headline sheet and fixed it under the wired board. "Extra, extra, another railway murder. Handless corpse found near Rugby. Extra" the vendor had shouted.

Stunned by the headline, Shaw panicked. It shouldn't have happened like this: they shouldn't have discovered the body until he had left Rugby tomorrow. Now he'd have to change his plans. He'd dashed back to his brother's house, had packed hurriedly and was on his way to the station to catch a train, any train, to take him as far away from Rugby as he could imagine.

He wanted Glasgow and luckily the next one to arrive happened to be heading there. He paid cash, as usual, for a first-class ticket. Although his father left him a moderate amount in his will, it wasn't going to last much longer. He'd bought property years ago near Glasgow and in Warrington, as well as Rugby. And he'd spent a good chunk of it helping his daughter get a flat in London.

The six-thirty came in on time from Euston hauled by a very large red engine with steam hissing from the top of its boiler, not that Shaw noticed. Dozens of doors opened and people gushed onto the wide platform; mostly it seemed, shoppers wealthy enough to have a Saturday spending spree in London. But at which end of the train were the first-class carriages? Pushing his way through the crowd he at last saw the bright yellow stripe running below the guttering of the first-class carriages towards the rear of the train.

Once settled aboard, he tried to relax knowing that as each minute went by he'd be another mile further from the incident

32

YOU ARE ON YOUR WAY TO CREWE AGAIN, AND WILL SOON KNOW the way as well as the driver. You aren't sure how many times you will be doing this trip to Crewe, because your elderly mother only has a few months left to live.

You'd have caught an earlier train, but that bloody boss of yours said you had to go in for an important shareholder's meeting. On a Saturday for goodness sake. But still, it's history now and you will be with your mother in just a few hours.

How many times have you done this trip? At least a dozen. You are beginning to recognise the staff on the train; the pleasant ones even greet you as an old friend. Helps to pass the time. And, it occurred to you, occasionally you recognise a fellow traveller, a familiar face.

Ah, you're coming into Rugby; not too long for you now.

The dining-car is pretty full, just a couple of spare tables. You've had your meal, and after coffee you ought to return to your first-class compartment. But you like it here.

You see an old man enter from the far vestibule. Hang on a minute, isn't that? Oh where the heck have you seen him before? He takes a seat at the spare table across the aisle from yours. A table for two. He looks pretty nervous and throws his overcoat onto the spare seat.

A tall, smartly dressed man is looking for a seat but walks past. The old chap is watching him and lets out a sigh as he passes by. He obviously wants privacy. Don't we all?

But the dapper man doesn't find a seat. 'Do you mind, sir,' he asks the old man. 'Is this seat taken?'

'I, er, I don't know. There may have been someone there,

perhaps they left.' He's looking around, hoping to find some trace of belongings which might indicate to the dapper man that this seat was occupied ... but nothing remained. 'Yes, looks like they left,' he said, through gritted teeth.

'Oh, that's good then. You see I don't like travelling with my back to the engine, especially if I'm having a meal as we go along. You can get the soup in your lap if they slam on the brakes.'

'Oh yes, yes, quite so,' and he gestured for the dapper man to sit. 'Going far?'

'No, not far really: Crewe; under two hours. Enough time for a little something though.'

The way Dapper speaks reminds you of Pooh Bear. The waiter arrives and asks them both if they are eating. The old man just ordered red wine then changed his mind when Dapper ordered roast beef.

You are still trying to work out where you've seen the old man before, when the train plunges into a tunnel. By the time you're out the other end you've remembered. He's not wearing his tartan suit, but he certainly is Tartan.

Dapper pulls out the evening paper from his brief case and studies the front page for some time. Then with a quick flicker of his wrists he flings the paper wide open and disappears behind it.

You can clearly read the headline.

RAILWAY MURDERS
SECOND VICTIM FOUND IN GOODS WAGON

33

SHAW IS LEANING FORWARD OVER THE TABLE READING THE ARTICLE on the front page of Crosier's newspaper ...

The body of the second railway murder victim in three years was found earlier this afternoon in a railway wagon used to carry track ballast. The ballast was part of a track replacement scheme in progress ten miles south of Rugby. British Transport Police and Rugby CID still don't seem to have a motive for this or the killing which took place three years ago on a branch line near Whitegate in Cheshire. They have not found any clues other than the man's bicycle which was discovered shortly afterwards in another wagon. The victim, who'd had both his hands amputated, was crushed beyond all recognition by the full load of ballast stones in the wagon. Police think it will be days before a formal identification will be made due to the highly compressed state of the deceased. This is the second railway murder being investigated by DI Crosier of the British Transport Police based at Crewe with the assistance of Chester and, now, Rugby CID officers.

There was a photograph of DI Crosier. Shaw knew he'd seen it before. Then the paper was lowered and folded away and the man in the photograph looked directly at him.

Shaw took a deep gasp of breath and almost dropped his wine.

I assumed the man was having a fit or something. Whatever it was he looked very shocked, and the colour had drained from his face. 'Are you all right, sir?' I poured him a glass of water from the decanter. 'Here, have a sip of this.'

'It wasn't supposed to work out like this,' he said. 'He should never have done it. They should never have done it.' He was almost shouting.

Passengers across the aisle turned to look at the commotion.

'Steady, sir, take it easy. Try to keep calm. Have some more water.'

'It's a stiff drink I need after that shock,' and he grabbed his wine glass, emptying what was left in a single gulp. 'They shouldn't be going about doing this sort of thing,' he said, jabbing his finger in the direction of my paper.

I looked at the paper and now understood what the man opposite was talking about.

'And that's you isn't it? That picture is you!'

'Yes it is, sir. But I'd rather you kept your voice down. I don't want everyone staring at me.' I smiled at the man who, for the moment at least, seemed to be calming down.

'So what do you know about who is killing them?' he said, nervously.

'I'm sorry, sir, I'm not at liberty to say. It is still a police investigation.'

'Sorry officer, of course it is. Stupid of me.'

Fortunately, for me — and those disturbed by the fellow's outburst — our meals arrived and gave me an excuse to break off this conversation. I glanced occasionally at the man opposite. Murder took people in different ways; just seeing it in the papers was often enough to frighten some, especially the elderly or the weak-minded. The man sitting opposite could easily be both.

The rest of my journey passed somewhat more quietly than it had begun. After the plates were cleared away, and my companion had polished off a third glass of wine, with little else to drink, he gradually fell into a deep sleep.

I looked up from my paper occasionally as he mumbled in his sleep: "I'll have to tell Nancy about them. Tell Nancy. Nancy, must tell her.' Then later on, still dreaming, he moaned, 'Tell her how, how bad they ..."

∗

The train was approaching Crewe. Passengers were gathering their things and getting ready to leave the train. It jerked as it passed over the points, disturbing the old man's dreams. He opened unseeing eyes briefly then was gone again.

I picked up my things and turned to leave.

"They shouldn't have happened, they shouldn't be doing this, too many dead", the old chap moaned. A few passengers turned towards him then rolled their eyes towards heaven.

'One too many, I think,' I said. 'Still, should keep him quiet the rest of the way to Glasgow.'

I walked along the carriage with the other departing passengers and stepped down onto the platform, closing the carriage door after us.

Walking back, past where I'd been sitting, I stopped to look in at the old man. Still asleep. "They shouldn't have happened, they shouldn't be doing this, too many dead" played back in my head. That was what the stupid old bugger had said.

The guard at the rear of the train was blowing his whistle and waving his green flag.

I put my case down then dashed back to the carriage door, opened it and rushed inside.

I heard the guard in the middle of the train blow his whistle. The train was about to leave.

The waiter was bringing a tray of coffee and we danced around each other so I could pass as someone slammed closed the door that I'd left open for my escape.

I hurried along the aisle to where the old man was snoring.

I heard the distant whistle from the guard at the front of the train, then engine whistled a response and the train began to leave for Glasgow.

I fumbled inside my pocket for my cards, found one and placed it the top pocket of the sleeper's jacket. The train was gathering speed as I turned and ran back towards the door. The last place I wanted to be now was Carlisle.

I lowered the window, leaned out to reach the handle outside, turned it and swung the door open. Hanging onto the door briefly, I jumped and hit the platform, running as fast as I could for a few seconds to stop myself from falling flat on my face.

The open door, now moving away at speed, was pushed shut by the guard, further along the platform, who shouted 'Now that wasn't very clever was it, sir. Don't you know how dangerous it is to jump from a ...

'Oh it's you, Oliver. Forgot something did you?'

'In a manner of speaking yes, I did,' I said, catching my breath.

I turned away and went back along the platform to pick up my case then headed for the way-out before the guard became more inquisitive.

34

13th NOVEMBER

MY DAY STARTED WELL ENOUGH. UP AT 7:30, I'D TAKEN MY TIME shaving and even gave my bushy eyebrows a trim. I must be getting older, I thought, noticing for the first time the hairs in my nostrils were becoming longer; they'd need cutting back before Alice noticed and complained. I'd send for one of those new-fangled trimmers they advertised in the *Daily Herald's* small ads.

Breakfast with Alice and the kids before they set off to school had been a real treat. I'd still be at the office early enough.

Letters fell onto the hall floor as the letterbox smacked shut.

Then the promise of an easy day turned sour.

I spotted the envelope as I got my jacket from its hanger in the hall. Maybe it's the newsagent's bill, I thought, but the envelope simply said, *Lost Crosier?*

Puzzled, I opened it. Inside, written by the same hand, was a brief note of well ... what exactly? I took it into the kitchen to read again.

Been 3 years Crosier
last King and Scotsman take Royal Scot Friday.
OR ANOTHER DIES!
His predecessor knows when.
The Boy.

I stared at the threat again — yes, it was a threat all right. Not a hoax. Could it have come from the railway murderer?

'Jesus,' I shouted, 'it's just been delivered!' I dashed out through the front door and looked up and down the road. Nothing. Nobody was about at all.

I telephoned Claire to get Dobbs and Smith in my office by ten sharp. I carefully placed the note back inside its envelope and found a paper bag to protect it from damage until I got to work. I felt a mixture of excitement and frustration as I cycled along to the meeting. Then I realised where I'd seen that handwriting before.

They were all seated in my office when I arrived and while removing my overcoat, I told them what had been delivered to my house within the last half an hour. 'And, we've seen that writing before,' I said, searching the case file. 'Look.' I pulled out the piece of brown paper carrying my name. 'These are both from the same person, the killer. Tell me what you make of his latest delivery? Claire?'

'It's obviously some sort of code, Oliver,' she said, reading the note now in a transparent folder. 'But what does it mean?'

'That's why we're here, isn't it?' Sometimes people, even bright ones like Claire, just back from her latest training course at Tadworth, asked the daftest of questions! She had joined the BTP in 1957 attending the first all-women course and gained top-marks.

Be calm, keep calm. 'What bothers me,' I said, 'is that whoever this is from, whether it is a real threat or some sort of prank, knows who I am, where I live, and that I'm working these two murder cases.'

'Well anyone reading the local papers would know you're working the cases, sir,' said Dobbs. 'They print your picture and name each time they report about them.'

'Getting jealous are we, Dobbs?'

'No, sir. I'm just saying that you shouldn't be bothered about the papers. But, I would be bothered about whoever wrote this threat knowing where you live.'

'They've seen your pictures, know where you work. It

wouldn't be difficult for them to follow you home,' added Smith.

'True. Anyway, putting those minor details aside for a moment, who has any theories?'

'Who was the last King?' asked Claire.

'King George the Fifth,' I said, stretching my head up and rubbing my neck, pleased with myself that I was able to recall the information so quickly. The neck rubbing tell, according to Alice, sometimes came out when I was pleased with myself. 'Surely everyone knows that! He abdicated in 1936 then ran off with some American woman.'

'That would be Mrs Simpson,' said Dobbs. 'If that's who he means.'

'Is there any other meaning?'

'What was the last King made?'

'What do you mean, Dobbs?' said Claire.

'It's possible he may mean which King locomotive was the last to be built. There's a class of engine called the King,' explained Dobbs. 'The GWR had all manner of posh classes: Halls, Manors, Castles and Kings, that sort of thing.'

'Okay, since you thought of it, Dobbs, get onto Swindon Works and find out the answer. And get all their numbers as well,' I said, to his disappearing back.

'So that leaves us with the Royal Scot and the Scotsman,' said Claire, stating the obvious again.

'There's the Flying Scotsman. Do you think he means the engine, sir?' said Smith.

'Highly likely. Our killer loves trains. But he is a nutter, fixated by them as a means of killing.'

'The Royal Scot is a named train, Claire,' said Smith.

'I know that! It runs each day through here. London to Glasgow and back again. Well not exactly the same train obviously. Do you think he means that train?'

'If I knew that, Claire, then I'd probably know a lot more about this idiot. Nip down to W.H. Smiths on platform four. See if they have any train spotting books and bring them up.

'Okay, sir, but I'll feel a bit daft buying spotters' books.'

'If anyone asks, tell them they're for your grandchildren,' I said, winking at Claire as she left my office.

'Meanwhile, Smith, get some coffee on. Thanks to Dobbs, we might be onto something already.'

Ten minutes later, the coffee was hot and Claire returned with some of *Ian Allen's* spotters books. She'd found what we were looking for. 'The Flying Scotsman is 64472 and the last King locomotive, King Edward VIII, is 6029. So together that makes err, 70,501!'

Before we could work out if this number was significant or not, Dobbs returned with his answers from Swindon. 'King Edward VIII is—'

'6029,' Claire and Smith said, together.

'How do you know?'

'Simple really,' said Claire, 'Mr *Ian Allen's* famous train spotters' books, courtesy of Smiths on four.' She passed one over to him.

'Ah, but was it the last King to be built?' asked Dobbs, who obviously had an answer ready.

'Out with it,' I said. 'We're all ears.'

'6029 was the last King built, but Edward VIII was not its original name. It was first built as King Stephen.'

'Don't be daft Dobbs,' said Smith. 'Whoever heard of a King Stephen?'

Claire burst out laughing and thumbed through the *Ian Allen* books again searching for supporting evidence. 'There's nothing in here about a King Stephen,' said Claire.

But I could see Dobbs was serious.

'You really mean that, don't you, Dobbs?'

'Yes, sir. According to Swindon, King Stephen was built in August 1930. Then it was renamed King Edward VIII in 1936, when the real Edward VIII abdicated.'

'So what does that give us? King Edward abdicates in '36, has the last King built named after him, in place of "the predecessor"

King Stephen.' Its number is 6029, which if we add it to the Flying Scotsman's number gives us ... 70,501.'

'Or subtract them and you get 58,557,' said Claire. We all looked at her. 'I know, just thinking aloud, sir.'

'All right, let's put that on one side for a moment and concentrate on what else we know,' I said. 'This message is signed *The Boy*. So who is he? He's giving us another clue. It's been almost three years since Gilmore was killed. Assuming this idiot did it, he probably has his foot in his freezer as a trophy.'

'Maybe he wants to be found or more likely wants to play with us just to boost his peculiar ego,' said Claire.

I nodded agreement.

'We know they're connected by the string and the motorbike tracks, sir,' said Smith.

'Yes, yes, for goodness sake. We know all that, Smith. Boy; I think we have heard the name before. Smith, get your notes from interviews with the Gilmore woman. It's bugging me, but I reckon we missed something,' I said, leaning back and slapping the back of my neck. 'Come on, Smith. Jump to it.'

Smith's metal chair made a loud scraping noise as he quickly stood and pushed it back across the bare floorboards.

I cringed as the sound set my teeth jangling. 'Thank you, Smith.'

He returned and gave me his notes. Smith didn't think I'd find anything useful in them. After a moment, I started to smile and gave my neck a beating. I turned the notes to face Smith. 'There,' I said, pointing to a line in Mrs Gilmore's statement. 'Correct me if I'm wrong, PC Smith.'

He blushed, then read out the line. 'It says, "Oh yes, there were a couple of bad-apples. Let me see now, Ronnie Boys, I think and somebody Sylt often hung around together. A thoroughly bad lot".

'Thank you, Smith.' I glared at my team. I slapped the table. Startled, they all jumped. 'Someone should have noticed this and followed it up.' I knew I should have checked that they had, but this gave me the opportunity to get their serious attention. It would do them no harm.

I'd had doubts about Smith's ability in particular, and made a mental note to speak to him later. Maybe too, if I could find the right form of words, I'd suggest to him that he seek medical advice about his worsening acne as well.

I reached for the telephone and asked the operator to get the Winsford police on the line. Nobody spoke. They waited in silence for the call to be connected. I could see they tried not to look at me as I pretended to study one of my railway posters on the wall opposite. Claire found some urgent attention was required to the hem of her skirt, while Smith's right hand rambled around his face in search of the latest eruption.

Dobbs deployed his joker and leaving the room said, 'I'll make you another coffee, sir.'

'Do you have anyone on file called Boy?' I said, after introducing myself to the sergeant on duty at Winsford. 'We think he might be a vicious character. Hung around with someone called Sylt we suspect.'

'Yes we know about them two. You're dead right. A thoroughly bad-lot if you ask me.'

There it was again; "a bad-lot".

'Who are they, Sergeant?'

'Ronnie Boyton, not Boy, and Phyliss Sylt. Last known address for Boyton was 98 Seaton Street.'

'Last known?' I got that sinking feeling in my stomach again.

'Last known indeed, we ain't seen nor 'eard of him for over two years now. So the chances are he's moved away. Until he does some more mischief, I doubt we'll know where he is, same for the girl.'

'What do you have on them?

'Boyton, GBH. Sylt, shop-lifting and she's been in remand as well. She beat-up a relative she was visiting once, so not entirely stable.'

'Do you have any photographs of them?'

'I think we do of Boyton, but not Sylt. Hang on, I'll get the files out,' and there was a long silence broken only by the sound of Hampson opening and shutting several filing cabinet drawers. 'Sorry to keep you. Yes, as I thought, we have a few copies of a mug-shot of Boyton we took here. Shall I post one to you?'

'No, I'll get a courier over to you now. Time is against us,' I said, finishing the call.

I turned, smiling, to my team. 'The good Sergeant Hampson, has a photograph of Ronnie Boyton, not Boys. Smith, organise a motorbike to go to the Winsford constabulary now.'

Smith left the room as Dobbs returned with my coffee and chocolate digestive biscuits in his ploy to soften me up.

'And I think you and I have seen him before, Dobbs,' I said, taking the plate of biscuits.

Dobbs looked puzzled.

'I'll bet you a fiver on it?'

An hour later, we had a copy of the Winsford files on Boyton and Sylt. The team were back in my office waiting for me to pull my rabbit from my trilby.

I reached for my own file on the Gilmore case and removed two press cuttings. One showed a group of people at the Whitegate site, the other, a group of people listening to the Mayor of Middlewich, as they sent off the last passenger train.

I slid them over to Claire and asked her to see if she could see the same woman on both photographs.

After a short period of nose wriggling, Claire pointed to her. 'It's not very clear, sir, but I think they match. She looks like Phyliss Sylt?' She passed the cuttings over to Dobbs.

'And do you see this man anywhere?' I said, producing Hampson's excellent photographs of Ronnie Boyton.

Dobbs nodded and pointed to the man in the two press cuttings.

I rubbed the front of my neck. 'Now who owes me a fiver?'

As expected there was no reaction from the team. 'Nobody owning up? Well this time, I'll console myself that at last we know what our killers look like.

'All we have to do now, is find the buggers.'

35

WEDNESDAY MORNING

MY THEORY, DELIVERED OVER TEA AND BISCUITS – AND TWO MARS bars for Smith — in five's buffet, seemed reasonable to everyone, and by the time we returned to my office we had agreed a plan of action.

I called Newall and Davidson to tell them the good news about the Boyton and Sylt IDs and the bad news about the threat, and what I thought we must do about it.

Newall in Manchester said, he was "open-minded" — or in other words, he hadn't a clue — and "it was time he dropped in, especially now things were hotting-up". Dropping in "to chivvy us along" no doubt, now there was something to get excited about. Typical top-brass interest. Like as not he'd already told Big Boss Mullard in London, before I could say Jack Robinson.

Davidson seemed to think our understanding of the message had some merit. 'So what do you suggest we do about it, Oliver? Do we have any alternative?'

'I don't think we do. As I see it we set up the train like he told us. It may save a life, maybe several lives, if my assumptions are correct. If they're not, well it's back to the drawing board.'

'No, Oliver. I think you are correct. You need to work out the logistics of all this. Can I come to see you later this afternoon, say three, and we can go through it first before you present your plan to Superintendent Newall?'

'Yes, and I'll bring in the people we'll need to actually organise it, you know traffic controllers and the like.'

'See you at three then.'

I had managed to gather together most of the people needed to carry out my plan. All I had to do now, was present it to them and hope, that if there were any dissenters, Newall would back me up.

'Superintendent Newall, gentlemen,' I began, standing to address them once everyone was settled. 'We have on our hands two unsolved murders. It is possible, though, that the murderer has chanced his arm. He posted through my letterbox yesterday morning, the message of which you each have a copy. This followed a few days after the same person sent me a very unusual package. Claire, ask Mrs Ward to bring it in please.'

A moment later, Carol entered the room. 'This what you wanted, DI Crosier?' and she handed over a container the size of a shoebox.

'Thank you, Mrs Ward. Please be so kind as to wait a minute.' I lifted from it the severed hand, and held it up so everyone could see it. Now I had everyone's full attention.

'This was the first part of Alex Bright I saw, but didn't know that when it was actually delivered here, for me! Most of the rest of him turned up four days ago, south of Rugby. His other hand is still missing.

'We're dealing with someone who wants his own way. He's a bully and, as we all know, bullies don't work alone.' I replaced the hand back in the box. 'Thank you Mrs Ward. Would you put it back in the freezer for me?'

She looked at me and, I could see from her expression, she was about to ask why, having admired its contents only an hour before. I turned to my audience before she could say anything. She left to do as I'd requested.

'It seems,' I continued, 'we have to have a certain train, pulled by certain locomotives from other regions, in a certain place at a certain time on Friday.'

'Too many *certains*, when actually, in reality, Crosier you are uncertain about everything,' was Newall's response.

I let his remark pass. His time would come.

'But it's worth a shot,' put in Davidson.

'What is it you need us to do, Oliver?' asked one of the traffic controllers, who'd recovered his composure now that the hand was back in the freezer.

'First, we need to get the engines named together. Someone needs to check where they are and arrange with their regional traffic controllers to get them to Euston and hooked up to the Royal Scot ready to depart, on time, at ten o'clock this Friday morning. Their controllers will have to find substitute engines for their normal duties while we have them. We have to show these killers we're taking them seriously. And there's a little tweak I intend to give them, so we'll need two sets of engines.'

'Why two sets?' Jackson the controller for the Midland routes wanted to know.

'Because, Arthur, we're going to switch the trains.'

Utter silence.

'Whatever this maniac may have in mind, the last thing we can do is to risk the lives of the travelling public. For all I know he might be planning a serious smash or a derailment.'

'Okay, so how do we switch six hundred tons of train dashing along at sixty miles an hour?'

'Simple really,' I said, 'you switch them in a tunnel.'

Everyone looked at each other, then at me.

'And transfer everything over to a second train; in the pitch black? You must be joking, Oliver,' said Jackson.

More mutterings of dissent moved about the room.

Newall smirked.

'I'm not joking and it is simple: one, you park a duplicate train in a tunnel which has two tracks in each direction. The duplicate is dressed up like the real express. Two: you bring the real express into the tunnel and stop it alongside. Three, you transfer the force from one train to the next in twenty seconds. It can't take longer as someone might be watching en-route. If we're too late and don't make the location on time, the killer may strike again.'

'So Oliver, you want a tunnel long enough with two tracks to park a train after its entered at sixty, bring it alongside another already waiting there, get your blokes moved over to the waiting train and get the dummy speeding out of the tunnel at sixty and all in twenty seconds? You don't want much do you?'

This time, a chuckle moved around the room.

Newall slowly shook his head.

'That's twenty seconds stationary, not moving,' I said. 'So where do you suggest it can be done, Arthur? It can't be too far out of London, though.'

'There's only one tunnel suitable: Watford,' he said, enjoying the limelight. 'It has four tracks. It would give us a chance to re-route some services, too.'

'Right then, we'll work around that. Can you organise everything, Arthur?'

'In principle yes.'

'In principle?'

'Everything will have to be cleared first from upstairs.'

'And how long will that take?'

'Might have something for you by Friday, Oliver.'

'Sorry. Not good enough. Upstairs will have to move a damn-site quicker. We don't have the luxury of time on our side. This exercise has to be carried out *this* Friday. It needs authorising by tomorrow morning. We have no choice.'

Arthur looked peeved and scratched his head.

I pressed on. 'Is there any other business gentlemen?'

'Yes, I've a question,' said the regional manager. 'Where is the location of the next murder likely to be?'

'Ah, good question indeed, sir. We haven't figured that out yet.'

'You mean to say, DI Crosier,' said Newall, 'we're going to all this trouble and you don't even know where?' He waved his arms around, giving us his best impression of an incompetent magician. Everyone had turned to Newall as he spoke.

The room was completely silent.

They waited for me to respond.

'That's correct, sir.' Making full use of my extra height over Newall, leaned forward slightly, so my fists were on the table, and looked hard into Newall's eyes. Lowering my head, I spoke quietly as if addressing a naughty child, 'I am not prepared to ignore this threat. Someone's life is at stake. Are you prepared to risk that life, *sir?*'

Newall squirmed in his seat, glowering at me.

Inwardly I gloated at the discomfort I'd caused this twit.

'Very well then. Proceed ... DI Crosier.'

My time with Newall had come earlier than expected, and with a good result. I returned to my upright position. Plainly the effect I had on Newall had also worked on some of the others, too. Jackson raised his hand. I nodded to Jackson.

'Do you have any ideas?'

'My guess is it will be in the North West region.'

'With respect, DI Crosier, it doesn't narrow it down by much. It still leaves an awful lot of track miles.'

'The criminals, I'm convinced there are two, have only acted in mid-Cheshire. They appear to know about the area in some detail. I can't see them going to the lengths of travelling to London or Scotland to carry out another murder. The victims are from local families who know of each other. So far, we don't know where Boyton, or the woman Sylt is. So a tunnel switch below Rugby is, I think, a safe bet.'

'Okay, Oliver, we'll see about the logistics,' said the regional manager. 'If you, in the meantime, could work out where this maniac is likely to strike again, it could save us all a lot of trouble. And, our passengers a lot of delays.'

Most had left having said or contributed nothing, leaving me, Claire, Dobbs and Davidson to figure out where The Boy might strike again.

'Nice tie, Oliver,' said Newall, on his way out, apparently wanting no further participation in my scheme.

I couldn't hold my dislike of Newall any longer.

Claire stepped between us as Newall turned and left the room.

'My tie! Was that all Newall was concerned about? My sodding tie?'

The others looked at me and, I think, silently agreed.

Since I lost my favourite one on the sleeper, I'd chucked the tired ones out and bought half-a-dozen new ones from Marks. I kept the black one which I'd no doubt need soon enough for more funerals; hopefully Newall's.

'Sir,' said Cardin, when everyone else had left the meeting.

'Yes, Claire, what's on your mind?'

'How did you get the hand back without our knowing? Forensic evidence isn't usually allowed out like that.'

'Quite right,' I said, smiling. 'It was a model.'

'What?'

'You heard, a model. I had a model maker make a plaster one up for me. He took a cast of my own hand and painted it.'

She burst out laughing.

'I really wanted to chuck it at Newall but I think its shattering around him wouldn't have got the result we needed.'

36

THAT AFTERNOON

'DI CROSIER, SPEAKING.'

'Oh I'm glad I got through to you, Mr Crosier,' said a Scottish female voice. 'You see I've been very worried about him. I've said to him, it's no use; you cannot carry on like this, Archie. It's too big a thing you are involved in to keep to yourself. But he doesn't listen to me, stubborn old fool. He needs some sense knocking into him, that's for sure.'

I was somewhat thrown by this unannounced caller. Her voice sounded like that of an intelligent being, but what she was saying didn't convince me she was.

'I'm sorry, who is this?'

'I'm his step-sister you see and he spends a lot of time with me and some with his brother in Rugby. He's with me now so you should really come up to Glasgow, Mr Crosier, and see if you can make him see sense. He might save you a lot of time, too. I'm sure he knows more than he's telling me. So, as I say, you should really come up here as soon as you can.'

'It's very kind of you to invite me to Glasgow, Mrs ...'

I was trying again to find out who this rambling woman was. She certainly sounded old, the more she rambled on, but she did have a lovely lilting voice which caused me to hold back rather than bite her head off right there and then.

'Ocht, don't think anything of it, Mr Crosier. I think once he has got this off his chest it will make him feel a lot better, I really do. Don't leave it, too, long now. Between you and me, I don't know how much time the silly old fool has left.'

'Well, I'll certainly try, Mrs?'

'If you have a pen handy I'll give you the address. It's about thirty minutes in a cab from Central Station.'

I reached for my pen, thinking I may as well humour the old bat a bit more, and then I can get her off the line and go for a sandwich. My stomach had started to rumble loudly and I was glad I didn't have anyone else in the office with me. 'Ready, what is the address?'

She told me, and gave her telephone number. It wasn't often I was given strange women's addresses and telephone numbers. Pity this one sounded so batty. 'Yes I have it written down thank you,' and I read it back to her as she'd instructed. 'And what might your name be, Mrs—'

'Ocht, you can call me Nancy, Mr Crosier.'

I made another stab at trying to find out why she was calling me, 'How do you know who I am, Nancy?'

'Oh, easy enough Mr Crosier. I found your card when I came to have his suit cleaned. It was in one of the jacket pockets. I said to him, Shaw, what's this card from a Detective Inspector doing in your pocket? What have you been up to now? And then he told me where you'd both met.' She rambled on a bit longer, but I wasn't paying any attention. I was remembering the old man who had sat with me when I boarded the train at Rugby. She had said Rugby; the old man had said Nancy in his sleep. It had to be them, but why?

I just had time to say goodbye before she hung up. I went over to my office door. Claire, about to leave on her lunch break, was chatting with Carol.

'Claire,' I shouted, 'have you ever been to Glasgow?'

37

THURSDAY 15th NOVEMBER

I'D EXPLAINED TO CLAIRE YESTERDAY WHY I'D ASKED HER TO COME: to get the female perspective. 'I think she's a bit batty, in which case I'll need specialist help. Archie certainly is ... well, he was on the train and I doubt he's changed.'

'That's really nice of you to say, DI Crosier. You think I'm batty?'

'Yes, and besides . . .' I'd stopped, not wanting to make a complete fool of myself.

She'd looked at me curiously. I had turned away from her gaze. I'd been becoming very fond of Claire and a return journey to Glasgow with her would be just the thing. With luck we might have to stay overnight; maybe a sleeper — no perhaps not after my last experience. Spending time, mostly alone, with an attractive woman who didn't argue with me was not to be missed. Let's talk about it in the Crewe Arms, I eventually suggested, which we did after work.

At the time, tomorrow had seemed an age away.

***

We'd travelled on an early morning train to Glasgow and now we were heading by taxi to meet Nancy.

We discussed the cases again on the way up and I repeated how I'd met Archie, by pure chance, in the hope I'd remember some clue or other. 'He seemed agitated to me, particularly after he'd seen the front page of the local rag I was reading. I thought at the time he was just a frightened old man, upset by the Bright corpse description plastered all over the front page. He rambled a lot in his sleep after we'd had dinner. It was only when I'd left the train, it occurred to me he might know something. I dashed back on as it was pulling out and left my card with him.'

'But why didn't you talk to him more?'

'He fell asleep which was, to be honest, a bit of a relief for me. I felt it wasn't fair to wake him. And we'd got to Crewe by then anyway. The chances of him really knowing anything are very remote.'

'Not if he is or knows the killer. Or his sister does.'

'I know, Claire, but he has to be in his eighties if he's a day.'

'As I said, he might know them. I guess we'll know soon enough.'

We were looking out onto the dreary tenement blocks as the taxi wound its way west out of Glasgow, towards the village where Nancy and Archie lived.

'I hope they don't live in one of these ghastly places,' said Claire. She cheered up when we saw we were entering the small village of Bridge of Weir, leaving the Glasgow grime very much behind us. 'You do realise,' she said, 'this whole trip might be a wild goose-chase?'

'Yes I do, but it's a chance we have to take. Shaw might know something about these murders, but for the life of me I can't see what or how.'

'If he knows the killer, or killers personally, you'd have to admit you'd be a bit shocked wouldn't you, to read about them in the press?'

'We're just about to find out if he does. I think we've arrived.'

The taxi pulled up outside a large granite bungalow standing in huge, manicured gardens to three sides. Claire stood admiring the gardens while I paid off the driver. Before we reached the front gate, the front door of the bungalow was flung wide open. From the brick lined arch of the porch a sprightly, short woman crunched along the gravel drive to meet us. She looked, to me, to be at least seventy.

'Mr Crosier I presume?' she said, in her lilting accent. I nodded. 'And who is this lovely young woman you have accompanying you? Is she not your wife?'

'No, she is not my wife,' though, at the moment I wouldn't have minded if she was. 'She's Sergeant Cardin, my assistant on the cases I am covering at present. You must be Nancy?'

'I am indeed and I'm very pleased to meet you both. Now get in here and take your coats off while I make us all some tea. I'll go and raise Archie. He's napping in the back room so you'll be patient for ten minutes or so while he comes to. Do you like Dundee cake?'

'That will be fine,' said Claire. 'Do you need a hand with the tea?' She followed Nancy into the kitchen leaving me alone to wonder what might happen next. I could hear the sounds of crockery being laid out and the chatter between the two women sounded as if they'd known each other for years. Then Nancy went into the back room to awaken the sleeper. I heard voices, but I couldn't discern what they were saying. Nevertheless, I sensed Archie for whatever reason was not happy.

The living room was full of black-and-white photographs, presumably of family and friends. I couldn't resist taking a closer look.

Some went back to before the first war by the look of the clothing and stern faces staring back at me. Others were much more recent. A family picture showed Archie and Nancy with a young couple. The man had his hands on, presumably, their daughter's shoulders. She looked about four years old. Standing to one side as if she wasn't ready to be photographed was a fair-haired woman who looked vaguely familiar.

I was wondering who she was when the door swung open and in bustled Nancy followed by her obedient servant.

'Ah, I see you're interested in our rogues gallery, Mr Crosier,' Nancy said, as she put the tea tray down on a small table and thrust a plate of Dundee cake into my hand.

'Yes, I love looking at old photographs. Seeing the way

people were, what was around them. Are they your family, Nancy?'

'Some are, and there are some friends, too. The ones you'd be most interested in are on the second shelf of the bookcase.'

'And why would I be interested in those?'

'Well you see, Mr Crosier, they've all been in cases Archie has helped the police with.'

I turned and looked at Nancy and then Claire who, caring for her figure, was trying not to choke on a digestive biscuit — it was no use, she burst out coughing.

Nancy was looking at her and saw the look which passed between her two visitors. 'Yes, Mr Crosier, I know it must seem a bit of a surprise to you both, but really, the local police have been very grateful for the way Archie has helped them. You should talk to Sergeant McBride if you need a reference.'

'Need a reference Nancy? And why might I need that?'

She seemed to be considering something.

'We've come all this way thinking you or Archie might be able to help us with our investigations.'

'That's true right enough, and as you'll see when he comes in, Shaw's abilities go far beyond answering a few of your questions.'

Nancy busied herself with her tea, making it obvious she wasn't telling us more until Archie blessed us with his mysterious presence.

A silence followed, broken only by the sound of a grandfather clock ticking the seconds away. It looked sternly at its new visitors; they should know better than question Nancy.

'Ah, I think I can hear Archie coming through now. Yes, here he is.'

The living room door gradually opened to reveal the man I had met on the train a few days ago. He looked much the same but was dressed casually in a thin tartan sweater and corduroy trousers — his suit, presumably was still at the cleaners. He seemed half asleep, unprepared to impress his visitors with his powers of ... well what exactly? 'Mr Crosier, we meet again. And who might this young woman be?'

'This is my assistant, Sergeant Cardin. She's working with me on the case you read about in my paper.'

'Oh, is she now? And a pretty assistant you have too, Mr Crosier, if I may say so.'

I decided to get straight to the point with him. 'Archie, you remember our short time together on the train up to Crewe last Saturday?'

'I do indeed: I was somewhat surprised to come face to face with the man investigating those murders.'

'You were saying something about them. Something like, "they shouldn't have happened, they shouldn't be doing this, too many dead", I think you said.'

'Did I now, I don't remember.'

'Maybe not. You seemed half asleep at the time. I left my card in your jacket pocket just before I left the train, in case there was something you later remembered which might help us.'

Archie shot Nancy a look as if to say I told you not to interfere. 'That is a pity, Mr Crosier. I don't remember any of that.'

The grandfather clock once again dominated the next minute or so.

Archie set about pouring himself a cup of tea and deciding whether to go for the chocolate digestives or the ginger biscuits. 'Yes,' he suddenly said, attracting our attention once more. We were expecting him to have remembered something important, 'I'll have the ginger biscuit after all.'

I thought, he really should be being eating the fruit cake.

'Archie,' said Claire 'is there anything you think could help us find out who is perpetrating these murders?'

Nancy seemed nervous all of a sudden.

'If not we will have to set off back to Crewe. We don't have any spare time.'

Claire had guessed we were about to go down a mystic road and probably wanted to be out of here as much as I did.

'Tell them, Archie for goodness sake. Tell them what you've told me man.' At least Nancy was voicing the frustration felt by Claire and me.

'I don't know if it will help, woman. I told you they shouldn't have come, but you insisted, and here they are.' An arthritic hand was flicked towards us as if something horrible was stuck to the end of its fingers.

'I'll tell them if you won't.'

I said, 'Somebody had better or I might charge you for wasting police time. Now, what is it you want to tell us?'

Archie sat there, calmly finishing his ginger biscuit, nibbling each crumb individually, oblivious to my warning.

We waited.

Some thought in Archie's brain looked to be making steady progress towards his lips. 'I have this feeling, a feeling that something tragic has still to happen, especially to those who are connected with the case.' Shaw was regressing into a state approaching that when I first met him. He was beginning to shake.

Nancy got up and stood by him, stroking his head.

'You think there may be another murder, Archie, or that something might befall me or DI Crosier here?' Claire asked, gently.

'I don't know for certain, but I'm sure there will be something horrible happen. I can't ... I can't say what ... I don't know.'

'Do you have any photographs, Mr Crosier?' said Nancy. 'Sometimes they help Shaw see things that you and I cannot.'

I dug into my briefcase and reluctantly — thinking the whole damn exercise was a complete waste of time — pulled out some photographs of crime scenes and pictures which had appeared in some of the newspapers. We'd come this far and might as well humour the old man for a few more minutes.

Nancy snatched them off me and passed them across to Archie. He sat with them on his lap for a moment before gazing at each one in turn. The expressions on his face showed that he was registering something, but what the heck it was, I couldn't tell. He stopped and jabbed the page with a crooked finger, as he looked straight into Nancy's eyes. 'These,' he said.

'What about them?' said Nancy, quickly moving to stand behind Shaw. 'Do you have any clearer pictures of these people, Mr Crosier?' She handed me a blurred shot of the Gilmore murder. Several people were looking at the wreckage of Gilmore's car, from the field which overlooked the crash.

I dug into my briefcase once more and found a slightly larger shot of the same scene.

Nancy gave it to Shaw.

The old man studied it for some time.

Nancy waited behind Shaw while Claire and I remained seated wondering how much longer this charade was to continue.

'Her,' he said, 'she has a red car.'

Claire looked at me.

I rolled my eyes.

Archie started panting then threw himself back in his chair, staring into space. His mouth moved, but no words were spoken. The photographs slipped from his hand.

'Thank you, Mr Shaw,' said Claire, as she crouched to collect them. Her skirt rode up over her knees — a very nice distraction from this fiasco. 'I think you've been very helpful.' She looked at me.

I managed to tear my eyes from her legs while nodding my agreement that we should leave. Claire was amused by my embarrassment, something not unnoticed by Nancy.

Archie was out of it.

I stood to repack the photographs. 'I wonder, Nancy,' I said, clearing my throat, 'if you'd be kind enough to telephone for a taxi for us. I think Archie has helped us enough for one day and we don't want to over exert him, now do we?'

'Yes, of course,' said Nancy. She'd invited — no pleaded with me — to come all this way, yet she seemed pleased we were going to leave without any progress. An odd smile, more of a smirk, crept over her face as she turned to leave the room to telephone.

We waited in silence. Archie had closed his eyes and seemed to be sleeping.

'It will only be a couple of minutes,' Nancy said, returning and looking through the lounge window. 'Cromwells' taxi is only a few streets away. Are you certain we cannot help you more? Although I have to say, he does seem completely washed out?'

'No thank you, Nancy. Oh, perhaps there is one thing. At which police station does McBride work?'

'Paisley. I'll tell the driver, if you want to go there.'

Within a couple of minutes a private car with a Cromwells Cab sign on the roof had pulled up in Rawfurly Road. We said our goodbyes as swiftly as possible.

Nancy walked ahead to give the waiting taxi driver directions.

'Will Archie be all right, Nancy?' enquired Claire. 'He seems exhausted. How old is he.'

'Yes, he'll sleep for most of the of the day now, but then you might, too, when you reach eighty-two, Miss Cardin.'

Then we were in the car and off to see Sergeant McBride at the Paisley constabulary.

'What do you make of that?' said Claire.

'If you want my honest opinion,' I said, before realising the cabby could overhear our conversation, 'I think we've been well and truly led up the garden path by the old boy.'

'Ocht now, you've not been spun a line by old Archie have yea? His sister reckons he can see things what we cannae. Says he's one of those clare-things, d'ye ken what I mean?

'Clairvoyant,' said Claire.

'Aye, that's it, lassie. They're always calling the police aboot something or other. You'll see now. You ask the local bobbies. They'll tell you right enough.'

'Thank you for your opinion, driver,' I said, forcefully. It seemed to shut the man up. Fortunately, we arrived at the police station in less than twenty minutes.

Inspector Jimmy McBride, tall with a full head of fair-to-ginger hair, sat behind a desk of similar colour, smiling with some amusement at the tale Claire was telling.

'You see,' he said, 'old Archie thinks he's some sort of medium, but in our experience he regurgitates information already in public-knowledge and then comes and tells us about it.'

'What about his sister? She seems almost as barmy as he is. Have they always lived together?'

'Aye, quite some time now; I'd say about twelve-years. She moved here from Craiglockhart, south Edinburgh.'

'Archie is lucky to have her here,' said Claire.

'Aye, she's used to looking after people. If I were you, I'd be catching the next train back across the border as soon as yea can. Leave the likes of Archie and Nancy to us heathens who have nothing better to do.'

I said, 'Thanks for your time anyway, Jimmy. It's been very good to meet you. Could you call a taxi for us, please?'

'I'll do better than that, Oliver. I'll have a car rush you to Central straight away.'

Ten minutes later we were checking the timetable. 'Look, there's one at three-thirty,' said Claire.

'And it's got a dining car on it. Lovely.'

'There you go again, thinking of your stomach.'

'Well we did miss our lunch and eating is a good way to spend time on trains.'

Claire gave me a sideways look.

'Anyway, we've half an hour yet. Fancy some tea and cake?'
She raised her eyebrows, but still followed me into the café.

Forty minutes later, refreshed and aboard the south bound
express to London, we discussed our visit to Archie and Nancy
Shaw. We were alone in a first-class compartment and could talk
freely about the case.

'So, Oliver, what do you think about all this clairvoyant
stuff?'

'I think it's all a load of hooey. How could anyone look at
someone in a photograph, touch the printed face and come up
with the stunning fact that she drives a car?'

'A red one at that.'

'I just can't see it myself, Claire.'

'That's the whole point, people like you can't. And people
like me, I should add.'

'And look at McBride's response; he's obviously had plenty
of help from them and doesn't think it's worth anything.'

'That's his story. We don't know because we're not being
told by the copper-knob whether he was really helped by them
or not. It wouldn't do his crime record any good would it,
revealing he'd been helped by a medium?'

'All right for finding cats lost up trees I suppose.'

'That's about the size of it, I think, so where do we go from
here, apart from home,' she said, and flashed her cheeky smile
at me.

'Tell me about yourself, Claire.'

'I wondered how long it might take you.'

'Sorry?'

'Why I'm half-cast you mean?'

'That's a horrible expression, but since you put it like that.'

'I thought, Oliver, you'd accepted me, unlike some of the
others.'

'Claire, I have accepted you. Have I ever said or done

anything to suggest otherwise? I'm just trying to get to know you better. That's all.'

'Really. So how is Alice?'

'Okay, one all, Claire. Now tell me. I genuinely would like to know.' I watched the Scottish hillsides rolling by while she decided whether to answer.

'I am English you know. Born here, well in Birmingham. My mother is English, my father is Italian.'

'Ah, that explains it.'

'Explains what?'

'The way you try to walk through doors for a start.' She saw the humour fortunately. The last thing I wanted was for her to clam-up on me.

'That's definitely from my father. Or at least, it's what my mother always told me.'

'You mean he's not around?'

'He left when I was five. Left me and my mother to look after my younger brother. He was two.'

'Can't have been easy for your mother, for any of you.'

'My father is a part of my life I prefer to forget, not that I remember him much anyway. I wouldn't recognise him if he walked in right now.'

'So where is he?'

'He went back to Italy before the war started. We never heard from him again. No letters. Nothing. Not even a postcard! Mother told us he would have joined up, fought with the Italians, said he was very always patriotic and would have happily died fighting; apparently. But I know there's more to it. I saw the looks that passed between her and her brother. They never explained. Always shut up when I entered the room.'

'Sorry to hear that, Claire.'

'Don't be, Oliver. Like I said, I prefer to think I never knew him.'

'You should keep an open-mind. You may want to know him one day.'

'He's dead. End of story.'

We were approaching Carlisle by the time Claire spoke again. 'So, as I asked you before, how is Alice?' She crossed her legs, her black uniform skirt rising just over her knee. I couldn't help myself and looked at her thigh. My cheeks started burning. She must have noticed.

'Is everything all right between you?' she continued, softly, uncrossing her legs and leaning towards me.

I looked away. Carlisle had stopped outside our window.

'Oh, we're fine,' I said, after a little hesitation. I knew we weren't. 'Yes, we're all right, fine.'

I felt Claire studying me, as I watched people dashing to find a carriage with empty seats. I knew she liked working with me and was especially pleased to be involved with the two murder investigations. It allowed her to spend more time with me and occasionally, like this, it was just the two of us.

I was not my usual self lately, at least not all of the time. Perhaps it was the job: the job that often gets in the way of relationships, leads to separations and sometimes, as it was becoming easier, divorce. Officers needed to be with someone in the force who understood the job and the hours it thrust upon you. Alice was not in the force, or any demanding job for that matter.

It was really why Claire's last boyfriend hadn't stayed around very long. He became angrier every time she had to break their arrangements because something had come up.

She was unattached, perhaps even available if the right man came along. She'd spilled those particular beans to me in the Crewe Arms one evening, about six months ago, at an office party when I'd asked her why she was looking so glum. And she seemed to understand the way I always looked at her afterwards, as if our relationship had taken on a new dimension. I was always concerned about her after that night. And now, here we were; alone in a train-compartment, dashing through the north of England's counties and heading ... where exactly?

I turned to face her and smiled.

She smiled back.

'Time for dinner,' I said, looking at my watch. 'Care to join me, Officer Cardin?'

'Yes please, DI Crosier. And you can call me Claire, when we're alone.'

I'd reached the door to the corridor. Claire was right behind me. The door was a bit stiff and didn't slide open easily.

'It's a bit stuck,' I said, turning round to face her. And when I did she was looking up into my eyes. We stood still looking at each other until she pulled me towards her so that she could stand on her toes and kiss my lips. I pulled away a moment later, but not too fast.

'Now that has given me an appetite,' she said.

Our relationship certainly had taken on a new outlook. I wished she'd be staying with me all the way to London, instead of leaving the train at Crewe.

But I had to be in London tonight, prepared for the train swap tomorrow.

38

16th NOVEMBER

FOR THE FOUR HUNDRED OR SO PASSENGERS RUSHING TO BOARD the Royal Scot Express from Euston to Glasgow, everything appeared to be normal. There was the usual noise and commotion before an express train departed; late comers running desperately to catch it, even though there was still a good twenty minutes before departure; doors banging shut, then opening again as other passengers dashed aboard to find a seat.

Porters trundled noisy metal-wheeled sack-trucks, along the platform, loaded with passenger's luggage. Smoke and steam drifted across the platforms from engines of trains that had already arrived. Last minute sales of newspapers and magazines were made at Smith's mobile bookstall, as distant whistles of guards, waving off other trains, echoed around the station. And always at least one pair of oblivious lovers were draped around one another, blocking the way to the carriage vestibule, so other travellers had to find an alternative way aboard.

Those who rode The Scot regularly, unless they happened to be towards the front of the train would have assumed all was normal, too. Some might notice it was to be hauled by two different locomotives. Of course, there always a few people, usually men with their sons, who'd wandered up to the front of the train to witness the final preparations before they set off.

One young man dressed in a brown suit too large for him, was discussing with the driver of the second engine, the Flying Scotsman, how he expected the run might go. 'Will you make a faster time of it with two locomotives today?'

'We're certainly hoping to. Might even beat the east-coast record up to Scotland, now the war's over. We've not had a decent race for years. It'll be very interesting to see how they perform once we cross the border. Beattock can be a bugger of a climb! All I know is we're under orders not to run behind our normal times anywhere on the way.'

The guards were blowing their whistles.

The young man thanked the driver, wished them a good trip and turned smiling to join others who were dashing to board the train.

But for most passengers the early morning start, required to get them to Scotland's second city by evening, would have numbed their senses. Only a few wide-awake travellers might have noticed there were quite a number of uniformed police who had just boarded the rear of the train before it left Euston. They would be unaware of the excitement planned to take place half an hour after departure.

**

'So, Hawksnose. This is a big day for you, eh?' DI Hunt had provided some extra police support.

'Yes, if it all goes to plan we should be able to give you an exciting show.'

'When do you think he'll really show himself?'

'I don't expect any action this side of Stafford.' We were seated in a first-class dining car towards the rear of the train and tucking into a hearty breakfast, not knowing at what time our next square meal might be or, for that matter, where.

'Morning, Oliver, some more coffee?' I might have known you'd be involved with this lot. Who's your friend?'

'Hello, Daisy, how are you keeping? This is a very special friend of mine. Meet DI Hunt.'

'Special as in Special Branch eh, Oliver?' she said, winking.

'He's having an early ride to Crewe with me. Decided he wanted to meet my family. Therefore he can't be a full shilling, so I'm warning you to beware of him. And yes some more coffee would be most welcome thank you, Daisy.'

'Would you like black or white coffee, Mr Hunt? I don't hold with DI this and DI that. You're all paying customers to me. Or perhaps not in your case, eh, Oliver?'

I dug her in the side of her ribs and she still managed to pour Hunt's coffee. 'See that? Not a drop spilt.'

'Lucky you didn't do that through Watford Junction, or everyone would have had some. See you boys later.' She waddled back to the kitchen car to get fresh supplies.

'How long before we do the switch, Oliver?'

'Well,' I said, examining my watch again, 'assuming we're on time — which we better be — I'd say in about thirty minutes. We'll get three long blasts on the whistle two miles out. Then it's every one of our men standing by the doors ready to walk the planks and cross into the dummy.'

'That then, just gives me time to have a few rounds of toast and marmalade.'

'And you were the one always complaining about my eating habits! Just don't go getting too full or you won't be able to waddle over in time. Remember, the dummy goes twenty seconds after we stop. Anyone not aboard won't be coming with us.'

Hunt polished off his toast and marmalade sat back then lit up a Players cigarette, offering me one.

I shook my head. 'Not for me — spoils the food, though there have been times when one might have helped.'

'Getting fed up with the job perhaps?'

'No, not really, it's that, there are times when, when—'

'When you need a change,' guessed Hunt, incorrectly before I could explain what was really on my mind. 'I know I do. I've been in this job too long. I feel sometimes I'm getting stale, not figuring things out quick enough and certainly frustrated with those upstairs.' He rolled his eyes to the carriage ceiling.

I knew all about "those upstairs" and nodded.

'And then, when I took a bullet at that warehouse robbery in Brixton — I know it only clipped my left shoulder — it made me think about getting out. Gypsies warning and all that. Twenty years is a long time in the Met.'

I nodded again and leaned back in my seat, saw Watford rushing by: not far now. The empty coffee cups started to rattle in their saucers. I sat forward, moving the cups to silence them. 'So what would you do?'

'Don't know yet exactly, but I'm sure you and I could do something together: a new challenge, something.'

I raised an eyebrow. I hadn't expected that.

The three shrill blasts, from the leading engine, had us to our feet; discussion on the matter stopped.

***

The real Royal Scot express was running on the down-fast line. The adjacent line — normally the up-fast to London — was where the dummy was waiting inside Watford tunnel. As a consequence, a period of wrong-way working was established until after the switch, and both trains, had left the tunnel. The Royal Scot entered the tunnel braking heavily and came to a standstill exactly alongside the dummy.

The swap engines had been rigged out with copy name and number plates, the leading one carrying an identical Royal Scot headboard on its smoke box door. At a glance nobody would ever notice the difference.

39

'HERE SHE COMES,' SAID DRIVER EDWARDS, TO HIS FIREMAN AND Morgan. Edwards and his fireman were in charge of the GWR engine, but as they weren't familiar with the route Morgan, who knew it well, was on board to help by pointing out the difficult stretches of the line.

'Thank goodness we're in this tunnel, not Primrose Hill,' said Morgan. The Watford tunnel was chosen not just because of its length, easily able to hold two trains on each line, but because it had breathing stacks which allowed the smoke from engines to escape up and out over the fields above the tunnel. The lead engine of the swap-train had already been waiting beneath the breathing stack for nearly fifteen minutes, causing havoc to the timetable of trains heading into London.

'Remember,' continued Morgan, 'twenty seconds after they stop and we're off, so be ready for some pretty hard stoking. We must be through Rugby by ten-fifteen.'

***

At the rear of the train, facing doors had swung open on the rear carriage of both trains just before they stopped. Officers on the swap-train placed eight-foot planks across the gap between the trains. Those on the real express dashed across into the waiting vestibules of the dummy — there would not have been time for them to jump down, cross the gap, and haul themselves up into the carriages.

***

'I think it's time we were off,' said Morgan, giving a blast on the dummy's whistle. Edwards opened the regulator and the train moved forward, with a deafening noise. Smoke filled the tunnel.

Harrowing

None of the officers had considered what to do with the planks once they'd crossed and, on hearing the engine whistle, simply let them drop between the tracks as the trains parted company.

40

FROM HIS SEAT IN THE SECOND-CLASS COACH OF THE REAL ROYAL
Scot express, the brown-suited young man heard the long three
blasts from the King's whistle. He was enjoying this ride
immensely. He could never have imagined he'd be on his way
to Scotland by a train hauled by two of his favourite
locomotives: King Edward VIII and the Flying Scotsman. They'd
got the wrong King, but he didn't mind, too much.

No sooner had the third whistle blast stopped when he felt
the train jerk as its brakes were applied hard. They were
definitely slowing as they entered a tunnel and were coming to
a stop alongside another train. Its name boards on the carriage
sides proclaimed it to be the Royal Scot. But the train he was on
was the Royal Scot. And he knew there was only one!

Intrigued by this unusual stop in Watford tunnel, he stood
and tried opening the window of his compartment to see what
was happening. It was jammed.

He hurried out of the compartment and along the corridor to
the vestibule door and dropped open the window. Leaning out,
he saw the two train crews talking from identical classes of
locomotives, dimly lit by the rays of daylight penetrating the
smoke rising in the ventilation stacks. It was quite a sight and
would make a good photograph or a painting. But this was not
a set up for a photo or picture. What was going on? This was
not supposed to happen.

He looked back and thought he saw torch lights moving in
the distance at the end of the trains. They were not coming
towards him, but crossing from his train into the opposite.

He heard the whistle and, by the time he'd returned to his

seat, the train opposite had begun to move.

He sat watching the carriage windows gliding alongside, mesmerised by the flickering patterns, as they gradually became faster. Not many faces. In fact the train, so far, looked empty. He saw some uniformed officers, and then the face of someone he knew suddenly flashed by.

He stared into the darkness left by the moving train, had the feeling he was moving slowly backwards.

He hadn't really set out to kill anyone today, merely have Crosier set up this ride for him — it was the least he could do. He could see now Crosier was devious and had tried to trap him.

He had to give the DI and his mates something else to think about.

His train resumed its journey north and by Crewe, he had the bones of a new plan worked out.

***

I looked out to find we were dashing through Rugby. 'Damn, one-minute-ten-seconds late. She'll have to get a wiggle on now if we're to get to Stafford on time.' Hunt was looking at me rather strangely. 'What's up?'

'I've just had a horrible thought, Oliver. You're not going to like it.'

'Try me.'

'What if Boyton was on the Royal Scot?'

'No, he won't be. Mid-Cheshire is his ground. Not south of Stafford that's for sure.'

'I hope you're right, Oliver.'

So did I. But I wasn't going to give Hunt the satisfaction of thinking he might be.

We were speeding north but Hunt's words began to niggle away at me. I'd assumed Boyton would be observing from some vantage point or other, making sure the train ran to time. If it didn't, was he prepared to throw his next victim under the wheels of a train? The consequences if he did, were frightening.

It was after mid-day by the time the brown-suited Boyton arrived at Crewe. Still an hour or so before staking out the snatch, he thought, and in fact, time for a drink at the Crewe Arms.

Mulling things over a pint of beer, he remembered how, weeks earlier, he'd followed the DI home and watched the Crosier house one evening.

On a balmy evening, he'd waited until the man whose photograph was in the *Daily Herald* emerged from the station. He followed him along Nantwich Road before turning right towards the town centre. Then into Myrtle Street, which led onto Alton Street.

Crosier's house, one-hundred-and-forty-one, had a nice view across the park. Less than a minute after their dad went in, the Crosier brats came out screaming, into the park, heading for the swings. The boy was about ten years old, the girl slight, definitely a few years younger.

Then, the idea of kidnapping one of Crosier's kids hadn't occurred to him. But now, especially after what their scheming old man had done, really appealed to him.

He'd be able to control the girl easier than the boy, but it still might not be easy. He decided he'd have to refine his plan. Handling a screaming child in front of him on a motorbike was likely to attract attention. A sidecar would work, if he could get one?

When he'd finished his beer, he enquired at the bar to see if there was a motorcycle dealer in Crewe. There was, but when he telephoned the number in the directory, he was told they were supplied to order. He phoned Liss.

'Hello, Boy, how's it going, where are you?'

'The bastard switched the fucking trains.'

'What trains? What are you talking about, Boy?'

'Never mind that now. I need a motorbike with a side car, and soon!'

'Where are you, Boy?

- 223 -

'I'm in Crewe. Change of plan. I'm going to give Crosier a little something to focus his attention. How dare he not follow my instructions.' As he outlined his plan she became excited about this new aspect of their adventures.

'I don't know of anyone with a sidecar. I'll ring around and see what I can sort out. You call me here in half an hour.'

Boyton was totally frustrated: his good plan was rapidly going to waste, all because of the absence of a ruddy sidecar! He stormed out of the bar and aimlessly started walking the streets. There wasn't even a bike with a sidecar passing by. None parked for him to nick in any of the driveways of the houses. 'She'd better get one or else,' he shouted out loud, 'what time is it now?'

'Nearly half past one, dear,' said an old lady, walking her dog. He was so involved in his scheming, he hadn't noticed her at all, and nearly jumped out of his skin when she spoke to him.

'Are you sure?' he said, spinning around to look at her.

'Yes, dear. Porky is late for his din-dins aren't you, dear?' The dog looked up at Boyton as if to say, she's mad. Little did Porky know, it was the man looking down at him who really was mad.

He was late. He had to ring Liss to see if she had found someone with a sidecar they could use. He came to a phone box on his way back to the Crewe Arms.

'Hello, that you, Boy?'

'Yes of course it's me. What you got for me?'

'Nobody has a sidecar. I even rang a few garages, but nothing.'

'Oh, that's just great isn't it? All you have to do is get me a bloody sidecar! You can't even do that for me.'

'Calm down, Boy. I have something much better.'

'Oh, yes and what might that be, my useless Syph?'

'If you're going to be nasty, I'm not playing this game any more.'

'Okay then ... what is it?'

'Say you're sorry and I'll tell you.'

'Say sorry, say sorry! What is it you found, you useless little shit? Just tell me.'

'Uncle Robin's three-wheeler,' she said, giving up her demand for an apology. 'He said I could borrow it anytime he was away. He doesn't use it much and I can drive it on my bike licence; so could you.'

'Your Uncle Robin's Reliant? Brilliant. Why didn't I think about that? Brilliant, absolutely fucking brilliant! When can you get to Crewe?'

In an hour or so she'd arrive and they could work out what they'd do with the kid once they'd snatched her. He had to admit it, this new plan was coming along nicely.

***

Crosier, Davidson and Hunt were nearly at Preston. 'So, Oliver how do you feel about it now?' said Hunt.

'To be honest, Tony, I think the whole exercise, although going to plan, is a farce. We're running around at the beck-and-call of this, this idiot, this maniac. Look at us. In Preston at any moment, and have we seen anything en-route to suggest where he might carry out his next murder? No, we have not.'

'Don't be too hard on yourself, Oliver.'

'I really don't think it's worth the time going on to Glasgow. I suggest we call it a day, get off at Preston and return home. I'll tell the train crew to stand down and call Control to get the train back to London.'

'I tend to agree with you,' said Davidson. 'There's little we can do from a speeding train.'

'Agreed then, we'll get the next train back to Crewe. Do you fancy coming to my place for dinner tonight, Tony? Alice cooks a far better meal than you'll get in the Crewe Arms. Your boys had better go all the way to London. There's only room for six at our dinner table.'

'That sounds a very good plan, Oliver, thank you. I will.'

41

SHE ARRIVED AT THREE O'CLOCK AND PARKED IN THE CREWE ARMS car park. Boy had been inside at the bar since they'd spoken and had eaten a roast beef lunch, washed down with two pints of Wilson's beer.

'Better talk about this in the car,' he said to her, without asking if she wanted anything to drink. 'Walls have ears and if I stay in here much longer I might not come out sober.' He slapped her bottom, ushering her out of the bar.

He had to admit the car looked okay, and not too old either.

'See, I get you the perfect getaway car and you don't even thank me for it. You still ain't said you're sorry to me either.'

'Get in the bloody car and stop moaning. We've got more important things to talk about than thanks and saying sorry.'

He told her to drive out into the country; it wouldn't do to be noticed in the car park. 'I reckon his kids will come home from school, have some tea and then be let out to play. It doesn't look like rain, so our luck should be in. They usually wait until after daddy gets home, but today of course he'll be kicking his heels in Glasgow on a wild goose chase, stupid sod. We'll strike about six o'clock, less than three hours to go.'

'Strike?'

'Don't worry, Liss, I have it all sussed out,' he started to laugh, 'God, I'm so fuckin' good at this. Mummy Crosier is about to be one brat down.

'What's the kid done to you? Nothing, absolutely nothing.'

'It's not what she's done to me. It's her stupid father not doing as I tell him. He needs to know who the boss, so we're going to teach him a lesson.' He saw she was dug in. He had to get her back on-side. 'And I think there will be another killing, maybe tonight and perhaps another on Sunday as well,' he said, studying her reaction: she smiled. She was back.

'Petrol's a bit low, better pull in here and fill her up, wouldn't do to run out now, eh? And put the top back up, we're too much on show with it down.' He went inside the garage.

She struggled to put the top back up. After that performance she got back in, leaned back in the driver's seat and lit a cigarette. She was becoming sick of all his instructions and was regretting becoming involved with him and his murderous plans, but at the same time ...

A bloke came out of the garage and started to put petrol in the car. He banged on the plastic window and shouted at her to put her fag out. Did she really want them to be blown to bits?

No she didn't and pretended to stub out the offending fag. The daringness of the murders was what hooked her, not so much the killing itself. The power she felt in helping take someone's life was better than any adrenalin rush she could think of. So long as they left no clues there was nothing to worry about, apart from the next one — and he'd said that might be tonight. And besides, once the last one was done — whoever it might be — on Sunday that would be it, wouldn't it?

Boyton had not told her very much at all, except it would be spectacular and he'd promised her she'd have a very good view. There were no worthy victims left, as far as she could see. Those families they'd hated for their wealth and good luck had paid the price: 'Boy's and my price,' she said to herself.

The attendant went back to the shop.

She took a long drag on the cigarette and smiling, blew the smoke out slowly through her nose. Would the next victim be Crosier's daughter? She hoped not, for although she didn't know the little girl, she knew she was not to blame. And her father would be able to rest after the next murder 'cause there'd be no more. It was the plan. And Boy always said you must plan the work and work the plan. So far they had. They'd done the groundwork, checked out the places, devised ways to trap their victims. So, Sunday was to be the last one. What, she wondered, would he do after that? She was never going to live with him: she liked him less each time they met.

Should she just drive off now and to hell with him and his plans? What if things didn't go to plan? What if they were seen and identified, worse still caught and put in prison? How long would she get, ten years? They'd killed twice now, well Boy had, so they'd add a few years for him.

Actually, when she thought about it, they hadn't killed anyone. They'd killed themselves, hadn't they?

Gilmore didn't get out of the car in time.

Bright didn't land feet first in the wagon.

So she couldn't be blamed. She'd definitely give this some more thought and use this argument if she should ever be in court. Maybe she'd be out by the time she'd be thirty five and by then she'd have inherited her dad's house. She smiled to herself. She'd keep this little plan up her sleeve. No need to tell Boy. 'I wonder who the last one will be?' she said to herself.

He came back to the Reliant, swung the door open and got in. 'What are you smiling about?'

'Oh nothing, Boy,' she said, starting the engine.

'Right, not long now. Better find a suitable street to park you in. Head back into Crewe. I've got a little note to write.'

She did as she was told remaining silent while he began to write on the notepad he'd nicked from the garage. Gradually, as they drove along, the time for his plan was drawing nearer and she felt that special buzz again.

He scrawled *Mrs Crosier* on the envelope and placed the note he'd written inside, sealing it with his spittle; don't want the kid reading it before his mum. 'Okay, this street looks good to me.'

They found a suitable place where she could wait for him, while he kidnapped the kid, on Kingsway; just a few streets behind where Crosier lived.

Back in the Crewe Arms car park, they sat waiting until a-quarter-to. He kept avoiding her questioning looks. The last thing he wanted now was for her to start getting cold feet. He checked his watch every few minutes as if it would make the time pass quicker.

'Time to go,' he said, at last, got out and walked towards his new bike whistling *girls and boys come out to play*.

Where had he got a new bike from she wondered. 'Not even said good luck, Liss, or anything, arrogant bastard!' She followed him then turned onto Kingsway to wait. He continued on to the park.

He was there in plenty of time. His view across to the other side was nicely obscured by trees and bushes, even though the park was well lit. As far as anyone would be concerned he looked like a rider stopped for a cigarette. He could see some kids playing in the park but none were Crosiers. Five-thirty, five-forty and still they hadn't come out to play.

Ten-to-six; the door of Crosier's house swung open and out dashed the boy and the girl, crossing the road without looking and headed to where the other kids were playing by the swings.

He checked inside his pocket once more for the envelope. One last drag. He started the bike, threw the cigarette butt away and set off along the wide path which led to the swings.

The four swings were fully occupied with kids competing for the highest ride. They watched him draw up, surprised to see such a big gleaming motorbike in their park.

'Hey, are any of you kids Mrs Crosier's?'

'I am,' said the boy.

'Me, too,' said the girl.

'Good. I have a letter for her. Would you, young man, mind taking it to her for me? I don't know which house is hers. Say I'll wait here for her reply. Be quick now. I don't have much time.'

Alistair snatched the letter from Boy's hand and was off. The girl looked a bit uncertain now without her older brother.

'Tell you what, who'd like a ride round the park on my new bike while I wait for Mrs Crosier to come out?'

The two boys begged him for a ride. 'Eh, manners boys, ladies first,' and he held out his hand for Crosier's daughter to help her up. 'You can sit in front of me, darlin'. Get a better view there.'

To his relief, the girl took his hand and he picked her up and sat her on the petrol tank. 'Hold tight to the bars now, and we're off.'

The bike roared into action, startling the boys who were so excited they'd get a ride next. They watched the bike's red light pass the gardener's shed, its bright headlight pointing through the gates at the west end of the park.

Then it was out of sight, gone.

The boys looked at each other, each feeling slightly scared.

***

Alistair dashed into the front room. His mum and I were talking to our visitor from Scotland Yard.

'Mum, mum,' said Alistair. 'A man in the park gave me this for you. He's waiting for you to go and see him.'

Mary took the envelope, pulled out the single sheet of scrawl, then froze.

Seeing her shock, I snatched the note from her hands. My heart sank, I recognised the handwriting. '*Oh no,*' I said, raising a hand to my head. 'It's from The Boy.'

Hunt was on his feet and heading for the front door.

I read the note again, my lips moving as I read, unbelieving,

Dear Mr Crosier

Loved you're train switch, most envintive, but it very stupid. So another on my list has to die tonight because of you. And maybe another on Sunday. Run the train as I want on Sunday or you won't see your daughter alive again.

The Boy.

I looked briefly at Alice, then dashed after Hunt, who now, was talking to the other kids. As I crossed the road I heard Alice's blood-curdling scream.

When I caught up with Hunt I found him squatting down in front of the other boys in the park, asking them questions. There was no sign of Ruth and they'd already confirmed to Hunt she'd taken a ride on a big new motor bike and were pointing out the direction in which it had left the park, about two minutes ago.

Hunt told the boys to stay where they were, and to come back to Mr Crosier's house if they saw the motorbike return.

By the time Hunt and I got back to the house, Alice had already dialled 999 for Crewe Police. When we entered, she held the telephone out and said, 'It's Crewe police Station.'

'Oliver,' said Hunt, 'I'll deal with this. You're involved now. Leave it to me.'

I nodded and let Hunt do the talking. I was too shocked to do much else.

Alice glowered at me. 'You and your bloody trains. Now look what you've done. This man, whoever he is, has my daughter.'

'Our daughter, Alice ... our Ruth.'

'Don't be so bloody pedantic. Find out where is she for god sake. Now!'

A thousand possibilities shot through my mind. I couldn't think clearly at all. I picked up the note again hoping there might be some clue as to Ruth's whereabouts hidden within it. But of course there was none. This person, who had so carefully sent us clues about his last escapade, had also cleverly omitted all clues from this missive.

I couldn't believe it: how did Boyton know about the train switch? Had Hunt been right all along? But worse, where was our daughter?

Hunt returned, 'I've told the local boys to get an all-cars look out for a man on a motorbike with a little girl on the front. There won't be many of those about. There's also a car on its way here with the local inspector. He and I,' he said, looking at me hard, 'will want to interview all those kids to see if we can get anything else from them. All I did get, was that he didn't have a helmet. He did have goggles, and they said his bike looked new. It's not got us very far, sorry.'

Helpless I turned towards Alice, sobbing in the armchair.

The sound of a police car's bell could be heard coming down the street. The car pulled up outside and was soon surrounded by the boys from the park and their mates. The news had certainly travelled fast.

*****

The man on the motorbike had travelled fast, too. The girl had not given any trouble so far either because she was petrified or enthralled by the ride.

They had bundled her into the Reliant without a problem. As far as they could tell, they had not been seen.

Boyton set off east, past the railway station. She'd go west in the car.

Their plan was to meet up in an hour, so long as he wasn't stopped. He assured himself they'd only be watching the major roads for a motorbike not the back lanes through Cheshire. He knew she'd have no trouble. The police wouldn't be aware his accomplice, with Ruth, had escaped in a car.

*****

Hunt and DI Humphries from Crewe CID had taken the boys into Crosier's front room and were asking them questions about the motorbike and its rider. Between them they'd remembered the motorbike had a red petrol tank. They didn't have its number. The rider was tall, wore black goggles. They said his hair was black, but they were not really sure. It was unlikely they would glean anything else from them so Hunt let them out, telling them they were to go straight home.

*****

By eight o'clock The Boy and Liss were back. They'd not attracted any police attention. The car and their motorbikes were in the garage. They'd taken the girl, unseen, into the house and locked her in the upstairs back bedroom.

'What do we do with her now, Boy?'

'Keep her up there. Give her some food and water and let Mog in with her. Be company for each other. Keep her quiet and locked in. We have to do another on my list tonight.'

'Jesus, Boy. I'm knackered after that drive. Can't it wait?'

'No it bloody can't. It has to be tonight. Crosier has to learn I'm serious. Very serious, understand?

'Yes, Boy,' she said, recalling the gun incident. 'Okay, where are we off to now then?'

'The Lanigan Club, Warrington.' He saw she was about to protest further and raised his hand ready to slap her. She backed down.

'That's better, Gal,' he said, nodding, 'that's much better.'

***

At one hundred-and-forty-one Alton Street, Alistair was alone in the front room looking through the bay window, keeping a silent vigil, waiting for his sister to come home.

Hunt and the Crosiers sat around the dining-room table staring into cold cups of tea, each pondering the same question: what would The Boy do with Ruth?

42

ELSPETH CURZON, FOUR-FOOT-EIGHT REDHEADED DAUGHTER OF Joseph Curzon, who owned a men's outfitters shop in Northwich, had recently moved to get a job in Warrington. She lived with her nice auntie: who had a nice big spare room; in a nice big house; surrounded by a nice garden on three sides; in the nice leafy area of Appleton.

Anyone who knew the Curzon tribe would also know they were well-to-do and always lived in the 'alf-a-crown end of town: in other words they were posh. It did not take long for Elspeth's school friends to notice this, too. She'd been taking elocution lessons from the age of eight and she did, in their parlance, speak proper.

She considered herself to be a very attractive, slim young lady. And although too short, in her opinion, she had courted many an admirer once she'd moved to Appleton. Her good spoken voice made it easy for her to land a job at the local estate agent, Hambletons in Stockton Heath. By the time she was nineteen she was able to drive, so became the ideal person to show the rich and famous the expensive homes Hambletons advertised.

She liked dancing, one reason why she was heading for Lanigan's Night Club this Friday night; the other being her latest admirer, the aptly named gangly bloke, Stanley Longworthy. She'd been out with Stanley a few times. He was a good young man who looked after her very well, in fact, too well. She was becoming tired of his continual attention. She wasn't sure if she could stick him much longer. It wasn't that he was too pushy, eager to bed her, quite the opposite: he was very old fashioned, very ... old school. She imagined how utterly boring life would become if they ever married. So, perhaps it was time for him to be replaced. She'd give him one last chance tonight.

She'd brought him to dance, part of his final test, even though Stanley wasn't the dancing type. His brave attempt left her nursing several bruised toes as they sat afterwards at a round table. He sat opposite, not beside her where she expected him to be, staring into his beer.

He didn't really have a clue about clothes either. His only concession to fashion was a one inch wide tie with horizontal coloured bars, a friend had bought for him on a holiday in Blackpool, knotted too short. His dark-green jacket, with bright metal buttons, resembled one he'd used for school, not imitation-leather that most of the other males were wearing. The brown suede shoes were okay in themselves, but didn't go with the black trousers. Plainly, Stanley hadn't come to style yet. If she were to stay with him, she'd need to invest some serious time fitting him out. If.

The darkest corner of the club suited her. From here she could gaze around the dance floor for new admirers. Her flirting glances at other men were more than good Stanley could take and he told her so.

'Elspeth, darling, why are you always looking at those other blokes? You are out with me, not them!'

'Oh, Stanley, this is only our third date. I'm not your darling yet and may never be if you continue in this jealous fashion.'

'Fashion, Elspeth? Can't you just talk normal English for once?'

'There's nothing at all wrong with my spoken English, Stanley, which is more than can be said for yours.'

'Oh, for God's sake.'

'Don't take the Lord's name in vain, Stanley.'

Those in earshot turned to look at her.

'It doesn't become you. It makes you sound stupid.'

'He looks stoopid an' all love,' a flashy, necklace-clad rocker shouted from the bar. Stanley ignored him.

'I'm not stupid, Elspeth. And keep your voice down. Everyone's looking at us. And you are my darling.'

Buddy Holly started up, *That'll be the day* — her sentiment exactly. A few couples began to jive around the floor. Stanley reached out and put his hand on hers.

'Right, that's it, Stanley.' She flicked his hand away. 'I've had enough of your jealous and possessive attitude, so I'm going.' She stood to leave.

Stanley stood, too. 'Going, Elsp'?'

'Yes, Stanley, you know what I mean. How would you say it? Ah yes, I'm buggerin' orf.' And with that, she picked up her feather boa and flounced out of the club and into the cool morning air. Her many admirers noticed she could flounce particularly well.

The Lanigan club had also been graced with the presence of two leather clad bikers who, after much enquiry and help from mates of their old school, had traced Elspeth Curzon to Appleton.

'Look at her Boy, snooty cow. She doesn't deserve any attention from a nice lad like him. Who is he?'

'How am I supposed to know? And how do you know he is a nice lad when you don't even know who he is? I do worry about your logic at times, Syph.'

'Yer well, it looks like he's a bit pissed off with her if you ask me. Take a look.'

Boy swivelled his bar stool round to get a better look at the fracas taking place at the dimly lit table in the corner. 'Eh, looks like she's doing a runner to me, what do you think?'

'Looks like it to me, Boy. Do you think we can do her now?'

'Keep you bleedin' voice down, plonker. You want everyone to know we're after her, eh?'

'Sorry, Boy, but it's a chance.'

'Maybe. We've not really sussed out the ground on this one 'ave we? I suppose we could follow her though, and see ... see if we get a chance.'

'Drink up, she's definitely going now.'

They threw their drinks back and watched Miss Curzon leave to some applause, then left the club as casually as they could. But anyone with a trained eye, would see they were like hounds going after the kill.

Outside they mounted their machines waited and watched her take the path in the direction of the railway.

**

It was just after one a.m. She'd left her car at her auntie's house, expecting Stanley would have taken her home on his moped. She stepped along at a brisk pace, glad of the cool air on her face. She glanced down the embankment which overlooked the railway and was startled by two men walking up the steps from the line.

Instantly, she recalled her conversation with that WPC. "Don't put yourself at risk, be vigilant, especially near the railway". It's okay, she told herself, it's only the post office chaps.

When they reached the top of the steps they said goodnight love, and got into their little van.

She decided the shortcut along the railway would be much quicker than going through town. After all there was nobody else about.

43

2 a.m. SATURDAY 17th NOVEMBER

GRADUALLY SHE CAME ROUND, COMING OUT OF A DEEP SLEEP; A very deep sleep indeed. But now, she wasn't sure. Had she been dreaming?

It's so noisy! The steady *clank, clank, clank* was making her head ache. She could feel the vibration of it as it faded into the distance, leaving her in silence.

The pain in her wrists told her she wasn't dreaming. Her face felt very swollen. There was something caked around her nose and mouth: blood. Her blood.

Blood too, throbbed in her head.

A squeaking came from above her feet as a thin shaft of orange light penetrated the darkness and flashed across her eyes as she swung.

Her bound wrists made it impossible for her to find hold of anything to help her move into a more comfortable position. She could feel something with her fingers though, like stiff pieces of paper, lots of them.

She remembered walking ... and suddenly those motorbikes had trapped her against the wall.

'Smack her one, Boy,' the woman had shouted.

Before she could turn and run, she felt the powerful blow full in her face. The back of her head and her shoulders hurt where she had fallen hard against the wall of the bridge. Then nothing except blackness.

The *clank, clank, clank* noise was back, but seemed to be moving in the opposite direction. Smoke drifted across the place where she was trapped.

She screamed, 'Help, help me, somebody please help me.' But it was late when she'd left the club, nobody would be around now.

Would Stanley come looking for her? Probably not after the way she'd spoken to him. "I'm buggerin' orf" she'd said.

But there were two men. Yes, she remembered now. They came up the steps, from the railway line, wearing grey jackets. They'd said, goodnight love, to her then got into their little red van and drove away.

The clanking faded. It was silent again.

Her calves hurt and her feet and ankles were cold. She could taste smoke in the air.

She shouted for help again. Those bloody elocution lessons she'd hated so much were no good to her now. Why did I have to speak posh anyway? Gradually, her speaking became different from all her friends. They'd deserted her. Nobody would be coming to help her.

She felt tears running into where her fringe should be.

Why was her head so cold on one side?

And who was Boy? The woman had said the name. There was something about that name. Boy, Boys, Boyle, Bowler?

Boyton! Yes, that was it, Ronnie Boyton: the worst thug in her school. He was different now, bigger and heavier, yet his spaggy eyes retained their spiteful look.

Why did they come for her? She'd had nothing to do with him at school. Just the opposite. Avoided him like the plague.

The police woman's warning had been right.

They had come for her.

She heard the shrill whistle and knew she was beside the railway. The clanking started again but faster; *clackerty-clack*, ... *clackerty-clack* until it, too, faded away like the others.

44

2:30 a.m.

'WE'LL BE CLEAR OF WARRINGTON IN ABOUT FIVE- MINUTES, LADS,' announced Assistant Superintendent 'Cockney' Clarke, on the southbound Travelling Post Office. He did this shift from Carlisle to Crewe on the Postal five times a week and was in charge of twelve men in the middle collection car — usually the same men if they weren't too tired to turn up for duty. Once at Crewe they'd get the northbound Postal back as far as Carlisle, where they'd clock-off and rest up until their next shift.

It was intensive work sorting the mail from large mailbags delivered to the main stations en-route or from those hanging from stands by the trackside. Not only did you have to work against the clock if the train ran to time, you had to put up with the constant rocking and rolling of the sorting car. Collecting letters into bundles and putting them into pigeon-holes could be tricky at speed, especially across points.

They often hoped the train would be running slow to give them a bit of a break, the downside of which was that you usually clocked off very late and weren't paid overtime. The 'AGG' — the aggregated pay system — was very definitely in force.

'Need to have the next pickup sorted of Crewe's mail by the time we get there. That'll give you lot around half an hour at this speed. We're running slightly ahead of time, by my watch,' said Clarke, proudly displaying a gold watch on a chain left to him by his grandfather. This ritual occurred at every mail pick up. 'If you need more hands, James let me know ASAP.'

James just touched his cap.

Working in windowless carriages meant you weren't able to see where you were, but after a while you learnt the sounds as the train crossed points or went under bridges. They could tell you precisely where you were.

'Cleared Warrington; standby for the pickup James.'

He did as he was bid and wound out the collection basket. Do it too soon, and you might hit a bridge, too late and you'd miss the pickup.

There was about half a mile to go before contact was made with the GPO mailbag hanging from its peg alongside the track. The pickup at this spot was often heavy with mail from many of the mid Lancashire towns destined for the south.

The driver blew two short blasts on the whistle as a signal they were nearly at the pickup point.

**

Elspeth heard the two short whistles, felt the vibrations getting stronger. The *clackerty-clack, clackerty-clack* started again, but this time, much louder, faster, closer. Yes, definitely coming closer!

She suddenly began swinging as the engine pushed air out of its path.

The orange shaft of light danced around her.

She remembered the van — the little red van — the red GPO van with its gold letters beneath the Queen's crown. It was a post office van. They were postmen.

They'd been to hang up the post to be collected by the night mail. And she was in their bag, hanging upside down ready to ... 'Help, help me,' she screamed for the last time. Nobody would hear her above the sound of the train.

It was alongside her. The engine had already passed.

The carriages were rushing along — *clackerty-clack, clackerty-clack*. The night mail had come for her.

The steel-framed collection net had been wound into position ready to scoop up the gruesome parcel. The roar of the moving train, and the sound it made across the rail joints, increased inside the coach. James sounded the alarm bell for everyone to stand clear, as the mail would be shot at speed across the carriage floor.

***

She waited, knowing it would be over soon — *clackerty-clack, clackerty-clack, clackerty.*

Maybe she'd survive?

It was after all, a net that caught the mailbags, wasn't it?

***

The thwump-sound, made as the mailbag was caught in the collection net made everyone who heard it stop working and turn to look towards James. This mailbag didn't shoot across the floor as expected, but hit it with a heavy thud.

'Blimey, Jimmy, what's in the bag tonight?' asked Clarke. 'Not a sack of coal eh, that's supposed to be on the Newcastle run!'

James wound the collection net back in before the next bridge could smash it to pieces and then stood with Clarke looking down at the sack.

A pair of feet, one in women's black patent-leather shoes and short white socks, stuck out from the top of the sack. Sometimes the Post Office guys would put something unusual in the sack for a laugh. At first it looked like it was a shop-dresser's manikin.

'Looks like the boys have sent you a new girlfriend, Jimmy. You were only saying the other day how you were fed up with the wife. I wonder how they knew.'

They stooped to open the sack.

Clarke grabbed what he thought were the dummy's legs. 'Blimey, Jim, they're warm! It's a real girl. Her legs are broken — look, bones are sticking out through her skin.'

They carefully opened up the sack. As well as the usual mail, this sack contained the real body of a small young woman, her hands bound behind her with green string. She looked very dead. Clarke put a finger to her neck to find a pulse. Nothing.

After a long pause, during which nobody spoke, Clarke stood and said quietly, 'Well, if she wasn't dead before we arrived, the collection at this speed would certainly kill the poor lass. We'll not stop the train here, James. Crewe is only twenty minutes away. No point in holding up Her Majesty's mail just yet, is there? Nothing we can do for her anyway. We can decide what to do with the mail when we get to Crewe and the RP have seen her. Better nip along and inform the guard. What happens next is not for us to decide. Back to it fellas.'

*****

It was a busy scene at three a.m. when the train arrived at Crewe's platform five. Post Office porters with trucks of mail sacks were waiting ready to do the mail exchange — they would have plenty of time tonight.

Normally, this night mail service into London's Euston station would stand at Crewe for twenty minutes while sorted mail from north of the boarder for Manchester and the North West district was taken off and new mail from them destined for Stafford, Rugby and London was loaded.

Unusually, the guard had broken regulations and had travelled in the sorting car once James had told him what they'd picked up.

As the night mail pulled into platform five, he jumped off before the train came to a stop and sprinted to the station master's office. Porters watched him dash into the office.

Station Master Pilkington got on the telephone immediately to give Crosier the guard's bad news.

*****

I'd insisted Alice go to bed without me, something she seemed very happy to do. 'Hello,' I said, wearily, hoping for some good news.'

'Sorry to call you at such an hour, Inspector. I'm the night SM at Crewe, Eric Pilkington. The Glasgow Postal has just pulled into five with a dead woman in the sorting car; picked her up at Warrington.'

'Warrington? Are you certain about that?' I was instantly wide awake.

'Hello ... are you still there?'

'Yes, I'm ... I'm still here. She should still be alive.'

'Who should, sir?'

'Elspeth Curzon.' Claire had warned her, telling her to be vigilant. How could this have happened?

'Can you get down here now, sir?' asked Pilkington. 'We need to know what to do with her and the train.'

'Yes, I'll be there in fifteen minutes. Don't move anything. The mail will have to wait for me for once.' I ended the call. With an even heavier heart, I was back upstairs dressing when Alice came out of her fitful sleep.

'What on earth are you doing, Oliver? It's gone three!'

'Sorry, love, there's another dead body turned up on the Glasgow mail. Don't worry, it's not Ruth.'

'But you're off the case.'

'I'm off Ruth's case, Alice. This is a new one.'

'So, you're quite happy to dash off to the bloody railway again to solve another murder, are you, Mister DI Smart-Arse-Crosier? While your own daughter is somewhere out there. Kidnapped! What are you, Oliver? Just tell me who in hell are you?'

'Alice, don't be like that. This incident is almost certainly connected to Ruth's disappearance. I have to go and find out before Hunt does. There might be something to help us trace Ruth. Can't you see that, Alice?'

'Okay, okay ... but—'

I raised a hand. She could see I was right. I stood silent, thinking.

'What is it, Oliver?'

'I think I know who she is. I've got to go.' I left Alice and ran downstairs, out through the front door just as a squad car arrived.

***

A large crowd of onlookers had gathered around the middle of the Glasgow mail-train; porters, GPO men and two night shift women from the buffet, which they'd left deserted.

'DI Crosier,' I said. 'Show me what you've got?'

'Not a very nice parcel I'm afraid, officer,' said Pilkington, who was guarding the scene.

I pointed to the opened mailbag inside the mail's sorting car. 'Has anyone touched this?' I said, climbing inside. The guard introduced me to Clarke.

'No, sir,' said Clarke. 'We picked up the mail south of Warrington, but with such a loud bang, we knew something was amiss. Then we could see the feet sticking out, and thought it was a shop dummy put in for a joke. The GPO boys do that sometimes.' He tried smiling, then gave up. 'Anyway, when we saw what was inside, we left her as you see her now.

'We'll leave her as she is for the pathologist to take a look.' I turned to Pilkington. 'We need to get this carriage detached from the train and parked in a bay platform away from onlookers. Can you arrange that? Is anyone from the press here yet?'

'No press boys yet, sir. Too early for them. I suspect *The Chronicle* sleeps at this time of night, unlike us! I'll get onto the signal box straight away to organise shunting. It might take a while; there are no spare engines. We could use the Irish Mail engine. She'll be here in five minutes and stop long enough to do some shunting for us.'

'Well this train isn't going anywhere with her on it, so take as long as you like.'

A BTP photographer arrived and set about taking pictures while I took the mail crew into the Station Master's office to take their witness statements. It wouldn't take long. There was little to report, so they should be able to complete their next shift on the mail back to Carlisle. The rearranged train would probably get to London an hour or so late, not too bad considering what had happened.

I called Cardin. 'Claire, is that you?'

She yawned into the receiver. 'Oliver, what's happening? It's four in the morning!'

'Yes, I know. I'm at the station. The Glasgow Postal has brought in a dead woman. They picked her up at Warrington. I think she's—'

'Elspeth Curzon.'

'Yes. I think we'll find out it's her. Do we ... do we have a description of her, Claire?'

'Oliver, it's not our fault.'

'Yes, I know, but we—'

'Yes, Oliver, we warned her. We couldn't do more, could we?'

I knew Claire was talking sense, but the feeling that we could have done something made me feel very bad about her murder. 'I know. Look can you get down here?'

The Holyhead train arrived and its engine ran around to the rear of the night mail to pull the uncoupled carriages back out of the station.

I climbed aboard to make sure nothing was disturbed whilst the mail coach was shunted into the end of a north-bay platform. This done, the rear of the train was pushed back into platform five and re-coupled to the front portion of the train, which set off for London within a few minutes, minus one sorting car and its dead body.

Claire arrived with Smith, who she thought might be useful. I must have sounded like I needed all the help I could get. Together, we set about moving Elspeth out of the mail sack. It was then we saw that most of her hair had been cut off from one side of her head — another trophy. A tell-tale sign left at the two earlier murders appeared: green gardening string, binding her hands behind her back.

She had a letter gripped in one hand. I gingerly prised it from her grasp. It had a Stafford address on it, a Mr West. I'd have Dobbs deliver it personally to check there was no connection between them.

We searched inside the mail sack for any further clues. It contained only unsorted letters, none of which bore anything other than an address. Some were blood-stained, probably Curzon's. The corpse was intact. Mortuary staff would identify the cause of death — a simple enough task.

Curzon's — it had to be her — was the third murder using the railway in this region. With three under his belt, the killer was virtually guaranteed to strike again. One or even two murders, maybe: three, was becoming a habit, a drug.

I wondered when and where the next might be — please God, don't let it be Ruth.

Feeling chilled by the morning air and the grisly circumstances of this third murder, me and Claire set off to five's café, leaving Smith to guard the scene with an official from the Post Office. We sat by the fire, drinking hot cocoa.

'You look absolutely exhausted, Oliver,' said Claire, quietly, not wanting the waitress to overhear our conversation. 'Do you want to rest at my place tonight?'

I was staring into the fire and turned to look at her, smiled, then shook my head.

'I'll call Elspeth's office number first thing to see if she has turned up for work,' said Claire, getting back to business. 'I assume estate agents work on Saturdays. If she's expected to be in and isn't, I'll ask them to describe her and see if their description fits with the dead woman on the train. And, if it does, her parents will have to be told.'

At five o'clock I decided Claire was probably right and everything else could wait until later. We walked back home, Claire checking again if I wanted to stay at hers for the night, before we headed off to our own beds. I was very grateful I had Claire helping me on this case. She looked stunning, even at this hour.

***

I crept back into the house without waking anyone and went

upstairs to check on Alice and Alistair. To my relief they were still in exactly the same position as I'd left them three hours ago.

It was pointless trying to go to bed, so I crept back downstairs to make some coffee. It was when I considered the events of the last twenty-four hours, it occurred to me that I was hunting for the first serial-killer in British railway history.

45

I THOUGHT A LOT ABOUT RUTH AND WHETHER, ONCE SHE'D BEEN recovered alive, I would remain in the BTP.

Alive!

God, the consequences for my sanity and my marriage if she was found dead or injured didn't bear thinking about. Alice had been dropping hints for months about how this string of cases was coming between us. Whilst she understood my line of work required disruption to family life from time to time, she was now definitely set against me continuing with it. What else I'd do — apart from beating the living-daylights out of Boyton — was not at the forefront of my mind just now: recovery of Ruth was.

It was going to be very tricky from now on to even get to know what progress was being made. "No Oliver, you can't. You're involved. Leave it to me" had been Hunt's mantra.

I was shocked at how my old friend had suddenly turned so bloody officious with me. He might have thought that's what he had to do: to take charge; to make sure things went his way, not mine; to make sure his standing was not affected, at the expense of mine. I doubted we could ever work together, in any capacity and would tell him so when the time was right.

But I could not just sit back and wait for others to act. Of that, I had no such intention.

Eventually morning came and I left my son and wife to continue their sleep. I cycled to the office, pondering on what greeting I was likely to get when I arrived.

When I did, it was pretty obvious the word had got out about Ruth. Most of the station staff, let alone those in the office, seemed at a loss to know how to speak to me.

I took the opportunity to dig out copies of Boyton's photograph, from the filing cabinet in my office, before Hunt showed up. I already had with me the newspaper cuttings of pictures taken at Whitegate and Middlewich from my scrapbook at home. They'd be good material, for what I had in mind, and I just managed to hide them inside my overcoat as Claire marched into my office.

'Oliver, I can't believe you didn't tell me about Ruth last night. If there's anything I can do you only—'

'Thanks, Claire,' I said, turning towards her and grasping her arm. 'There is. The most useful thing, would be for you to let me know what's happening here with Ruth's kidnapping.'

I couldn't believe my own ears: the words shocked me and I paused to compose myself.

Claire placed a hand over mine.

'I am officially off her case, other than as an adviser, unless Hunt decides he needs me — which I doubt. You'll have to be careful, assuming—'

'That'll be my problem, won't it.' She released my hand. 'Don't worry about me, Oliver.'

Hunt's arrival stopped any further discussion on the subject.

'I suppose you've heard about the presumed Elspeth Curzon murder?' I said.

'Elspeth who?'

'Curzon. She arrived dead on the night mail at three this morning.'

'Night mail from where?'

'Glasgow. It picked her up in a mail bag at Warrington.'

'She was one of those potentially at risk from Boyton,' said Claire.

'We warned her, before you start thinking we can't do our jobs properly. All her details are in the file,' I said, pointing to the stack on my desk. 'Should you care to read it.'

'Don't come all snotty with me, Crosier. How come you

know all about it?'

'I was here last night. The station master called me out.'

'But you are off the case, or had you forgotten?'

'Ruth's case,' I reminded him.

'Who else knows the details?'

'Claire does.'

Hunt gave us a knowing-look.

Claire left.

'Okay, this is how we play it from here. I need access to all of your files plus anything your assistants have related to these murders, witness statements. Everything. And then you go home to Alice and Alistair. I will be in constant contact with Crewe CID. *If* you are needed here, I'll call you. Is that clear?' He went to the door and bellowed, 'Cardin, get hold of Smith and Dobbs, the Regional Traffic man and that new bloke in Manchester, what's his name?'

'Newall,' shouted Claire.

'That's him, Superintendent Newall. And Train Operations, too. They are all to be in the conference room by nine-fifteen, got it?'

'Yes, sir,' said Claire, winking at me as she went to round everyone up.

'And when you've done that, get in here and bring me up to speed on the Curzon murder.'

'Presumed murder,' I said.

'Still here, Oliver?'

'I can't go home. My daughter has been kidnapped, or had you forgotten. For God's sake, there has to be something I can do. I know the way Boyton's mind works. I'm close to him now, I can feel it.'

'Then your err, how shall I say it, intuition yesterday must have been a touch under par.'

We exchanged angry looks.

'Sorry, Oliver, there was no need for that, I'm sorry.'

I turned on my heels and left, slamming my office door shut

as hard as I could — the frosted glass just about stayed intact.

I passed Claire, who'd just spoken by telephone with the Regional Manager. 'Look, Oliver,' she said, 'it's still early days, but if I'm around at lunchtime I'll meet you in the Crewe Arms at say, one o'clock?'

'Thanks, Claire, that's much appreciated. I'll see you at one.'

'Oh and, Claire,' shouted Hunt, from *my* office door, 'add the officers from Northwich and Chester to the list. Here by nine-fifteen, not a minute later.'

Before he'd finished shouting instructions, I was stopped by Carol on the front desk, who asked if there was anything she could do. I shook my head, already preoccupied about my next move: a visit to the local rag.

There was no need for this case to remain under cover any longer, regardless of what Hunt or Crewe CID might think. The more pictures in all the local papers, the better. The national press, too. I hoped the *Crewe Chronicle's* crime reporter had good contacts, otherwise I'd have to take a trip to Manchester to see Jabberson.

***

'Oh, that will be Bob Browning,' said the receptionist, and went to the back of the office. She spoke with a stockily built man who looked up to see me waiting. He seemed to be in his early forties; not too young to be green, but getting to the age where if he didn't break away from here soon, he'd probably be spending the rest of his reporting life in this very room. He took a drag from his cigarette, stubbed it out and came over.

'Mr Crosier? Bob Browning. I've already heard a bit about last night's sorry business. How can I help you?'

'Is there somewhere we can talk privately?'

'There certainly is, follow me.' We marched through the main office and upstairs into a meeting room.

'I'll come straight to the point, Bob. Last night, as I suspect you already know, my daughter ... rather, our daughter, was kidnapped from the park opposite our house. I want a full story in the *Chronicle* and also the papers in Warrington, Winsford, Northwich, Chester and Manchester for starters. It's crucial that you get it on all the front pages tomorrow, Sunday. You do have contacts with the nationals?'

'You have no worries there. I know everyone, although it isn't often that we have such a scoop.'

'Well I'm going to give you your exclusive on the kidnapping of Ruth by British Railways' *first* serial killer, plus everything to do with three other murders I've been working on.' I could see the reporter trying to hide a smile, a smile that was saying if I get this right, it might be my ticket out of here.

'A serial killer, eh?'

'Right. Here are several pictures of my daughter Ruth aged three, five and six. The last was taken during her first year at primary school in York. Here's some family ones. And here, one of Ronnie Boyton from the Winsford police files. This one is not so good. She's Phyliss Sylt; I cut her from your own paper. Your original film stock will be much better.'

'I'll take a look-see, Inspector.'

'Yes, please do. Check what you have of the Middlewich closure and the Whitegate crash. We know they were at both but didn't know then what we know about them now.'

Browning picked up the phone and spoke to the photographer.

'Print them all if you want,' I said, 'because I need as much publicity as you can generate. The more people who see these pictures, or read the story, the more chance there will be that someone will recognise the kidnapper and where he, or more probably they, might be hiding.'

The reporter was all but rubbing his hands together.

'They took Ruth and it's a ninety-nine percent certainty they killed Gilmore and Bright. Last night they added Elspeth Curzon to their hit list. We're waiting for Mr Curzon to formally identify her body. I should be able to tell you more this afternoon. All we have to do now is find them, and that's where you come in.'

Browning could hide his smile no longer. 'Any common ground?'

'All the murders have taken place on the railways of mid-Cheshire. If you need to add some gore to your story, I'll tell you one piece.'

'Anything bloodthirsty? The tabloids love anything like that.'

'The killers took Gilmore's left foot, amputated Bright's hands and Curzon lost half her head of hair. Boyton sent me one of Bright's hands.'

'A sick present, from a sick bastard,' said Browning, nodding and turning a little pale as well.

'Boyton went to school at Winsford Secondary Modern, was only good at history. Left at fifteen, had several jobs. None lasting. He was either well off enough to buy a new motorbike, or he was given one. Or nicked it. Winsford police have a record on him. Other than suspected GBH, there are no serious convictions. It appears his two loves are bikes and trains.

I've now tracked down his older sister. She works in London and I hope to get to meet her later today. I'll let you know from London if there is anything I learn from her that can be used in your story. Both their parents are dead. As to where Boyton might be living, we have no idea. We've contacted a lot of his old school chums, if that's the right word. None we've spoken with had anything to do with him since school or very little at it. He was a vicious fighter and almost got expelled in his fourth year. My view is someone, probably Phyliss Sylt, noticed this.

'Is that enough to keep you going, Mr Browning?'

'It's a bloody good start. I tell you what. Can you come back about three this afternoon? I'll have a copy draft you can take a look at and any better pictures we can dig out. If there's anything new or something you need to add, we'll still have time before I telex it out to all the evening papers. We have a bit longer for the Sundays. It should get them all interested. I'd be amazed if they didn't front-page it. The locals, I'm afraid, won't be out until next week.'

'That's a big setback, Mr Browning. You see we suspect he's hiding out somewhere in the North West, so the local rags, sorry papers, could be of great help to us.'

'I'll see what I can do with the *Manchester Evening News*. I might persuade them to add a pull-out in this evening's issue.'

I got home about ten-thirty. Alice was up and dressed, saying she'd let Alistair stay in bed.

She turned to me. Her eyes were red from crying. I put my arms around her ... held her tight. She felt very frail. 'Where have you been, Oliver?'

'I went to the office to see what's going on. Hunt virtually had to chuck me out. He's taken me off all the cases and moved into my office. Newall agrees with him, useless twit. Sounds daft, I know. It's standard procedure when an officer has become personally involved, regardless of whether he wanted to or not. He's dropped his own cases in London for the moment.

Claire might ring or call here. I had a word with her. She's going to let us know what's going on. She's sticking her neck right out for us, love. She could be suspended if she's caught.'

'I know its official policy, and all that, but to lose the man closest to these damned murders, and *now* of all times. Keeping you off Ruth's kidnapping seems like rule-book hogwash to me.'

'Crewe CID is handling Ruth's kidnapping.'

'Don't split hairs with me, Oliver. You know damn well what I mean.'

'Sorry, love.'

'So what's next? Do we sit here and wait?'

'Officially, but I'm meeting Claire later in the Crewe Arms.'

Alice looked at me. Was I mentioning Claire's name a little too often?

'She'll tell me what's happened during the morning.'

'And, after that? What will Claire do for you next?'

'I have an idea or two. Neither involve her. If I'm not in the office I can still make some enquiries of my own. Sorry love, you will have to stay in. They might come round. If they want me you'll have to think of something. Say I'm out walking and I'll call in. I'll ring here every hour or so. If they call you can tell me their news, if they have any.'

Alice burst into tears again. I regretted my caveat.

'I need to call Claire now. She should be out of the case meeting.' I went into the hall and dialled the office number.

'Transport Police Crewe', said Carol.

'Can you put me through to Claire please?'

'Oliver, I'm sorry. Hunt has said nobody is to speak to you except him. Shall I put you through?'

'No, Carol, it doesn't matter. It can wait.' I hung up. 'Damn, damn, damn.' It will be another two hours before I see her.

I went back into the kitchen and made some coffee. The morning's events had made me hungry so I tucked ino a bowl of cornflakes as well.

'I don't know how you can eat at a time like this, I really don't.'

'I know, love, but I have to keep going. There's things I need to do and I need some energy to do them, if that's all right with you.'

'It has to be all right with me. Doesn't it? I don't have much fucking choice do I? You are hardly ever here. And even when you are, you have your head up your arse thinking about these bloody murders. And it didn't do any good because right now Ruth might be the next one on ... on Boyton's bloody list!'

I stood there, looking at her ranting.

The kitchen door opened slowly. Alastair stood, tears rolling down his face. He turned and went back up to his room.

I made to go after him but Alice pushed me away and headed upstairs.

There was nothing else for it, I would have to go and sit it out in the Crewe Arms and wait for Claire to bring me up to date. I left my half-eaten cereal, put on my coat and walked to the hotel.

It was a long wait. Fortunately nobody who knew me came in. The last thing I needed was talking to others about Ruth. Claire didn't arrive until one thirty. At least I'd had a decent meal, without being nagged, to set me up for whatever the rest of the day had in store.

'So what's happened, Claire?'

'Well as you know, Hunt is well and truly running the place. He's bringing some of his mates up from The Smoke as well.'

'What happened at the meeting? Have they got any sort of plan worked out?'

'The first hour was taken up by reviewing the files, photographs etc.'

'Yes, Claire, but does he have a plan?'

'No, not really. He's sending teams out to interview everyone again to see if any can give a lead as to where Boyton might be. I don't think it will yield anything though, I was present at—'

'Has her father identified her as Curzon?'

Claire nodded. 'It's her. We both knew, Oliver, the likelihood of her being someone else was . . .'

'How is he?'

'Much like you: absolutely devastated. He'll be here later to make the formal ID. Apparently, he lost his wife in 1953. She died in hospital in Edinburgh after being hit by a car.'

'Is Hunt going to talk to Boyton's sister?

'No.'

'Why in heavens not? She's the most likely to know more about her killer-brother than even she realises. I need you to get me her telephone number in London. I'll talk to her. Maybe something will come out.'

'Okay, I can get that. Stay here and I'll phone it through to reception. Have you done anything yet, Oliver?' she said, looking at me with her knowing smile, one that said I won't believe you.

I shook my head.

She grabbed the sandwich I'd bought for her earlier, said

goodbye, squeezed my shoulder and headed for the door.

A quarter of an hour later I had the number of Boyton's sister. I asked the manager if he had a telephone I could use in private and was shown to his office. I didn't speak for very long on either of the two calls.

It was only two o'clock and my meeting with Browning was still an hour away. I decided to call him to see how he was getting along with the draft copy. He was making good progress, so we decided to meet again as soon as I could get to the *Chronicle's* office.

'Thanks for seeing me. I need to go to London as soon as possible.' Browning took me into a private office and passed me a draft copy. He was doing well. All the main facts were written in a manner that would maintain the reader's interest, and hopefully, trigger a response. Just one could be enough.

I went home to see how Alice & Alistair were doing and to pack a small travel bag in case I had to stay overnight. 'I've arranged to meet and interview Boyton's older sister in London. If nothing else I can see if her picture matches the ones you picked out.'

'London! Do you really have to go? What's wrong with the bloody 'phone? Can't she come here for goodness' sake?'

'It's not as simple as that, Alice. I found out from her flatmate that she's in hospital, so she can't travel.'

'Can't Hunt send someone from Scotland Yard?'

'I'm closer to Boyton than any fresh DI could ever be. I'll have the photographs, too. Hunt doesn't know I'm going.'

'So why aren't you telling him?'

'He doesn't think she'd have anything worth saying.'

'And you do, do you, DI Crosier? Well you always did know best!'

'Yes Alice. That's why I'm going now. If anyone knows Boyton, it has to be her. Boyton's parents are dead; there isn't anyone else close to him to ask. I'm hoping a face-to-face meeting with the father of the girl her brother has kidnapped might get her thinking. It's a long shot, I know, but do you have anything better in mind?'

She turned her back on me and marched out of the room.

I left for the railway station. We hadn't even said goodbye.

There was a train at ten-past-three. I just had time to walk back to the station. I managed to get down onto the platform without any of the station staff approaching me to ask how I was coping.

The train was already standing there, waiting for the off. Doors were slamming shut as the last passengers boarded and the guard was blowing his whistle. As I jumped aboard, the train moved off.

Hunt was walking across the footbridge. He saw me board the train and started running down the steps to the platform. At the bottom, he turned and ran alongside the accelerating train hoping to catch my attention.

He was too slow.

I was on my way south, leaving Hunt behind, out of breath, out of ideas and, no doubt, wondering what the hell I was up to.

46

I SAT STARING THROUGH THE WINDOW AS THE UNSEEN COUNTRY-side slid by. The rhythm of the wheels on the track was hypnotic after my bad night's sleep or rather no sleep at all. I felt my head lolling as sleep began to catch up with me.

I was almost at Watford before I came round. It was pitch black outside and the light in my compartment was off. I thought for an instant I'd slept right through to London and was now on my way back north. Then I realised I was in a tunnel, illuminated by the lights from the carriages ahead, and I saw the faint outline of breathing-stacks flash by. It was the same tunnel where we'd carried out the train switch — over twenty four hours ago!

Yesterday, everything seemed to be going to plan; but now my plan was shot to pieces ... and my Ruth was still missing.

**

Euston. Smoke and steam cleared as I reached the engine and, as if by magic, presented me with a distant view of a familiar figure. Bombastic, autocratic and tending to fat, I could spot BBM a mile away. Worse, he had already seen me! Hunt must have realised my destination and tipped him off. Nowhere to hide, I had seconds in which to think about what I was going to say.

'Oliver,' said Mullard, 'an unexpected surprise! First, accept my sympathy about ... you know. If there's anything I can do. Second, tell me, what the hell are you up to?'

I accepted Mullard's short lived sympathy. Was it a sign the man had feelings after all? I didn't see any point in dodging Mullard's question, so told him why I'd come to London.

'Come on. I'll take you to Hammersmith myself. I've a car waiting — I guessed you might need a lift somewhere.'

'Thank you, sir. But when we get there, I want the interview to be private, just Boyton's sister and me.'

'So long as you bring me up to date.'

I nodded, hoping that no elaboration would be needed.

'The sooner we get there, the sooner we can have you on a train back to Crewe and your family.'

I was glad of the lift to the hospital, saving me the time of clambering around Euston Square and the Metropolitan Line which ran out to Hammersmith. Mullard dropped me at the hospital's main entrance, wishing me luck as he drove away to find somewhere to park.

I eventually found Sarah Boyton's home, for the next few weeks at any rate: the women's orthopaedic ward on the third floor. Why was it when visiting the sick, the ward you wanted was located at the end of a very long corridor? Was it to give you extra time to think about what you might be going to find when you finally arrived at the patient's bedside?

I passed all manner of sinister-looking equipment parked in the corridors. Some reminded me of when I used to visit an auntie of mine, when I was very young. She had a new-fangled upright vacuum cleaner which stood much taller than me and made a frightening racket when used. It scared the living daylights out of me — like some of the stuff I was walking past.

As it happened, Matron was entering the ward as I arrived. 'Excuse me, Matron. I'm DI Crosier. Was it you I spoke to earlier this afternoon? I've come to see, Sarah Boyton.'

'Ah yes, Inspector Crosier. I remember. She's this way, follow me.' Matron turned to me before we reached Boyton's bed. 'Now she looks pretty fit, Inspector, but if you are going to question her, as you suggested you might on the telephone, be prepared because she will be shocked by your revelation.'

'I'll take it easy on her. As I told you, I think her brother kidnapped my daughter last night. Miss Boyton, even if she doesn't realise it, might have information as to his whereabouts.'

'I hope you are right, Inspector.' She turned and marched me to Boyton's bedside. 'You have the visitor I told you about, Sarah.'

Sarah, obviously a popular woman, was lying on top of the bed, dressed in stripy pyjamas, the left leg rolled up to display a plaster signed by several visitors. I put her somewhere in her mid-twenties.

Matron drew the curtains around us, then left us to it. We both smiled when we overhead her giving orders to a nurse, as only Matrons can.

'I can see why you're in here, Miss Boyton!' I looked at her carefully — there was little resemblance with the face of the man in the incident photographs. Her lower jaw jutted forward, like a small scoop. Her brown eyes were perfectly positioned, an indication, I hoped, that sanity lay behind them.

'Simple really, got my leg broken yesterday on a trip, literally, by falling down some steps at The Tower of London. I assume my flatmate told you when you called her?'

'Yes she did. At least they didn't keep you in there with the ravens and some old Beefeaters for company.'

'True, Inspector. I understand this is not a social visit by the message you left with Matron. What can I do for you, Mr Crosier? Won't you sit down?'

I put my trilby on the foot of the bed, pulled the heavy wooden seat around so I could face her, slipped off my overcoat and hung it on the back of the chair. I gave her my card, at which she glanced, as I sat.

'I'll come straight to the point, Miss Boyton, I don't have much time. You may or may not know, we think your brother is connected with three murders that have taken place on railway property. In fact, I'd go as far as to say he committed them, probably with help from someone else. If that is true, Miss Boyton, it makes your brother a serial killer. This is your brother?' I said, passing her the best picture I had.

There, the worst part of it was out. I watched her closely for a reaction. It was simple enough: she was completely stunned and she stared at me open mouthed. But she did not break down or burst into tears as I'd expected.

She nodded slowly as she looked at the photograph again. After a moment she said, 'You can't be certain, Inspector ... can you? Why do you think Ronnie has killed three people?'

I passed Sarah Boyton a copy of her brother's note. 'It is his hand writing I assume?'

She studied it and began nodding again. 'Yes,' she said, 'that's his scrawl. One of his teachers once said the only way to read it was to stick it to a wall and read it as you dashed past. It's interesting that it's so poor considering he was a reasonable student at school, study-wise at least. Though, he only passed history exams.'

I was surprised she'd made such a humorous remark so soon. Maybe she wasn't as close to her brother as I'd expected. 'And now he has my daughter.' I said. 'He's threatened to kill again. I can't let him kill Ruth. Where did Ronnie go wrong, Sarah?' I hoped using their Christian names might help her relax. 'You must have spent time with him. At what point did he change into someone who takes lives ... innocent lives?'

'Yes, I spent time with him when we were much younger. Remember, Inspector I am some years older and when Ronnie left school, I'd already been in London for three years.'

'What sort of things did you do together? It's very interesting that each murder involved the railway. Why might that be?'

'He was very interested in trains. He wasn't a train spotter, like a lot of kids. He never saw any sense in that. He wanted to know how they worked, where did they go, how the signals operated, that sort of thing. We both played on the track; you know putting half-pennies on the rails to see if they'd be turned into pennies. When I look back now, I'm horrified we had the nerve to do it. My dad would have leathered us if he'd ever found out.' She half-smiled at the memory.

'It seems his interest in the railways has continued. Did you give up yours?'

'As I said, I'm a few years older and have, as you say, given up my interest in them. I hope you don't think I've been helping Ronnie to do all this, all this—'

'It had crossed my mind earlier, Sarah. I can see now it was a foolish notion.'

'Other things start to interest teenage girls, Mr Crosier, sorry, Detective Inspector. I remember once we'd been to the pictures: usual sort of Saturday afternoon flicks. "Take Ronnie to the matinee, Sarah. Get him out of my hair" mum used to say.

The Indians had tied the heroine to the track and the train was on its way. Standard plot. Then the hero arrived and started to untie her and Ronnie started to shout, "No, no; leave her there, let it kill her, let it chop her head off." I was shocked. He wasn't laughing like the other kids: he was deadly serious. When we were walking home afterwards I asked him, "Why did you want her to be run over, Ronnie?". He said it would be a better thing to happen. But really what shocked me was when he said, "I wanted to be the engine driver. So *I* could kill her". I guess he must still harbour that feeling, though fortunately for us, he can't drive a train.'

'What sort of friends did he have?'

'Vicious ones mainly; he was always in some scrap or other and sooner or later all his mates dropped him. He got too risky to be with.'

'But why, if he was reasonable at his school work, did he not go on to further education?'

'He had his first girlfriend by then, you see, and that's when his schooling deteriorated. After a while he was only interested in history. He had lots of history books at home. No other subjects mattered; subjects which might have helped get him a steady job.'

I filed away *history*, was this why his threat was about Kings?

'Did you ever meet her?'

'No, thank goodness! I never heard anything good said about her, not that I had much opportunity to meet her anyway. I'd have gone out of my way not to. Fortunately, I went to St John's, a different senior school than her and Ronnie.'

'Did you know her name?'

She drifted off to think about it for a few moments. 'No sorry, Inspector, I don't recall it.'

'What about your parents? What sort of relationship did he have with them?'

'Dad had died when he was five. I doubt he remembers him. Mother died when he'd be sixteen.'

'About the time this girl friend came along?'

'I guess so. I'd not really thought about it quite like that.'

'I need to know more about the girl. You see in the first two murders he definitely had an accomplice. Probably the third, too, but we're not certain of that or if she is helping him.'

'Mum had met her once or twice before she died, wasn't too happy about her. She never said a lot to me, but she reckoned she was a nasty piece of work, said they deserved each other. She didn't live much longer to have any positive influence over him and, as I said, I was down here.'

'When did you last see your brother?'

'That was just before I came to London. We'd had an argument the day before. He demanded I should stay at home and take over from mother, didn't see why anyone would want to come all the way down here to live in a flat. Strange really how he was such a bully, yet dared not leave his own little patch.'

'All bullies are cowards, Sarah.'

'I hated him. Hated the way he tried to dominate mother after dad died, the way he tried to trap me in the same house as him. I hated him more as he grew older and I hated his outlook on life. He couldn't keep a job for long, while those he went to school with could. So long as he had enough money to put petrol in his motorbike and go to the pub he was happy. When this girl turned up, I suppose, he had everything.'

'There's a good chance then she is his accomplice.'

'Maybe she'll lead you to him. I still can't really believe he would do all this.'

'I rather hoped you might know where he's living? He's not been on any of the local police forces' radar for some time and he's not at any previous addresses they have on record.'

'I'm sorry, Inspector. I don't know where he is. I don't want to know. I don't care about him. Does that sound unkind?'

'No, not really, Sarah. Your feelings are not uncommon. I should really be on my way now.' I stood to put on my overcoat, picked up my overnight bag and faced her. 'It may not feel like it to you, but you have helped me get a better picture of him, and his girlfriend.' But it still wasn't enough for me to catch him.

'Sarah,' said a nurse, swinging back the curtain. 'You have another visitor.'

I turned to look at the new arrival.

A tall young woman of Sarah's age, with long blond hair, came and stood next to the bed and began eyeing me up and down.

'Lorraine,' exclaimed Sarah,' how nice to see you.'

'I hope you like grapes,' said Lorraine, leaning over to kiss Sarah's cheek, 'but they're really for the visitors to nibble when they get bored.'

'Lorraine, you've come just at the right moment. I'll explain in a minute. First, though, you remember that awful girl my brother went out with don't you?'

Lorraine thought for a moment then nodded.

'Do you know where she lives?'

Lorraine considered some more.

I waited, hoping she could.

'Well, I'm not absolutely certain. I think Peter said she'd moved into Northwich. Near the bus station, Drill Field road or

Drill Hall something or other, I think.'

'I don't suppose you remember her name?' I said.

'Sort of. Her mates called her Liss, obviously an abbreviation.'

'How about Phyliss?' said Sarah.

Lorraine turned to me and said: 'Phyliss Sylt! All those s-sounds in a row. Yes, that's her. But why do you want to know?'

'It's all right Lorraine, this is DI Crosier. He's looking for Sylt and his daughter.'

'You've been most helpful. Thank you Miss?'

'Costello.'

'Do you know if she's still living in Northwich?'

'I don't. Peter, my boyfriend, might know where she is.'

'Lorraine,' said Sarah, 'I'll explain in a minute. I think DI Crosier has to go.'

I thanked them both. I couldn't believe my luck. She'd confirmed the name of Boyton's girlfriend and maybe this Peter could direct me to her. 'Might I have Peter's address or telephone number?' I said, proffering my notebook. 'Just in case he can help our enquiries further, you understand.'

Lorraine wrote them down.

'I hope you find your daughter soon, Inspector,' said Sarah.

I was taken-aback by Sarah's words. For a second or two, I'd been on a high, but Sarah reminded me of the painful and difficult a task that still lay ahead.

She saw my sadness.

We shook hands, I thanked Lorraine again then slipped between the curtains leaving Sarah to tell Lorraine that in all probability, her own brother was a serial killer.

47

MULLARD WAS WAITING FOR ME, JUST OUTSIDE THE HOSPITAL entrance, strolling back and forth on his tiny feet. One thing that always fascinated me about this large man: why were his feet so petite? They'd be more suited to a small woman than a seventeen-stone copper. They never looked able to support his weight.

'So how did it go, Oliver?'

'As I suspected, I have a lead. Her younger brother apparently had a nasty piece of work for his girlfriend, who came on the scene just before his mother died. He became more aggressive to his mother and when she did die, he expected his sister to take her place. Sarah Boyton was not too keen on that arrangement. They argued until she left and came down here to look for work. And when the girlfriend came on the scene, his education went down the tubes. There must have been a lot of anger building up in this young man and its release, probably, was murder.'

'So she knows where he is?'

'She thinks Sylt might be in Northwich: Drill Hall or Drill Field Road, or at least she did live there.'

'Come on, if we dash you can make the eight-thirty back to Crewe. I'll call Hunt once you are on it and tell him what you've got.'

'Call him now, sir, please. The sooner he knows about the girlfriend's address, the more time he'll have to find her.'

While Mullard called Hunt from the car, I found a telephone in the hospital reception and put in a reverse-charge call to Browning to tell him about the suspected whereabouts of

Boyton's girlfriend. I wanted Browning to revise his copy to the national press, which he was only too pleased to do saying, "It would add local interest" — an understatement if ever there was!

Then I put through a second call to Claire, to see what was going on in the team. I was fortunate Carol had gone home and that Claire picked up the call on the second ring. She had no developments to report, so I told her about my latest discovery, and that if Hunt didn't move on it as soon as Mullard had spoken to him, she should try to trace Boyton's girlfriend herself.

Finally, I gave her Lorraine's boyfriend's address and telephone number asking her to find out if he could remember anything as to the whereabouts of the Sylt woman.

'I'll meet you off the train if I have anything for you.'

'That would be very nice, Claire, but I suspect Hunt will be doing that. We don't want to give him the wrong idea about us, do we?' I heard her sigh, said goodnight and hung up.

'So, how's your wife coping?' asked Mullard. 'She pleased you'll be home tonight?'

'I don't know. I didn't call her,' I mumbled, looking at the ground as I reached his car. He knew not to ask any more questions. We drove in silence for most of the way.

'Oliver,' Mullard said, as we were crossing Tottenham Court Road, 'you know Hunt was livid you'd come down here without telling him. I calmed him down, though, now we have a new lead, thanks to you. He's promised to get the team out tonight to see if they can trace the girlfriend.'

'Oh, very decent of him, I'm sure.'

48

I DOZED A LITTLE ON THE WAY BACK. AND WHEN I WASN'T DOZING didn't come up with a single new idea on how to prevent Boyton from carrying out his deadly scheme. I pulled myself together to await Hunt's good news; or his wrath.

BBM must have told him which train I'd be on. He was waiting at the steps which exited the platform. We walked up them together, not saying a word until we were out of earshot of others leaving the station.

'Come on,' said Hunt, 'I think we both need a drink.'

Nursing two large whiskies courtesy of Hunt — the least he could do — in the Crewe Arms' lounge bar, we stared at each other.

Hunt had to break the silence. 'We followed up your lead on the girlfriend.'

I knew they'd wasted their time, otherwise it would have been the first thing Hunt had told me when we met.

'Northwich officers went to that address. She's not there, hasn't been for over a year.'

My heart sank again; she could be anywhere after a year.

'Neighbours think she might be either in Manchester or Warrington. Officers from Winsford made several late-night calls to some of her school teachers and her classmates. She'd been living in Northwich with her aunt who moved out at the same time.'

'And nobody knew where they moved?'

Hunt shook his head.

'So, you don't actually know where she is then?'

'No, not yet.'

'And what, pray, have you come up with for the big event tomorrow?'

'There's nothing new.' Hunt studied his whiskey then took a gulp, hiding his embarrassment.

'I thought as much. So the only progress made on the case today has come from the bloke you threw off it! Am I right?'

Hunt wriggled uneasily in his seat and looked up from his glass of whiskey. 'It's procedure, Oliver,' he said, with his hands spread wide, palms open. 'You know it's what happens when a case goes personal.'

'Fuck procedures! What do your procedures tell you about Ruth, DI Hunt? What do I tell her mother when I get home in ten minutes? The collective brains of New Scotland Yard, four local forces and the RP haven't come up with a single new lead. Is that what I tell her?'

'Steady on, Oliver.'

Other early-morning customers in the lounge stopped talking and turned to look at us. Hunt glared back at them.

'Steady on, my arse. I'm going home. Tomorrow, I am coming into the office, no into *my* office to lead the team again, procedures or no fucking procedures. If you don't like it, talk to that useless twit Newall, or Mullard.'

I slammed my empty glass down on the table.

'Here, check if Winsford went to this address.' I ripped the page out of my notebook that Lorraine had written on. Call me if you hear anything. Thanks for the drink.'

I walked home fuming after my outburst at Hunt. I consoled myself by thinking at least some progress had been made. But so far it didn't really amount to much. Boyton and Sylt were still at large, with someone very precious indeed.

I passed a telephone box and decided to give Claire a call.

She confirmed what Hunt had already told me, adding some details but nothing new. Finally, to complete my depression, she said, 'There wasn't reply from Lorraine's boyfriend either.' It was nice to hear her sympathetic voice, though. She even asked me if I would like to come round, 'for a coffee'.

I declined her offer. I had to go home to my wife and son, not get sidetracked by anything that might possibly develop between me and Claire, tempting as it might be.

I arrived to a tearful Alice. I was glad I'd come straight home. She had calmed down a lot given the circumstances. She made me some hot cocoa and, as I hadn't eaten much on the return journey from London, a ham sandwich too.

I told Alice about the interview with Boyton's sister and that we now had a lead on his girlfriend.

But as to the missing person closest to our hearts, there was no news.

49

AGAIN THAT SCREAM. MY FEET POUNDING THE COBBLES. MY feet. Running fast, fog everywhere. She was there. I saw her. Gone now. There. I'm close. My arms shrink. Hers outstretched, yet she's fading. That fog. The enormous hand gun, its bullets coming slowly ...

I sat up shaking, wiped the sweat from my brow. Just a bloody dream! I swung my legs out of bed and sat until I had my bearings. 3 a.m. Sunday. *The* Sunday. The Sunday I hoped to recover Ruth.

I looked at Alice. I didn't seem to have disturbed her and hoped she wasn't having the similar terrors. I dared not go back to sleep. I shouldn't have had that bloody cocoa and ham sandwich so late. I slipped my dressing gown on.

The kitchen clock said three-fifteen. I brewed coffee; no point in going back to bed now. I sat and read Boyton's note again for what felt like the hundredth time. The Royal Scot would be leaving Euston in just over six hours, be in Crewe within nine.

I still thought the chances of Boyton doing anything south of Crewe were slight. I'd been right so far and hoped my judgement would be right this time. Boyton's sister had said as much yesterday. I forced myself not think about the consequences if I was wrong.

There would be plenty of police on the train as it left Euston and I'd decided not to switch the trains again in the tunnel in case Boyton was on it. Pictures and descriptions of him would be given to everyone on the case, including the officers on the

Royal Scot, who were going to get hold of copies of the Sunday papers, if they carried the story and had decent pictures. We still needed a decent photograph of Sylt and might get one later today, though probably too late to get them to the officers on the train before it left Euston. They'd have to distribute them when the train came into Crewe.

I would go to the newsagent at the end of the street to get all the national papers to see how Browning's report turned out. They should print the good picture of Ronnie Boyton I'd given to Browning. They had to lead with this story on the front page of every Sunday paper. But would it be out in time to get any useful leads from the public? Time would tell and there was very little of that left.

There had been no telephone calls since I got back from London, so presumably the Sylt woman's whereabouts was still unknown.

I sat, both frustrated and extremely worried, looking at the bastard's note again.

I woke at six-fifteen slumped across the kitchen table with my head on my arms and was surprised to see my full cup of cold coffee on the table.

Alice came into the kitchen. I'd never seen her look so old, her face drawn and pale, almost grey, her hair dishevelled. She couldn't stop yawning. She saw my cold coffee.

'I'll make us a fresh pot of tea. It's what you are supposed to do at times like these isn't it?'

'I believe it is, Alice. I believe it is.'

'So what's going to happen today?'

I went and put my arms around her. 'I can't answer that, not because I don't want to, but because I haven't the slightest idea. I'm going up to Askey's paper shop in a minute to see what the press have said.'

'I'm glad Hunt has done something useful,' she said.

'He didn't tell the papers. I did.'

She was about to get the milk from the pantry but stopped to look at me.

I must have looked like Alistair when he'd been caught out.

Now she realised I'd been working my own investigation and not kicking my heels waiting for something to turn up. She seemed grateful and kissed my cheek.

'Does he know?'

'He probably will do in ten minutes, if the Crewe Arms delivers the Sunday papers to his room.'

She smiled. The kettle boiled. I stood ready to leave.

'Get this in you first,' she said, offering me a fresh cup of tea. 'Askey won't be open yet anyway. And you'd better change out of your dressing gown and pyjamas before you go.'

Fifteen minutes later, I was back in my working suit and setting off to Askey's shop.

'I thought you might be in early, Mr Crosier,' said old man Askey, 'so I took the door off the latch as soon as I saw the papers. I'm very sorry to read about young Ruth; take 'em all, no charge today. I've put a bundle up for you. There's plenty to read. I saved you last night's *Manchester Evening News* as well. They printed a pull-out sheet, anything to beat the Sundays. You'll have to thank Jabberson for that one day.'

I was touched by the old man's kindness. I nodded a thank you, then left for home.

They all had the story on the front page with Boyton and Sylt's pictures printed large, though hers was fuzzy. There were pictures of my family with a big one of Ruth next to Boyton's. Some had Ruth between Boyton on one side and me on the other with brash headlines . . .

WHO HAS RUTH? WHICH MAN NEEDS HER MOST?
BOYTON AND SYLT: BRITISH RAILWAYS' FIRST SERIAL KILLERS
KIDNAPPED: CAN MY DADDY RESCUE ME IN TIME?

and of course ...

WANTED: PHYLISS SYLT AND RONNIE BOYTON

All had a version of Bob Browning's story and made the most of the murders being the work of a serial killer. On the whole it was very good publicity for Ruth's case. I prayed that a reader somewhere, just one from the thousands who would be reading her story this morning, would call in with a useful lead.

'So, what happens now, Oliver?' Before I could answer Alice, the telephone rang in the hall.

'So, Oliver, you went to the press I see.' Hunt didn't sound too upset. 'They made a good story out of it, I'll give you that. Let's hope someone can link this bastard to the woman Sylt.'

'But there's so little time. The Royal Scot will be leaving Euston in under three hours and be in Crewe in six! What are you going to do, DI Hunt?'

'First we need to crack the code.'

'I know that. I've been trying, doing virtually nothing else. Who's working on that apart from me?'

A long silence.

'Well?'

'The same team and me, Oliver. We're meeting again at seven.'

Hunt didn't have anything new to offer. The silence between us hung in the air, palpable. I cut his call and went back into the kitchen.

'Another case review,' I said, 'and I'm going to it.'

'But you're off the case, Oliver.'

'Well, ... I just put myself back on it.'

50

I FELT A BIT FRESHER AFTER I'D HAD SOME CEREAL, TOAST WITH marmalade and very strong coffee. I was almost looking forward to going back to my office, determined to take it back.

Alice was looking at a copy of the first note the killer had sent.

'Have you worked out the hidden meaning in this sick bastard's notes yet?'

'We don't know for sure. We suspect it's something to do with the last King locomotive built at Swindon. It was renamed in 1936 from King Stephen to King Edward VIII, the last King of England. Went off with that American woman Simpson.'

'But, Oliver, Edward VIII was not the last King of England.' I looked at her stunned. 'King George VI was the last. God, don't you know any history?'

'Oh shit.' I heaved on my overcoat and left.

✳✳✳

I arrived at my commandeered office to find Hunt, Claire and Dobbs going through the case notes yet again.

'We're on the wrong track.' They stopped talking to turn and look at me, none laughing at my unintentional pun. 'The last King locomotive was King Edward VIII. The last King of England was George VI. How could we get it so wrong?'

They all realised it was me who'd been wrong, and could see I was rightly embarrassed.

'So, it will be a different number!' said Claire, grabbing the spotter's book again. 'Yes 6028.'

'So what have we got now, people?' said Hunt. He'd obviously decided not to turn me away. Rules or no rules, I was the only one coming up with new information.

'So if we add the numbers we get 70,500 or take them away to get 1,556. I still don't see what we have here,' said Hunt.

'All we have are the numbers,' I said. 'They have to mean something. Dobbs, call your contact at Swindon again. See if 6028 was renamed as well.' Dobbs left the room, smiling again now I appeared to be taking charge of the team. Ten minutes later he was back.

'6028 was originally named King Henry II but they changed it to George VI in 1937, the year after Edward VIII abdicated.'

Inside, I was kicking myself at being reminded of my blunder. My old history master was right, even now.

Hunt was looking at the first note the killer had sent and was still scratching his head when Smith, obviously excited, barged into the office and ignoring Hunt, slapped a note down in front of me.

'Sir, we have a lead on the Sylt woman.'

51

7:30 a.m.

'A WOMAN IN WARRINGTON RUNG HER LOCAL FORCE. THEY'RE going round there now,' said Smith. 'Seems she recognised Sylt and Boyton from the pictures in the papers. Said she'd seen them at a house across the street several times during the last week. They both have motorbikes. One looks very new and, get this: recently, if she is Sylt, she's been using a car.' Smith could hardly contain himself.

'Then there's a good chance they used it to snatch, Ruth,' I said. 'No wonder Traffic didn't see her on a motorbike; she was in a bloody car! How could we be so stupid?' I was pulling my overcoat back on and heading for the door. 'We need get up to Warrington now.'

***

We'd arrived at Algernon Street within half-an-hour. The local police were already installed and drinking tea in Mrs Birtles' house.

I'd never seen such a round woman before. She was drenched in Eau-de-Cologne, either to impress her visitors, or in a vain attempt to cover the smell of an elderly collie lying in front of a roaring fire. It occasionally opened an eye, but refused to move even when its fur was burnt by flying sparks.

'Mrs Birtles, I'm DI Crosier, Crewe Transport Police. You spoke with my assistant this morning. This is DI Hunt from London's New Scotland Yard.'

'Yes, I know you. I saw your picture; in the paper,' she said, pointing to one on the coffee-table.

'We need to go through again what you probably have already told our colleagues from Warrington.'

The Warrington officers looked at each other, no doubt wondering what was going on, with the BTP and NSY marching in and taking over the questioning. Hunt raised a hand to silence them before either spoke.

'So it's your daughter who's missing then is it?'

'Yes it is, Mrs Birtles. Which house are they at?'

'Number thirty-eight, directly opposite, maroon window frames, terrible colour, doesn't go at all with the neighbour's.'

Hunt and I peered at number thirty-eight, from behind Mrs Birtles' net curtains, a large thirties semi-detached house with a garage built onto the right side.

'And when did you last see either of them? This morning?'

We were still looking at the house as I asked her. No sign of any activity. Perhaps they'd escaped out of the back when they saw the police cars arrive, or maybe they were still in bed, unaware our man hunt had arrived on their doorstep.

'Oh, that would be Friday night about half-past-seven when the car came back. He was on his bike and arrived a little while after her.'

'That fits the time when Ruth disappeared,' Hunt said, pointlessly.

'Are you sure it was her, Mrs Birtles?'

'I couldn't see them really because it was dark. But I'd seen her before, and him.'

'Tell me when that was?'

'Friday afternoon. She came out about two o'clock in ever such a tiz-was. Ran round to the garage and drove out in a car.'

'You're certain it was her?' asked Hunt.

'Positive, Inspector. The roof was open, I know it was her.'

'What type of car was it?' I was desperate to know.

'Oh I'm not much of a one for cars, Inspector, don't know the make or anything. It's one of those daft cars, neither a car nor a bike.'

'Sorry, I don't follow you.'

'You know one of those silly three-wheel things. Nice red colour, though.'

I stood frozen, and even though the room was stiflingly hot, I felt as if someone had walked over my grave. I sat down before I fell down. Archie Shaw had said there was a red car involved and, maybe, he'd pointed to the picture of the woman we were now hunting. Why hadn't I, or Cardin, looked at the woman he'd pointed to when we were in his front room? Jesus!

'You all right?,' said Hunt, 'you don't look well. Can you fetch him some water please, Mrs Birtles.'

She returned from the kitchen. 'Here you are, Inspector. Take a swallow of this.'

I drunk half the glass in one draft and was starting to regain my wits. 'So tell us what she did next?' I said, looking up at her.

'She locked the garage door, ran back to the car and whizzed off as fast as she could.'

'And you haven't seen her since Friday night?'

'No, sorry. Not seen anyone there at all.'

'Could they still be inside?'

'No.'

'Are you certain about that?'

'Very, Inspector. You see, late last night I heard the car drive away. I was in bed. By the time I got up to look through the window, I just saw the back of the car as it went round the bend.'

'So they're lying low somewhere overnight,' said Hunt.

'I think the car belongs to Mr Wilson. He's retired and spends a lot of time with his sister in New Brighton, I think he said. He's been retired years so I suppose he lets her use the car and the house when he's not here.'

Hunt instructed one of the local officers to call his station and see if he could get registration numbers for red three-wheelers in the district registered to a Mr Wilson.

I knew the chances of tracking down Wilson were slim but,

if we could find him, he might know the whereabouts of the Sylt woman.

'Did you see anyone with her, a child perhaps?'

'No, no one at all. Although, I think a child could easily have been hidden in the car. You can get into the house through the side door of the garage without being seen. And I've seen him a few times too.'

'When?' asked Hunt.

'I've seen him come here a few times. He looks proper shifty, something about his eyes. He's only there for ten minutes and then goes. He's probably feeding Mr Wilson's cat for him.'

I looked at Hunt, who flicked his head towards the door. It was time for us to visit the house.

Outside, Hunt asked me what had come over me.

'I'm not sure really; probably the shock of being so close to Ruth and then just missing her.' I was hardly going to tell Hunt about my 'clairvoyant' experience I'd had in Scotland. 'I need to put a call through to Alice. I'll use the car's radiophone. You check number thirty-eight.' I went across to the police car, but didn't call my wife.

'Claire, it's me.'

'Hello, Oli—'

'Listen, Claire. I need you to put a call through to Nancy and Archie Shaw. The neighbour saw Sylt leave in a red three wheel car.'

'So, whatever we thought about Archie Shaw, well, we were wrong.'

'Somehow, he knew something. I don't want to tell everyone here about him just yet. It's a long shot, but he might be able to help us further. I'll call you back in ten minutes or so to see what he's had to say.'

'You okay, Oliver?'

'Just make the call, Claire.'

At number thirty-eight there was no sign of life. I was very tempted to break the front door in, but Hunt held me back.

However we found the side door to the garage unlocked and went inside. No car but there were two motorbikes and the biggest, with the red petrol tank, looked brand new.

'I'd say these are the bikes,' I said, looking at its tyres. 'I'd swear this one is a match and that one,' I said, pointing to the large gleaming motorcycle, 'matches what the kids from the park told us.'

I scanned the almost empty garage for any other clues and noticed an old chest-freezer, as its compressor started up. I looked at Hunt and tipped my head towards the freezer.

Hunt opened the lid and searched under bags of frozen vegetables. He pulled out Bright's other hand and Gilmore's foot, frozen for just over three years. We'd found enough evidence in the garage alone to hang Boyton.

'Come on, maybe we can force the back door of the house,' said Hunt. 'There's enough here to clear us from a charge of breaking and entering without a warrant.'

One of the Warrington constables put a brick through the kitchen window, climbed inside and unbolted the door. It was still locked, so another eager officer from Warrington had his chance to shoulder it open.

Once inside we went first to the living room. I instructed a constable to go through the desk in the corner to see if an address could be found in New Brighton for Mr Wilson's sister.

A cat shot down the stairs to see what all the commotion was about and then went into the kitchen where it stood at its empty food bowl and shouted to be fed. The constable who'd shouldered the door open obliged by opening a small tin of Kitty Kat he found in a cupboard.

Upstairs in the front bedroom we found, lying on the double-bed, a folder containing press cuttings taken at Whitegate and Middlewich. Boyton or Sylt had even pencilled circles around their faces. They obviously craved the publicity, confirming my theory that he in particular was a showman.

And hanging over the bed-head was a very strange picture; a

face, neither male nor female. It was only when I took a closer look I saw that it was made up entirely of strands of hair painstakingly, yet badly, glued to its card backing. It had to be Elspeth's hair.

In the back bedroom I found signs that someone had stayed there recently. The dimple in the single-bed's pillow was warm where the cat had been sleeping.

I bent down to pick up a small handkerchief with pink edging. 'Ruth's been here,' I said to Hunt, as he came in from the front bedroom with the folder and 'artwork'. 'This handkerchief is one of hers and it still feels moist to me. The bastards brought her here, but where is she now?' I put Ruth's handkerchief in my pocket — it might be my last connection to her. 'I'm going to make another call from the car. Then we'll decide what to do next.'

I called Claire. She picked up on the first ring.

'Hello, Oliver. I thought it might be you.'

'Did you speak with them?'

'I only spoke with Nancy. I explained the situation and about the red car. She seemed to accept it as if it was obvious, nothing at all unusual. Then I asked if there might be any way Archie could help us, with him being so far away.'

'And?'

'She asked me how I knew.'

'What do you mean?'

'She meant with Archie Shaw not being there.'

'You mean he's gone away somewhere?'

'In a manner of speaking, yes. He died in his sleep last night.'

52

8:30 a.m.

'THERE WAS ONE OTHER THING NANCY SAID, OLIVER.'

'What?' I said, still struggling with the fact that one possible source of hope, like Ruth, had vanished overnight.

'She said the last thing Archie had whispered, was "not Warrington", whatever that's supposed to mean.'

Again I was struck by the mysterious, inexplicable way Archie was connected to this case. Was his meeting with me on the train really a coincidence. He was a cantankerous old-sod and I'd not believed a word he said. And now I was sorry I'd underestimated him.

'It means, Claire, somehow or other, Archie knew I was going to come here damn him. Why did he have to die now?'

'So what's your next move, Oliver?'

'I'm not sure. How am I going to explain this to Hunt? He thought I was off my rocker in thinking these cases were inspired by jealousy! Introducing a clairvoyant at this—'

'I think you should come back. You should see Alice. She rang me ten minutes ago, very angry that you were not keeping her informed.'

'You're right, Claire. I have been blanking her out for the last twenty four hours. I needed to think more clearly, something I find very difficult to do when she's around fretting.'

'Okay, Claire. Keep me posted if anything else comes in. Did the photos of Sylt arrive? They need to be on that train when it gets to Crewe. Someone on it might have seen her.'

Claire said they had but, as they were blow-ups of the shots in the newspaper, they weren't very good. I got out of the car and went across to Hunt.

'There you are, Oliver, what's going on now? Are you all right? You look like you've just seen a ghost?'

I felt like I had too. I'd have to tell Hunt before long about Archie Shaw, but for now I'd see how the conversation went. 'I've been thinking; there's nothing to keep us here.'

Hunt looked hard at me.

'You need to put pressure on the local boys to see if they can find her locally,' I said, 'but I don't think they will.'

'You're right. Boyton has to be close to a railway line by now if he's going to carry out his threat. I'll get onto the Chief Constable. Keep the pressure up.'

Hunt then told me they'd found the address in New Brighton that Mrs Birtles had referred to. My hopes were raised, only to be dashed a second later. He'd already got the local boys to call New Brighton CID, from the other squad-car, while I was talking to Claire. He'd asked for an officer to visit Mr Wilson's sister's address, 28 Preston Park Avenue, to find out if he knew where Sylt might be living. They called back within minutes, adamant. There was no such address in New Brighton.

Another dead-end.

'But there's more, Oliver,' said Hunt.

I waited.

His expression told me what he was about to say was not good news. 'The constable who found the address, found something else.'

'What?'

'Bullets.'

'And a gun?'

'No ... no gun.'

Now all I felt was despair.

53

9 a.m.

THROUGHOUT THE JOURNEY BACK TO CREWE, HUNT AND I TOOK IT
in turns to read a copy of Boyton's note I'd kept since Friday.

Dear DI Crosier.

Loved yer train switch. Most envintive but to can play
that game. Another on my list has to die tonight. Run the
train Sunday and dont try any more triks or you mite not
see your girl alive.

The Boy.

We passed it back-and-fro, each time scratching our heads in
turn. We came up with no new ideas. I looked out of the
window, thinking about where Ruth might be. The missing gun
was a real worry.

The journey had seemed to take forever, but we were back in
my office by eight-fifty-five; the driver, under orders from Hunt,
had put his foot down.

The team were gathered for a final brain-storming session. If
we didn't work out now what Boyton meant, we all knew Alice
and I might never see Ruth again.

'I don't think that the engine numbers mean anything,' I said.
'No matter which way we combine them. Are they map
references?'

'No,' said Claire, 'I already looked at that possibility while you were in Warrington. They bear no resemblance to any of the numbers we have, no matter how you adapt them. In fact the longitudes become negative.'

Everyone looked at her, she flushed a little. 'Remember too, that Boyton's best subject at school was history. So, I'd say the numbers have to be times.'

The telephone on my desk started jangling. Nobody spoke while I took the call. Carol, who'd come in specially to man the phones, said, 'It's London Region for you, Oliver.'

I looked at my watch: five-past-nine. 'Put them through, Carol, please.' I listened to the controller, then slowly put the handset back on its cradle. Everyone in the office was looking at me. 'The Royal Scot is on its way. And it's on time.'

'15:56 is too late anyway,' said Hunt, getting back to the debate and trying not to be eclipsed by Claire. 'The train will almost be in Scotland by then. 10:50 might work. Claire, get the Royal Scot's timetable and see where she'd be at 10:50.'

'That's less than two hours from now and it's nothing to do with *the predecessor!*' I said. 'Could someone call Boyton's history master from his old school? He'd know when Henry II was on the throne. The years must mean times?'

Dobbs got to his feet to call the history master, who by now might have finished his Sunday breakfast.

'At 10:50,' said Claire. Studying the timetable, 'she'd be this side of—'

'Claire, don't bother with that. We need more on King Henry to work this out. Where's Dobbs got to?'

He returned after a few minutes. 'Sorry, I had to wait until Mr Millar finished his Sunday morning bath. I asked his wife to put the question to him and for him to call me back. He's just 'phoned. Born 1133, came to the throne in 1154.'

'So now we have two possible times when he may strike again, both of them in less than three hour's time!' I said, starting to really worry now about Ruth's safety.

'The train would be north of Tamworth at 11:33 if it's on time.'

Hunt asked, 'What's at Tamworth?'

'Not a lot,' I said. 'But more importantly, it is not in the *North West*. His sister said "he was afraid to leave his own patch". Remember?'

'11:54 at Stafford,' said Claire.

I jumped to my feet, dismissing the Stafford possibility. 'Dobbs, you didn't say when Henry died, did you?' We all looked at Dobbs.

'1189, sir.'

'That doesn't make any bloody sense at all does it, Dobbs?' I banged my fist hard on the table. 'Are you sure?'

'Positive, sir. Millar read all the dates to me from one of his history books to make certain he was right.'

'So,' said Hunt, 'do we concentrate on Tamworth or Stafford?'

'No, no, *no*,' I said, 'they're not in Boyton's region.'

'What about here? Crewe?'

'The train would be here soon after twelve,' said Claire. 'None of the dates are after twelve.'

Davidson arrived and asked for a quick review. After some discussion and rejecting all Davidson's ideas, I began to slap the back of my neck.

Everyone in the room stopped talking and watched me pacing around the room. Eventually I said, 'Supposing it was 11:89. If you carry the twenty nine minutes and put them onto twelve o'clock, it would be 12:29.'

'Winsford,' said Claire, before anyone asked her.

'That's in the North West region all right. It's slap-bang in the middle of Cheshire, where all three murders have taken place,' I said, almost starting to smile again.

'Remember it doesn't normally stop until it reaches Carnforth to change crews,' said Claire.

'Well, we're going to stop it here, distribute the photographs of the killers and we'll swap the engines over onto our own carriages. She should arrive early being double-headed. That should give us the extra time.'

'Smith,' said Hunt 'get onto Northwich to see if they have anything on the Sylt woman yet.'

'Dobbs,' I said, 'call the regional operations controller in Stafford. Make sure nothing gets in the way of the Royal Scot. Then get the carriages for our own train sorted. We need to consider every way Boyton might carry out his threat and how we are going to rescue my daughter. The possibility he will kill her, if the train does not run to time, is not going to happen.'

I thought he'd try to kill her regardless of the timetable, but kept that to myself for the moment, though it had probably occurred to everyone.

I sat down wearily. 'I think we need to cover as much as possible of the line from here to Warrington, paying particular attention to Winsford.'

Now I'd worked out the clue — or at least I hoped I had — it was time to set up road blocks, especially in the Wharton and Stanthorne districts, where the London to Scotland main line passed through Winsford.

Davidson organised both the Northwich and Winsford police forces. They'd be on the ground, while the BTP would cover from the train. What Boyton did not know was that we knew about his red car, and we were on the lookout for it.

But when it came down to it, I knew all we could do was watch and wait, hope that the puzzle was solved and that we'd be in the right place at the right time.

54

10 a.m.

BOYTON, SYLT AND RUTH SPENT SATURDAY NIGHT IN THE LITTLE Reliant, holed up in the lanes which ran from the village of Moulton to Wharton on the Eastern side of Winsford. It was easy to hide in them and apart from a few farmers, nobody travelled along them.

He'd picked a spot that was once part of the deserted brine workings which had left several shallow pits in the ground. Farmers never came here; only rough grass grew there once the salt workings closed. He knew of one in which you could drive a small car so that it was completely hidden. There had been little rain for almost a month and the porous soil, strengthened by the coarse grass, allowed water pits to drain away so the ground was almost solid under foot.

Sylt had made them all salmon paste sandwiches. She'd brought apples as well.

Ruth had tucked into them with relish before they slept. Until then, she'd not eaten at all since they kidnapped her. She didn't like Boy, as the woman kept calling him. He was too strict with her and the woman. He was always bossing her about, and if the woman didn't do what he said right away, he'd slap her face. The woman never cried. She was strong in Ruth's eyes, and friendlier towards her, making sure that Ruth and Moggie had enough to eat and drink.

'Okay, Boy,' said the woman, 'what do we now? I'm getting a bit tired of you not telling me what we're doing next.'

'You'll see my beauty ... all in good time.' Then he turned

round to Ruth and smiled that evil smile he made when he was being very horrid towards her, one eye looking at her, one looking outside.

She shivered and turned away from him. The taste of the salmon paste sandwich was suddenly as horrid as Boy's grin. A tear ran down her cheek.

Seeing it Boyton turned back. 'Not too long now. The King and the Scotsman will be along soon.'

'What the fuck are you talking about, Boy? You've had us sleep in this, this ditch all night and now you're on about Kings and Scotsmen. You're going mad, Boy that's what you are.'

He hit her again, but not too hard. It was difficult to throw a punch in this confined space. The woman hit him back and now the car was rocking violently from side to side as they each struggled to hit each other again.

'Stop it, stop it,' screamed Ruth, 'stop it.'

They did and turned to face her, then turned back and stared through the windscreen. The woman didn't like not knowing what their next plan was, let alone being beaten by Boy who was becoming more violent as the hours rolled by. He was getting more nervous she could tell. She was frightened that he had some plan which involved Ruth; plans to hurt her, or worse, kill her. Sylt didn't care to be involved in any of that. She'd have to wait to see what was going to happen. Maybe she'd have a chance to help Ruth escape.

Boyton had become equally sick of Phyliss Sylt. He wanted her out of the way. She questioned everything he did and even asked him last night not to kill Ruth. They had argued about that several times. She'd said there wasn't anyone else they'd hated, but he said there was only one more he wanted rid of, then he'd stop.

But of course, Phyliss Sylt was too stupid to realise he was talking about her.

55

11 a.m.

I HAD SPOKEN AGAIN TO SARAH BOYTON BY TELEPHONE, TO SEE IF she had any idea where her brother might strike. She'd been very helpful.

We were working out our next move to foil Boyton's scheme, when Alice entered, demanding to know what was happening and what progress we'd made to recover Ruth. Claire had telephoned Alice earlier to say Hunt and I were back in Crewe. When Alice had asked Claire about their progress, Claire had told me she had not known what to say.

Claire's silence was enough to spur Alice into action. Twenty minutes later she arrived at the RP Crewe headquarters and was now in my office.

'Hello, Alice,' said Hunt, as she entered, trying to keep things affable between the four of us.

'Alice,' I said, 'you shouldn't be here. Where is Alistair?'

'Don't you worry about him. He's safe with the neighbours. Where's Ruth, DI Crosier?'

'We're still working on that, love.'

Hunt flashed an embarrassed smile at her and gestured she take a seat. He knew all along I should really be with my family, but he could see I was torn between that and my duty to find my own daughter. And after all, only my progress had brought anything new.

'Well?' Alice demanded, scowling at each of us in turn.

'We think we've figured out where he will strike. The note inferred that if the train reached this place dead on time, he'd spare the life of whoever he'd been planning to kill next.'

'And do you believe him, Oliver? Do you, Tony?'

'My experience tells me, Alice,' said Hunt, 'that when a killer has killed twice then he's always a killer. There's never been a case to my knowledge where they decide to stop. It's like a drug to them. They enjoy the thrill of stalking their quarry, the kill, the publicity which follows and the risk of being caught. That's why he sent us those notes. He wants to heighten the chase. He wants to tease us, to play with us like he might play with a cat. He knows we have claws, but he also knows we don't know where to scratch him. At least, he thinks we don't.'

Davidson nodded his agreement with Hunt's synopsis.

'So, where are you going to scratch him?' asked Alice, keen to put a stop to Hunt's verbal diarrhoea.

'I called the Hammersmith hospital again,' I said, 'just before you arrived and spoke with Boyton's sister. I remembered something she'd said about Boyton when I visited her yesterday, after they'd been to the pictures together. I asked her where they used to play near the railway.'

'And?'

'By the line, as it passes through Winsford Junction.'

'And when will the train be there?'

'If we let it run to time, it should pass through Winsford Junction in about an hour and a half. When it gets here we're going to hold it while we go through it to see if either Boyton, Sylt or Ruth are on it. We have pictures to—'

'You mean, you are going to hold up the train? Don't you realise our daughter's life is at stake here, Oliver?' She questioned me angrily and so loud the people in the next office heard her.

'Alice,' I said, as calmly as I could, while moving around the table.

She wasn't looking at me, but at the photograph of us taken on our honeymoon in Eastbourne. It lay face up and was almost covered with files.

I moved the stack of files to one side so I could half-sit on the desk to face her.

Now the picture was completely covered.

She looked back at me with eyes which asked, what is going wrong between us?

Taking her hand, I continued. 'When the train reaches Crewe we'll check to make sure they are not on it. We'll detach the engines and they'll pull another similar set of carriages north. It's running early so we'll have plenty of time. Boyton will only see the engines with their name plates: he won't know that the rest of the train is only carrying police officers, not passengers. We cannot risk the lives of those passengers should Boyton be trying on something more dramatic.'

'What could be more dramatic, Oliver, than Boyton killing Ruth for God's sake?'

'Alice, give us some credibility. We already have Winsford Junction surrounded. If Boyton shows up there he won't be able get anywhere near the track or the train.'

She looked at us one by one: Hunt, Davidson and Cardin, before standing to face me. 'And if he isn't there? What then?'

I stared at Hunt, then the ceiling — we hadn't thought of that.

56

11:50 a.m.

PASSENGERS LOOKING OUT ON THE LEFT OF THE ROYAL SCOT, couldn't fail to see the line of police officers stretched out along the platform as it came to its unscheduled stop almost ten minutes early. Armed with the pictures of Boyton and Sylt, they boarded the train and started to question everyone to see if they'd seen anyone on the train that looked like the suspects. Nobody had, although some proffered their Sunday paper in response.

There had been some frantic moving of carriages onto the adjacent platform to save time in running the double-heading engines onto it. The spare rake came in on platform-two just as the Royal Scot arrived. While the King George and the Flying Scotsman were uncoupled from the express, the shunting engine that brought in the empty rake was uncoupled and the engine rapidly moved off. The King and Scotsman were called forward by the shunting signal about eighty yards beyond the head of the platform. Points were changed and they reversed onto the empty carriages. The fireman of the Scotsman jumped down onto the track behind the tender and began coupling. The fireman rejoined his driver and they waited for the all-clear to depart.

Officers emerged from the Royal Scot empty handed: nobody had seen either Boyton or Sylt and they certainly were not aboard the express. After reporting to me and Hunt, they boarded the empty train on the adjacent platform. Claire, Davidson, Smith and Dobbs had taken seats in the first carriage.

Hunt and I walked to the front engine King George, and climbed onto the footplate after first asking the crew of the Scotsman to join us.

'Whatever may happen in the next half-an-hour,' I said, 'we must have the best view possible.' I briefed both engine crews on the likely scenario. The crews were aware of the basic idea, but now they were told the likely location was Winsford Junction. They should be extra vigilant and be prepared to stop as quickly as possible should something happen that might risk the lives of those on the track or on the train.

The crew had no questions and the Scotsman's driver and fireman returned to their locomotive. The home signal was raised to caution; the guard blew his whistle, waved his green flag and boarded the last coach.

Our train moved off slowly at first until it crossed onto the down fast line, where it gained speed rapidly. We were late leaving Crewe and both engines would have to work hard to make up time before we reached Winsford Junction, about sixteen minutes away.

The target time was 12:29 and it was now 12:15 p.m.

57

'TIME TO GO,' SAID BOY. HE'D LEFT IT AS LONG AS HE DARED.

'I want to go to the toilet,' said Ruth.

'You'll have to wait. We have a train to catch.'

'She can't wait,' said the woman. 'Let her out, she'll only be a minute.'

Boyton looked at his watch; twelve-ten. He still had eighteen minutes.

'Okay, but you go with her. And no funny business, or else.'

Boyton waited. They hadn't returned after two or three minutes. He got out of the car to see where they were. He saw movement behind the bushes and hoped they would be back soon. He double-checked in the back of the car that he had the green string and leather straps. They were essential to tie them to the track. He wanted to blow the horn to get them moving, but feared someone might notice them. So far his plan was going well, but now time was slipping away.

He knew Crosier would be on the footplate of the King. He wanted to make sure he had time to select a place where he'd have a good view of his daughter tied to the line next to Sylt — she wouldn't be a problem for much longer. His dream to have an engine chop off a woman's head was about to come true. Crosier's kid would be a bonus, even though he wasn't being paid for their deaths.

She appeared with the girl and came towards the car.

He grabbed them and bundled the girl into the back, then hit Sylt hard in her stomach.

She doubled in pain.

Boyton forced her into the car.

Ruth went white with fear, cowering on the back seat.

Boyton started the engine and they set off to Winsford Junction with Sylt moaning in pain.

He followed the lane to where it joined Wharton Road. He stopped and looked to see if there were any police about. He saw none and drove towards the railway. As he came over the hump-back bridge he was confronted by a police road block.

He laughed out loud. 'They're useless. They think I'm going straight on, but I was turning right anyway. Idiots,' and he swung the car sharp right onto another lane that the police had deliberately not blocked. Now, unknown to Boyton he was trapped.

Two police officers scrambled back into their car and set off with its bell ringing loudly. They radioed to the other cars which began to close in on the junction.

The dirt lane was dry and Boyton's three-wheeler sent up clouds of dust. The police were gaining on him and maybe they could nudge them off the lane. But as the driver was about to try, Ruth sat up in the back seat and looked back at them. They backed off, not wanting the girl to be hurt if the car left the road.

Boyton fumbled about under the steering wheel and pulled out the gun.

'Jesus, Boy, don't use that thing on—'

'Shut it, Syph. I've got to try and keep them back.'

The lane dipped down onto a level crossing. He turned right and stopped dead. He wound the window down and took aim at the police car's windscreen, trying to hit the driver.

Sylt leaned across Boyton to try and get the gun from him. In their struggle, Boyton pulled the trigger.

The sound inside the car was deafening. The police car's windscreen shattered. The policeman in the passenger seat slumped forward as his mate skidded to a stop and picked up the radio-phone.

'For fuck sake, Syph, see what you've done, you stupid bitch. You've made me hit a copper.' He gunned the engine.

The Reliant took off at speed along the narrow dirt track beside the single track line leading to the junction with the main line.

The broad Wolsey police car followed slowly but with difficultly; its offside wheels kept hitting the sleepers. The driver tried hard to keep the car straight. Suddenly he lost his grip on the steering wheel as it spun fast to the right when they hit yet another sleeper.

The car mounted the track and came to a halt across the railway line, its rear wheels spinning in free air.

The driver got out and tried to push the heavy police car back onto the track. It was jammed across the rails. He'd have to pursue on foot, leaving his mate in the car to call the ambulance that was waiting nearby.

Boyton was losing them. But now that the police were close by, he couldn't carry out his plan to tie his passengers to the line in the path of the express. His bold plan was unravelling fast. He must escape.

He continued alongside the line as it curved left to run parallel with the main line. The little car bumped and jolted along the narrow track. The further they went, the more difficult it became. The car lurched to a halt: the centre wheel stuck in a large pothole.

'Get out and push,' Boyton screamed at Sylt.

The woman got out leaving the passenger door open. She went round to the back of the car and saw Ruth looking back at her. She pointed to her and the open passenger door trying to get the child to make a dash for it.

The kid was bright and took her chance to escape, scrambling out before Boyton realised what was happening.

Sylt pushed as hard as she could, the pain in her stomach unbearable. She tried again, scared she might be caught and arrested. She didn't want to spend ten years in prison.

The car lurched forward and stopped.

Boyton got out ready to chase after Ruth who had run up onto a grassy bank and was looking back down at them. He aimed the gun at the child and shouted for her to come back.

Sylt tried to grab the gun from Boyton. He turned and smashed it into her teeth.

'Let her go, she's no use to us now,' Sylt moaned, searching her mouth for broken teeth.

They heard the police whistles close behind.

He forced Sylt back in the car, climbed in and floored the accelerator. The car moved off at speed.

They were approaching another much wider level crossing. Boyton had to decide whether to turn left onto Deakin's Road then follow the lanes, or to go right over the main line railway.

The crossing-gates were open. A large truck had just crossed, and had stopped on the far side. Its driver was getting out of the cab, ready to shut the gates.

Boyton got closer to the crossing, saw a second police car approaching from the left.

He had no choice. Could he make it across before the truck driver closed the gate?

He had to try.

Try to cross the main line.

58

12:25 p.m.

THE EXPRESS WAS MAKING GOOD TIME AND WOULD ONLY BE A FEW seconds late when we reached Winsford Junction. I was looking out on the right. Hunt, on the left side of the footplate, was standing behind the driver as we passed through Winsford Station at seventy miles per hour.

The next signal was at caution indicating we may soon have to stop. Something ahead was about to slow us down: maybe Boyton.

Although the driver did not apply the brakes, he reduced steam pressure. 'About half a-minute now to the junction,' he shouted, over the noise of the engine.

I nodded, then took a call on the radiophone. Hunt saw my face turn white. 'Boyton has just shot a police officer.'

'Any sign of Ruth?'

'She's in the car, with Boyton.'

We were both stunned by this news, and hadn't expected Boyton to use the gun. None of the officers were carrying firearms.

The train rattled on and I gripped the handrail to lean out further for a better view as the line began to curve left and under the new bridge that carried Wharton Road over the electrified railway. With the train slowing to sixty miles an hour, we were under the bridge with smoke billowing around us, obscuring our view.

Hunt rubbed his eyes attempting to remove coal smuts from them. Everyone's faces were already becoming black.

The smoke cleared, the line straightened.

'It should have been here, but there's nothing,' I shouted. 'Do you see anything on your side?'

Hunt shook his head and looked out again.

'There, at the crossing,' shouted the driver pointing ahead.

At first I could only see the glistening-silver surface of four parallel rails coming to a single point in the distance — but there was something, a movement.

A small red car was bumping alongside the line, about five hundred yards ahead, and would soon be obscured from my view by the locomotive as it stretched out in front.

I crossed over to where Hunt was standing.

The car was starting to turn right.

It was going to cross in front of us!

I shouted for the driver to stop as fast as possible.

He applied brakes.

The fireman held the whistle wide-open.

Boyton stopped the car across our track.

There was no way the heavy train would stop before it reached the car. It was only three hundred yards away now: five or six seconds at the most.

Was Boyton considering his chances of getting across, or ending his life along with whoever else was in the tiny car?

There was another train too, a long heavy goods appeared, moving slowly towards us, gaining speed as it left the siding just beyond the signal box.

I moved back to the right side just as the car began to move slowly off our track. Then it stopped again, between the north and southbound lines. If Boyton stayed put, at least we wouldn't crush the car.

I could see a stationary truck, its driver pulling the crossing's gate back open so Boyton could escape. The signalman seemed to be waving at the driver to close the gate. The driver either didn't hear him, or chose to ignore him.

We were a hundred yards from the crossing.

Harrowing

As if leaving it until the last possible second, Boyton lurched the car forward over the wooden sleepers forming the roadway between the rails.

He misjudged and stalled.

There was no time to start the engine.

The oncoming goods train clipped the front of the lightweight car, ripping the body from its wooden chassis and spinning it towards our track.

Our engine passed over the crossing without hitting it.

I looked down from the cab to see bodies inside the car flung out as the vehicle shattered and the remnants of the car were crushed under the wheels of both trains as their drivers fought to bring them to a standstill.

The image of the occupants of the car being slung out like dolls from a child's toy box was to haunt me for years to come.

59

BEFORE THE EXPRESS CAME TO A STANDSTILL, I'D CLAMBERED down the steps and was hanging on until I could jump down without breaking any limbs.

The brakes of both trains were squealing. Steam was hissing from the safety valves above the express' huge engines. The noise was almost deafening.

The signalman furiously swung levers to set all the signals to danger.

I jumped down, closely followed by Hunt, before the train had stopped completely. As I stood collecting myself, everything fell silent.

For a split second, it seemed the world was standing still. I was aware of the giant apple-green wheels of the Flying Scotsman towering above me and the goods train almost at a halt on the other line. When Hunt slapped me on my back, it felt like someone had turned the sound back on.

The goods train was still squealing, its trucks banging to a halt.

Officers were leaning out of the carriage windows. Then they were opening doors and jumping down onto the track.

I started to walk towards the wreckage some hundred yards back down the line. The image of the bodies so violently ejected from the car kept replaying in my mind and I froze where I stood. I could not go on. I didn't want to find Ruth crushed below one of the trains.

Hunt careered past me, becoming smaller by the second.

The goods train had stopped and the steam from the expresses had shut off. For a moment, it was silent.

The loose-coupled goods wagons started to recoil from the engine, as the pressure built up in their buffers and pushed the wagons apart. They sounded like a giant's steel-domino set slowly crashing over. At last they stopped.

It was deadly quiet.

I was standing by the first carriage when I thought I heard Alice's voice — I must be dreaming.

'Oliver.' She was screaming at me, from above. 'Get me down from here.'

I looked up, astonished she was actually here and standing by an open carriage door. I came to my senses and helped her jump onto the narrow path between the tracks.

We ran towards the wreckage, Alice screaming for Ruth at the top of her voice.

Claire and Davidson were already ahead of us.

Dobbs and Smith were probably searching on the other side of the express.

When we reached some of the wreckage Hunt had found Boyton unconscious. An officer was attempting to staunch the flow of blood from Boyton's severed wrist, by tying the sleeve of his tunic around his upper-arm.

Sylt was found almost immediately, separated from us by thirty yards or so. Hunt and Alice ran to her.

'That's all I can do for him now, sir,' the officer said, and went off in his shirt sleeves to join the search leaving me alone, face to face, with the bastard who had kidnapped my daughter.

I released the officer's tunic a little so that Boyton's wrist started to bleed again. It was his turn to suffer.

He kept drifting in and out of consciousness. I grabbed him by his jacket, forcing him to sit, then slapped his face as hard as I could trying to bring him round and hoping it hurt like hell. This evil creature was going to tell me where Ruth was if it was the last thing he did.

He looked at me, first with one eye then the other.

'Where is she? What have you done to her?'

He moved his right arm towards my face, then looked at it with his wandering eye, surprised to see his hand was missing. All the time, his other eye watched me.

I took a pen from my pocket and jabbed it in the stump of his wrist. 'Now you know how Edward Bright must have felt, except you chopped off both his hands. Shall I chop off your left hand too, so you can really feel his pain?' I worked the pen once again, then stabbed the bloody mess so hard with it that only an inch protruded.

He just sneered at me, not seeming to feel the pain at all.

'Where is my Ruth, you evil piece of shit?'

The sneer turned to a grin.

Even in his condition, he probably realised I didn't have an axe at hand. I heaved him up and propped him against the wheel of a truck, then hit him hard in his guts.

This pain he felt, and I enjoyed watching it develop across his hideous face. My hands found his sweaty throat, my thumbs pressing hard onto the windpipe.

Still the grin remained. He wasn't going to tell me a thing; he'd sunk as deep as he could go and I was going to squeeze the life out of him — and I didn't give a damn.

The next thing I knew, I was on my back and staring up at Hunt's silhouette set against bright-blue sky.

'For God sake. That's not going to tell us anything is it, Oliver?'

'He has to die. He's killed innocent people and Ruth.'

'You don't know that Ruth is dead.'

Boyton began to shake but only for a few seconds before slumping forward.

Hunt crouched to feel the pulse in his neck, then shook his head before looking hard at me. 'I don't think what you did actually killed him. I wouldn't have blamed you if you had. He's lost a terrific amount of blood,' he continued and eased my pen from Boyton's wound. He tossed it into one of the freight trucks and helped me to my feet. 'Come on, Sylt is trying to tell Cardin something. She's with her now.'

Sylt was on her side under a carriage; her arm pinned down by its wheel, though not completely severed. Her face, like Boyton's, had taken a battering. She was still alive, just.

Cardin was kneeling over her in the confined space, her ear close to Sylt's mouth, trying to hear what she was saying.

She repeated as Sylt spoke: "'I tried to ... tried to free ... tried to . . ." I think she said.'

An officer was stopping the flow of blood where her arm had been trapped by a wheel, by tying some green string he'd found around her elbow. Sylt stopped breathing; he stopped trying.

Alice was under the carriage before I could stop her. 'Where is my daughter?' she moaned and started to pound her fists on Sylt's chest.

'She's dead,' said Claire. 'She can't tell us anything. Come on, Alice, let's crawl out and look for Ruth.'

Hunt, on his hands and knees, was looking under the carriages near the wrecked car for any sign of Ruth.

We ran to him.

'She's not here. Maybe they didn't bring her. I did find this, though,' he said, in my ear as he shielded Alice from his discovery.

Boyton's right hand, still holding the revolver, lay just inside the rails. It would have it bagged later and sent to ballistics. Maybe they could trace where the gun had come from. I couldn't believe I was still considering procedures.

A young officer arrived breathless, 'She's nowhere to be seen, sir.'

'Keep looking, man,' said Hunt, to get rid of him, 'she has to be.'

I held Alice tight. Her body shook as she sobbed, expecting the worst news to come at any moment.

Suddenly she pushed me away. 'You and your bloody trains. I hope you are happy now?'

The crews from the three engines had joined in the search. Men were crawling under the length of the two trains to examine every scrap of the wreckage they could find. There was surprisingly little. Apart from the car's red broken body, shattered windows and wooden chassis, there were parts of its engine, wires, twisted wheels and deformed seats, some leather straps and a bundle of green string. Boyton had obviously intended to put the green string to some last gruesome act of killing. But with Boyton and Sylt both dead, any clues as to Ruth's whereabouts were gone with them.

Hunt crawled out from under a carriage. He was looking at Alice and me, but he didn't have to speak.

'Ruuuuth,' screamed Alice, then dropped to her knees, sobbing.

I looked towards the two engines of the express. I wanted to be as far away from them as possible. Yet I knew that until Ruth had been found, it would be impossible.

The signalman was leaning from his signal box, blowing a whistle and waving a red flag, trying to attract someone's attention. He started shouting something which neither I nor Alice could hear. Then he pointed above the express with the flag.

I ducked low, to look under the carriages, and shouted for Alice to come.

On the other side of the sidings, we could see a policeman's head slowly rising above the top of a low embankment.

Alice screamed.

The policeman held Ruth in his arms.

60

WE WERE AT HOME, THE DAY AFTER RUTH'S RESCUE, WHEN NEWALL rang. The look I got from Alice, when she heard the telephone ringing, said it all. She stomped out of the house, slamming the back-door behind her.

I felt very confused about Alice. We'd had an early night last night and had actually made love for the first time in years which gave me some hope she might, at last, begin to settle down here. Gardiner had his usual turn of phrase for situations like this, when his wife was in an unpredictable mode: "I don't know whether I'm having a shit or 'n 'aircut." I knew what he meant.

After a few minutes with Newall, I went into the garden. Alice was just standing in the middle of the lawn.

I guessed what was going through her mind. 'It's okay love,' I said. 'That was the twit Newall, telling me to take two weeks off and for us to take a holiday somewhere.' At least it wasn't Claire who'd called.

She smiled, 'I'm sorry for stomping out like that. I just thought—'

'Hey, it's all right. He said we could go first-class, as if he was really giving us something. I always go first anyway,' which reminded me of Claire's bad mood after Lorna had put her in her place.

'Management are very skilled at looking like they are considering their staff's welfare,' Alice said. 'I expect they go on charisma courses, to develop their charm.'

We laughed, such a relief.

It wasn't long after she said she wanted — no demanded —

for us to stay with her parents in York. That cut short my relief. I remembered Gardiner's expression again and consoled myself that a holiday by the seaside wouldn't be much fun anyway at this time of year.

The first week in York was all right. I caught up with my father, who passed me a letter with an American stamp on its envelope; it had to be from David. It contained the usual pleasantries, and finished with a suggestion that I could join him in New York in a couple of months time. He even said he'd buy my air ticket, as my pay was obviously too low for such a joy ride.

To make matters worse, Alice hadn't taken well to David's invitation for me to go to America. She wasn't invited, probably because my brother didn't care for her much, rather than the cost of us both going.

Having seen all our old friends, I was often bored. My mind kept drifting back to work. Despite much team back-slapping and congratulations from the top-brass — who thought the case had reached a successful conclusion — I knew the Boyton-Sylt case should not be closed: there was more to it than my superiors were prepared to believe.

On the pretext of going for a walk one afternoon, I decided to visit my old colleagues. The BTP office at the station was only half a mile away. Nobody wanted to come with me — which, unlike the weather, was fine — and it would allow me to make some free calls.

'I've been tidying up the loose ends on the Boyton case, as you requested,' said Claire, once our small-talk was out of the way.

'You sound a little unsure. What's the problem?'

'Oliver, I've been thinking about the motive for the killings. Everyone thought, it was jealousy, right? We thought, as did Hunt, that—'

'I agree, Claire, it isn't enough. There's something else, a connection somewhere. It doesn't sit right.'

'And now both killers are dead, so we can't ask them.' She was as frustrated: a noise like files being slapped hard onto her desk made me hold the receiver away from my ear.

'And so, too, is Archie bloody Shaw,' I said, once I felt the coast was clear.

'A type of justice was done,' she said, 'but not what we worked for. They should have gone to trial, and then, perhaps, we'd know more about them. Maybe even understand them.'

'And then hang them.'

'A suitable end, I think, don't you?'

'I certainly do. I'd have happily pulled the lever myself if anything had happened to Ruth. But that pleasure is no longer an option. If they'd got away, would they still be out there planning another killing?'

'So what are we going to do about it?'

'It's a long shot, I know, but I'm going to call Nancy, see if she can throw any light on it.'

'Hello,' said a Scottish female voice. It wasn't Nancy's. 'Can I help you?'

'Is Nancy available?'

'I'm afraid not, who's calling please?'

'This is DI Crosier.' There was no reaction. I wondered if it took a while for speech to go uphill to Scotland. After a short wait, I added, 'from the Railway Police. I was hoping to talk to her.'

'She's not here, Mr Crosier.'

'Do you know where I might find her?'

'She's been staying with a friend since Archie died. You knew Archie had died, didn't you?'

'Yes. I was sorry to hear about that, I liked him, though I only met him a couple of times. When will Nancy be back?'

'The funeral is Wednesday, should you be thinking of attending. She may come back here afterwards. She may not. We'll have to wait and see.'

'What time is the funeral Mrs ... sorry, I didn't catch your name?' I hoped I wasn't going to have to go through the same rigmarole I'd had before trying to extract Nancy's name.

'Oh, it's okay. I'm Vera. I live across the way, and keep an eye on the place if they're, sorry, if she's away. The funeral is at eleven o'clock.'

That made up my mind. I could travel up via Edinburgh, stay the night in Glasgow and be in plenty of time for the funeral next day. I called Claire again.

'I'm going to the funeral. Travelling up tomorrow.'

'I'd be happy to come with you. I'd like to see Nancy, as well.'

'Maybe another time, Claire. We can't both be away for two days. People will talk.'

I heard the files slammed down again and waited for her verbal response.

'And what are you going to tell Alice, Oliver?'

It was a good question, though I got the feeling Claire didn't require an answer.

The response I'd get from Alice, when I did tell her, would be anything but good.

61

TODAY, WAS THE DAY OF ARCHIE SHAW'S FUNERAL. FUNERALS were bad enough at the best of times, but in early December, with grey skies to match our moods, I was glad it wasn't someone close to me.

I had spent the night in the Railway Hotel on Glasgow Central station. I didn't fancy another sleeping-car experience so I travelled to Scotland in relative comfort yesterday morning which gave me time to hire a dark suit.

I got a taxi take me over to the bungalow which Archie shared with his sister.

∗∗∗

'The cortege will leave in about fifteen minutes,' said Vera, as she invited me in. Within seconds, I was standing with a cup of tea in one hand and one of Archie's ginger biscuits in the other. She left me alone, so I took another look Nancy's "rogues".

I didn't see anything of relevance until my eyes wandered up to the shelf above. From there several of her family gazed down on the mourners, one group framed in a large oval bronze frame.

Looking back at me were Archie with two men and a woman, each in their thirties, plus two young girls.

I picked the frame up for a closer look and was drawn to the two girls. They looked very alike. There was something familiar about them as if I'd seen them before. I couldn't put my finger on it.

I wished Claire had come with me— after all, women in my experience are always much better at analysing faces.

I was about to ask a woman, standing nearby, if she knew

who they were when Vera announced that the hearse had arrived. 'If anyone requires transport would they please use one of the two taxis behind the hearse.'

I filed out with the rest of the mourners, the well-heeled of whom rushed off to their own cars. The first taxi was full with people who obviously knew each other and I found I was the only passenger in the second cab; the same cab and driver which had taken Claire and me to Paisley police station a few weeks ago.

'I did'nae expect to see you again so soon,' the driver said.

'Nor me, you.'

'It's a sad do. Poor old Archie. Was he of any use to you when you were here last?'

I almost told the driver to mind his own business, but then thought better of it. Maybe I could pick up some information about Archie. 'No, he wasn't, not really. I'm afraid I don't go in for all this fortune telling mumbo-jumbo.'

'Me neither.'

'Had you known him long?'

'Let me see noo. I'd say aboot five years. He was always a bit of a funny old stick. His wife died years ago. Long before I knew him. So then, Nancy came to stay. He improved after that, for a while at any rate.'

**

The church nestled precariously on the hillside above the main road to Paisley, some hundred feet below, and the very steep hill from Archie's place.

The driver struggled to find a space to park.

'It might have been better if I'd walked. Plainly, a lot of people had known Archie.'

'Aye, they did that right enough.'

'Look, are you going to wait until after the service? I'd like a lift back to his place afterwards. I don't like the look of this hill.'

'I'll not be waiting here, man. I'm going in to pay my respects, too.' He smiled at me through the rear view mirror.

When he got out I could see he was in black, but not his usual chauffeur's uniform. We followed the mourners in silence, bringing up the rear, then took a pew at the back of the church.

Forty minutes later the mourners filed out into the churchyard for the committal. It was a chance for me to examine the faces of those passing by. God, I wished I brought Claire along. Some definitely resembled Archie, but how?

We were walking back to the taxi, when our attention was drawn to a heated conversation behind us. I stopped and turned to see what was going on.

A short, shabbily dressed man with long grey hair was shouting and pointing at Nancy, as she was getting into the funeral car.

'What on earth's going on?' said the cabby.

'Just hang on a moment, I'm going to see if Nancy is all right.'

The driver decided to tag along. We hurried towards the argument.

Several mourners had stopped to watch it, some it seemed, were preparing to put a stop to it.

I saw Nancy pass an envelope to the man, who immediately quietened down. Was it cash?

He glanced towards me and, seeing my approach, stuffed whatever Nancy had given him into a pocket of his raincoat. He dashed down the steep hill towards the junction of four roads.

I followed and, breaking into a run, wondered how I might safely stop at the bottom.

Facing me, on Preston Road, was a pale-blue Morris Traveller; the driver revving its engine hard.

Our quarry waved and the car moved closer to the junction. He reached the car, rushed around the front and was climbing into the passenger seat. His door closed as the car sped away, narrowly missing me and a coal truck on the main road.

I made a mental note of its number plate, then crossed back

over the road intending to check on Nancy, but her car, too, was speeding away up the hill.

The cabby joined me. Both getting our breath back, he said, 'I'm not as fit as I used to be. Did you recognise him?'

'No,' I said, wondering if this was a family argument I should keep my nose out of. 'Did you?'

'No, but I've seen the car, right enough, outside Nancy's place.'

'Can you remember when?'

'Not exactly. A few times over the year.'

'You said something earlier, on the way down here, that Archie was all right for a time, after his sister arrived. What did you mean?'

'Ocht, I can tell you'll make a good copper one day. Do you remember everything people say?'

'That's one of the things they pay me to do. Go on.'

He sat on a low wall. 'Well ... I guess we'd all take a turn for the worst if we'd lost three of our close family.'

I tried not to show my excitement. 'What do you mean, exactly?'

'It was aboot ten years ago ... '53, I think, sometime around then. Before the Coronation anyway. I'd taken Archie, his son and his granddaughter to Central.' He waggled a finger towards Glasgow. He could see I hadn't cottoned-on. 'To catch a train, man! To London. Anyway, a week or so later, I gets a call from Nancy asking if I'd pick her up and take her to Central Station, too.'

'And?'

'All she said was, Archie didn't feel well, and she was going to London so she could travel back with him to look after him.'

'But weren't his son and granddaughter coming back with him. What about his son? Did he have a wife?'

'Died in childbirth, poor lass. Like I said, he lost them all.'

'They were all killed?'

The cabby nodded.

'Terrible it was, caught in that train crash near London.'

'That wasn't 1953. You mean 1952, don't you?'

'Aye man, I do. Harrowing it must have been for them.'

'Where's the nearest telephone box?'

'Claire, it's me. We were right; There's definitely a link. I'm not sure what, exactly, but it's to do with Archie's family.'

'So he wasn't clairvoyant after all!'

'Probably not, but we don't know for sure. If my hunch is right, it's irrelevant anyway. I need you to pull the Government Inspectors' report. It was published just after Elizabeth's Coronation. If we don't have it, Mullard will. Check through it for any familiar names.'

'Okay, Oliver I'll see what I can dig up for when you're back. Will that be tomorrow?'

'Maybe. Depends upon what I can get out of Nancy later. She may not be in a talkative mood today. I may have to come back and see her tomorrow.'

'So, that would have been two nights in the Central hotel. Did they give you a good room?'

'They only had one available.'

'A double I suppose?'

'Yes, it is actually.' I heard her sighing wistfully at the other end of the line and I cut the call before it became too heavy.

***

Back in Archie's front room, I mingled with the others Nancy had asked to come back for 'a wee-dram'. The scotch was very good. I must ask her what it was next time she came round.

I went over to look at the photographs again. I could see some people who were at the funeral; all much older now than when the pictures were taken.

The other unattached male, who I'd seen arrive before we'd set off to the church, came over to me. 'How do you do, sir? I'm an old friend of Archie's, William Morris.'

'Hello, pleased to meet you, Mr Morris.'

'Your accent doesn't sound Scottish.'

'I'm English. Oliver Crosier,' I said, holding out my hand. 'Archie was helping my enquiries into a case I'm working on. I thought I'd come to see how Nancy was making out.'

'Oh, you're a bobby, eh?'

'I'm afraid so.'

'She's taken his going very badly. For some reason she thinks it's her fault; Archie having a heart attack.'

'Really, I can't see why. She seemed to keep a good-eye on him, as far as I could tell, but I only met her once before.'

'Yes, she was a good sister. A professional one, too, before she retired.'

'Yes, I'd learnt that about that half-an-hour ago, he went downhill pretty badly after the rail crash. Understandable.'

'Poor bugger. I mean that in the nicest way, sorry. He could be a bit deceitful right enough.'

I lifted an eyebrow.

'I don't mean to talk out of place,' I could smell the whiskey, working on him, as he leaned closer, 'but when I was in the army with him, he was always in trouble and blaming others for it. Loved to stir things up, if you know what I mean?'

'Well, I am surprised,' I said. But I wasn't a bit surprised at all. The longer I stayed up here, the more I learnt about Archie. The latest snippet, being he might not have always been sweetness and light.

'Bit of a bugger, that kerfuffle outside the church.'

'Yes it was. Do you have any idea what it was about?' I said.

'Haven't a clue, old boy. Funerals are strange events. You never know who, or what, turns up at funerals.'

I'd heard that phrase before somewhere.

Mr Morris turned away in search of some more whiskey.

I was thinking of doing the same, but was halted by an odour which had crept up behind me; one I'd first detected in my office. Strange how smells can instantly take one back.

'Hello, Mr Crosier.'

Her voice confirmed its owner. I turned round to look at Lorna.

'Lorna? Sorry, I didn't notice you here before we all left for the church. I only just arrived in time myself.'

'I wasn't here. I travelled with the undertaker from his office. Anyway, decent of you to come,' she said.

I looked her up and down. 'But what are you doing here?

'Still asking questions I see. Why shouldn't I be here? Archie was my father.'

'Your father? But—'

'You didn't know? Come on, Inspector. You can do better than that.'

I looked at her, the question forming in my mind. 'But, you said your name was Todd-Dunscombe.'

'And so it is. It's my married name.'

'But you let us call you Miss.'

'I didn't think it relevant at the time, Inspector. More pressing things on my mind. Don't be too annoyed with me.'

I looked at her again, waiting to see if she had any other surprises to reveal.

'Yes, I know, Inspector. Who'd want to marry a woman who looked like she was set to be a spinster for the rest of her days? Look here.' She turned to the rogues' gallery, 'This is how I looked before you and I met. Before the crash. It was taken in the summer of 'fifty-two at my wedding.'

I held the photograph and picked her out. That's why the people in the picture looked familiar. 'So, this woman is Mary?'

Now it was her turn to be surprised. 'Yes, it is. These are—'

'Robert with his daughter Emily, and an older girl; Mary's daughter—'

'Phyliss Sylt,' she spat.

'Yes, it's her all right.' I thought I'd said that to myself, but Lorna must have heard me. Did she know that Sylt was dead? If she did, she'd have been certain to say.

'How are your nightmares these days?' I said, playing for

time. 'Is it wise for you to be looking at these?'

She seemed to be probing my mind about something but answered, smiling. 'Thank you for your concern, Inspector. They're much better since . . .' she said, not meeting my eyes and pulling me away from the photographs.

'Since?'

'The pictures aren't so bad now,' she said, refusing to answer my prompt, 'but mist can still occasionally trigger them.'

'Did you ever find any professional help?'

'No. I'm testing time, seeing if it's the healer that everyone says.'

I was about to ask her again, when determined to change the subject, she said, 'What did you mean earlier, about Phyliss, Inspector?'

'I err I'd seen her before. I saw her at Vincent Sylt's funeral.'

'You were there!'

'Who was?' said Nancy, who came to stand next to Lorna.

'Mr Crosier was just saying how he'd been at Vincent's funeral. Why didn't you tell me when we first met?'

Those nearby overheard Lorna's courtroom-voice starting to boom and they turned to look at us.

'Do you two know each other?' said Nancy.

Lorna and I, it seemed, were simultaneously deciding if we should tell her, but neither of us spoke.

To my relief Nancy said, 'It's very nice of you to come, Mr Crosier. Did you not bring that nice young woman with you?'

Lorna looked at her, then me again her legal mind trying to piece things together.

'No, I'm afraid not,' I said, to avoid talking about the funeral in case I revealed something that was best kept quiet — for the time being anyway. 'We can't both be away for long periods together. Short staffed,' I said, before she made up her own explanation.

'Oh that is a pity,' she said, raising a hand to stifle a yawn.

'Nancy, I was wondering if I might, at some point, ask you a few more questions about the cases I'm working on? I know now is not a good time. If it's more convenient for you, could I come back in the morning.'

'Yes, come back in the morning, Inspector. I'll ... I'll be here.'

'I have one question you may be able to answer now.

'I'll help if I can,' she said, looking a little flustered.

'I heard you were a nurse in Edinburgh and wondered if you ever met a Mrs Curzon? She died in 1953 as a result of a car accident.'

Nancy glanced at Lorna who, for once, looked flustered and took a drag from one of her stinking miniatures before deciding it was safer to talk to Mr Morris.

'I knew you'd be back, sooner or later,' said Nancy, flopping onto the arm of the settee before passing out backwards. Her black, thick-stockinged legs stuck up across its arm — not at all ladylike.

62

THE NEXT MORNING, I WOKE WITH A START AT THE SOUND OF THE telephone jangling on the desk over the other side of the bedroom. It was eight-twenty. I shot across the room to reach it before the caller hung up.

'This is your wakeup call, DI Crosier. Rise and shine.'

'Claire, is that you?'

'How are you today, Oliver? You sound like you've had a good night on Sauchiehall Hall street.'

'A bit ... a bit sleepy if you must know. I didn't get out on the town and I didn't get off too well last night; had a bad dream about funerals.'

'Um, still sorry you didn't bring me along?'

'Yes I am, but not for the reason you're thinking. I could have done with you to recognise a few faces for me, but I got them worked out in the end.'

'Is that all?'

'Yes. Now what did you really call about.'

'Are you sitting down?'

'Claire!'

'Okay, okay. I've been thinking. The post mortem on Bright's body reckoned he could have been dead for anything up to a month before he was found. The Harrow accident took place on October the 8th 1952. I think Alex Bright was murdered, not just on any old day but, ten years to the day!'

'Coincidence.'

'Oh come on, Oliver. Ten years, to the day! This was planned. And I bet you, it was—'

'Archie bloody Shaw.'

'Yes. You're going to have to go and see that nice Nancy again.'

'Already booked the appointment, so long as she's up to it. She passed out yesterday while she was talking to me and Lorna.'

'Lorna?'

'Yes, turns out she's Archie's daughter.'

'His daughter?'

'Claire, stop playing parrots and listen. Nancy said she knew I'd be back, then flaked out.'

'She knows something, Oliver. Believe me. Believe my woman's intuition.'

I felt much better after my bath, and now I was in need of a good breakfast to see me through what might turn out to be a difficult day.

I took it in the dining room and was browsing through today's issue of *The Scotsman*, when I stumbled across Archie Shaw's obituary — very quick off the mark.

It was quite a long article and even had a picture of him from around 1935. It went on to describe his Great War career and the tragedy that befell him in 1952. Also listed were names of some of the close relatives and mourners, including one Lance Sylt.

How right Mr Morris had been. I realised where I'd heard his statement before, except it wasn't just at any old funeral: it was at a Lance's brother's. "You'd be surprised what turns up at mob-funerals, and who!" Hunt had said, over ten-years ago.

My mind started racing. Lorna turning up yesterday had unwittingly unlocked the case for me. I gulped down the rest of the poached haddock as quickly as possible — criminal really.

Lance Sylt ... was it just coincidence that he had turned up yesterday? Albeit distantly, he was a relative of Archie's. Lorna had confirmed that when we first met. I decided to call Claire.

'Claire, pin you ears back. I think I've got something.'

'Oliver, I wasn't expecting to hear from you just yet.'

'I saw Shaw's obit' this morning in the paper. Someone called Lance Sylt attended.' I heard Claire gasp. 'There's the possibility he's directly connected to Archie Shaw and the murders. And Lorna is Archie's daughter.' I paused, letting the jigsaw pieces in Claire's mind click into place. 'Claire, you still there?'

'Yes I am.'

'And he's got record.'

'What are you talking about?'

'Listen, he was in my dream last night.' I heard Claire sighing down the line. 'But, Claire, it wasn't a dream at all.'

'Oliver you're losing me again.'

'I must have been remembering where I'd seen him before.'

'Lance?'

'Yes. I saw him at the funeral a week before the Harrow crash. I told you about it after Lorna left us, remember. I was finishing a training attachment with The Yard. I saw him at his brother's funeral: Vincent Sylt's funeral. And I reckon it was him who was threatening Nancy yesterday.'

'Yesterday?'

'I'm sure it was him. After the service he was ranting at Nancy until she passed him an envelope. He created quite a scene and I went to help. He saw me, ran and was picked up by a mate who drove him off at speed.'

'It still doesn't link the murders to the funerals though, does it?'

'No, not yet. It might do after I've seen Nancy later this morning. She'll probably collapse again when I ask her about Lance. I'm going round at eleven. I'll stay on this number until ten-thirty in case you have any news.'

I looked at my wristwatch — still well over an hour to wait.

I sat in the back of a very old and tatty taxi, on my way to see Nancy, mulling over things. No calls from Claire — she'd obviously not found anything fresh — though she should have a copy of the crash report from Mullard's office later this morning.

As the cabby turned into Kilbarchan Road where Nancy lived, an ambulance, its bell clanging impatiently, careered round the junction, causing the taxi to swerve and mount the pavement.

My heart sank: premonition or not, I knew Nancy was in it and on her way to hospital.

The taxi pulled up outside her bungalow. I asked the driver to wait. The helpful neighbour was just about to leave as I dashed up the gravel drive.

'Oh, Mr Crosier, I'm afraid Nancy is ill. She just been taken in the ambulance.'

'Taken ill?'

'Yes, proper poorly she is.'

'How? In what way poorly?'

'I came across to see her about a half-an-hour ago. She was lying unconscious on the settee. The ambulance men seemed to think she might have had a heart attack. I suppose the stress of yesterday was a bit too much for her.'

I was briefly at a loss again, then started to slap the back of my neck.

Vera looked at me, curious.

'Can I take a look inside? I was coming to see her and it's possible—'

Vera held up her hand. 'Nancy called me about nine o'clock this morning. She said you were coming, but that she had to go to the post office first. If she wasn't back, I was to let you in.'

I stopped, having opened the door to the lounge, and scanned the room looking for clues as to what might have happened to Nancy. I went across to the shelves of photographs and studied the family group again. Was one of them Lance Sylt? Was he really the man I saw at Vincent Sylt's funeral? It looked like it. I heard Vera enter the room.

'I expect you might like a cup of tea, so I brought one

through for you.'

Had I really been studying the photographs that long? 'That's very kind of you. Thank you, Vera,' I said, taking the tea from her, but there was really no time to enjoy it.

'Oh, and I found this in the kitchen for you.'

I looked at the envelope bearing my name, and sat down on the settee upon which Nancy had collapsed the day before.

'Strange, why has she left me a note? She knew I was coming.'

'Ocht, that's typical of Nancy, organised to the end.'

We stared at each other. Vera had her hand over her mouth. We were both thinking the same thing.

I ripped the envelope open and found inside it a single small sheet of pale-blue Basildon Bond paper, with equally small neat writing.

Dear Mr Crosier,

I'm sorry I wasn't there to explain what's happened and why, but I decided that I'd had enough and now that dear Archie has left me I couldn't face the music alone. That nice young policewoman Claire will be able to tell you all about it tomorrow, when you get back to Crewe.

Yours sincerely,

Nancy Shaw

'She's tried to commit suicide! Which hospital would she have been taken to?'

'The ambulance men said Glasgow Royal Infirmary.' I dashed from the lounge to the bathroom, then into her bedroom, finding nothing to indicate what she'd taken. 'Vera, go back into the kitchen and see if there are any drugs about, pain-killers, sleeping pills, whatever. I'll check the dustbin for pill bottles.'

'You might well be wasting your time there. They were emptied over an hour ago.'

'Damn,' I said. A minute later I was back. 'Nothing, just as you said. They're empty.'

'There's nought in the kitchen, too.'

'Looks like Nancy really was organised and got rid of the evidence one way or another. Okay, I'll call the hospital. It'll be up to them now, if it's not too late.'

I was told she hadn't arrived yet but was expected within minutes. I would go to the hospital and wait to see if she would recover, but first, I decided to search Archie's study — after all Lorna had found something here, maybe I would, too. What I really wanted was to find something, other than them being relatives, to link either Archie or Lance Sylt, to the murders.

Sylt still remained a mystery but having had a brief look through Archie's files, on my way to the hospital, I knew the motive for the murders.

63

I'D BEEN WAITING OUTSIDE THE EMERGENCY WARD FOR OVER AN hour. Inside, Nancy was having her stomach pumped while doctors fought to save her life. I felt like a concerned relative, not a DI desperate to know what was going on inside the head of the woman who, at first, appeared so harmless.

I'd telephoned Inspector Bryce before I set off to the hospital. Sooner or later Nancy's suspected suicide would become his problem. For now, I had to wait and tried, in the midst of the chaos of the emergency reception, to piece together what had really happened. Had Archie become instrumental in the deaths of Gilmore, Bright and Curzon, maybe even responsible for them?

From an article in *The Times* of 1953, which Shaw had in his bedroom along with many photographs of the crash scene, a picture was cut out which obviously meant a lot to Shaw. The press photographer had caught two women sitting on the paved platform. Between them lay a young girl: she had to be Emily. Lorna had her back to the camera and through the fuzzy image facing me, Phyliss Sylt stared.

More importantly were four photographs printed on square glossy black and white photographic paper taken, it would appear, from the footbridge over the tracks at Harrow and Wealdstone station. One showed the wreckage from the Perth express after it had ploughed into the commuter train. In the next — a shot much closer — a couple were looking up into the camera and waving. Another showed several people standing on the northbound platform before the second smash happened. The last, pictured how the wreckage from the third train had obliterated everything on the north-end of the down platform.

I studied the people looking at up at the camera. They were the same faces as those in the framed picture I'd removed from Nancy's lounge. Towards the end of the platform, I could just make out two girls sitting on a bench-seat with an older woman, who had to be Lorna. They were too far away for me to recognise them, but I knew they must be the girls in Archie's family photographs: Emily and Phyliss. Archie must have taken these after stopping to buy a book or a paper. It must have been the last time he saw his close family alive.

'D I Crosier?' said a firm, Scottish voice. I stood and nodded, wondering what was coming next. Before I could speak, the white clad doctor took me by my elbow and led me through the jammed reception and outside into the fresher air.

Bluntly he said, 'I'm afraid she didn't make it. We did what we could. We were too late. I'm sorry. There was no sign of drugs in her stomach, as far as we could tell. I think she knew what she was doing though.'

'How do you mean?'

'One of our nurses recognised her name. Turns out Nancy Shaw used to be a nurse, then a sister at Edinburgh until three years ago. They'd worked together. It's likely she'd have known which drugs and how many were needed to take her life.'

'And she would have access to them.'

'Quite, probably stole them from Edinburgh. At this stage we don't know what she used. A post-mortem might tell us more but injections of drugs, insulin for example, are impossible for us to detect yet. 'I'll let the local police have the details and they will probably send them on to you if you request them. That's all I can tell you. Sorry.'

'Thank you, Doctor?'

'Drummond, Nigel Drummond.' And after the quickest of smiles, he was rushing back towards the hospital, his open white coat flapping behind in its struggle to keep up.

The journey back to Crewe was frustrating. I hadn't solved the riddle and would have to wait almost another twenty hours before Nancy's confession, if that's what she'd posted, arrived on Claire's desk.

I hadn't slept at all well. The house was cold, and didn't feel the same without Alex and Ruth running about at the crack of dawn. Alice had decided to keep them with her in York. For how long she wouldn't say, so I didn't I know yet whether I'd be welcoming the New Year here in Crewe, or York. Perhaps I'd give it some serious thought this evening once I knew the contents of Nancy's missive.

'The post doesn't arrive until about eleven,' Carol said, when I rang in.

I'd thought about sleeping late, but it was pointless. On the one hand, I felt like a kid waiting for a present to arrive and, on the other, sad. The crash at Harrow was enough in itself, without at least five others dying ten years later because of it.

***

I arrived at the station just after nine. 'Any post yet?' I asked, stumping past Carol's desk.

'Good morning, DI Crosier. I'm afraid not. You've forgotten already! I told you, it isn't usually here until eleven.'

Claire followed me into my office. I slung my overcoat across my desk, knocking over the framed picture of Alice.

'My, we have got out of bed the wrong way,' she said, straightening Alice's picture and hanging my overcoat on its hanger on the back of the door.

'Sorry, Claire, it's just so frustrating. So close yet—'

'So far. I know. Strong coffee I think?' She poked her head out of the door and gesticulated to Carol.

'Has Hunt come up with anything?'

'He rang this morning. He went to see Lance Sylt yesterday, but he wasn't in. The neighbours hadn't seen him for days.'

'He went to Shaw's bloody-funeral. I assume you told him?'

'Of course I did.'

'I'm certain it was Sylt arguing with Nancy. Sod him. And damn Nancy-bloody-Shaw as well.'

My telephone rang. A woman, obviously out of breath, was trying to speak to me but not making any sense. 'Hang on,' I said. 'slow down. Who's calling?'

'Don't you remember me, Inspector Crosier? We met a few weeks ago, when you were searching for your daughter.'

I realised where I'd heard the woman's voice, and distinctly smelt singeing fur as I said her name, 'Mrs Birtles, is that you?'

'Yes, Mr Crosier.' She seemed calmer now I'd recognised her.

'What can I do for you?'

'Since you were here, the house opposite has been very quiet. I suppose because those killers are dead now.'

I started slapping the back of my neck, as if it would dislodge a blockage in her line of thought. I knew another part of the jig-saw was about to fall into place.

'So what are you saying, Mrs Birtles? Is someone there now?'

'Yes, I think there is.'

'Who?'

'I don't know.'

'Describe him for me.'

'Well, he's short ... '

The pips started going and I had to wait until she had put several more pence into the coin box.

'Hello, are you still there, Mr Crosier?'

'Yes. Is he short? Does he have long hair? Was he wearing a grey raincoat?'

'Yes. Collie heard a car pull up late last night.' I got burnt fur again. 'I looked through the window and two men went into the house. One short, one quite tall.'

'Are they still there?'

'I think so, their car is anyway.'

'Describe the car, Mrs Birtles.'

'I'm not good with cars, as you know, but it's a pale-blue

van-thing, with woodwork at the back.'

***

An hour later, I was behind the wheel of a split-windscreen Morris, the Railway Police's pool car, waiting until eleven o'clock. With me, PCs Dobbs and Long Len, who was always handy to have with you if there might be a brawl. Claire had insisted she come along, too, and after a moment I relented.

Behind us, a large police van from the Warrington Force was waiting. Inside, four officers were eager to race Long Len into breaking number thirty-eight's front door off its hinges. Four more were already in place round the back.

'Eleven o'clock, it's time,' I said, starting the engine. I drove along Algernon Close up to the house, parking it in the drive to block the Morris Traveller's exit.

Mrs Birtles' net-curtains twitched.

The police van arrived, swerving across the road, effectively sealing-off the narrow cul-de-sac. Its officers sprinted to the front door, truncheons at the ready. The largest amongst them shouldered the door, which flung wide open on his first attempt.

'Next time eh, Len,' Claire said. Long Len looked crestfallen.

Once inside, an officer shouted, 'Police.' We followed them into the house to find two officers marching Lance Sylt down the stairs. Two more had grabbed his friend. The officers held Sylt in front of me. He looked more than ten-years older, but there was no doubting who he was.

'Oh, it's you, Crosier. Knew it was you I saw yesterday. Looks like you beat Hunt-the-c—'

'Lance Sylt,' I said, addressing the man standing in just his underpants and smirking at Claire, 'I'm arresting you for the murders of Alex Bright and Elspeth Curzon.'

64

2 a.m. 8th OCTOBER 1952

'THIS MIST IS THICKENING,' THE RELIEF FIREMAN SAID, CLOCKING-ON for the early shift. 'We need a good breeze, but something tells me we'll not be in luck this morning.'

'The sleeper's already running late through Preston,' said his driver. 'Still, better late than never. Eh, lad?'

'That's what they say, John—'

'Better this mist than dodging Gerry's bombs I can tell you.'

The fireman had heard John liked to talk about driving in the war days. 'I'll take your word for that,' he said, sticking his clock card back in its slot.

The sound of the supervisor's office window sliding open got their attention. 'Fifteen late now. She's just cleared Bank Quay. I should get yourselves over to five. Talk to the crew when they get here. See if there's anything you need to know about her.'

Sid was grateful for the supervisor's interruption. The last thing he wanted was a four hour trip to Euston and a driver droning on about being bombed.

'Come on, lad, still time for a cuppa before she gets in.'

***

The station announcer attempted to stir the few passengers who were destined for London. A minute later the sleeper thundered in, brakes squealing, enough to wake everyone on board as it came to a stop. The engine was uncoupled and a fresh one, fully watered and coaled, brought over from the south sheds. The crew who'd brought the express reported on its load and jokingly apologised for the delay caused by fog, most of the way down through Cumbria, Lancashire and Cheshire. Glad to be off the footplate they were looking forward to some rest.

The driver checked the locomotive, 46242 City of Glasgow. His mate made the fire up just the way this class of engine liked it. If they were going to make up half-an-hour of lost time on their way to Euston, one thing they'd be certain to need was a good fire.

The guard blew his whistle and waved his green flag.

At four-thirty-seven the regulator was gradually opened. High pressure steam eased the five-hundred-ton train smoothly out of the platform; wouldn't do to wake those sleeping behind a second time.

Dawn started to creep in as they passed through Wolverton, some fifty miles north of Euston. The driver hoped it would help clear the mist but it would still take a little while yet.

They were approaching Watford, its tunnel some half-a-mile ahead. The distant signal warned them they'd have to stop before reaching the tunnel.

Next, the home signal, stood at danger and the driver pulled the train to a standstill.

A northbound freight began to exit the tunnel as their home signal changed to caution. The Perth train moved forward slowly: full steam couldn't be applied due to the 15mph speed limit through the tunnel.

They were inside the tunnel now. The fireman was busy stoking and the driver was looking into the blackness ahead. He turned to see how his mate was coping and was amazed to see two strangers, dressed in black boiler suits, standing on the footplate. The noise from the passing freight train and his own engine pulling away inside the tunnel had masked the sound of their arrival. One of them pulled from a canvas holdall a sawn-off shotgun and stood smiling at the driver who slowly raised his hands.

The other man grabbed the shovel from the fireman and

swung it across the back of his head. He fell unconscious onto the footplate. The man with the shotgun swung its butt into the driver's stomach then laid him out, crashing it down on the back of his neck.

'That went easier than I thought. You sure you can drive this thing, Spade?'

'Positive, Donnie. You just get on with stoking the fucking fire. We're not in the clear yet. Once you've got a good fire, like I told you how, get ready to chuck the gun. We'll be through the tunnel any minute.'

Spade turned back to watch the line. 'Right,' he said, 'get ready.'

The train left the south tunnel mouth. Donnie flung the shotgun into the grassy bank separating the twin tunnel entrances.

'Nobody will find it for years. I hope you wiped the prints clean.'

The look on his mate's face said it all. 'Don't tell Lance for fuck sake. Promise me, Spade.'

Spade opened the regulator. The train picked up speed.

'So how long now 'fore we get to Wembley?' pestered Donnie.

'Shut it. I'm listening to the engine. Got to find out how much regulator I can give her without spinning the wheels. Can't concentrate with you on my back.'

'You mean ... you don't know?'

'Jesus, all engines are different. Like women. Some like it gentle, some can take it rough.'

'And how's this one taking it?'

'Pretty good, she's better than them shunters at The Cross.'

'Shunting engines? You told me you'd driven expresses.'

'No I didn't. What I said was, one day I'd be able to drive expresses. It was taking them so long to promote me from fireman to driver, I quit.'

'It's why they all call you Spade, isn't it? You ain't a proper driver at all, are you?'

'Like I say, engines are basically the same. Stop worrying. We'll be through Watford Junction any second, then continue for half-a-dozen or so stations and bingo, we'll be in Wembley before you know it. Franky will be waiting for us with the motor. I'll pull this beauty up in the station, we'll get off — all calm-like — walk up the steps and through the barrier. Don't you speak to a soul, not a single fuckin' word. Got it? And rub some coal dust in your cheeks. Don't want to appear too clean now, do we?'

They were passing through Watford Junction now, and Spade exchanged a wave with a ganger standing by the line, then with the man in the signal box.

'You know 'em then?'

'Don't be so stupid, 'course I don't know 'em. I didn't work this line, did I now? I was at The Cross. And I don't mean New Cross, that dump you call home.'

'Mist's thickening, Spade.'

'I can see that for myself, you idiot. Shut it and sling a bit more coal on. There's nothing to hold us back unless we catch up to the last express. I doubt we will. She's got at least ten minutes on us. All downhill from here, matey, plain sailing. You'll see.'

'I hope you're right.'

'Once and for all, Donnie, I've been watching these trains for the last week, since Lance told us about the job. Thought we'd need a better escape route than the fuck-wit Lance planned. Better than going by road an' all.'

They sped through another station.

'Where was that, Donnie?'

'Bushey, maybe. Didn't notice.' Spade turned to give Donnie a mouthful, but to his surprise saw Driver Curzon coming round and trying but failing to get to his feet.

'You haven't a clue where we are have you?' said Curzon.

'Shut it, or else.'

'Shall I smack him again, Spade? Looks like trouble to me.'

'You don't know even how to stop her, do you?' persisted Curzon. And we're running late, so they might well switch the locals onto this line.'

'Is he right?' said Donnie. 'Looks a bit delirious to me.'

'He's talkin' bollocks. Whoever heard of the locals being given right of way over the expresses?'

'Is that true?' he said to Curzon. 'About the local.'

Curzon nodded. 'We're not the Liverpool train. We're the sleeper from Perth. Help me up. I have to see where we are and stop this idiot from killing us all.'

Curzon was on his feet and lunging for the regulator. Spade pushed him back down onto the footplate.

'Shit, Spade. What if he's right?'

They shot through another station. Curzon thought it was Hatch End and could tell they were gaining speed on the downhill run into Harrow and Wealdstone. Neither of the idiots were checking the way ahead for danger signals.

Fireman Bright was coming round. Curzon tried to prop him up against the side of coal tender. Spade stepped back then went to kick Curzon in his belly again. Curzon sidestepped Spade's boot but fell back onto fireman Bright.

'We've got to do something,' gasped Bright in Curzon's ear. Get them to check the way ahead,' suggested Bright, 'then maybe we can overpower them. If you can get to the vacuum brake, we'll still be okay.'

'And the gun?'

'I can't see it. It must be in his bag. I'll try to get it.' Curzon stretched and managed to get his foot around the bag's handle and dragged it over. 'Good, it's not here, just a few trinkets.'

'You'd be better looking out for where we are,' shouted Bright, 'instead of trying to kill us all.'

Spade told Donnie to look out from his side of the cab.

'They seem distracted enough, John.'

Curzon and Bright were on their feet. Bright flung himself on

Donnie. They tangoed around the rocking footplate, neither one able to get the advantage over the other.

Curzon swung on the regulator, managing to close it, then held the whistle wide open.

Spade seemed to have given up the fight and was still leaning out of the cab, peering out into the fog.

'He's seen something, Sid,' shouted Curzon.

Three ear piercing emergency detonators exploded below the engine's wheels. The crew exchanged glances knowing the danger that lay ahead.

Curzon applied the vacuum brake, but had to release the whistle.

Donnie broke free from Bright but didn't know what to do next.

Curzon took up his proper position and looked forwards to see the local to Euston train standing just a hundred yards in front, on the same track! It would have scores of passengers aboard.

'Donnie,' screamed Spade, ignoring the crew. He ran across the footplate. 'We've got to jump. The bastard was right. Leave the fuckers here to die. It's our only chance.'

'But we must be doing fifty.'

Spade didn't argue, opened the folding gate and pushed Donnie through it and blindly followed him.

The crew stayed put; helpless. They knew that if they jumped from the footplate at this speed, they'd be certain to die.

Curzon saw young Bright looking back at him in despair. Urine was running down the lad's legs and pooling on the footplate.

Curzon couldn't watch Bright die. He turned away, hung onto the whistle chord ... and prayed.

65

I MADE HUNT'S DAY WHEN I PHONED AND TOLD HIM OF SYLT'S arrest. His joy was short lived, however, when I asked him to track down the wives of two men who, according to Sylt, might have been killed in the crash.

As Carol was on her lunch break, Claire duplicated copies of Nancy's letter. It had arrived just a few minutes after we left to bring in Sylt. 'That bloody Gestetner! I'll be glad to see the back of it. Just look at my hands. All just to print off a few copies of this! It had better be worth reading.'

I knew exactly what she meant. I always tried my best to avoid the machine, happy to let Carol — who had dominated the decrepit printing beast from their very first meeting — do it instead. There would probably be a party if and when the new Xerox we'd heard about arrived.

Nancy's letter wasn't exactly what Claire and I expected: a confession right enough; and a revelation. We read it again to make sure we made sense of it.

Dear Mr Crosier,

I would hope that by now, you have pieced together what has happened to our family. I refer of course to our 'association' with the Sylts and to the appalling train crash at Harrow & Wealdstone. Archie was there. He saw it all happen, witnessed his son, daughter and his youngest granddaughter Emily slaughtered by the third train. He escaped the crash, only because his war-wound slowed him down so much, he hadn't crossed the footbridge before the second accident.

He was, as you might imagine, never the same again.

The report, that came out the following year, put the accident down to the relief train-crew of the express from Perth passing danger signals. That festered in him for years. The possibility of technical problems, or anything else, was irrelevant to Archie. He, who knew nothing of trains whatsoever, rejected them as did the Board, and preferred instead to stick with the report's conclusion that the train-crew was at fault.

What made it worse, was his elder granddaughter Phyliss survived. Emily, who lived nearby to us, did not. We used to see a lot of her. The two girls were often mistaken for sisters. They had quite different characters, mind you: Emily was good, while Phyliss Sylt remains the opposite.

'Doesn't look like the old bat knew Phyliss was dead?' said Claire. She's written about her in the present tense.'

I was on duty at the hospital, so I couldn't attend Vincent's funeral. I was fortunate to have escaped the crash, but I was still damaged by it. Not as much as dear Archie who, as I say, witnessed the whole thing from the footbridge.

If only there was something I could do to help Archie improve and, eventually, I convinced him to pay to have the train crew's family killed. Revenge, plain and simple; an eye for an eye. And we knew someone who would do anything for cash: Lance Sylt. It would be easy for him to do it if Archie asked him. He and his deceased brother had been 'well connected'. He demanded more money than we had, but I knew someone I could work on.

Then, after Bright died, you came on the scene, so I invited you to our home: I needed to know if you could scupper my plan. Happily, you didn't know a thing but I could see you were frustrated by the clairvoyant theory and wouldn't stick with it for long. I told Archie to try and arrange for Bright's murder to be on the tenth anniversary of the crash. I was toying with whoever would investigate his death; a big clue, wouldn't you agree? I was very surprised you didn't see it. You should pay more attention to history.

I hope you catch Sylt. He and his brother were hated by us. Scum, nothing more. A pair of London thugs. At least we were able to exploit Lance for a change. He wanted more than a lot of money. He wanted somewhere to live. You'll find him at 18 Algernon Street, Warrington. I was giving him a spare key and the final payment, passed to me by the undertaker, when you saw him shouting outside the church.

You will not know that Moira Curzon was my first victim? I murdered her in August 1953. By coincidence, she came into my ward after a car accident. I recognised her name from the reports in my paper, two months before. Her husband unwittingly gave me sufficient information for me to be certain it was her, and The Scotsman had named the train crew's family, too. It was a rare chance, too good to be true. I don't regret it. And that experience, years later, set me thinking about how I could exploit Sylt.

Archie continued to get worse. He rambled a lot, as you witnessed yourself. When you came, he was at his worst. I thought you might put two and two together and arrest him, although he was completely innocent. Well, almost. You didn't, but I knew you would be back one day.

He couldn't have taken a trial and imprisonment. So I put him to sleep, in the same way I did for myself. He didn't suffer, nor did I.

I said, 'Interesting, how she happily admits to murdering Moira Curzon, yet when it comes to her own flesh and blood she—'

'Puts them to sleep,' said Claire. 'Who cares if she suffered?'

'Not me, that's for sure. If we believe her, and I'm minded to, she was the root-cause of every one of these killings. Can you imagine what life must have been like for Archie. There he is, doing his best to come to terms with the tragedy, while all the time this ... this ding-bat is whispering in his ear that he'll feel a lot better if he arranges for some innocent relatives of the crew to be bumped off.'

'She doesn't explain Gilmore's death.' Claire read my mind. 'Maybe we'll never know why he died.'

> I wanted Archie buried first, to at least afford him some dignity. His friends remain ignorant of what happened. I hope they continue to be, Mr Crosier, but that is up to you. What is so sad, is if Vincent had been murdered at a different time none of this would have happened.
>
> I sent this letter to Claire, because I can see you are close. Perhaps working together, will bring you closer. Forgive me if I've interfered, yet again.
>
> Yours, without regret—

We sat taking in what the scheming old woman had set in motion. I thought I could judge a person's character, but this time, Nancy had taken in both Claire and me, totally. The only normal part of her letter, I hoped, was the last paragraph. I watched Claire's face, as she read to the end. She looked at me; a feint blush had developed on her cheeks. 'There's one thing I'm certain about,' she said, trying to get back to business. 'Had Ronnie Boyton not played games with us, he and Phyliss Sylt might not be dead but richer and still at large.'

By now it was mid-afternoon and I looked at my overnight bag, slung on a spare chair. 'There's one thing we still have to do, sergeant.'

66

'IT'S BOTHERING ME, SO IT HAS TO BE DONE,' I SAID. 'FACE TO FACE. Not over the telephone. I could delegate it to Hunt, but I know it will be better coming from us.'

Claire looked at me, trying not to show she knew what was coming. She left the office and returned a few seconds later with her own small case, and a big smile.

On our way out, I passed the telephone number of our destination to Ward, asking her to make certain the occupant would be at home after eight o'clock.

***

As soon as our train pulled into Euston I found a telephone box and dialled Whitehall-one-two-one-two. I asked to be put through to Hunt's office, in Scotland Yard, eager to hear his news.

He'd tracked down and spoken with one of the wives of the missing men. She confirmed they'd both remarried, so it looked like Sylt, for once, might be telling the truth — or at least had made at pretty good stab at what may have happened.

***

It was almost nine in the evening, a misty evening with a gentle breeze, by the time we reached Lorna's house in Kensington. Luckily, she was at home. And so, too — by the sound of operatic 'singing' emanating from the back of the house — was her husband. She gave us her best smile and invited us inside.

'Please ignore my hubby. Minister or not, he'll be really embarrassed when he finds out we have guests.'

We were shown into a large sitting-room, where we sat together on an enormous leather sofa, while Lorna made and brought through some very welcome coffee. It gave me time to double-check I had brought the copy of Nancy's confession with me.

'So, Inspector. Claire. What can I do for you?'

'We have news relating to the crash, Lorna.'

'Oh, really?'

'This letter is from Nancy.' I passed the confession over for her to read. She did, twice, before looking at Claire, then me.

'This *is* genuine ... I recognise her hand writing.'

'Why would you expect us to show you anything else?' I said, relieved I'd cut out its last paragraph.

'Sorry, Inspector, it's just the way things are in my line of work.'

'There's more you should know, Lorna.'

'Isn't Nancy's 'confession' enough? What more could there possibly be?'

'We have Lance in custody.'

'That's good to know, Inspector. But, he's irrelevant to the crash, surely?'

'He admitted to being put up to take the lives of several of the train-crew's relatives. But he also claims he didn't kill anyone, ever.'

'So who did kill them, Inspector?' she said, concentrating on her coffee.

'That we don't know, yet, Lorna,' I said, playing it canny.

A welcome break from Figaro gave her an opportunity to look over her left shoulder and study the hall-door; in anticipation of her husband's imminent embarrassment?

I waited a little longer for her attention to return, then said: 'He also claims he knew why the crash happened, though he has no definite proof.'

'The prospect of leniency loosened his tongue, eh? Go on.' The coffee cup in her hand began to rattle in its saucer. She placed it on the table between us and reached for her cigars.

'In the early hours on the morning of the crash, he admitted to robbing a jewellers shop in Hemel Hempstead. Him and two accomplices. After the robbery he drove their haul to Rugby.

'To Archie's place?'

'Indeed. But he dropped his mates near the railway tunnel north of Watford.'

Again, she wasn't looking at me — preferring instead, to fiddle with her lighter — so I paused until she did. 'The plan was for them to get to Wembley by road. But they might have feared being remembered if they were picked up by a passing vehicle. The railway was nearby—'

'So they caught a train?'

'Sort of.'

'Either they did or they didn't, Inspector. Which is it to be?'

'Neither. They held one up.'

'Don't be ridiculous. The man's a born liar.'

'Fantastical, I know. It's what Lance reckons happened.'

'And you believe him?'

'He knew one of the men had worked on locomotives for over ten years, on the line from Kings Cross. Spade might have noticed the speed restriction in force at the time through Watford tunnel, as they walked near the line. Trains were slowed before the tunnel mouth and halted if they were gaining on the train in front.'

'You're suggesting they could board one if it had to stop?'

'The express sleeper from Perth was the first to be stopped,' I said.

'Yes, I'd read that somewhere in the report. Carry on.'

'If Lance's suspicion is correct, Spade convinced his accomplice it was possible for them to climb onto the engine of a train as it moved slowly off into the darkness of the tunnel. And, to make it easier for them, Spade carried a gun.'

'But there would be gunshot wounds, surely?'

'Yes, if the gun was fired. Not if they clubbed to death the driver and fireman. Their injuries would look as if they were sustained in the crash.'

'You make it sound as though they knew there would be an accident. So where are these *accomplices* now?'

'That's another mystery. According to their wives, they never came home.'

'So you think they died on the footplate?'

'Highly likely. Two bodies were recovered at Harrow without any identification. They were never claimed.' I waited for this information to sink in.

Lorna took on that far-away look I'd first seen when she visited my office; a look that seemed to doubt what I'd just said. She got up and went to look through the window, its curtain undrawn.

'I got the records checked this afternoon,' I said, turning to address her back. 'They confirmed two bodies were never identified.'

'I don't ... think they did.'

'Sorry? You don't think who didn't, Lorna?'

'I don't think they died on the footplate.'

Claire and I exchanged glances.

Lorna was off somewhere with the fairies again and turning something over, remembering something . . .

'My thin reflection in the window is offering me no protection from him ... the mist lurking outside, is sucking me in ... I don't understand what's happening to me. Try not to panic. Why here, trapped in this ... lurid greyness? I see two rails, they almost meet in the distance, not far off. Perspective. Yes, that's what it's called, a perspective leading me towards ... towards what?

'Behind me, the rails just fade away, no perspective, no escape. I'm stuck in this fog ... thick, orange-grey fog. I must stay calm.'

Claire and I exchanged worried looks. 'Like she says,' I said, 'stay calm.'

'Has she hypnotised herself again?'

'She said it herself: the mist outside. And she's stressed by what we've told her.'

'What's going to bring her back?'

'Figaro, perhaps. Maybe her husband has seen her like this a before. Let's wait. Don't go dashing into his bathroom just yet.'

'There must be a boundary somewhere, has to be or I'd already be out in the clear, not in here, captured. Beyond, at the station, I know it's a clear day. I was there only a few seconds ago. I must get free, find a way back.

'A mirrored barrier. Skin-like. I think that's what it is, separating this fog from the clear air. It's swaying, a sail of skin in the gentle breeze.

'A face is growing on it, blurred. I don't think this is a cinema. In focus now, I see: it's Phyliss, immense. She's wearing her favourite sneer. Never looked at me any other way. Trust her to turn up when she's not wanted. I doubt she knows the way out, ignorant child.

'She's looking down her avian nose at me. Thinks I'm her prey. Her head turns and I duck fearing her nose will knock me over. My hair ruffles as the vast beak wafts over me. She could at least try to find the way out instead of toying with me like this, but she just wiggles her fingers then ... she's gone, instantly.

'I startle myself, but it's only me reflected in this wobbly fairground mirror. I have to get out there with my family, in the clear air, not standing between the rails, captive. How can I protect them when I'm stuck here?

'I'm walking along the track towards the mirror. My steps are rushing, I have no choice: the wooden sleepers are moving beneath me. I try to keep to them. I'm not making any progress at all. The mirror is just as far away as when I started. Only a few leaps and I catch my foot on a heap of stones between sleepers, go my length and fall flat on my face. My hand checks for loose teeth. The bruising stones taste oily. And they smell of drains.

'The sly track slows then stops moving. I'm back where I began. It must be in cahoots with the fog. And Phyliss. Looks like I'll be stuck here until the sun is well up.

'Try standing. My hand grabs a rail for support. It's cold. It's steel and ... it's vibrating. Something mechanical is moving beside me, levers, rods. I move my hand just in time to stop it being trapped. The detonators have been set. Oh, no.

'I hold the rail again. My arm quivers and feels numb. There's a metallic sound. Is someone tapping on a water pipe? The rails are singing, louder, the beat rising.

'Phyliss is back. Her huge image, still sneering, treats me to a wink. Come to see me die has she? But I won't die on the tracks like her. She's smiling now, her evil smile. She must have seen it, the train coming fast and heavy. The mirror is trembling, jagging her features. Can she feel the train coming, too?

'I reach for her, but she's waving and mouthing "bye, bye". Her face fragments, fingers drift from her palms. Blooded red fingers, the only colour, waltz around bits of her face. One by one her features dissolve.

'Good riddance, I say and turn to look back along the track. An ominous shape is swelling in the murk. The ground is shaking violently. The train is coming for me.

'I hurl myself over a rail and end up on my back. I'm not having a fit, but shaking just as much as the ground. Frantic, I untie my red scarf and wave it in a last attempt to warn the train. Fog swirls, the engine looms then flashes by, ignoring my warning. I glimpse its name over the wheels: Princess Anne. She's still working hard pumping steam and smoke. Such noise, steel on steel, I cover my ears but still hear the three detonators explode.

'Anne has changed her mind, has decided to slow; her

driver has applied the brakes. Fireworks of hot sparks fly from every passing wheel. I smack away their hot needles jabbing at my cheek then shield my eyes.

'I roll over just in time to see the driver push the fireman from the footplate. He jumps too. They hover, flying beside the engine, then punch a hole in the barrier. There is sunlight outside!

'I see colour, too. I'm on my feet, running beside the slowing train.

'I can see beyond the smashed boundary: see through the clear air; see my family waiting, not knowing what is about to happen to them.

'The train-crew hit the ground. I stumble over them. There's no movement from them. They are dead. But what I see beyond them is far worse. Anne's train doesn't want to crash, be smashed to pieces, but she's too late, far too late and she will be.

'Agony or warning? Her whistle screams long, loud blasts.'

Lorna grabbed the thick curtains for support.

Claire's beside her in a flash. 'She's coming out of it. She must have heard the whistle in her head,' Claire said, guiding Lorna back to her armchair.

A minute must have gone by before Lorna spoke again. 'All this time ... and I didn't realise I'd known all along.'

'Known what, Lorna?' said Claire.

'The answer ... Why they are dead.'

'Is there something you're hiding from us, Lorna?' Claire probed. 'Something we should know about?'

'I thought it was the nightmares playing tricks with my mind. But a part of them never made sense. But my dreams, they were true after all.'

Claire tried once more. 'What didn't make sense, Lorna?'

'I saw them jump, just after the detonators went off.'

I said, 'Are you sure? Your memory might have been—'

'It was them. I'm sure, falling just as the engine burst from the fog. Then the engine's whistle started screaming long blasts.' Lorna looked at us, waiting for the realisation to strike.

'Meaning,' I said, 'there had to be someone else on the footplate. The train crew: they were trying to stop the train and they died on the footplate.

'I told you about two men, laying dead between the tracks. Remember?'

'Yes, I do,' said Claire, 'when you told us about Lieutenant Sweetwine.'

We waited while Lorna's mind had rearranged her memories.

'So, it was just as I thought,' she said, at last. 'Not just Vincent. Lance compounded things by robbing a pathetic little jeweller's shop; he was the one who'd done something so dreadful that caused so many to suffer and die. It was Vincent who started my family's destruction. And Lance who completed it. All the time, he knew. Yet he still came to me for—

'God, if only Mary hadn't married him.'

After a moment of coming to terms with the revelations, Lorna seemed to lighten her mood. She'd been looking for the key to her puzzle for over ten years, yet the clue to her search for closure — the smallest detail — had evaded her. Until now.

It had been locked inside her own head.

67

'LORNA,' SAID CLAIRE, 'WOULD YOU MIND IF I COULD CHANGE OUT of my uniform? It has been a long day. We thought we'd go into town when we're done here.'

'No. No, not at all. You can use our bedroom. You'll have to be quick, mind. I expect my husband will be out of the bathroom soon.'

'I will be, thank you,' Claire said, picking up her overnight bag and leaving us. The marriage of Figaro, this time with splashing accompaniment, attempted to re-enter the room, but was eased back into the hall by the closing door.

I told Lorna about the kidnapping of my daughter, which didn't elicit a response. But there was something that might. 'You said in your dream, Lorna, you wouldn't die on the tracks, like Phyliss had.'

A short stab of disgust stiffened Lorna when I mentioned her niece, but otherwise she listened with equal disinterest — her mind, presumably, was still going over what she'd unlocked.

'Yet when we met at Archie's funeral you never mentioned you knew. You even pointed her out in the photographs as if she was still alive, yet said nothing.'

'Didn't seem important. Like I told you, I'd always hoped one day she'd rot in hell. Pity her uncle hasn't!'

I finished my cold coffee in the short silence which followed and then I told her about the Boyton-Sylt murders. I had the impression there still was something she wasn't going to tell me. 'Oh, I almost forgot,' I said, reaching into my briefcase.

Lorna was definitely on edge as if expecting me to reveal something which she was trying to hide. 'I borrowed a picture from Nancy's "rouges gallery". It's not needed any longer for my investigation.'

Lorna looked relieved, sighed and took the framed picture from me, running her fingers over the faces of Mary and Robert. She studied it a little longer then walked over the room and stood it on the sideboard. 'Thank you, Inspector. They belong here now, with me; there's no one in Scotland for them.'

Claire returned and fixed me with a determined look — her plan for a night out, I assumed. It was only the second time I'd seen her made up and out of uniform. I had trouble taking my eyes off her and hadn't noticed Figaro had stopped singing when she entered the lounge.

Lorna's husband arrived a few seconds later, to stand in the doorway, his dressing gown wide open. It was just the picture the press were desperate for.

It was time for us to take our leave.

Ten minutes later, although we'd eaten on the train, my stomach really started to grumble. We went inside the first restaurant we found, a new Chinese. It was late but the restaurant was noisy and crammed — its customers more interested in this new-fangled cuisine than the hour. I was very tired, but determined to enjoy the pleasure of being off duty with Claire. Hopefully, the food would boost my energy level and keep me awake until we found a room each for the night.

The first course of our meal arrived. We tucked in, saying little for some time. Claire took a break, while I soldiered on.

'So, Oliver. How would you rate Lorna's performance tonight?'

'How do you mean?'

'She knows more than she's letting on about.'

I'd almost got the knack of using the chopsticks but, as my interest was piqued by Claire's words, I flicked a pea into her meal. She laughed. So did I. I felt good for the first time in months and began to relax. 'You mean because she didn't react much to learning about Lance's involvement?'

Claire reached over and placed her hand over mine. How she'd got duplicating ink on the back of it puzzled me. 'I know something else, too,' she said.

'Oh, yes? Tell me.'

'I will ... when we're ... alone.'

From that moment, my mind raced with a mixture of excitement and curiosity. We threw our dinners down our necks as fast as possible, and left refreshed and eager to find a bed for the night — a double or single, either would do.

*****

'I've forgotten where certain parts of a woman's anatomy are hiding. It's been years since Alice and I were ... you know, intimate,' I said, not being entirely truthful.

Claire kissed me, then becoming impatient, guided my hand between her legs to the parts she enjoyed most.

Afterwards, in my arms, she said, 'You're very pensive all of a sudden, Oliver. Not feeling guilty already, are you?'

'I am pensive, but no, I'm not feeling guilty.'

'What's the matter? Am I not up to Alice's standard?'

'We provided a lot of information for Lorna tonight,' I said, ignoring Claire's gibe. 'And, it seems, she now has the answer to the question she'd asked when we first met in my office.'

'We still don't know for certain if the robbers caused the crash,' said Claire, 'but it looks highly probable. Hunt's enquiries virtually confirmed it.'

'Lorna is a determined woman,' I said. 'I think she's the type who never gives up. She'll follow Sylt's trial with great interest. No doubt she'll inveigle herself onto the prosecutor's team.'

'Oh? I'm not quite so sure about that, Oliver.'

I'd completely forgotten about her comment in the restaurant. 'And why might that be, my lovely Sergeant?'

'First, I have to check something out in the morning. I'll ring Carol early, ask her to confirm an address. I'm not going to call now. I don't want to give the idiot Gardiner the satisfaction, and besides, I have someone far more interesting laying beside me.'

I was nibbling her nipple, and took a breath to say, 'Stop teasing me, Sergeant. What's this secret you're nurturing?'

'Well ... when I went to change into my mufti, I noticed a *For Sale* document on their dressing table.'

'So?'

'It was for a house.'

'They often are.'

'But this one was for 28, Preston Park Avenue.'

'Can't have been. Hunt had it checked out, if you remember,' I mumbled, as I returned to her breast. 'It doesn't exist, does it?'

'No,' she said, hooking a finger under my chin and forcing me to look into those dark eyes once more. 'Not in *New Brighton*, it doesn't.'

Next morning, I woke and felt the warm sheets where Claire had been sleeping. I checked my wristwatch: seven o'clock. She'd probably gone to call the office, leaving me to snooze after my energetic night.

I first noticed the four envelopes, propped against the dressing table mirror, on my way back from the bathroom. Two hadn't been posted. The other two had a York postmark and a New York postmark and they'd been sent to my office.

I opened the New York one first. Inside a picture of a huge American steam engine. On the back, my brother had written *Happy Birthday Bro* — very American — followed by *get your arse over here soon*. God, I'd completely forgotten I was forty!

I recognised Alice's spidery writing and — amazed the postman had managed to decode the address — tore open the envelope. A card pictured a Coronation Scot engine and, carried in the white smoke billowing from its funnel, the words *Happy 40th Birthday*. Alice, never one for anything romantic these days, had added in as few words as possible . . .

Best wishes from Ruth, Alistair and me.

The other cards, depicting locomotives dashing through

glorious countryside, were from Mrs Ward and Claire. I placed them on the dresser and crawled back into bed, catching my toe in Claire's bra. I remembered everything about the night before and wished we were just arriving. Why do such magical nights have to pass so quickly? Why can't they last forever, or at least be twice as long?

The bedroom door was suddenly flung wide open, as if it had taken it upon itself to wake everyone in the adjoining rooms. I was very glad not to have been standing behind it.

Claire, wearing her uniform, stood in the doorway. Having my full attention, she stepped into the room. 'Do you want the good-news or the bad?' she said, heeling the door shut.

'And good morning to you, too. Do you always wake your latest lover in this manner?'

'Answer the question, officer. Good or bad?'

'The bad, get it out of the way.'

'I was in luck and got hold of Carol. The idiot Gardiner went home sick.'

'Must have eaten the pork pie that's been stuck in his moustache for years ... food poisoning, hopefully.'

'Carol came in early to cover for him. The bad news is she's quit. Handed in her notice.'

'Why, for heaven's sake? She likes working with us. Did the damn Gestetner get the better of her?'

'She applied for a job in Bradford and got it.'

'Bradford?' I don't know anyone in the force there.'

'It's academic anyway you might say; she's going into a Technical College. Not the force. Reckons it will become a university one day. Wants to be in on the ground floor, so to speak, when it does.'

'Academic all right ... bugger. I'll miss her.'

'Me, too. She goes at the end of the year. Anyway, don't let's think of her just now. I have a really nice present for you. Would you like it now?'

I guessed what was coming. After moment of teasing she

removed her uniform to stand naked before me.

'And the good news?' I said, after we'd got our breath back.

Those eyes were fixed on mine again. She rolled on top of me.

The weight of her supple body seemed to force even more warmth into mine.

She began to stroke the bridge of my nose with one finger and said, 'You're going to have to call Hunt pretty soon, Birthday Boy. I've been right all along.'

She whipped the sheets off the bed, rolled off me and padded her naked body over to the dressing table to pick up Carol's and Alice's card. 'Happy Birthday, Oliver,' she said, turning to sit on the dresser.

Just then, I was as happy as Larry. But not for long. As Claire held the cards up to read them, I glimpsed a few lines written on the back of Alice's card. Claire looked at Carol's first then read Alice's card, checking the back of both before slowly looking over them at me. 'Maybe I should move to Bradford, too,' she said, before flinging them at me.

I grabbed Alice's card, wondering what it was that Claire already knew. I wished I hadn't.

Claire paused at the bathroom door and turned to face me, watching for my reaction.

Alice's to-the-point-missive carried no emotion whatsoever:

I'm still in York.
I'm staying in York,
I'm pretty certain I'm pregnant.

Claire went into the bathroom and slammed the door hard. 'Thanks, Alice. Happy bloody-birthday!'

68

LORNA FINISHED DRESSING AND THREW BACK THE BEDROOM curtains to look out onto High Street Kensington. She knew, beyond the early morning mist, the actors would not be waiting for her to join them, on the platform at Harrow.

They pestered her less frequently since the day Nancy confided in her about Moira Curzon. They'd virtually stopped altogether, when, a year later, Lorna sent a envelope, fat with money, to a man in Warrington.

Nevertheless, last night had been a bit nerve racking. But, having thought about it, she was confident her visitors hadn't seen her loss of control. Her dreams, now she knew their secret, were almost as impotent.

She sat and brushed her hair. Then at last, satisfied she'd done her best with the unruly mop, stood and looked outside.

The plane trees had shed their leaves two months ago. According to the BBC's Home Service, winter had definitely arrived: snow forecast for tomorrow. The garden already lay dormant, thankfully. It wouldn't need much attention until spring.

She took breakfast with her husband, as usual, and afterwards returned to the bedroom to collect her handbag and her red scarf. Red made her feel cosy. She tightened it around her neck, and tucked the ends into her overcoat. It looked so cold outside.

Beyond the mist she noticed two black police cars arriving from the direction of Scotland Yard.

A knot began to form in her stomach.

Her hand fumbled inside her bag for the small-tin of cigars.

It wasn't there.

The cars were drawn-up now and parked on the broad pavement outside her gate. A female officer climbed out of the first car, to stand guard.

From the second, came three figures. Along the garden path they trouped then, as one, stopped when they noticed Lorna watching them.

She could see their faces clearly; Hunt, she knew from her dealings with the Flying Squad, was smiling, but not Cardin, or Crosier.

They stood beckoning, through the faint mist, for Lorna to join them.

Crosier stepped forward, waiting for her.

For Lorna, a new nightmare was about to begin, and once again, her thin reflection in the window offered no comfort.

More about this story

The Harrow & Wealdstone rail crash of 8th October 1952 is, at the time of writing, England's worst. Three hundred-and-forty people were injured, many seriously. One hundred-and-twelve lost their lives. Many survivors will have suffered the trauma of it for years afterwards and it has not been my intention to demean their anguish.

The accident report, published in 1953, concluded that the crew of the Perth express were to blame, but fails to establish why they ignored several warning signals. Sadly, they were amongst the dead, so we'll never know.

Railway, and other transport, accidents occur because of a series of events leading up to the disaster. Often at least three are enough to cause a crash. In this case, there was bad weather along the west coast that night. This caused the Perth sleeper-train to be delayed. The weather, though improving, was still not clear by the time the train was north of Harrow. Train speeds were reduced to 15 mph, through the tunnel north of Watford, adding further to the delay. Finally, the local train for Euston was, by routine, given priority over the delayed expresses and routed from the southbound slow line onto the fast line.

The one single thing which might have prevented the crash was ATC: Automatic Train Control. ATC applies the brakes of a train passing danger signals.

Modern versions are widespread today. British Railways did not, then, have ATC on the London Midland Scottish Region — though it inherited the precursor to it, invented and used by the G.W.R. on its Western Region. It was forced to introduce it after this crash.

For those who know Winsford's railway history, you will have to forgive my artistic license in using the line that ran through Whitegate — the line where Gilmore was killed. I know it closed many years before 1962, but the Middlewich closure did take place on the date in the story and today there is a move to revive it. The actual place of Gilmore's demise never existed. But a similar crossing existed on the line from New Mills just west of High Lane, where the twisty country road from Poyton crosses it. And of course, you'd not be able to fit even a small woman inside the Night Mail's pouches!

I hope you enjoyed this novel and thank you for purchasing it.

Further reading
The Railways Archive:
railwaysarchive.co.uk/eventsummary.php?eventID=108
The book 'The Railway Policeman' is out of print, but second hand copies may still be available from Amazon.
To learn more about the British Transport Police, the world's oldest police force, see:
btp.police.uk   and for their historical website:
btphg.org.uk/?page_id=5
For newsreels of the day, visit:
youtube.com/watch?v=YU60PgAjh0Edna
britishpathe.com/video/harrow-rail-crash and
bbc.co.uk/news/uk-england-london-19873951
http://www.youtube.com/watch?v=FkLoDg7e_ns

Connect with the author: details on next page.

Connect with Me

Follow me on Twitter: twitter.com/edwintip
Friend me on Facebook: facebook.com/edwin.tipple
Sign up to my blog: edwintipple.wordpress.com

If you would like to help indie authors, you can easily by placing an on-line review on Amazon or Smashwords, even if you didn't purchase their books from those retailers. Please make your review honest.

Printed in Great Britain
by Amazon.co.uk, Ltd.,
Marston Gate.